W9-DED-782

THE FEDERAL THEATRE, 1935-1939

THE
FEDERAL
THEATRE, 1935-1939
Plays, Relief, and Politics

JANE DE HART MATHEWS

PRINCETON, NEW JERSEY
PRINCETON UNIVERSITY PRESS · 1967

Publication of this book has been aided
by a grant from the Duke University
Dissertation Award Committee

Printed in the United States of America
by Princeton University Press, Princeton, New Jersey

For my Mother and Father

Preface

A PROJECT of the Works Progress Administration[1] for unemployed theatrical people, the Federal Theatre embodied all of the aspirations, ambiguities, handicaps, and frustrations of Franklin Delano Roosevelt's New Deal. Spawned by the misery of the great depression and the hopes of humanitarian reformers, the Theatre Project, like all WPA programs, was based on the novel proposal that the unemployed deserved socially useful jobs rather than the humiliation of handouts and bread lines. The task of this new artistic venture was twofold: to preserve the talents of unemployed actors, directors, designers, and stage-hands and to bring the results of that talent to an audience of Americans virtually untouched by commercial theatre. Shaped by individuals committed to the creation of a theatre with regional roots and socially relevant plays, it would hopefully become the foundation of a permanent, national theatre. At once a relief measure and a work program, an emergency stopgap and the foundation of a much desired national theatre, the Project reveals in its brief, turbulent history all the conflicts of ambiguous origins and various ambitions. Its demise is an excellent illustration of how politicians, seizing upon those ambiguities, made of this controversial New Deal experiment a symbol —and a scapegoat.

Part of the social and cultural history of this depression decade, the Federal Theatre is also a chapter in the continuing search of artist for patron, of dramatist and actor for an aesthetically sound, restlessly original national theatre. Unlike those European nations where state and municipality have assumed the function of patronage formerly belonging to the crown, the United States has had no firmly established tradition of government aid to the arts.[2] The theatre—banned by Puritans interested in a holy commonwealth and ignored by the new democ-

---

[1] The name was changed to Works Projects Administration in 1939.

[2] For a survey of such contacts between government and the arts as have been made prior to 1940, see Grace Overmyer, *Government and the Arts* (New York: W. W. Norton & Co., 1939).

racy bent on mastering a continent—achieved maturity as an art form only in the twentieth century. With this newfound maturity came a demand on the part of a few pioneering spirits for a permanent, decentralized national theatre released from the social and geographical confines of Broadway. Created in the "seedling period of national drama"[3] when these ideas were being articulated by theatrically conscious men and women throughout the country, the Theatre Project offered an opportunity to build a federally subsidized theatre of broad geographical scope. Although its origins as a relief measure vitally affected the nature and operation of the institution which emerged, the Federal Theatre nevertheless affords a dramatic illustration of the problems encountered by an art form subsidized by a democratic, representative government. The largest, perhaps the most productive, and certainly the most socially committed and controversial of the WPA Arts Projects, it serves as precedent, inspiration, and warning to those who continue to look to government subsidy for support of the decentralized repertory theatre which this nation still lacks.

At its height, the Federal Theatre employed approximately thirteen thousand people in projects scattered over thirty-one states. The records available to the historian are commensurate with its size. Located principally in the National Archives, they have served several scholars, most notably the Project's National Director, Hallie Flanagan, whose monumental and moving account, *Arena*, was written with a sense of immediacy, urgency, and personal involvement which only she could provide. Writing from a different perspective and with a different purpose, I have relied on those sources which seem to me to reveal most about the nature of the Federal Theatre as a national institution—its origins and administration, the personalities, ideas, and circumstances which shaped it, the problems it faced, and the contributions it made. The resulting study contains neither the detailed

[3] "The World and the Theatre: Dedication to G[eorge] P[ierce] Baker]— National Theatre Conference . . . ," *Theatre Arts Monthly*, XVII (July 1933), 483.

account of individual projects which those interested in local history might wish, nor the kind of literary and dramatic analysis expected of persons trained in dramatic criticism.

For help in using the copious material available on this WPA Theatre, I am indebted to archivists at the following institutions: the National Archives, the Franklin Delano Roosevelt Library in Hyde Park, the Archives of American Art at the Detroit Institute of Art, the New York Public Library. Mr. William E. Woolfenden at the Detroit Institute of Art was particularly gracious, allowing me access to material not yet ready for general use. To Mr. Roy Wilgus, formerly of the National Archives, I owe a special debt of gratitude for the constant assistance and unfailing interest he showed throughout my long stay in Washington. Librarians at Duke University and at Princeton University have also been helpful.

One of the advantages of writing about so recent a period as the 'thirties is the accessibility of those directly involved. In this respect, I have been particularly fortunate. Although ill for many years, Mrs. Hallie Flanagan Davis not only submitted most graciously to interviews and question-laden correspondence, but also placed her personal records at my disposal. Her interest, encouragement, and injunctions to "tell both the good and the bad" are appreciated both for their intent and for what they reveal about the kind of director, coworker, and friend she was to those serving with her on the Federal Theatre. To Mrs. Shirley Rich Krohn I owe a special debt of gratitude. As a friend and former student of Hallie Flanagan's, she interrupted the task of cataloguing Mrs. Davis' library to serve as her secretary and my frequent host and aid.

The following people, whether members of the Federal Theatre, supervisors, critics, supporters, or interested observers, took valuable time to discuss the Project—often at considerable length—to my very great benefit. They are: Arthur Arent, Brooks Atkinson, Philip Barber, Howard Bay, John Mason Brown, Marc Connelly, Howard Da Silva, George Freedley, Joseph Freeman, Rosamond Gilder, Sam Handelsman, Alfred

Harding, Venzuella Jones, Florence Kerr, George Kondolf, the late Maida Reade, Elmer Rice, the late Eleanor Roosevelt, Hiram Sherman, Herman Shumlin, Bernard Simon, James Ramsey Ullman, and Ellen Woodward. For his generous assistance in locating some of those involved in the Theatre Project, I am also grateful to Dick Moore, formerly of Actors' Equity Association.

To those members of the academic community who have contributed to this study, I am particularly indebted. Professors I. B. Holley, Jr., Richard L. Watson, Jr., and Harold T. Parker of Duke University have taught me much of what I know about research and writing, as this study grew from a seminar paper into a book. To Professor Holley who read many earlier drafts and made many suggestions, I owe special thanks. Professor Robert A. Lively of Princeton University also read portions of an earlier draft. More recently, my Rutgers colleague, Professor Emery Battis, examined the manuscript, offering helpful comments as did Professor Arthur S. Link of Princeton. For Professor Link's careful editing and valuable counsel, I am especially grateful. The Rutgers University Research Council also offered me its assistance.

Finally, I wish to thank one person in particular. As a fellow scholar, Donald Mathews has read, criticized, edited, and reread these pages more times than either of us cares to remember. As a husband, he has borne both me and the manuscript with fortitude, patience, and generosity. His abundant help and unfailing support were indispensable and, for both, I am deeply grateful.

Princeton, N.J.   J.D.M.

Contents

ILLUSTRATIONS

following page 116

The Witches Scene from *Macbeth*, La Fayette Theatre in Harlem
69-TS-22Z-33 (National Archives number)
Hallie Flanagan and Harry Hopkins in New York City
69-N-1504
Eleanor Roosevelt, Harry Hopkins, Fiorello LaGuardia at
   Opening Night of *Swing Mikado*
69-TS-24Y-905-2
The Nativity Players in New York City
69-TS-23-843-2
Inventiveness of *Power*
69-TGS-33N-1
Orson Welles as Dr. Faustus
69-TS-21S-28
Regional Theatre in St. Mary's Park, the Bronx, New York
69-TGS-31J-1
Audience for Circus Performance at Bellevue Hospital
69-TS-20-17
Pinocchio with Edwin Michaels and Allan Frank
69-TGS-31P-1
One-Third of a Nation
69-TGS-33D-2
Androcles and the Lion at New York's La Fayette Theatre
69-TGS-32E-1
Power in New York City
69-TGS-33N-2
Joseph Cotton in *Horse Eats Hat*
69-TS-22G-28
Daily Scene in Lobby of the Adelphi Theatre in New York
69-TS-22N-22
Revolt of the Beavers with Jules Dassin
69-TS-24J-400-3
Murder in the Cathedral
69-TS-23-13
Harlem's *Swing Mikado*
69-TGS-32L-1

Photographs reproduced with permission of the National Archives,
   WPA Collection.

xii

THE FEDERAL THEATRE, 1935-1939

Manuscript Abbreviations for
Material in the National Archives

Approp. Comm. on WPA—Appropriations Committee, Sub-Committee on Work Projects Administration

Aud. Survey Reports—Audience Survey Reports

Barber Correspondence—Correspondence of Philip Barber, Director of the New York City Project

DI Records—Records of the Division of Investigation [WPA]

FTP Records—Records of the Federal Theatre Project

FTP-PC—Federal Theatre Project Press Clippings

Gen. Correspondence-FT Mag.—General Correspondence Regarding the Federal Theatre Magazine

GSS—General Subject Series

Narr. Reports—Narrative Reports

NOC—National Office Correspondence

NOC-Reg. I-V—National Office Correspondence with Regional Offices I-V

NOC-State—National Office Correspondence with State Offices

NOPM—National Office Publicity Material

NOTL—National Office Testimonial Letters

NSB—National Service Bureau

RG 69—Record Group No. 69; Records of the Work Projects Administration

RG 233—Record Group No. 233; Records of the House of Representatives

Woodrum Comm.—Woodrum Committee [House Appropriations Committee Investigating the WPA]

WPA-CF—Works Progress Administration Central Files

210.13—File 210.13, Memoranda

211.2—File 211.2, Drama (Federal Theatre Project)

211.29—File 211.29, Miscellaneous Correspondence

CHAPTER ONE

The Chance of a Lifetime

IN THE HARSH MONTHS between Franklin Delano Roosevelt's election in November 1932 and his inaugural in March 1933, actors, stagehands, designers, and directors were only a few of the fifteen million unemployed Americans searching hopelessly for jobs that did not exist. To Harry Hopkins, these dejected men and women, standing in line for free meals at the Actors Dinner Club of New York or for packages of food and clothing from the Stage Relief Fund, were a source of real concern.[1] In the early days of the depression, when he and his colleagues from the New York Tuberculosis Association were dabbling in work relief on an after-hours basis, this restless, gangling, young social worker had seen men carrying violin cases beg for work they obviously were not fit to do.[2] Some of these destitute musicians he had managed to steer away from heavy manual labor into lighter tasks, but he was well aware that the kind of work supplied by the Park Commission would hardly return artists to their profession with talent and skill unimpaired. As deputy administrator of the new Temporary Emergency Relief Administration (TERA) subsequently created by New York's enterprising Governor Roosevelt, Hopkins had tackled the job of running the largest, most ambitious state relief program in

[1] The scope of these actors' charities is described by Burns Mantle, editor of *The Best Plays of 1932-33 and the Yearbook of Drama in America* (New York: Dodd, Mead and Co., 1933), pp. 4-5 and *The Best Plays of 1933-34 and the Yearbook of Drama in America* (New York: Dodd, Mead and Co., 1934), p. 4.

[2] In 1939 William Mathews of the Association for Improving the Condition of the Poor obtained $75,000 from the Red Cross to use for work relief. With this sum he, Hopkins, and Dr. Jacob Goldberg of the New York Tuberculosis Association arranged for the Park Commission to supply jobs for unemployed men. Each night after work at the Tuberculosis Association, Hopkins and Dr. and Mrs. Goldberg went to AICP headquarters to assign jobs to applicants for work relief. See Robert E. Sherwood, *Roosevelt and Hopkins: An Intimate History* (New York: Harper and Bros., 1950), pp. 29-30.

3

the nation with customary energy and efficiency. But in those uncertain times, when the return of prosperity seemed just around the corner, his primary concern was relief—nothing more. Called to Washington in 1933 to head the Federal Emergency Relief Administration (FERA), Hopkins faced a task which, although vastly larger, was much the same. A part of the great war on depression, the FERA had one all-absorbing purpose: to get federal funds to the states and thence into the pockets of the needy with the greatest possible speed. At a time when state and local agencies were still trying to meet the needs of jobless millions with antiquated methods and inadequate resources, Hopkins' insistence on cash payments sufficient to provide clothing, shelter, and medical care, as well as food, marked a major improvement in relief practices. Not until the autumn of 1933 and the establishment of a federal work program under the Civil Works Administration (CWA) did its director have a chance to experiment with the notion that a man out of work through no fault of his own deserved more than a relief check and the confidence-eroding idleness of unemployment.[3]

· I ·

Convinced that society ought to conserve the talents of workers in the arts as well as in factories, Hopkins had set aside CWA funds in January 1934 for projects using unemployed artists. Across the nation, penniless painters, including many listed in *Who's Who in American Art*, were put to work decorating public buildings; opera singers were sent out to tour the Ozarks; and in New York, a hundred and fifty actors were kept

[3] *Ibid.*, pp. 31-34, 44-49; Searle F. Charles, *Minister of Relief: Harry Hopkins and the Depression* (Syracuse, N.Y.: Syracuse University Press, 1963), pp. 23 *passim* 43; Corrington Gill, *Wasted Manpower* (New York: W. W. Norton & Co., 1939), pp. 132-176; Arthur E. Burns and Edward A. Williams, *Federal Work, Security and Relief Programs* (Washington: U. S. Government Printing Office, 1941), pp. 11-35; Harry Hopkins, *Spending to Save* (New York: W. W. Norton & Co., 1936), pp. 97-107. For evidence of Hopkins' concern for destitute theatrical people, see Marvin H. McIntyre to Ed Jacobs, February 13, 1935, Roosevelt MSS, Official File 80, Franklin D. Roosevelt Library, Hyde Park, New York.

busy presenting vaudeville, marionette, and legitimate shows in the city's schools and hospitals. Although these theatrical performances lifted the spirits of the young and sick, this "free show thing," as Broadway promptly dubbed Hopkins' dramatic experiment, was a makeshift, hand-to-mouth affair. Funds, appropriated on a month-to-month basis, were sufficient to employ only a fraction of the thousands who stormed union headquarters when news of possible employment leaked out. Actors who did get on the project soon felt the stigma of relief and requested that their names not be used on programs. The anti-New Deal press denounced white-collar projects as "boondoggling"; the Republican National Committee scolded the CWA and its administrator for "gross waste"; and disgruntled Southern Democrats managed to persuade Roosevelt to abandon the thirty-cents-an-hour minimum wage on CWA projects. At the same time, conservative advisors persuaded him that if government-made jobs were available, people might choose to remain on the public payroll indefinitely. Consequently, in the spring of 1934, the President ordered the dismantling of the CWA to the bitter disappointment of its director and many supporters.[4]

Local and state relief agencies, and particularly the FERA, were able to take over. Theatrical unions, unable to care for their own, pushed for a more extended program; additional people were employed by the Public Works Division of the FERA; and open-air performances in city parks enabled thousands of New Yorkers to exchange the realities of heat and hardship for a world of make-believe and laughter. With a supplementary grant of $300,000 from the federal government, twenty touring groups were sent out to entertain jobless youths in Civilian Conservation Corps (CCC) camps in six Eastern states. These three hundred troupers, however, were but a fraction of the

[4] Jack Pulaski, "The Year in Legit," *Variety*, January 1, 1935, p. 134; Edwin Bruce, Address to the Cosmopolitan Club, n.d., Edwin Bruce Papers, Archives of American Art, Detroit Institute of Arts; Hallie Flanagan, *Arena* (New York: Duell, Sloan and Pearce 1940), p. 15; Sherwood, *Roosevelt and Hopkins*, pp. 55-56; William E. Leuchtenburg, *Franklin D. Roosevelt and the New Deal, 1932-1949* (New York: Harper and Row, 1963), pp. 122-123.

5

number of unemployed actors, stagehands, lighting technicians, and costume designers who waited, like cast-off stage props, hoping someday to be put to use.[5]

While they waited, the nation, like the awakening Gulliver, had begun to stir. Told that they had nothing to fear but fear itself, the American people looked to Washington for action: this time they were not disappointed. Mobilized by a confident Chief Executive, Congress embarked on the most extraordinary legislative session in the country's history. In a few short months, bills had been passed that took the nation off the gold standard, repealed prohibition, regulated Wall Street, guaranteed small bank deposits, authorized huge public works projects, pledged billions of dollars to save home and farm from foreclosure, and began a far-reaching experiment in regional development. Pressed by the President, Congress committed the nation to an unprecedented program of government-industry cooperation, accepted responsibility for the welfare of the jobless quarter of the labor force, and promised millions in benefits to farmers who would adjust the production of staple crops. Here, at last, was action—action as Roosevelt had promised. It was invigorating and exhausting, and it caught the imagination of the nation; but it did not end the depression.[6]

As farmers with checks from the AAA and workers with relief checks crowded into shops and stores, the *New York Times* Weekly Business Index climbed from 72 in October 1933 to 86 in May 1934—and there it stalled. National income rose $8 billion in 1934 to a little more than half what it had been in 1929. In New York City, restaurants in the financial district, empty the year of the President's inaugural, filled with lunchtime customers; but in towns and cities across the nation millions of unemployed men and women could scarcely pay the price of a cup of coffee and a doughnut. Clearly the country had weath-

[5] Pulaski, "The Year in Legit," *Variety*, January 1, 1935, p. 134; January 22, 1935, p. 53; February 27, 1935, p. 59.
[6] Leuchtenburg, *Franklin D. Roosevelt and the New Deal*, pp. 41-62; Arthur M. Schlesinger, Jr., *The Coming of the New Deal* (Boston: Houghton Mifflin Co., 1959), pp. 1-23.

ered the crisis, but it had not recovered; and, like a patient on the mend, it irritably refused to recover in silence.[7]

Aroused by the display of presidential initiative, groups at both ends of the political spectrum began to display a vitality of their own. The business community, much of which had readily supported Roosevelt in the dark days after the inaugural, had become increasingly disenchanted with the President and his policies. Disturbed by their experience with the National Recovery Administration (NRA) and indignant at the passage of legislation to regulate the stock market and communications industry, more and more businessmen were convinced that the New Deal meant government control of business. As federal spending pushed the national debt ever higher, they could only regard the prospect of continued meddling and spending as a threat to business recovery. For some the threat was moral as well as economic. Conservatives were soon denouncing the New Deal as an aberration destructive of traditional American freedoms and demanding a return to self-reliance, a balanced budget, and limited government.[8]

While the newly formed Liberty League, an organization of conservative Democrats and certain wealthy businessmen, crusaded on behalf of property rights and private enterprise, an oddly assorted band of prophets on the left won huge followings with schemes for new and radical departures. Minnesota's Governor Floyd Olson, with his Cooperative Commonwealth; Louisiana's shrewd, flamboyant "Messiah of the Rednecks," Huey Long, with his Share-the-Wealth program; the Detroit Radio Priest, Reverend Charles E. Coughlin, with his diatribes against bankers and Bolsheviks; California's benign Dr. Townsend, with promises of pensions—these promoters, whatever their proposal, found ready supporters in a nation newly alive with ferment, indignation, and discontent.[9]

[7] Leuchtenburg, *Franklin D. Roosevelt and the New Deal*, pp. 93-94.
[8] *Ibid.*, pp. 91-92.
[9] *Ibid.*, pp. 95-106; Arthur M. Schlesinger, Jr., *The Politics of Upheaval* (Boston: Houghton Mifflin Co., 1960), pp. 3, 15 *passim* 69.

Despite these radical rumblings, most Americans remained intensely loyal to the President; in the fall of 1934 they went to the polls to prove it. In a landslide victory that astonished the most optimistic of the administration's prognosticators, the party of Franklin Delano Roosevelt emerged from an off-year election with 322 seats in the House, 69 in the Senate, leaving the Republicans weaker than at any time since the Civil War. To that dean of American editors, William Allen White, the election results signified that Roosevelt had been "all but crowned by the people." To jubilant New Dealers in Washington, these same results seemed a clear-cut mandate for further reform, a second Hundred Days. None was more elated than Harry L. Hopkins. "Boys—this is our hour," he announced to his staff on the way to the races. "We've got to get everything we want—a works program, social security, wages and hours, everything—now or never."[10]

Prodded by administration liberals like Hopkins in the weeks following the election, Roosevelt found himself forced to choose between the increasingly critical leaders of business and industry, and a population tired of suffering from "old inequities." In January 1935, the President of the United States went before Congress with a proposal to replace the dole with a public employment program that would provide work for three and a half million able-bodied, but jobless, men and women. With the eloquent incisiveness that had become familiar to a nation, Roosevelt declared: "The Federal Government must and shall quit this business of relief. I am not willing that the vitality of our people be further sapped by the giving of cash, of market baskets, of a few hours of weekly work cutting grass, raking leaves or picking up papers in the public parks." While the Senate debated the virtues of the "security wage" proposed by the President for relief workers as against the higher "prevailing wage" preferred by New Deal liberals and the A. F. of L., relief

[10] The *New York Times*, November 7, 1934, pp. 1-3ff.; "The Congress," *Time*, XXIV (November 19, 1934), 12; "The Presidency," *ibid.*, 11; Sherwood, *Roosevelt and Hopkins*, p. 64.

officials, leaders of Actors' Equity Union, and other interested persons met to explore the extent and remedy of unemployment among musicians and stage people. By mid-March 1935, *Variety* confidently predicted that, unless Congress put "too many strings" on the appropriations sought by Roosevelt, more federal relief for show business was quite likely.[11]

After much grumbling about "blank checks" for the White House, Congress finally handed over nearly $5 billion for work relief to be spent largely as the Chief Executive saw fit. It was several months, however, before the President himself saw fit to decide whether the money was to be spent by the crusty, cautious Public Works administrator, Harold Ickes, or the dynamic, impulsive Hopkins. Since quick reemployment and a sharp stimulus to consumer purchasing power were key goals, Hopkins' plan to channel funds into the pockets of men on relief rather than into self-liquidating public works projects seemed more desirable to him. To the Iowa-born administrator, Roosevelt finally assigned a division of the new works organization to be known as the Works Progress Administration (WPA), and the authority to "recommend and carry on small useful projects designed to assure a maximum of employment in all localities."[12]

Both men agreed that one of these "small useful projects" should be designed especially for actors, artists, musicians, and writers. Deciding upon the desirability of such plans was far easier than finding imaginative men and women in the arts who could conceive, set up, and administer them within a governmental framework. Whoever the administrator, he would have to use to full advantage the talents of a destitute, highly indi-

[11] "Annual Message to the Congress, January 4, 1935," *The Public Papers and Addresses of Franklin Delano Roosevelt*, comp. Samuel I. Rosenman (New York: Random House, 1938), VI: *The Court Disapproves* (1935), p. 20; Leuchtenburg, *Franklin D. Roosevelt and the New Deal*, p. 124; *Variety*, March 13, 1935, p. 60.

[12] Sherwood, *Roosevelt and Hopkins*, pp. 66-69. For a detailed account of the "angling, planning, and wrangling" involved in the creation of the new relief organization, and especially the Hopkins-Ickes rivalry, see Charles, *Minister of Relief*, pp. 94-127.

9

vidualistic group within the anti-individualistic confines of relief requirements and Washington bureaucracy. Fully aware of his problem, Hopkins confided to a friend in his usual pungent language: "God, if I've had trouble before, what do you think I'm going to have now." Nevertheless, beneath that characteristic air of cynicism and defeatist irony was a "buoyant—almost gay—conviction that all walls fall before a man of resource and decision." In an equally characteristic display of both, Hopkins picked up the telephone, and, on May 16, 1935, called Hallie Flanagan, director of the Vassar College Experimental Theatre. Would she come down right away to talk about unemployed actors?[13]

This was not Mrs. Flanagan's first invitation from Hopkins. The year before, as CWA administrator, he had urged her to come to New York to help him out. However, the Vassar director, about to sail for England to set up an experimental theatre at Dartington Hall, had refused to change her plans despite Hopkins' abrupt mutterings that he "didn't know what an American would do in an English theatre." Later at Dartington, when she suggested that the new theatre be headed by an Englishman, Mrs. Flanagan recalled Hopkins' misgivings. But in the ancient hillside theatres of Greece where she and her new husband, Professor Philip H. Davis of Vassar, pored over classical inscriptions, basking in the Mediterranean sun and their new-found happiness, the Relief Administrator and his unemployed actors seemed far away. On her return to America, however, Hopkins and his still jobless actors could not be so easily dismissed. This time Hallie Flanagan consented.[14]

Stopping first in New York, the Vassar director began telephoning people who she believed might have given serious thought to this impending union of government and the arts. As

[13] F.D.R. to Hopkins, May 10, 1935, Roosevelt MSS, Official File 954; Florence Kerr, tape recording, October 16, 1963, Archives of American Art; Schlesinger, *The Coming of the New Deal*, p. 266; Flanagan, *Arena*, p. 7.
[14] Flanagan, *Arena*, pp. 3-6; Flanagan, Autobiographical Notes for Jane Mathews.

Hopkins had already discovered, however, neither union officials, editors of theatrical periodicals, nor directors of local work projects seemed to have on hand imaginative workable plans for nationwide theatres employing destitute actors. Silently bewailing her failure to turn up a single original proposal, this tiny woman with the pleasant, intelligent face, large brown eyes, and bobbed hair went to the Pennsylvania Hotel to meet Elmer Rice. Promptly at five o'clock, he emerged "unpressed, rumpled, rosy," and full of ideas. A Pulitzer Prize-winning playwright, known for his dramas of protest and expressions of dissatisfaction with the commercial theatre, Rice was presently engrossed in the formation of the Theatre Alliance, a new cooperative, nonprofit, repertory group.[15] Hoping to secure government funds for the

---

[15] Rice's expressionistic drama, *The Adding Machine*, produced first in 1923, remains one of the most significant experimental plays written by an American playwright. After the Pulitzer Prize-winning *Street Scene*, which Rice himself directed in 1928, the playwright turned out other dramas of protest, notably *We, the People*, a pageant of the depression, and *Judgment Day*, a protest against Fascism. For criticism of Rice's work, see Barrett H. Clark, "Broadway Brightens Up a Bit," *The Drama Magazine*, XIX (March 1929), 170-171; Robert Littell, "Brighter Lights: Broadway in Review," *Theatre Arts Monthly*, XIII (March 1929), 164-166; Francis R. Bellamy, "The Theatre," *Outlook and Independent*, CLI (January 23, 1929), 140; R. D. Skinner, "The Play: *We, the People*," *The Commonweal*, XVII (February 8, 1933), 411; Barclay McCarty, "Three Designs for Living: Broadway in Review," *Theatre Arts Monthly*, XII (April 1933), 258; Joseph Wood Krutch, "The Prosecution Rests," *The Nation*, CXXXVI (February 8, 1933), 158-160; "Two Playwrights With a Difference," *The Literary Digest*, CXV (February 11, 1933), 15-16; Richard D. Skinner, "The Play: *Judgment Day*," *The Commonweal*, X (September 28, 1934), 509.

Rice's feelings about the commercial theatre are expressed in various articles and books, among them: Elmer Rice, "Towards an Adult Theatre," *The Drama Magazine*, XXI (February 1931), 5, 18; "The Elmer Rices Buy a Theatre for *Judgment Day*," *Newsweek*, IV (August 11, 1934), 20; Joseph Wood Krutch, "Elmer Rice and the Critics," *The Nation*, CXXXIX (November 21, 1934), 580; Elmer Rice, *Two Plays: Not for Children and Between Two Worlds* (New York: Coward McCann, Inc., 1935), Introduction.

For a discussion of the Theatre Alliance, see Elmer Rice, "Theatre Alliance: A Cooperative Repertory Theatre Project," *Theatre Arts Monthly*, XIX (June 1935), 427.

11

Alliance, he affably confessed to his Poughkeepsie friend that he had gone to Washington to present his request only to have Hopkins moan: "Katharine Cornell has been here, and Frank Gillmore and Edith Isaacs and Eva Le Gallienne and they are driving me crazy. . . . When I talk about plans for an American theatre, each one talks about his own little problem. Isn't there any *one* person in America who has no axe to grind?" After three manhattans, the bespectacled playwright gallantly insisted that he had replied, "Hallie Flanagan"—to Hopkins' great satisfaction. More important, Rice himself had returned to New York and, with the Relief Administrator's encouragement, sketched the broad outlines of a plan to transform local theatres into community art centers. Coordinated on a national basis, each theatrical company would produce first rate programs ranging from Shakespeare to modern farce, folk plays, and topical works by American dramatists—in short, whatever plays would meet the needs of a particular community or region, at prices that community could afford.[16] As he expounded on possibilities that for nearly twenty years had been no more than a dream, Hallie Flanagan interrupted with questions and ideas of her own, until both were talking in unison—"plagiarizing each other," Rice laughed—in their excitement over this magnificent chance to create a decentralized national theatre.[17]

Full of hope and ideas after her evening with Rice, Mrs. Flanagan arrived in Washington only three days after receiving Hopkins' call. Escorted by Jacob Baker, who was to head the white-collar division of the WPA,[18] she walked from the Willard Hotel to Hopkins' office listening to Baker talk about the Presi-

[16] Rice to Hopkins and Jacob Baker, April 28, 1935, Personal Papers of Elmer Rice, Stamford, Conn. An abridged version of the letter is printed in Elmer Rice, *The Living Theatre* (New York: Harper and Bros., 1959), pp. 150-153.

[17] Flanagan to Philip Davis, May 17, 1935, Personal Papers of Hallie Flanagan, Poughkeepsie, N. Y.

[18] Baker had also supervised the work program for the FERA and CWA. Prior to joining Hopkins' staff, Baker had been a high school teacher, a mine superintendent, a personnel expert, and the organizer of Vanguard Press. See Charles, *Minister of Relief*, p. 30.

12

dent and absorbing the overwhelming sense of adventure, cocky assurance, and ceaseless activity which in two short years had transformed the capital city from a placid, easygoing Southern town into a lively metropolitan center. When the rickety elevator in the Walker-Johnson Building on New York Avenue finally stopped near Hopkins' small, drab office with its peeling walls and overflowing ash trays, she found the lanky Relief Administrator much as she had remembered him—"nice, brown and humorous." But the harness-maker's son from Grinnell had little time for reminiscences about the quiet, Iowa town where they had gone through grade school, high school, and college a year apart.[19] Tossing out a folder containing plans and programs submitted by various people connected with the theatre, Hopkins said: "I wish you would spend a week here and go over these things and tell me what you think." As they talked about a theatrical organization that would involve the entire nation, Hopkins suddenly remembered a garden party at the White House that afternoon. "You'll want to [come and] talk with Mrs. Roosevelt," he urged. "She's interested in all these art projects." The First Lady was indeed interested. Recalling her acquaintance with the Vassar Experimental Theatre during the years when Roosevelt had been a trustee of the college, she promised to ask Vassar's President MacCracken to give his director a leave of absence. Not until she returned to the hotel, to wait for Hopkins to take her to a ball at the Russian embassy, did this soft-spoken young woman pause long enough to ponder what so far had been an "incredible" day.[20]

Had Hallie Flanagan been in Washington longer, she would have realized just how incredible it was for the frantically busy Hopkins to devote the better part of a day and evening to any visitor, whether sent for or not. But the Relief Administrator could consider the time well spent. Although aware that the

[19] Mrs. Flanagan was graduated from Grinnell College in 1911; Hopkins, in 1912. Henry Alden to Florence Blakely and Jane Mathews, November 7, 1960.

[20] Flanagan, Personal Notes, May 19, 1935, Flanagan Papers; Flanagan, *Arena*, pp. 8-12.

Vassar director was totally lacking in administrative experience, Hopkins wanted her to take over his unemployed actors—and with good reason. A woman of immense integrity, originality, and drive, Hallie Flanagan possessed an extraordinary ability to fire the imagination and energy of others, a sensitivity to current problems, and a broad knowledge of drama and the theatre. That she had also acquired an international reputation as one of the leaders in experimental theatre may have seemed a bit surprising to those, like Hopkins, who remembered her as Hallie Ferguson, a pretty, popular co-ed whose only plan was to marry Murray Flanagan, a handsome Irishman of the Grinnell College class of 1909.[21]

· II ·

Hallie Ferguson Flanagan Davis would have been the first to agree that her career hardly fitted the traditional "Who's Who" pattern—at least not in the beginning. Born of German-Scotch ancestry in Redfield, South Dakota on August 27, 1890, she had lived in various midwestern states before her parents, like Hopkins', finally settled down in the college town of Grinnell. Despite frequent moves and fluctuations in family fortunes, the Fergusons had given their three children a secure, serene childhood—one filled with recollections of horses named after characters in novels; of plays written and acted by two small sisters; of a quiet, gentle woman who painted pastels and kept the cooky jar filled; and of a gay, volatile, dynamic Scotsman who read aloud from Scott, Dickens, and Thackeray, and who somehow communicated his own unswerving conviction that all men *were* created equal, and that life was full of changes, each a new adventure. This ability to accept change was perhaps Frederic Ferguson's most important bequest to his elder daughter whose adult life would be filled with tragedy. It reinforced not only her own will to survive, adjust, and overcome, but also her

21 Florence Kerr to Jane Mathews, April 10, 1962.

14

overwhelming belief that the theatre, if it would remain vital, had to respond to a changing world.[22]

Hallie Flanagan's private world had changed abruptly in March 1918. Her father suffered a severe financial loss and her husband contracted tuberculosis and died a year later. A widow with no previous thought of a career, she now had to make a living for herself, two small sons, and aging parents.[23] Summoning the vast reserves of energy stored in her small frame, she set out in 1919 to persuade the head of the Grinnell College English Department that acting experience in the college dramatic club—actually only an extracurricular activity—along with the classroom experience she had acquired the previous year at Grinnell High School were adequate preparation for teaching a course in drama. After some talk about the lack of a Master's degree, he consented.

Grinnell College had no cause to regret the decision. One year later this indomitable young woman published a prize-winning play, *The Curtain*. Writing, rather than acting, the author had reasoned, would allow more time with her children. Convinced that any play to be fully understood had to be performed rather than merely read, she next persuaded Grinnell authorities to let her use an art room one night a week for a new course called "Basic Communication." It was the beginning of a theatre whose productions soon attracted the attention of Professor George Pierce Baker and won for their director an invitation to the famous 47 Workshop as Baker's production assistant during his last year at Harvard. Her excitement tempered by grief over the death of her precocious seven-year-old son, Hallie Flanagan and five-year-old Frederic journeyed east to Cambridge.[24]

In 1923, when Hallie Flanagan arrived at Radcliffe, the 47

---

[22] Flanagan, Autobiographical Notes for Jane Mathews.

[23] *Ibid.*

[24] *Ibid.*; Biographical Notes on Hallie Flanagan, Record Group No. 69: Records of the Work Projects Administration, Records of the Federal Theatre Project, National Office General Subject File (RG 69, FTP Records, NOGSF).

15

Workshop already occupied a unique and venerable position in the world of American theatre. Although the stately Baker with his pince-nez and gray buttoned-up suit hardly fitted the stereotype of the pioneer, he had been among the first to believe that a potential playwright could be taught the essentials of his craft through study and application of principles followed by dramatists in the past. How well the student succeeded, Baker had soon realized, could only be determined when the play was staged and acted in a working theatre exactly as conceived by its author. Inspired by the famous Abbey Theatre in Dublin, which had started from such small beginnings, the Harvard professor in 1912 had turned the first playwriting course offered in the United States, English 47, into the 47 Workshop, a cooperative, self-sustaining, theatrical laboratory. By thus combining the study of dramatic technique with the practical problems of production, he had provided a new method of training brilliantly justified by the contributions of such former students as playwrights Eugene O'Neill, Sidney Howard, Philip Barry, Edward Sheldon, Percy MacKaye, George Abbott, and Josephine Preston Peabody. Among the others who had studied with him were producers Winthrop Ames and Theresa Helburn; designers Robert Edmond Jones and Lee Simonson; critics Robert Benchley, Van Wyck Brooks, Heywood Broun, and Kenneth MacGowan.[25]

Hallie Flanagan had soon proved no exception. Working with such fellow students as Donald Oenslager and John Mason Brown and, of course, Baker himself, she filled in enormous gaps in her knowledge of the theatre, absorbed the principles on

[25] Wisner Payne Kinne, *George Pierce Baker and the American Theatre* (Cambridge, Mass.: Harvard University Press, 1954); George Pierce Baker, *Dramatic Technique* (New York: Houghton Mifflin Co., 1919), vi-xii; Boyd Smith, "The University Theatre as it was Built Stone upon Stone," *Theatre Arts Monthly*, xvii (July 1933), 521-530; LaFayette McLaws, "A Master of Playwrights," *The North American Review*, cc (September 1914), 459-467; George Pierce Baker, "The 47 Workshop," *The Century Magazine*, ci (February 1921), 420-421; John Mason Brown, "The Four Georges: George Pierce Baker at Work," *Theatre Arts Monthly*, xvii (July 1933), 538; "Two 'Baker Maps,'" *ibid.*, 552-553.

which the 47 Workshop was based, and completed a satirical comedy, *Incense*, with which the Harvard professor chose to open his first season at Yale. Her talent polished by much needed training and experience, she returned briefly to Grinnell, not to devote herself to playwriting as Baker wished, but to a more financially secure position as head of dramatic work at the college. Quickly transforming "Basic Communication" into the Grinnell Experimental Theatre, she began a season of productions ranging from a spectacular *Romeo and Juliet* to *Ace of Thirteen* by a then unknown playwright, Michael Arlen. Acclaim was immediate. Frederick Keppel of the Carnegie Foundation attended a performance as the guest of Grinnell's president, J. H. T. Main. Delighted with what he had seen, he promptly sent off an article on the Grinnell Theatre to *The Atlantic Monthly* and arranged with Baker to sponsor its director for a Guggenheim grant. No less impressed was Vassar's president, Henry Noble MacCracken, who invited the Grinnell director to establish an experimental theatre at Vassar similar to the one she had started in Iowa. Mrs. Flanagan accepted.

Encouraged by the humorous, humane MacCracken, she set about creating a smaller version of the 47 Workshop on a campus where the only stage had to be shared with public lecturers, musicians, and freshman hygiene classes. Her efforts were soon interrupted, however, for in the spring of 1926, she received a grant from the Guggenheim Foundation for a comparative study of the European theatre—the first to be awarded to a woman. A unique opportunity to search out the best in contemporary theatre, the year abroad would convince Hallie Flanagan that truly creative theatre was theatre which responded artistically and socially to a changing world.[26]

Planning originally to spend a month in each of twelve countries, Mrs. Flanagan went directly to London. Trafalgar Square at sunset and Buckingham Palace with its Milne-like toy soldiers

[26] Flanagan, Autobiographical Notes for Jane Mathews; Hallie Flanagan, *Dynamo* (New York: Duel, Sloan and Pearce, 1943), pp. 15-16. *Dynamo* provides an excellent account of Mrs. Flanagan's work with the Vassar Experimental Theatre.

were unforgettable sights, but the vigorous lusty theatre of Shakespeare's England had long been dead. What remained was a glossy, empty shell surrounded by an air of propriety and elaborate ritual—an art untouched either by a war that had destroyed England's youth and ended a glorious century, or by the economic and social changes which had come with an uncertain peace.[27]

Although languages and landscapes changed, theatres did not. In the famous old Viennese theatre, the venerable Comédie-Française, and the prosperous state theatres of Germany, she found technical proficiency but no life, no willingness to interpret a new age, save in those few theatres where expressionism held sway. A failure to believe characterizes the contemporary theatre, Gordon Craig told his young American visitor. Not until actors and spectators are united in a common belief, the famous scene designer insisted, would plays again become a revelation of the inner life and values as they had been with the Greeks. But if the union of actor and spectator did not exist in most of the theatres of Western Europe—and for Craig it did not—it existed for Hallie Flanagan in Russia in all its strength and vitality.[28]

In 1926, when she arrived in the U.S.S.R., the worst ravages of war and the excesses of War Communism had passed. With the reintroduction of limited capitalism under the New Economic Policy, this huge and varied nation had recovered its economic vitality while continuing the social transformation that was to create a new soviet citizenry. Dominated by men of rare artistic gifts who were willing to take part in this new task, the Russian theatre, strong since the middle of the eighteenth century, flour-

[27] Hallie Flanagan, *Shifting Scenes of the Modern European Theatre* (New York: Coward McCann, Inc., 1928), pp. 8-13.

[28] *Ibid.*, pp. 72-73. Craig, the son of British actress Ellen Terry, was a noted designer of scenery and a considerable influence on American stagecraft particularly in the 1920's. For a brief discussion of Craig and his influence, see *A Treasury of the Theatre From Henrik Ibsen to Arthur Miller*, ed. John Gassner (New York: Simon and Schuster, 1956), pp. 258, 260-261.

ished as never before. Under the direction of its founder, Constantine Stanislavsky, the Moscow Art Theatre, re-invigorated by new talent, new plans, and almost complete freedom, enjoyed the international reputation for inspired, authentic productions it had known under the tsars. But it was in the workshops of Stanislavsky's former student, Vsevolod Meierhold, and of Alexander Tairov that Hallie Flanagan found the new artistic developments that would make the Russian stage the mecca for actors, directors, and designers throughout the West. A confirmed innovator and dedicated Communist, Meierhold had found in the new order a chance to experiment with new artistic forms and new methods of acting. In his great, bare theatre filled with a jostling, laughing audience of workers, students, and soldiers, this impressionable young woman watched with a mixture of antagonism and amusement as roughly clad actors appeared on a curtainless stage in a satire called *The Death and Destruction of Europe*. It was propaganda, she realized, but in the hands of an artist like Meierhold, it was also theatre transforming actors and audience into one.

So it was throughout Russia. In theatres, schools, prisons, peasant villages, and factories, she saw plays performed, sometimes crudely and primitively, but always with dedication and belief. A few years later she would deplore the Stalinist policies that transformed the stage into an indoctrination center and drove Stanislavsky and Meierhold into exile. But in the Russia of 1926, Hallie Flanagan had discovered a theatre of great artistry and tremendous vitality, a theatre which seemed to serve a force beyond itself—one which had dared to respond to a changing world.[29]

[29] Flanagan, *Shifting Scenes*, pp. 82 *passim* 114. Some awareness of what was happening to the Russian theatre under Stalin is indicated in articles written for *Theatre Guild Magazine* upon her return from the Russian Theatrical Olympiad in 1930. See "Blood and Oil," viii (October 1930). 27-29; "The Tractor Invades the Theatre," viii (December 1930), 36-38; "The Dragon's Teeth," vivi (February 1931), 24-28. For other accounts of the tremendous vitality of the Russian theatre in the late 1920's, see P. A. Markov, *The Soviet Theatre* (London: Victor

In the years that followed Mrs. Flanagan's return to Pough-keepsie, the Vassar Theatre continued to gain stature as one of the nation's leading experimental theatres.[30] It won for its director the fanatical loyalty of students, the admiration of theatrical leaders abroad, and the respect of Broadway critics who journeyed up from New York for major productions. Whether an original student play, an experiment in form, or a play in the original Greek, Vassar's theatrical productions, according to its president, were a source of intellectual stimulus for the entire college.[31]

Perhaps none was more stimulating than *Can You Hear Their Voices?* Produced in 1931, before the appearance of documentary books such as Erskine Caldwell's *You Have Seen Their Faces,* Dorothea Lange and Paul Taylor's *An American Exodus,* or even before John Steinbeck's *Grapes of Wrath,* the play was as experimental in form as it was controversial in content. In her carefully documented dramatization of Whittaker Chambers' account of the Arkansas drought, Hallie Flanagan and a former student, Margaret Ellen Clifford, told a moving story. Seven scenes, played with no intermission, related the narrative of dirt farmers who starved while Congress "dilly-dallied on the

Gallancz Ltd., 1934) and Marc Slonim, *Russian Theatre From the Empire to the Soviets* (New York: The World Publishing Co., 1961), pp. 228ff. Slonim points out that by 1927 there were 24,000 theatrical circles in Russia; drama schools were swamped; theatres crowded; and experimentation encouraged. "Interest in the theatre resembled an epidemic unprecedented in modern history," p. 240.

[30] According to Alistair Cooke, the Vassar Theatre bore comparison "with some of the most distinguished experimental theatres in Europe." See "A National Theatre on Trial," *Fortnightly* (December 1936), p. 726; also John K. Hutchins, "Vassar's Hallie Flanagan," the *New York Times*, September 22, 1935, Sec. 10, p. 1.

[31] Henry Noble MacCracken, *The Hickory Limb* (New York: Charles Scribner's Sons, 1950), p. 79. MacCracken himself was a frequent actor in Experimental Theatre productions. For additional information on these productions, see Hallie Flanagan, "Experiment at Vassar," *Theatre Arts Monthly*, XII (January 1928), 70-71; "The Tributary Theatre . . . ," *Theatre Arts Monthly*, XVII (July 1933), 566; Flanagan, *Dynamo*.

dole." The production, according to a reviewer for the *New York Times*, consisted of a

> series of black and white vignettes . . . capped by small blackouts and interwoven argumentively with the stark facts of Congress's inaction thrown at you from printed slides on a huge white screen. Dominating the picture was the barbed lampoon of the quarter million dollar debutante party which startled Washington at the height of the drought.

At the end, the screen was brought down as the prison-bound father sent his sons to Communist headquarters in the hope that they could "make a better world." A voice is heard saying to the audience: "These boys are symbols of thousands of our people who are turning somewhere for leaders. Will it be to the educated minority? Can You Hear Their Voices?" It was, said the *Times*' critic, "a play in which propaganda did not defeat drama, as usually happened, because it was all propaganda—scaring, biting, smashing propaganda." As such it was a novel experiment in an age when playwrights, according to Joseph Wood Krutch, were still trying to "fictionalize" history, economics, or current events; when they were not content to present their information and arguments pure and straight, but tried to slip them in between the lines of a conventional play.[32]

As effective as it was novel, *Can You Hear Their Voices?* made itself heard far beyond the walls of Vassar's Experimental Theatre. In Poughkeepsie, students collected clothes, medical supplies, and money for the relief of suffering farmers. They wrote letters to congressmen and to local newspapers. Meanwhile the play was performed across the country by players at Jasper Deeter's Hedgerow Theatre, students at Smith College,

---

[32] Flanagan, *Dynamo*, pp. 106-110; the *New York Times*, May 10, 1931, Sec. 8, p. 2; Joseph Wood Krutch, *The American Drama Since 1918: An Informal History* (New York: George Brazillier, Inc., 1957), p. 282. Krutch gives credit to the Federal Theatre's Living Newspaper for being the first to present information as a thing interesting in itself. In fact, *Can You Hear Their Voices?* was a precursor of the Living Newspaper in its use of factual material, charts, statistics, loud-speakers, and blackouts. See *Dynamo*, p. 107.

and farmers in North Dakota. It was done by the Cleveland Playhouse, by Negro groups in Cleveland, by students at the Commonwealth College and at the Beaux Arts Theatre in Los Angeles. In Milwaukee, Lansdale, Philadelphia, Newark, New York, and Vancouver there were productions. When Vassar published the play, copies were ordered by theatres in Greece, China, Hungary, Finland, Denmark, France, Russia, Spain, and Australia. Not even Broadway was exempt. *Theatre Guild Magazine*, abandoning its usual procedure of reviewing only professional plays, wrote of the Vassar production: "Disregarding the accepted conventions of dramatic art, *Can You Hear Their Voices?* deeply moved its audience." *Theatre Arts Monthly* called it "native material, well characterized, handling experimental technical equipment skillfully, worth any theatre's attention." As for subject matter, conservatives found the play too radical; radicals, too conservative. Communists complained that it was not to the educated minority, but to the Communist Party that the working class must turn for leadership. To the Vassar director, however, *Can You Hear Their Voices?* was simply theatre at its best—experimental, challenging, and, above all, relevant to a world of hunger and privation outside the tree-filled campus in Poughkeepsie.[33]

In Washington, the plight of several thousand jobless actors was a forceable reminder that the kind of theatre created in Poughkeepsie existed only in a few isolated communities, certainly not on Broadway. As she studied conditions in the commercial theatre contributing to unemployment, Hallie Flanagan rediscovered an ailing, frequently irrelevant institution that seemingly had come of age artistically and socially too late. Like most enterprises at the turn of the century, the commercial

[33] *Can You Hear Their Voices?*, *Theatre Guild Magazine*, VI (July 1931), 24-25; "Theatre Arts Bookshelf: *Can You Hear Their Voices?*," *Theatre Arts Monthly*, XV (November 1931), 952; Flanagan, *Dynamo*, pp. 107-110. Plays of protest, incidentally, were not confined to Vassar in the spring of 1931. Princeton's Theatre Intime produced Ernst Toller's *Men and Masses*; Yale, Harold Igo's *Steel*. See "The Colleges Protest," *Theatre Arts Monthly*, XV (July 1931), 535-536.

theatre had succumbed to the monopolistic, profit-making devices which were a part of the economic revolution transforming America. The list of such practices was long: gambling in theatres as real estate; syndicates fostering a cross-country touring system; a monopoly booking system; the "star" system; long-run shows that destroyed repertory; type casting that stifled an actor's development; the staging of the "tried and true" rather than the work of a new playwright with ideas. The result was predictable—an art stumbling toward maturity had been transformed into a primarily commercial enterprise.

How little the American people needed such a theatre had become strikingly apparent with the coming of motion pictures. Almost overnight theatres across the country had closed and reopened as movie houses. Road companies and vaudeville became virtually a thing of the past, as thousands of actors struggled westward to Hollywood hoping to find jobs as extras. With the "legitimate" theatre now almost the exclusive property of New York City, Broadway producers began charging as much as five and six dollars for admission in order to make a profit after paying rental prices, union wages, and extensive advertising costs. The select audience thus created gradually demanded, and got, productions that reflected interest in the theatre as art rather than exclusively as business. Although it had always been a small audience, it was made still smaller by the depression, as Hopkins' records so plainly indicated. In 1933 one-half of the theatres in New York were dark; more than one-half of the actors unemployed; and one-third of the plays produced were revivals of past successes. Talk about reforming the theatre "when the end of the present system comes," once confined to a few dissident individuals, was now heard from leaders of Actors' Equity Union as well as the managers, actors, and playwrights who flooded Washington with schemes for subsidizing the performing arts.[34]

[34] Edith J. R. Isaacs, "Portrait of a Theatre: America-1935," *Theatre Arts Monthly*, XVII (January 1933), 32-42; "The World and the Theatre: Reforming the Theatre," *Theatre Arts Monthly*, XVII (May 1933), 331-

The theatre which was to benefit most from these reforms was located along a half-mile area in the heart of Manhattan, but, as Hallie Flanagan well knew, it was by no means the only live theatre in America. In the heyday of the progressive crusade to police industrial monopolies and restore popular democracy, would-be reformers of the theatre began talking about that enterprise as a "communal instrument," dedicated to "public, not private ends." The catalyst that caused countless drama groups to spring up all over the United States seems to have been the touring Irish Players who followed the Abbey Theatre's founder, W. B. Yeats, to this country in 1911. Struck by the contrast between the natural, authentic folk art of the superb Abbey Players and the often feeble productions of their own highly commercialized stage, a few imaginative individuals had resolved to create the kind of theatre that commercial managers, with a few exceptions, would not supply.[35]

In 1912, the same year that George Pierce Baker's 47 Workshop produced its first plays by aspiring young Harvard dramatists before a Cambridge audience, "little theatres" were founded in Chicago and Boston. Although the latter flourished but briefly, others sprang up across the country in what proved to be a veritable mushrooming of university and community theatres. At the University of North Dakota, and later at the University of North Carolina, a former Baker student, Frederick H. Koch, urged his own students to look to their environment

---

333; Rice, *The Living Theatre*, p. 149; Flanagan, *Arena*, pp. 12-16; Sheldon Cheney, *The Theatre* (New York: Longmans, Green and Co., 1930), p. 500; Sheldon Cheney, *The Art Theatre* (New York: Alfred A. Knopf, 1925), pp. 30-31; Willson Whitman, *Bread and Circuses* (New York: Oxford University Press, 1937), pp. 10-15; Kenneth MacGowan, *Footlights Across America: Towards a National Theatre* (New York: Harcourt, Brace and Co., 1929), pp. 59-70.

[35] Percy MacKaye, *The Playhouse and the Play and other Addresses Concerning the Theatre and Democracy in America* (New York: The Macmillan Co., 1909), p. 5; Glenn Hughes, *A History of the American Theatre, 1700-1950* (New York: Samuel French, 1951), p. 369; Edith J. R. Isaacs, "Come of Age!," *Theatre Arts Monthly*, XVIII (July 1934), 478-488.

and traditions as did the Irish playwrights.[36] The result was a repertoire of remarkably effective folk plays by such writers as Thomas Wolfe, Paul Green and Dorothy and Dubose Heyward.[37] At the University of Iowa, E. C. Mabie developed native playwrights and communitywide interest in the theatre, as did Thomas H. Dickinson at the University of Wisconsin, A. M. Drummond at Cornell, and Glenn Hughes at the University of Washington. By the 1920's those colleges and universities which permitted drama to be lifted out of the classroom and into a professionally equipped playhouse were sending graduates, often men and women of considerable talent and originality, to the New York stage as well as the scarcely less professional community theatres around the country.[38]

[36] One of Koch's former students wrote: "Applying principles which are closely akin to those of the Abbey Theatre, Koch approached the dream of an American People's Theatre even as Yeats, Synge and Lady Gregory had striven for an Irish Theatre. For one who has worked with the Carolina Playmakers, it is impossible to avoid this comparison. The spirit of the Abbey Theatre Players is ever present." See Kai Heiberg-Jurgensen, "Drama in Extension," *The Carolina Play-Book*, Memorial Issue (June-December 1944), p. 61.

[37] The best of these plays were edited by Koch and published in *Carolina Folk Plays* (New York: Henry Holt and Co., 1941). One of the most effective of these pioneers in university and regional theatre, Koch's ideas and contributions are amply documented. See, for example, Frederick Henry Koch, "Towards a New Folk Theatre," reprinted from *The Quarterly Journal of the North Dakota University* (1930); Frederick H. Koch, "Making a Regional Drama," *Bulletin of the American Library Association*, XXVI (August 1932), 466-473; Frederick H. Koch, "Drama in the South," *The Carolina Play-Book*, Memorial Issue (June-December 1944), pp. 7-19; Samuel Seldon, "Frederick Henry Koch: The Man and His Work," *The Carolina Play-Book*, Memorial Issue (June-December 1944), pp. 1-5; Samuel Seldon and Mary Tom Sphangos, *Frederick Henry Koch: Pioneer Playmaker—A Brief Biography* (Chapel Hill: University of North Carolina Library, 1954); Montrose J. Moses, "Native Drama," *The Carolina Play-Book*, XVI (March-June 1943), 64; Thomas Wolfe, "The Man Who Lives With His Idea," *The Carolina Play-Book*, Memorial Issue (June-December 1944), pp. 15-22.

[38] Isaacs, "Come of Age!," *Theatre Arts Monthly*, XVIII (July 1934), 478-488; Glenn Hughes, *The Story of the Theatre: A Short History of Theatrical Arts from Its Beginnings to the Present Day* (New York: Samuel French, 1928), pp. 360, 367-370; MacGowan, *Footlights Across America*, pp. 52-53, 117-122.

25

Founded at the time university theatres were being established, many of these little theatre groups had folded after a few years or become a mere springboard for local egos. But those blessed with an energetic director, possessing the combined talents of artist, businessman, and social leader, had gradually grown into permanent institutions with strong local roots and broad creative influence. Such were Gilmor Brown's Pasadena Playhouse, Frederick McConnell's Cleveland Playhouse, Thomas Wood Steven's Goodman Memorial Theatre in Chicago, Jasper Deeter's Hedgerow Theatre outside of Philadelphia. Nor was New York exempt from this grass-roots renaissance. Greenwich Village gave birth to the Washington Square Players and the Province-town Players, both veritable storehouses of talented young men and women rebelling against the old-fashioned drama and stage-craft of the commercial theatre.[39]

Because of these insurgents and reformers, a new modernizing breeze had swept over the commercial stage in the years after World War I. Perhaps more important, in this "seedling period of national drama" theatres with deep local roots had grown up throughout the country—theatres which were responsive to the needs of a particular community, and hence became an artistic and social force in an entire region. Loosely organized into the National Theatre Conference (NTC) in 1933, they were tribu-taries which men like George Pierce Baker hoped would even-tually come together to form a permanent national theatre. Deeply rooted in a particular locality, yet with the power of growth and change, this theatre would represent the ultimate reform of a commercial enterprise crowded into a few neon-lit streets around Times Square.[40] From these practical, imaginative

[39] Cheney, *The Art Theatre*, pp. 64-82; Hughes, *The Story of the Theatre*, pp. 358-365; Hughes, *A History of the American Theatre*, pp. 372-373, 375; Jean Carter and Jess Ogden, *Everyman's Drama: A Study of the Noncommercial Theatre in the United States* (New York: Amer-ican Association for Adult Education, 1938), pp. 13-17, 31-32; Mac-Gowan, *Footlights Across America*, pp. 53-58, 98-100, 298-299.

[40] "The World and the Theatre: Dedication to G[eorge] P[ierce Baker] —National Theatre Conference . . . ," *Theatre Arts Monthly*, XVII (July 1933), 483-491; "The American Theatre in Social and Educational Life:

26

pioneers of tributary theatres Hallie Flanagan would soon seek ideas and leadership for the Federal Theatre.

With her first trip to Washington, came the confrontation with that inevitable dilemma—how to have art and relief in the same package. As she labored over volumes of testimony from NRA hearings on the theatre and motion picture industry, critical appraisals of dramatic work done under FERA and CWA, innumerable requests for government funds from tributary theatres and commercial managers, she began to wonder if the dilemma were insurmountable. Whether displaced technically or simply out of work because of the depression, unemployed stagehands, designers, directors, costumers, actors, vaudevillians, and circus performers numbered an estimated twenty thousand. Previous government projects employing only a small fraction of that number were commendable humanitarian ventures, but hardly theatre. Although vaudeville performers in Boston delighted hospitalized children, these old troupers needed imaginative direction and extensive retraining if they were to perform creditably, much less return to the commercial stage.[41] Whether a theatre worthy of the name could be developed from whatever talent these people possessed, Hallie Flanagan did not know. But she was certain that not one of the many proposals submitted to WPA headquarters demonstrated how thousands of men and women on relief rolls could be put to work in productions of a thoroughly professional caliber under government auspices. She also decided that whatever was done would require the services of a social worker, not someone in the theatre.[42]

Hopkins did not agree. Both he and Roosevelt wanted theatre projects sprinkled over the countryside by a qualified director who was not associated with the Broadway stage. Urging his

A Survey of its Needs and Opportunities," *Theatre Arts Monthly*, XVII (March 1933), 235-242; Isaacs, "Come of Age!," *Theatre Arts Monthly*, XVIII (July 1934), 478-488; MacGowan, *Footlights Across America*, pp. 312-325.

[41] Report to Jacob Baker on FERA Drama Projects in Massachusetts, n.d., RG 69, FTP Records, National Office Correspondence (NOC).

[42] Flanagan, *Arena*, pp. 12-18.

guest to postpone a final decision, the wily Iowan suggested that she "come on out to Henry Alsbergs" where the heads of the Art, Music, and Writers' Projects had gathered for the evening.[43]

It was one of those evenings, Mrs. Flanagan later recalled, when everything seemed possible. Alsberg outlined plans for a series of Writers' Guides for every state in the union; Nikolai Sokoloff expounded on the symphony orchestras which he believed could be formed throughout the country; Holger Cahill talked of setting up community art centers across the nation, of sending unemployed artists into the countryside to capture the architecture, painting, glassware, and early functional art for an Index of American Design. Caught up in the tremendous possibilities of a new people's art, Hallie Flanagan soon began talking about touring small towns where living theatre was seldom seen. As she launched into a description of how huge casts of unemployed actors doing bit parts could be used in a series of Living Newspapers—a kind of newsreel on stage—Hopkins could afford to indulge in self-congratulations. "When can you get to work?" he demanded as they drove away. Brushing aside all reservations, he argued that the Theatre Project was a noncommercial venture and must be run by someone who knew and cared about the theatre outside New York City. "I know something about the plays you have been doing for ten years," he insisted, "plays about American life. . . . It's a job just down your alley." It was also the chance to create the theatre that a whole generation of thoughtful men and women had dreamed of, talked about, and worked toward—a living theatre, flourishing in the particular soil of a particular region and acting as an artistic and social

[43] *Ibid.*, p. 18; Roosevelt had been insistent from the beginning that the fine arts be distributed "to the smaller communities." See Memorandum, F.D.R. to Marvin McIntyre, May 15, 1934, Roosevelt MSS, Official File 954. According to George Freedley, curator of the New York Public Library's theatre collection, Roosevelt was reputed not to have wanted anyone from the commercial theatre as head of the Federal Theatre because he felt such a person would be too Broadway centered. Interview with George Freedley, December 29, 1960.

28

force on the people of that region. This was *not* a job for a social worker. Hallie Flanagan accepted.[44]

· III ·

Since she was already committed to directing a summer theatre in Poughkeepsie, the Vassar director returned to New York; but her thoughts were on the stages across the nation soon to be filled with unemployed actors, stagehands, designers, and directors. How many unemployed people there actually were, who they were, and where they were, could only be determined when volunteer boards were set up in each state to audition applicants on relief rolls. In the meantime an overall plan had to be worked out, if the tremendous potentialities of the government's relief venture were to be realized.

Throughout June and July Hallie Flanagan toyed with the problem of how best to meet the needs of both people on relief and people in the audience over a vast geographic area. As she discussed with Elmer Rice ideas for a national network of decentralized theatres, the Vassar director became increasingly convinced that the community theatre must be at the heart of any plan. When she proposed organizing one hundred such centers throughout the nation to E. C. Mabie, his enthusiasm matched her own. The young Iowa director exulted in this unique opportunity to "change the entire course of American drama for years to come." Encouraged by Mabie's response, Mrs. Flanagan urged him to help her adapt to new needs the ideas for a regionally centered national theatre so much discussed in the tributary theatre world. His imagination fired by this "amazing opportunity," the Iowa professor promised to begin with his own plan for regional theatres, drawn up originally for NTC.[45]

Hallie Flanagan could scarcely have enlisted the cooperation of a better person. A careful planner and a man of enormous energy, Mabie was thoroughly aware that the nature and quality

[44] Flanagan, *Arena*, pp. 18-20.

[45] Mabie to Flanagan, June 26, 1935; July 1, 1935; July 9, 1935; FTP Records, National Office Correspondence with Regional Offices, IV (NOC-Reg. IV).

of this government theatre would depend in large measure on
the nature and quality of the ideas supplied to its creator.[46]
Within days his letters and bundles of notes began to arrive in
Poughkeepsie with a seemingly unending supply of "wonderful
ideas."[47] Mabie also asked if Mrs. Flanagan and Hopkins could
attend a theatre conference in late July at the university during
the Relief Administrator's forthcoming visit to Iowa City. If
they could, he promised: "I will see to it that in some way the
ideas I have been using in lectures for the last two years are
projected into the Conference," along with those of directors
of university theatres, playwrights, and critics who would come
prepared to discuss subsidized regional theatres. Did she agree
that Gilmor Brown, who had recently succeeded George Pierce
Baker as president of NTC, should be asked to draw up a "constructive plan of broad social vision?" Such a plan, coming
from an organization outside New York City, Mabie predicted,
would have the support of "people of vision" in the East such
as Barrett Clark, Edith Isaacs, and Elmer Rice. As for the
regional organization outlined in his own plan, "nothing," he
wrote, "should be allowed to upset [that]." Like most of those
who hoped for a national theatre, he was convinced that if this
government venture were to achieve permanence, it had to
"grow up out of the soil as an expression of the life of the
people in many regions. . . ."[48]

With the help of Mabie and Rice, Hallie Flanagan gradually
hammered out a plan for five great regional centers to be located
in New York, Chicago, Los Angeles, possibly Boston, and possibly New Orleans. Each would be a production and touring
center for a professional company; a retraining center for actors

[46] Rosamond Gilder, "Who's Who in the Tributary Theatre," *Theatre
Arts Monthly*, XXVI (July 1942), 462; "A New University Theatre,"
Theatre Arts Monthly, XVIII (September 1934), 702; Isaacs "Come of
Age!," *Theatre Arts Monthly*, XVIII (July 1934), 487.

[47] Flanagan to Philip Davis, August 28, 1935, Flanagan Papers.

[48] Mabie to Flanagan, June 26, 1935; July 9, 1935; July 10, 1935; July
10, 1935 (Telegram); Mabie to Gilmor Brown, July 16, 1935; Mabie to
Glenn Hughes, July 29, 1935; FTP Records, NOC-Reg. IV.

30

of varying ability and background; and a service, research, and playwriting center for the network of community theatres in that area. Each, too, would work with nearby university and community theatres to develop playwrights who could build up a body of dramatic literature springing from the history, tradition, and customs of that particular region. General policy and program would be outlined in Washington, but carried out with appropriate modification by each region and state. Unlike the national theatres of Europe this Federal Theatre would be, as its name suggested, a federation of regional theatres which could become organic, permanent parts of the regions which nourished them.[49]

Assured by Mabie that the political advantages of such a plan were so obvious that the administration would willingly support it, Mrs. Flanagan submitted her proposal to Hopkins. As Mabie predicted, the Relief Administrator gave it his enthusiastic endorsement and suggested that Mrs. Flanagan's appointment be announced at the Iowa Conference as further indication of the Project's national scope. In a jubilant letter to the Iowa director, she wrote that the regional plan was to "go through" and that she was now empowered to appoint "key people." Could two hours be available during the conference for "you, Hopkins, Rice, and other regional possibilities to confer," and "could you send me a list of people to be there, checking your recommendations for regional directors?"[50]

Regional directors were not the only subject of queries in the two weeks before the conference. Although the broad outlines of the Federal Theatre had been approved, hundreds of details were still undecided; crucial facts still unknown. Aware that time was running out, Hallie Flanagan bombarded the Wash-

[49] Theatre Project for Works Progress Administration. Enclosed in letter from Hallie Flanagan to Bruce McClure and quoted in *Arena*, p. 29; Flanagan to Mr. and Mrs. Charles Coburn, September 5, 1935, FTP Records, National Office Correspondence with State Offices (NOC-State).

[50] Mabie to Flanagan, July 9, 1935; Flanagan to Mabie, July 13, 1935; FTP Records, NOC-Reg. IV; Flanagan, *Arena*, p. 24.

ington office with questions. Were the estimated ten thousand prospective Federal Theatre employees a definite fixed group already tabulated on cards in various cities, or just any ten thousand unemployed theatrical people? Where were they? What proportion of them were actors, musicians, stagehands, etcetera? How would the new Equity ruling on minimum wages affect the Theatre Project? Had an appropriate sum been allotted for regional directors, production costs in regional theatre, and office expenses in Washington? If not, was it her job to draw up such a plan? Would this sum come from their appropriation or would any part of it, such as office expenses, come from another budget? By way of reply, a WPA official was sent to Poughkeepsie.[51]

A few days later, Mrs. Flanagan and Hopkins left for Iowa City. The whole experience was exhilarating. With her usual sensitivity, Hallie Flanagan caught the spirit of it at once: the train trip punctuated at each stop by newspapermen armed with cameras and questions; young, overworked, tremendously alive WPA officials carrying briefcases and complaining furiously about Washington bureaucracy. There were also Hopkins' earnest lectures on the trials and tribulations of spending public money, and the government's obligation to insure its citizens a decent life—to build housing projects for those pale listless children whom they saw sitting on fire escapes as their train passed through Chicago slums. And the role of art in all of this? Hopkins and Mrs. Flanagan agreed that theatre could do more than entertain children in city parks and in small towns; it could throw a spotlight on these ramshackle tenements and unite an audience in the conviction that something must be done.[52]

The conference itself, at which some fifty playwrights, critics, and directors of university and community theatres had gathered, went according to plan. Elmer Rice led a discussion on the regional theatre and Harry Hopkins addressed an audience

[51] Flanagan to Bruce McClure, July 19, 1935; McClure to Flanagan, July 20, 1935; RG 69, General Subject Series, File 211.2, Drama (Federal Theatre Project) (GSS-211.2).

[52] Flanagan, *Arena*, pp. 24-28.

which included many of the Federal Theatre's future regional directors. Speaking of the new theatre which was being created in America, he concluded with a ringing declaration: "I am asked whether a theatre subsidized by the government can be kept free from censorship, and I say, yes, it is going to be kept free from censorship. What we want is a free, adult, uncensored theatre." A "free, adult, uncensored theatre"—this was Harry Hopkins' promise, and Hallie Flanagan would do her utmost to hold him to it, as she turned the spotlight of the Federal Theatre on problems besetting a changing world.[53]

For those involved in the creation of this theatre, the brief weeks following the Iowa Conference were a time of continued planning and preparation. Barrett Clark, theatrical critic, writer, editor, and always an advocate of high standards, suggested that if the question of relief were not involved, there should be a delay of "at least one year" during which "we could clarify our ideas." But the question of relief *was* involved. With twenty thousand unemployed theatrical workers begging for jobs, there was simply no time to clarify ideas, ponder how best to help the commercial theatre, or reflect on problems of federal subsidization of the arts. There was not even time enough to plan a carefully conceived theatre project.

Pressed by harassed Washington officials for decisions which neither she nor anyone else was equipped to make, Hallie Flanagan could only encourage those interested in regional theatre to contribute ideas. As always, Mabie did his best. Perhaps a company might be established in Seattle near Glenn Hughes' Penthouse Theatre at the University of Washington, he wrote. As for Chicago, he wondered if the sponsorship of President Hutchins and the University of Chicago might not solve the problem of leadership in the Midwest. Hallie Flanagan agreed; but her own thoughts were centering more and more on Washington and the frequent conferences that drew her to WPA headquarters. The whole Project, she confided to Mabie after her most recent

[53] For NTC calendar of events, see Mabie to Flanagan, July 23, 1935, RG 69, FTP Records, NOC-Reg. IV; *Variety*, July 24, 1935, p. 53; Flanagan, *Arena*, pp. 28-29.

trip, "is even more limitless in opportunities than we imagined," but tied up in "miles of red tape."[54]

In the meantime, letters poured into and out of Poughkeepsie. As news of federal subvention spread, hundreds of people eager to help the government spend its money flooded WPA offices and Mrs. Flanagan's mail box with a variety of schemes. From women's clubs throughout the United States came promises of support for the Arts Projects. From fifty of the Vassar director's best students came confidential reports on theatrical activities in their scattered communities. To Frederick Koch, Samuel Seldon, and Paul Green went a request to consider ways in which a subsidized regional theatre could be related to the University of North Carolina and the surrounding country. Could Herbert Kline, editor of *New Theatre*, suggest young playwrights on relief rolls who might wish to work with a regional theatre group? Would Frederick McConnell consider the directorship of the Ohio area, using his Cleveland Playhouse as a regional center for Indiana, Ohio, Kentucky, and West Virginia? And most important, could she, under existing governmental regulations, possibly provide challenging, useful work for the thousands of men and women from relief rolls in so short a time? This last question haunted the Vassar director as she hurriedly prepared to bid good-bye to her husband, three young stepchildren, an eighteen-year-old son, and the housekeeper who had promised to run the pleasant Poughkeepsie home in her absence.[55]

Hallie Flanagan was officially installed as National Director of the Federal Theatre Project on August 27, 1935. Newspapers and periodicals briefly traced her academic career from Grinnell College to the 47 Workshop, and then to Vassar College and

[54] Barrett Clark to Flanagan, August 8, 1935, RG 69, FTP Records, NOC; Mabie to Flanagan, August 12, 1935; Flanagan to Mabie, August 15, 1935; RG 69, FTP Records, NOC-Reg. IV.

[55] Flanagan to McClure, August 15, 1935, RG 69, GSS-211.2; Flanagan to Frederick Koch, August 16, 1935; Flanagan to Herbert Kline, August 14, 1935, RG 69, FTP Records, NOC-State; Flanagan to Frederick McConnell, August 24, 1935, RG 69, FTP Records, NOC-Reg. II.

Europe. The more gracious accounts referred to the tiny director as a "practical idealist," a producer of plays on themes "vitally related to modern life," one who had "the confidence of important people in the professional theatre and yet remains out of it." Other accounts were less enthusiastic. Among "old-timers" on Broadway, there was much dubious headshaking. Whether this appointment represented art or politics, or something like the little theatre movement, they did not know. They did know this: that an old-line Broadway manager, wise in the devious ways of the commercial theatre, was needed for the job, not some college professor from a girls' school. As if to explain this apparent aberration on the part of New Dealers, *Variety*, that hard-boiled trade journal of the entertainment world, erroneously stated that Mrs. Flanagan was considered to be "an intimate of the Roosevelt family being especially close to Mrs. Anna Roosevelt Dahl Boettiger, the President's daughter."[56]

Although the appointment of a national director was now official, the Federal Theatre was still only a paper plan. During the hot days of late August, Hallie Flanagan worked frantically in her stifling, Washington cubicle to convert that plan into a project. Bombarded by the sounds of electric fans, riveting machines, and hammering workmen, she alternated between hope and despair as she read the letters of men and women pleading for work and struggled with the red tape, confusion, and delays involved in working out financial and labor policies. The long-awaited decision to pay relief workers $30.00 to $94.00 monthly, depending upon their locality and skills, and to grant supervisory personnel between $1,200 and $2,500 yearly seemed a kind of milestone. In fact, it was only the beginning of a series of decisions that had to be made on such matters as box-office control, promotion policies, and the collecting and spending of admissions. Insisting that "the thing can be done *if* we can find

[56] The *New York Times*, July 27, 1935, p. 15; "Federal Pulmotor for Arts," *The Literary Digest*, CXIX (October 12, 1935) 24; "The National Theatre Approaches Reality," *The Literary Digest*, CXIX (June 22, 1935), 23; Hutchins, "Vassar's Hallie Flanagan," the *New York Times*, September 22, 1935, Sec. 10, p. 1; *Variety*, September 4, 1935, p. 55.

a way to do it," she cursed the bureaucratic bungling that had sent the Federal Theatre's allotment to the National Youth Administration. She prodded and encouraged WPA officials, legal advisors, statisticians, and Treasury Department employees to figure out how the government could handle royalties, lease theatres, acquire equipment, tour theatrical companies within and across state lines. Although she might privately confess that "cutting" through these legal and bureaucratic "knots" was difficult "beyond anything [she] had ever encountered," like everyone on Hopkins' staff, she refused to admit defeat. Somehow answers were found, decisions made.[57]

Labor policy had, in effect, already been determined. Hopkins had insisted from the outset upon complete cooperation with all unions, so long as there was no discrimination against the non-union worker on relief. Other forms of discrimination—race, creed, color, political activities, or party affiliation—had been specifically forbidden in the Relief Act itself. To the Federal Theatre Director belonged the task of securing the cooperation of a whole network of union groups and associations, each with its own regulations. It was no minor endeavor in an industry so highly organized that the opening of a single play required the combined efforts of at least twelve different unions, representing everyone from dramatists and actors to bill posters. Nevertheless, on September 18 leaders of nearly twenty different unions gathered in Washington to discuss wage scales, hours of work, and regulations for touring that would be acceptable to both the WPA and the unions.[58]

[57] Flanagan to Philip Davis, August 28, 1935, Flanagan Papers; Flanagan to Mr. and Mrs. Charles Coburn, September 9, 1935, RG 69, FTP Records, NOC-State.
[58] Flanagan, *Arena*, pp. 35-37. The unions to which invitations were sent included: the Dramatists' Guild; the Associated Actors and Artists of America, representing Actors' Equity Association; Hebrew Actors; Hebrew Chorus; the American Federation of Actors (vaudeville); White Rats (vaudeville); the United Scenic Artists of America (scene designers, scene painters and studio operators); the American Federation of Musicians; the International Brotherhood of Teamsters and Chauffeurs; Theatrical Wardrobe Attendents; International Alliance of Poster and

Leaving her assistant to transpose these decisions on procedure, finance, and labor into an instruction manual for the Federal Theatre, Hallie Flanagan went to New York to find directors for regional and community centers across the nation. Perhaps no decisions were more crucial, for the success or failure of community and university theatres had revealed time and time again the direct relationship between good leadership and good theatre.[59] Understandably, therefore, top regional positions would go to directors who had already proved themselves effective pioneers in the tributary theatre. Hopkins, moreover, insisted that projects be established where strong leaders had built up geographically strategic centers.[60] But the men who would work in subordinate posts had yet to be chosen. With Edith Isaacs and Rosamond Gilder of *Theatre Arts Monthly*, Gilmor Brown, and Mabie, Mrs. Flanagan spent hours going over names suggested by these NTC officials. To find directors from the commercial theatre for posts in Chicago, New York, and other Eastern cities was even more difficult. These projects needed professional theatre people with vision enough to see the possibilities of a regionally centered national theatre and executive ability enough to set up and administer, under stringent governmental regulations, huge self-contained centers employing a thousand or more people. When Mrs. Flanagan consulted Sidney Howard for suggestions, the playwright thought the plan magnificent, but predicted that, with the exception of Elmer Rice, the kind of men she wanted to carry it out simply could not be found. He was right. Even Hallie Flanagan at her persuasive best could not dispel doubts about the caliber of

Billers; Association of Theatrical Agents and Managers; National Theatrical Treasurers' Association; Theatrical Protective Association; Variety Managers' Protective Association; Theatrical Press Representatives of America; and the League of New York Theatres.

[59] See, for example, Hughes, *The Story of the Theatre*, p. 365; Robert E. Gard and Gertrude S. Burley, *Community Theatre: Idea and Achievement* (New York: Duell, Sloan and Pearce, 1959).

[60] Flanagan to Mrs. Charles W. Collier, July 29, 1935, RG 69, GSS-211.2. See also Lester Lang to David Russell, September 17, 1935, RG 69, FTP Records, NOC-State.

actors from relief rolls, fears of excessive red tape, or the fact of meager salaries. Her offer to the energetic, young, Broadway producer almost invariably met with an emphatic "No." Yet somehow people were found—often men not connected intimately with the commercial theatre—and appointments made; yet the skepticism remained.[61]

Determined to win what support she could from the commercial theatre, Hallie Flanagan devoted much of her time to appeals for joint sponsorship of various projects proposed for the huge New York center. She outlined the advantages of a Children's Theatre, described the possibilities of a theatre for Negroes to the Urban League, and talked about resident drama instructorships in CCC camps for Federal Theatre employees. With the Dramatists' Guild, she discussed payment of royalties and sponsorship of an experimental theatre for playwrights; with the editors of *Theatre Arts Monthly* and the *New Theatre*, a research and publication project; with Chorus Equity, musical comedy plans. To the League of New York Theatres, she suggested the sponsorship of managers' tryout theatres in which federal actors would tryout plays for managers who wished to gauge their commercial possibilities. The League, however, was skeptical about taking part in a relief enterprise. To officials of Actors' Equity, she proposed that the union sponsor a federal unit with rotating companies in three New York boroughs; but Equity's kindly president, Frank Gillmore, reported that the Council was unwilling to let the union become involved.

Undaunted by these rebuffs, she accepted the invitation of John Mason Brown, Brooks Atkinson, and Percy Hammond to meet with drama critics to discuss the entire venture. Afterwards she left for Washington confident that at least among the critics were a few who believed a theatre, and not a relief project, was about to be born.[62]

[61] Flanagan to Philip Davis, September 6, 1935, September 9, 1935, Flanagan Papers; Flanagan to Frank Gillmore, September 9, 1935, RG 69, GSS-211.2; Flanagan, *Arena*, p. 37.

[62] Conference schedule for September 19-21 enclosed in a letter from Flanagan to Jacob Baker, September 10, 1935, RG 69, GSS-211.2. For a

The newly appointed regional and state directors arrived on October 8 at Arts Project headquarters in the old McLean Mansion at Du Pont Circle, the "grandest, showiest, most expensive" house which its newly rich owner could build in Washington of the 1890's. An incongruous setting for a relief enterprise, the huge old building, with its pastry-tube ornamentation, high ceilings, brocade- and fresco-covered rooms, reminded Hallie Flanagan of the luxurious Moscow palaces housing the arts in space once belonging to the aristocracy. More important, it seemed to epitomize an era when art had been the exclusive possession of a privileged few rather than the heritage of an entire people. To restore that heritage and create a new kind of theatre for a vigorous new audience of the people were the tasks of regional and state directors.[63]

The men she greeted were of diverse backgrounds and achievements. A few came from Broadway, but there were many more from community and university theatres across the country. Eddie Dowling, Broadway actor-producer and recent participant in F.D.R.'s campaign, was on hand as national director of vaudeville. Playwright-producer Elmer Rice, director of the New York City Project, was there with his assistant, Philip Barber, a graduate of the Harvard 47 Workshop who had worked as a dramatist, actor, and stage manager of the New York Group Theatre. Director for New England was the actor and director, Charles Coburn; for Pennsylvania, Jasper Deeter, a single-minded, intuitive artist who had left the Provincetown Playhouse to found the tiny Hedgerow Theatre, one of the few genuine repertory theatres in America. Director for the Midwest was, of course, E. C. Mabie of the University of Iowa Theatre; for Chicago, Thomas Wood Stevens, a pioneer from the University of Wisconsin Players who had established a remarkable

---

more complete listing of activities, see Flanagan, Address to Regional and State Directors of the Federal Theatre, Washington, October 8, 1935, RG 69, FTP Records, NOGSF.

[63] Flanagan to Philip Davis, September 11, 1935, Flanagan Papers; Flanagan, *Arena*, p. 43.

Department of Drama at Carnegie Institute in Pittsburgh before taking over the Goodman Memorial Theatre in Chicago. From the flourishing Pasadena Playhouse had come director-administrator Gilmor Brown as director for the West. On hand as his assistant was J. Howard Miller, former actor and stage manager for Max Reinhardt. Frederick H. Koch, creator and director of the Carolina Playmakers, and John McGee, director of the Birmingham Little Theatre, were to share the South. Present as director of the Bureau of Research and Publication was Rosamond Gilder, Associate Editor of *Theatre Arts Monthly*.[64]

For hinterland pioneers as well as Broadway veterans, the task of creating regionally centered national theatre with thirteen thousand unemployed, unknown, theatre workers was a formidable challenge. With that challenge came the added complication of governmental procedure—an aspect so novel to men accustomed to the highly individualistic world of the theatre that five days before the meeting Hallie Flanagan had hastily sent telegrams cautioning all directors to hold on to receipts for railroad and Pullman transportation.[65] Their real initiation into the wonderland of bureaucracy began when Jacob Baker explained that, of the nearly $5 billion made available in the Emergency Relief Act of 1935, $27 million had been set aside for unemployed musicians, artists, writers, and theatrical people under WPA's Federal Project No. 1, one of the several professional projects for which he was responsible. Describing the organization of the WPA, Baker undoubtedly explained that, like the other assistant administrators in charge of labor, women's work, finance and statistics respectively, he was responsible to Hopkins and the latter's second-in-command, Aubrey Williams. Within

[64] Flanagan, *Arena*, pp. 42-43. For additional information on Hughes, Deeter, Stevens, and McConnell, see Gilder, "Who's Who in the Tributary Theatre," *Theatre Arts Monthly*, XXVI (July 1942), 460-473; "The Tributary Theatre . . . ," *Theatre Arts Monthly*, XVII (July 1933), 570; Harriet L. Green, *Gilmor Brown: Portrait of a Man—and an Idea* (Pasadena, Calif.: Burns Printing Co., 1933); "It's Most Useful Citizen," *Little Theatre Monthly*, II (April 1926), 264.

[65] Telegram, Flanagan to Regional Directors, October 3, 1935, RG 69, GSS-211.2.

the state organization, the major operating unit of the WPA, this same hierarchy was roughly duplicated. A state administrator and various directors corresponding to Hopkins' assistant administrators served as intermediaries between the Washington office and local district offices. Usually these district and state officials approved and operated projects conducted by the WPA, but the Arts Projects, Baker continued, were an exception since they were to be run directly from Washington. As federal projects they were the responsibility of national directors who would appoint their own personnel and be in charge of their own program. For reasons of economy, however, the Arts Projects would operate administratively through district and state WPA offices.[66]

An introduction to WPA hierarchy was only the beginning. Finance officials discussed Treasury regulations and demonstrated how to put relief and non-relief people on the payroll. The WPA, they explained, would pay labor, supervisory, and production costs only if certain provisions were met: production costs could amount to no more than 10 per cent of labor costs; supervisors could not exceed the proper ratio (one non-relief supervisor for twenty relief workers); and projects had to conform to the proper wage classification. Once these conditions had been met and the proper forms been approved, special funds earmarked for the Theatre Project would be released through the finance division of the state WPA. Next, labor division experts reminded the new directors that Congress had stipulated that 90 to 95 per cent of all WPA workers should come from relief rolls. Finally, Federal Theatre officials went over the instruction manual, explaining in detail how to set up audition boards, establish the various kinds of projects permitted, requisition labor and supplies, and fill out reports for the Washington office.[67]

Lest governmental regulations appear too difficult and oppres-

[66] See Agenda of Regional Directors Meeting put out under the heading "Federal Theatre Project Presents a Premier Performance of Regional Directors," Washington, 1500 I Street, October 8-9, 1935, Flanagan Papers; also Flanagan, *Arena*, p. 44.

[67] Flanagan, *Arena*, p. 44; Instructions for Federal Theatre Projects of Works Progress Administration, RG 69, FTP Records, NOGSF.

sive, Hallie Flanagan sought both to reassure and to challenge her new staff. She recounted what had already been accomplished: procedure worked out; wage classifications set up; an instruction manual compiled; regional directors appointed; the cooperation of unions and commercial theatre managers enlisted; plans made for the reclassification of jobless theatre workers in New York City; field surveys begun in the South, Midwest, and California. Turning to the centers themselves, she emphasized once again that Hopkins demanded quality rather than quantity. "Our best efforts must be spent in finding intelligent and imaginative theatre plans, excellent direction and adequate [local] sponsorship for such plans," she insisted. Only if theatres "vital to community needs" could be created would there be a basis for permanence.[68]

Gazing out at the men around her—slight, jaunty Koch, with his ever-present pipe; darkly handsome Mabie; Rice, with his round, hornrimmed glasses and thinning, red hair—Hallie Flanagan challenged them to insure that permanence by rethinking the theatre in terms of contemporary art and economics. Let us, she urged, supplement the New York stage with experimental plays by unknown dramatists, plays emphasizing regional materials. Still better, let us create a theatre conscious of the past, but adapted to new times and new conditions. Reiterating her belief that a theatre relevant to the present could make itself necessary to the American people after the need for relief had passed, she declared:

> We live in a changing world: man is whispering through space, soaring to the stars, flinging miles of steel and glass into the air. Shall the theatre continue to huddle in the confines of a painted box set? The movies, in their kaleidoscopic speed and juxtaposition of external objects and internal emo-

[68] Flanagan, Address to Regional and State Directors of the Federal Theatre, Washington, October 8, 1935, RG 69, FTP Records, NOGSF. Portions of the speech may also be found in *Arena*, pp. 45-46 and *Theatre Arts Monthly*. See Hallie Flanagan, "Federal Theatre Project," *Theatre Arts Monthly*, XIX (November 1935), 865-868.

tions, are seeking to find visible and audible expression for the tempo and psychology of our time. The stage too must experiment—with ideas, with psychological relationship of men and women, with speech and rhythm forms, with dance and movement, with color and light—or it must and should become a museum product.

In an age of terrific implications as to wealth and poverty, as to the function of government, as to peace and war, as to the relation of an artist to all these forces, the theatre must grow up. The theatre must become conscious of the implications of the changing social order, or the changing social order will ignore, and rightly, the implications of the theatre.

Flinging to her listeners a final challenge, she recalled a scene in a recent play depicting the initial, long-postponed encounter between a worker and an intellectual. "Is it too much to hope," she asked, "that the Federal Theatre Project in America, in 1935, may be indeed, for the[se] two great forces, in need of each other, the appointed time and place [for meeting]?"[69]

The conference was over. Directors, conscious of being poised on a threshold, left for locations as diverse as the people themselves. With few exceptions, they were bound by a common goal: creation of a relevant theatre with regional roots. But that goal had to be realized on a relief project created in a nation ravaged by depression. Because of this crisis, there had been no time to plan a carefully conceived work program, much less a theatre; no time to assess present problems or anticipate future ones; no time to develop imaginative solutions, realistic procedures, or a strong base of support. Yet plans were somehow made under the pressure of necessity. The attempt to carry out these plans in an institutional context complicated by humanitarian, bureaucratic, and political pressures is the story of the Federal Theatre.

[69] *Ibid.*

CHAPTER TWO

A Theatre Is Born

WITH Hallie Flanagan's challenging words still ringing in their ears, her new directors set out to build a "free, adult, uncensored theatre" in regional centers across the country. Some had founded theatres before, but none were prepared for the complications, frustrations, and sheer hard work involved in the unprecedented, uncharted task ahead. With no stages, no properties, no costumes, no plays, and no offices, they started quite literally from scratch. Understandably, Hallie Flanagan's first instructions after the Washington conference concerned the most elementary matters: make "your first travel . . . a courtesy call" on the state WPA administrators and through them meet the state directors of Professional Projects; "make necessary arrangements for securing office staff; use WPA stationery [being sent from] the Washington office; secure a rubber stamp to imprint your own office; . . . make three carbons of all correspondence, letters, and telephone calls; each week send one [copy] to Washington." Finally they were reminded with bureaucratic precision that project proposal form Number 320 had to be filled out in sextuplicate.[1]

Such instructions, even on the most routine matters, proved difficult to carry out. Hopkins, in his appointment of state administrators, had tried to find men who were sympathetic to both the WPA and the particular senators who had demanded the privilege of senatorial courtesy as the price for their support of the new work-relief program. In general, however, the Relief Administrator found little cause to be enthusiastic about the quality of the men appointed;[2] nor could he guarantee their sympathy for a nationally directed theatre within their state, but largely beyond their control. As might be expected, state admin-

[1] Flanagan to Regional Directors, October 11, 1935, RG 69, GSS-211.2.
[2] Charles, *Minister of Relief*, pp. 178-179. Only those persons receiving an annual salary of $5,000 or more had to be approved by the Senate.

istrators, also in the throes of organization, received their callers with varying degrees of cordiality. The California administrator and his staff were most receptive to the tactful Howard Miller.[3] Kansas, Minnesota, and Nebraska officials promised cooperation, but expressed strong doubts that the government would ever come through with money for anything like an Arts Project.[4] The Iowa state administrator refused to be bothered with such an outright boondoggle until construction projects had been handled, and then, only if he could exercise control by naming the assistant regional director of the Theatre Project. Then Mabie could appoint his own stenographer—possibly a young man who had done such a "good job of keeping records and counting hog carcasses in connection with their farm program." With such meager talent and vision to contend with, the Federal Theatre would not soon develop a regional center in Iowa. Realizing this, Mabie made one last request for an administrative assistant. He was told to consult his Democratic county chairman. The local politician's nominee, however, was unsatisfactory.[5]

In spite of Hopkins' insistence that state WPA officials cooperate with Arts Project representatives, Mabie's inability to secure office facilities and secretarial aid was not unique. Jasper Deeter, promised both necessities by cooperative, but harassed Pennsylvania authorities, discovered that his office was unfurnished and the secretary incompetent. Until a desk and chairs could be rented from a secondhand furniture store, he handled appointments "in strange but convenient barrooms and coffee shops (no expense account)." His own assistant, he explained, had simply taken correspondence home at night to retype.[6] Less fortunate regional directors were forced either to use the facilities of the theatre or university with which they were connected, or

[3] Miller to Flanagan, October 25, 1935, RG 69, FTP Records, NOC-Reg. v.

[4] Telephone Conversation, Mabie and Flanagan, November 16, 1935, RG 69, FTP Records, NOC-Reg. IV.

[5] Mabie to Flanagan, October 28, 1935, RG 69, FTP Records, NOC-Reg. IV.

[6] Deeter to Lester Lang, December 13, 1935, RG 69, FTP Records, NOC.-Reg. II.

else to rent offices and hire secretaries at their own expense, hoping that eventually they or the institution would be reimbursed.[7]

As frantic letters describing these tribulations poured into Hallie Flanagan's office, she did her utmost to help, only to find that her original request to speed up the appointment of assistants and secretaries had been referred by Jacob Baker to the Treasury Department where it was somehow "lost."[8] Desperate, she warned Washington officials that her regional directors were fast losing confidence in the national office. Even those state administrators who were "friendly" regarded Federal Theatre directors "as advisors only." "Unless something is done immediately," she predicted, "we will definitely lose some of these people—with a great deal of unfavorable publicity."[9] Permission to charge office facilities and secretarial aid to the precious 10 per cent allowance for supervisory costs was scant consolation. To WPA officials she patiently explained that the 10 per cent exemption was "barely adequate" to provide the directors so crucial to the success of the Project.[10] The artistic direction of a theatre not yet in operation was not, however, a relief agency's most pressing concern.

The real problem in these difficult days was to locate and organize thirteen thousand prospective Federal Theatre employees. When regional and state directors examined WPA files to determine the number of unemployed theatrical people on relief, they found that, with the possible exception of those in New York, Chicago, and Los Angeles, only a few individuals had indicated that they were members of the theatrical profession when they signed up for relief. Dubious about ever finding work in the theatre, they had called themselves everything from saleswomen to garage mechanics. Thousands more, who, until now, had been kept from starvation by savings and occasional

[7] Flanagan to Harold Stein, November 7, 1935, RG 69, GSS-211.2.

[8] Flanagan to Charles Meredith, November 19, 1935, RG 69, FTP Records, NOC-Reg. III.

[9] Flanagan to Harold Stein, November 7, 1935, RG 69, GSS-211.2.
[10] *Ibid.*

46

earnings from odd jobs, simply were not on relief rolls under any category.[11] For those who had not signed up for relief before the November 15 deadline, Federal Theatre directors could do nothing, no matter how great the need. But they could try to find those "lost in the files." It was a formidable task even when WPA supervisors chose to help. California and Florida officials, eager to have a theatre project, conducted surveys of theatrical people in their prospective states with care and thoroughness.[12] Officials in Georgia and Tennessee only consulted old records.[13] In Oklahoma, the state director of Professional Projects was much interested in the Federal Theatre, but he simply threw up his hands in despair at the amount of work involved in trying to pluck qualified individuals out of the thousands on relief rolls.[14] When state administrators would permit, regional directors appointed qualified volunteers—usually little theatre directors or college drama teachers—to make surveys and serve on audition boards. If they were fortunate in their choice of volunteers, they were sometimes able to get beneath the surface of the records and discover most of the qualified theatrical folk on relief rolls.[15] Otherwise, there was nothing to do but hope that news of a theatre project would reach those eligible.

In New York, five thousand unemployed theatrical people did not have to be sought out. They literally swarmed into the dilapidated old bank building on Eighth Avenue which had become Federal Theatre headquarters. The unemployed profes-

[11] For a more detailed description of this problem, see Helen Schoeni to Flanagan, December 18, 1935, RG 69, FTP Records, NOC-Reg. II; Guy Williams to Pierre de Rohan, December 19, 1935, RG 69, FTP Records, NOC-Reg. V; John Dunn to Flanagan, December 7, 1935, RG 69, FTP Records, NOC-Reg. III.

[12] John McGee to Flanagan, November 9, 1935, RG 69, GSS-211.2; J. Howard Miller to Flanagan, October 25, 1935, RG 69, FTP Records, NOC-Reg. V.

[13] John McGee to Flanagan, November 9, 1935, RG 69, GSS-211.2.

[14] John Dunn to Flanagan, December 7, 1935; Charles Meredith to Flanagan, November 13, 1935, RG 69, FTP Records, NOC-Reg. III.

[15] John McGee to Flanagan, November 9, 1935, RG 69, GSS-211.2.

47

sional, the girl who had been in summer stock, the old vaudeville star, the untried genius, and the outright faker—they represented every shade of color, political opinion, religious faith and nationality.[16] But they had one thing in common: all were out of work. Not far removed from breadlines, many were desperate— one man so desperate that he went berserk while applying for a job and began beating his head against the wall. But it took time to fill out forms on the professional experience of each applicant, evaluate his ability, and place him in a balanced theatrical company with the right proportion of actors, stagehands, and technicians. It took still more time to fill out project proposal forms indicating the

> . . . description of and purpose of the individual project; the number of relief and non-relief workers with classification of each (actor, painter, seamstress, etc.) . . . ; the names and obligations of the cooperative sponsor; a statement as to whether the project involved rental or travel and if so for what purpose; a statement of non-labor cost (not to exceed 10 per cent of labor costs) broken down under: equipment, material and supplies. . . .[17]

Once the required number of copies were filled out, directors and applicants alike had to wait while the proposal made its way along the chain of command from the regional director, through Hallie Flanagan and Jacob Baker, to Aubrey Williams, deputy administrator of the wpa, who finally authorized the Treasury Department to release necessary funds. An error found meant repeating the entire procedure and a wait of as much as seven weeks for the successful applicant, whose home relief dole had been discontinued some five weeks before.[18] Such safeguards, necessary where the spending of public funds is involved, made the process of putting men on the payroll a slow one under the

[16] Flanagan, *Arena*, pp. 51-52.   [17] *Ibid.*, p. 32.

[18] Flanagan to Jacob Baker and Bruce McClure, November 15, 1935, rg 69, gss-211.2; *Variety*, December 11, 1935, p. 61. Home relief payments were discontinued sixteen days after an individual had been requisitioned for a work project.

very best of circumstances; under the worst, an occasion for real hardship. "The most shocking part of the whole business," Rice confessed to Hallie Flanagan, "is the way the human values are lost sight of in this maze of procedure, routine, and politics."[19]

These much publicized delays, if not so shocking to the Washington office of the WPA, were certainly no less annoying. Hopkins had wangled relief funds on the assumption that he could put three million people to work by the end of November, and his staff was understandably impatient with what seemed to be the deliberate slowness of Theatre Project directors.[20] Why, they asked, could not Federal Theatre officials just send out a request for two hundred actors in the same way supervisors of a road-building project sent out a call for two hundred unskilled workers, thereby quickly getting them on the payroll without any appearance of favoritism?[21] Hallie Flanagan and New York director Elmer Rice carefully pointed out that the Theatre Project was not a construction project, and that, if it were to be a theatre rather than a purely charitable venture, they must have time to obtain the most able, experienced people possible. As late as November 27, after working two months to hold auditions so that they could requisition people individually rather than en masse, the New York City WPA under Victor Ridder ordered that henceforth no one below the professional level be requisitioned by name.[22]

Hallie Flanagan fired off vigorous protests to the director of Professional Projects in Washington, explaining that this directive threatened to undo all that had been accomplished. But Jacob Baker, already under pressure from his superiors as well as from delegations of disgruntled job applicants, was in no mood

[19] Rice to Flanagan, November 19, 1935, Flanagan Papers. Some adjustment of procedure was eventually made, however. The original November 1 deadline—the date by which perspective employees had to have been registered on relief rolls—was changed to November 15. For controversy over the deadline and the hardships entailed thereby, see the *New York Times*, Nov. 16, 1935, p. 19; December 4, 6, 24, 31, 1935, pp. 27, 31, 4 and 10 respectively.
[20] Charles, *Minister of Relief*, p. 138.
[21] Flanagan, *Arena*, p. 53.   [22] *Ibid.*

49

to heed her request. Blaming the delays on the "stupidity" of local officials, he announced that if people were not put on payrolls and the allotment spent "darn soon," the money would be withdrawn.[23] Worn down by pressure from Washington and constant complaints from the press, the New York director complied. Reasoning that this was after all a relief project and that the government could well afford to pay $23.86 to anyone on relief who claimed to belong to the theatre, Rice decided to forego auditions.[24] Hallie Flanagan argued that signed statements of professional status were no guarantee of ability, but Rice assured her that misfits and incompetents could always be fired later.[25] The tenacity with which this troublesome minority would fight for their jobs and the constant headache they would constitute for his successors were of scant concern to the distraught New York director, as he simultaneously signed requisitions, held conferences, and answered a constantly ringing telephone.[26]

What did concern both Rice and Hallie Flanagan was the rental of theatres. Once workers were put on the payroll and money allotted, actors worthy of the name would have to have stages on which to perform. Despite the number of unused theatres in New York, the outlook was not auspicious. Mrs. Flanagan's earlier suggestion that managers supply "dark" theatres for "tryouts" of new plays had been promptly squelched by union groups, who feared that "tryouts" with relief actors would draw crowds from commercial productions.[27] Even if he could persuade managers to rent "dark" theatres in the Broadway area, rather than the neighborhood theatres preferred by union leaders, Rice had no assurance that he could sign the necessary

[23] The *New York Times*, December 21, 1935, p. 1. For evidence of Baker's concern about the withdrawal of funds, see Baker to Bruce McClure, —— Ozer, Harold Stein, October 24, 1935, RG 69, Works Progress Administration Central Files 210.13, Memoranda (WPA-CF 210.13).

[24] Interview with Elmer Rice, November 15, 1961.

[25] Flanagan, *Arena*, p. 54.

[26] Rice Interview, November 15, 1961.

[27] The *New York Times*, October 2, 1935, p. 12; October 30, 1935, p. 23; December 31, 1935, p. 18; *Variety*, October 23, 1935, p. 53.

papers for, after weeks of "dreadful, frustrating conversations," WPA and Treasury officials still had no provisions for theatre rentals worked out.[28] While Mrs. Flanagan prodded and nagged about procedure, her embattled director began negotiations with the League of New York Theatres. Cries of competition immediately went up from Equity officials, who were afraid that actors playing in commercial productions would suffer if already meager audiences were drawn to nearby federal theatres.[29] League members chimed in with similar protests in what proved to be a masterful disregard for logic on the part of managers, who had earlier complained about the "substandard" production to be expected from actors on relief.[30] To get the use of "any theatre whatever," amidst all the heat and furor, became a task requiring the "utmost ingenuity."[31] Only after months of negotiations did the New York director finally secure an agreement permitting the Federal Theatre to stage regular productions in theatres outside the Broadway area.[32]

While Rice was negotiating with the League of New York Theatres, other unions seemed frustratingly uncooperative with their countless protests, meetings, and delegations which soon made labor matters the greatest single administrative problem in the New York City Project. Despite the hue and cry about competition raised by actors and stagehands, Equity officials were primarily concerned about the wages of members in Federal Theatre productions. Although Frank Gillmore had previously agreed on a wages-and-hours policy based on the WPA's security wage system, the union's executive council refused to

[28] Telephone Conversation, Flanagan and Leonard Gallagher, November 16, 1935, RG 69, FTP Records, NOGSF.

[29] The *New York Times*, October 19, 1935, p. 21.

[30] *Ibid.*, September 24, 1935, p. 28; October 28, 1935, p. 16.

[31] Rice, *The Living Theatre*, p. 156.

[32] *Ibid.*; the *New York Times*, November 13, 1935, p. 24; November 14, 1935, p. 16; December 10, 1935, p. 6; December 17, 1935, p. 30; December 31, 1935, p. 18. According to the terms of the agreement, the Federal Theatre Project could not rent theatres in the area between Fortieth and Fifty-Second Streets, the East River and the Hudson.

endorse the president's decision.[33] Those vociferous members belonging to Actors Forum demanded that delegations be sent to Washington to insist that WPA salaries equal prevailing union wages, lest commercial producers lower wages for all actors. Clamoring for union rights, they refused to understand why the Federal Theatre could not maintain a closed shop.[34] Months of struggle within the union itself, the threat of resignation from Gillmore, and weeks of conferences with Federal Theatre officials finally spawned a compromise. Actors would receive the WPA wage of $23.86 rather than the Equity minimum of $40.00, but they would give only six performances a week and rehearse no more than four hours a day—a crippling limitation when new plays were being readied for opening night.[35]

The demand for a closed shop was not really negotiable. Local administrators did agree, however, to separate union and non-union members whenever possible.[36] In New York, this promised to be virtually no problem, since the Socialist-inspired Workers' Alliance was fast absorbing non-union workers on all relief projects. Formed in 1935 as a union for WPA employees, the Alliance made every effort to convince potential members that the individual without the security of union membership would be "lost in a maze of assistant to assistant to assistant supervisors."[37] Duly impressed, clerks, janitors, timekeepers, stenog-

[33] Under the security wage system, workers would be paid a salary greater than the sum received under direct relief but less than the prevailing union wage. Attacked by the unions, the security wage system was supported by WPA officials because it permitted them to place more people on jobs. Almost from the beginning, however, adjustments were made in the number of hours worked by various types of workers. For additional information, see Charles, *Minister of Relief*, pp. 150-152.

[34] The *New York Times*, October 18, 1935, p. 27.

[35] *Ibid.*, October 30, 1935, p. 23; December 21, 1935, p. 4; Irving Kolodin, "Footlights, Federal Style," *Harper's Magazine*, CLXXIII (November 1936), 623.

[36] *Ibid.*

[37] The *New York Times*, October 27, 1935, Sec. 2, p. 2. Organized at the Socialist Party Convention on March 2-4, 1935, the Workers' Alliance had as its stated purposes the following: action on behalf of the unemployed to press their grievances with relief bureaus and the WPA,

raphers, washroom attendants, and unaffiliated theatrical people
—often those who had slipped into the Project when auditions
were stopped—were quick to sign up. Thus, to the offices of
harassed Theatre officials came not only representatives of nearly
two dozen old, established unions, but also those from the Alliance and its white-collar affiliate, the City Projects Council.
Few in number, but with a zeal and energy in no way commensurate with its size, the Alliance soon made its militant, and
sometimes irresponsible, spokesmen familiar figures at Federal
Theatre headquarters.

Indeed, in these incredible, problem-ridden days, Federal
Theatre offices never seemed free of spokesmen from some group
or other.[38] Eager to create a theatre, Project officials found themselves spending more than half of each day listening to grievances and complaints. Delegations accused them of discriminating against everyone from dancers and stagehands to Chinese,
Negroes, and Jews—the latter charges which never ceased to
amaze Elmer Rice, with his Hebrew heritage and devotion to
civil liberties.[39] Actors, ashamed of being on relief, weepingly
pleaded with Mrs. Flanagan not to put their names on Federal
Theatre programs; actors who had not gone on relief complained
bitterly because they could not be hired. Representatives of the

---

prevention of discrimination, and pressure for higher wages on WPA
jobs. The Alliance also called for unionization of all workers as well as
"independent working class political action." With its union with the
Communist Party's Unemployed Councils in 1936 during the Popular
Front period, the Workers' Alliance came under the control of Herbert
Benjamin, a leading Communist and the former head of the Unemployed Councils. In many states, the Alliance became the official bar-
gaining agency with the WPA. It also worked closely with both the A. F.
of L. and the CIO, and served to create a growing "union consciousness"
among its members, many of whom later became members of the
unions mentioned above. See Bernard Karsh and Phillips L. Garman,
"The Impact of the Political Left," *Labor and the New Deal*, eds. Milton
Derber and Edwin Young (Madison, Wis.: University of Wisconsin Press,
1957), pp. 79-119; also Sidney Lens, *Left, Right and Center: Conflicting
Forces in American Labor* (Hinsdale, Ill.: Henry Regnery Co., 1947),
pp. 259-263.

[38] Flanagan, *Arena*, p. 42.

[39] *Ibid.*, p. 52; Rice Interview, November 15, 1961.

commercial theatre protested against the charging of admissions for shows with relief actors. *Variety* complained that the Project was headed by a "pedagogue" with pronounced "leanings" toward "little theatre"; that the heads of the New York Project's experimental unit were not thoroughgoing professionals; that some, like Elmer Rice, were even of "distinct radical leanings."[40]

Variety, perhaps the Federal Theatre's most frequent critic, was by no means the only one. In nearly every batch of press clippings that poured in from across the country, Hallie Flanagan found references to the government's ill-advised venture into show business—this theatrical boondoggle on which, as was to be expected, no curtain had gone up. "*You* try getting up a few curtains," she would remark savagely in one of many imaginary exchanges with the editor of *Variety*.

> I'd like to see you sign a thousand requisitions in triplicate without going to Alcatraz. I'd like to see you satisfy at once the demands of governmental procedure and of ten different theatrical unions, every one with a different wage scale. I'd like to see you break this contract jam without breaking heads and landing in jail.

"The number of editors and critics thus profanely apostrophized (mentally) . . . would have staffed our much needed and non-existent . . . promotion department," she later recalled.[41]

In spite of the frustration and anger behind the invectives she silently hurled at the press, or the exhaustion and despair that, at times, overwhelmed her, Hallie Flanagan would not be worn

---

[40] *Variety*, October 30, 1935, p. 59; November 27, 1935, p. 53.

[41] Flanagan, Federal Theatre-1937, address, n.d., no audience designated. RG 69, FTP Records, NOGSF. In this speech, Mrs. Flanagan recalled that in these early days melodrama had been mixed with tension. In Chicago relief and local politics had become intertwined. Prior to a visit there, she had received telephone calls threatening physical violence if she investigated too closely the professional status of groups inherited from the older FERA drama program. Although initially inclined to dismiss the threats, she had finally been persuaded by Louis Craus, head of the Stagehands Union, to avail herself of the services of a bodyguard, who trailed her about throughout her stay in Chicago.

down. Working furiously with her directors, particularly those on the huge New York Project, she urged, cajoled, and half-threatened the relief administrators who were her superiors, and comforted and encouraged the theatre people whose superior she was. Convinced that the Federal Theatre was "vast, exciting, discouraging, but still potentially superb,"[42] she assured Rice that his "standing by in the face of all . . . delay" was simply "magnificent," and that his "belief and fortitude" would soon be justified.[43] In a period of constantly changing rules emanating from Washington, she expressed admiration at the "fortitude and ingenuity" with which all her directors adapted, and assured them that such changes were no less distressing to her.[44] Nor was her own frantic staff in Washington neglected. Hoping to restore their sense of humor and perspective, she hurriedly penciled an absurd little farewell gift for a departing member entitled: "A Day in a Federal Theatre Office: An Original Realistic Drama by Hallie Flanagan."[45]

While few faced problems of such sheer magnitude as those confronting Elmer Rice in New York, other regional directors gratefully availed themselves of whatever balm the National Director could offer. They, too, were under pressure to get men on payrolls immediately. In Massachusetts, WPA officials interested only in relief insisted that old FERA drama groups be transferred intact to the Theatre Project at once. Assured that all were professionals, director Hiram Motherwell agreed, only to find that the Massachusetts Project, which was to have been a strong regional center for New England, had on its payroll people who were obviously unqualified. Many had never been remotely connected with the original drama program.[46] Elsewhere, directors

[42] Flanagan to John McGee, November 15, 1935, RG 69, GSS-211.2.

[43] Flanagan to Rice, November 19, 1935, RG 69, GSS-211.2.

[44] Flanagan to Glenn Hughes, November 20, 1935, RG 69, FTP Records, NOC-Reg. V.

[45] "A Day in a Federal Theatre Office: An Original Realistic Drama by Hallie Flanagan for Esther Porter," November 21, 1935, RG 69, FTP Records, NOC-Reg. II.

[46] Motherwell to Flanagan, November 11, 1935; Motherwell to Donald Meeker, November 20, 1935; Motherwell to Lester Lang, December

usually held out for auditions, but then the problem became one of judgment. Where was one to draw the line between the qualified and unqualified in a theatre that was also a relief project? In states like Virginia, where actors numbered only a dozen or so and politicians expressed interest in a project, Theatre officials were not likely to agonize over standards, hoping, instead, to work out a recreational program, perhaps with the National Youth Administration.[47]

In other parts of the South and Midwest, where actors were few and scattered, directors faced a somewhat different problem. To form a strong regional center they had to bring these theatrical folk together in a nucleus which could be supplemented by relief workers from New York or local volunteers. Despite Hopkins' earlier belief that the Federal Theatre's best hope lay in just this plan, obstacles soon appeared: WPA officials pointed out that Theatre Project employees could not be transferred outside the area where they had initially registered for relief or, in Indiana, even across county lines; and union leaders objected to professional actors working with amateurs.[48] Thus, delayed by the necessity of having to seek out theatrical workers and thwarted frequently in their attempts to bring together those they found, most regional directors were slow to send project proposals to Washington, slow to receive allotments, and slow to report the number actually on their payrolls.[49] That WPA officials could not even say how many people were enrolled on the Project or what

7, 1935; Motherwell to Conrad Hobbs, January 4, 1936, RG 69, FTP Records, NOC-Reg. I; Lang to Flanagan, December 27, 1935, RG 69, FTP Records, Narrative Reports (Narr. Reports).

[47] Lester Lang to Colgate W. Darden, December 19, 1936, RG 69, FTP Records, NOC-State.

[48] Flanagan to Mrs. Charles W. Collier, July 29, 1935, RG 69, GSS-211.2; Thomas Wood Stevens to Lester Lang, December 11, 1935, Stevens to Flanagan, February 18, 1936, RG 69, FTP Records, NOC-Reg. IV; Lee Norvelle to Flanagan, February 15, 1936, RG 69, FTP Records, NOC-Reg. II.

[49] Flanagan to Glenn Hughes, December 4, 1935, RG 69, FTP Records, NOC-Reg. V; Lester Lang to Regional Directors, December 7, 1935; RG 69, GSS-211.2.

plays were being rehearsed was a situation too tempting for *Variety* to overlook. Its December 11 issue contained an account of the confusion, uncertainty, and lack of cooperation prevailing in the Federal Theatre.[50]

By the end of 1935, the Federal Theatre was, in fact, a combination of chaos and emerging form. The confusion, so apparent to *Variety* reporters, was real enough. Everywhere directors, some of whom still had no telephone or typewriter, found it virtually impossible to get supplies. In Pennsylvania, a requisition for sewing supplies languished in state WPA offices at Harrisburg for two months before it was returned with the request that Federal Theatre officials specify "the length of needles required in the requisitioned two packages of assorted needles."[51] In New York, only a week before rent was due on six theatres, Rice still had no agent cashier authorized to make the necessary payments, in spite of Hallie Flanagan's urgent messages to Washington to speed up procedure.[52] Nowhere had directors received authorization to collect the admissions so vitally needed to help meet production costs.[53]

In the midst of these administrative tangles, however, there were signs of hope. As a slightly belated Christmas gift, the comptroller general presented the California Project with forms for signing on agent cashiers.[54] Three days later Harry Hopkins told WPA field representatives meeting in Washington that state officials were neither to ignore nor try to control Arts Projects. In a blisteringly clear demand for cooperation, he said, "I want it distinctly understood that these projects are directed from

[50] *Variety*, December 11, 1935, p. 53.

[51] Harry Archibald to Jasper Deeter, March 22, 1936, RG 69, FTP Records, NOC-Reg. II.

[52] Telephone Conversation, Flanagan and Leonard Gallagher, November 16, 1935, RG 69, FTP Records, NOGSF. Agent Cashiers were authorized by the Treasury Department to collect and disburse admission funds, sign leases for rental of theatres, and supervise box office attendants.

[53] Flanagan to Baker and McClure, January 2, 193[6], Flanagan Papers.

[54] Flanagan to J. Howard Miller, December 27, 1935, RG 69, FTP Records, NOC-Reg. V.

Washington by the Federal Directors. These directors and their Regional Directors make all appointments, decide what people go to work and what sort of projects they work on." One job of all WPA staff was "to expedite these projects by helping those in charge."[55] And on New Year's Eve came news of the California Project's opening production complete with box office and ticket agent—news, said Hallie Flanagan, that "has reduced us all to a state bordering [on] imbecilic rapture." At last, out of the chaos birth was taking place—perhaps, she thought, "the birth of a politically and economically literate theatre in America."[56]

Slowly, but surely, the feat of the California Project was duplicated elsewhere. By February, the Federal Theatre could claim nearly nine thousand people on its payroll and production groups in twenty states.[57] By March 13, when regional and state directors again assembled in Washington, the figures were even more impressive: eleven thousand workers, twenty-two producing centers, and a weekly audience of one hundred and fifty thousand people.[58] Of the productions themselves, Hallie Flanagan said, "we wish there were more and we wish they were better," but at least "they prove the thing can be done. . . ." "In the main," she told directors, "administrative problems . . . are settled: we know what no one knew six months, three months, or even one month ago—that we can work through the State offices of the WPA; that we can rent theatres; pay royalties; appoint agent cashiers; take in admissions and let them accrue to the project; travel companies; and pay a subsistence wage."[59]

She had only to look around to realize that the cost had been high. Of the twenty-four directors who had gathered at the Mc-Lean Mansion exactly six months before, only eight remained.

[55] Flanagan to Regional Directors, January 8, 1936, RG 69, GSS-211.2.
[56] Flanagan to J. Howard Miller, December 31, 1935, RG 69, FTP Records, NOC-Reg. V.
[57] Flanagan to Rice, November 19, 1935, RG 69, GSS-211.2.
[58] Flanagan, "Federal Theatre Project" [statement for public information?], February 17, 1936, RG 69, FTP Records, NOGSF.
[59] Flanagan, Address to State and Regional Directors, March [14], 1936, RG 69, FTP Records, NOGSF.

Charles Coburn had given up the New England directorship within days after the first Washington conference: a salary of $3,600 was scant compensation for the herculean task of building a theatre with governmental regulations designed for a relief agency.[60] Shortly thereafter, Frederick Koch had decided that his commitments at the University of North Carolina left him neither the time nor energy needed to search the vast area between the Potomac and Savannah Rivers for relief workers that could not be brought together in an effective regional center. He promised, however, to give the Theatre Project the benefit of his backing and advice by serving in an advisory capacity.[61] Mabie, after three months of coping with the meager talent on relief rolls in the Iowa area and with state administrators who, more often than not, opposed the whole idea of a Federal Theatre, had also resigned. "My faith in the objectives originally set and my enthusiasm and admiration for your leadership" remain, he wrote the National Director; but there is "little possibility of realizing any results significant to the theatre" in the Midwest so long as state administrators refuse to supplement mediocre variety units with outside talent.[62] Within weeks of Mabie's resignation, Elmer Rice had taken leave of the New York Project, convinced that Hopkins' promise of a "free, adult, uncensored theatre" would never be realized. Thus, the very men who had contributed most to planning a theatre found running a relief project too fraught with frustrations to continue.

Relief, with its administrative problems, had not only thwarted the planners, but affected the plan. The very core of that plan depended upon building decentralized theatres, for only such theatres could attain the kind of grass-roots support necessary for permanence and, at the same time, relieve the overconcentration of theatrical workers in two or three large cities. But

[60] Flanagan to Coburn, October 14, 1935, RG 69, FTP Records, NOC-Reg. I.

[61] Koch to Flanagan, January 6, 1936, RG 69, GSS-211.2.

[62] Mabie to Flanagan, January 6, 1936, RG 69, FTP Records, NOC-Reg. IV. Mabie had managed to set up projects in only two of the seven midwestern states under his jurisdiction.

regulations preventing the transfer of personnel outside the area where they had registered for relief made it virtually impossible to gather together theatrical employees from over a large region, much less transport them in large numbers from the over-crowded centers of New York, Chicago, and Los Angeles. In some areas, state administrators made it impossible to set up projects of any size. Thus, Hallie Flanagan, who had intended to create strong regional and community centers, found herself in charge of three huge metropolitan projects and many small, often weak units in various cities and towns. The foundation stones for a regionally centered national theatre had, in short, been dumped in three large piles with a few pebbles scattered about elsewhere.

Hopkins was convinced for both cultural and political reasons, however, that the regional plan should be salvaged wherever possible. Although large numbers of workers could not be moved from overcrowded theatrical centers, he encouraged the Federal Theatre Director to send traveling companies out of New York, Chicago, and Los Angeles into rural communities of the South, Midwest, and Southwest. In a burst of optimism, she passed on this advice to her directors, assuring them that the regional plan, "apparently submerged in the first terrific pressure of getting the big units . . . started, is now assuming its original impor-tance."[63] With caution born of a six-month struggle with govern-mental procedure, she later added that they would move com-panies only "in one or two test cases."[64] Her caution would prove more realistic than her optimism.

· II ·

When Federal Theatre directors gathered at the McLean Mansion in the spring of 1936, Hallie Flanagan's first concern was with the choice of plays and standards of production, whether in New York City or Omaha, Nebraska. Of these relief

[63] Flanagan to Regional Directors, January 8, 1936, RG 69, GSS-211.2.
[64] Flanagan, Address to State and Regional Directors, March 14, 1936, RG 69, FTP Records, NOGSF.

projects, which now had to become production centers, she said, "I think none of us feels that we have attained more than twenty-five per cent efficiency." Unless we can make our theatre units more effective, give better plays in more exciting ways, build public opinion and audience support, "our administrative efforts will be worth absolutely nothing."[65]

These criteria were more than a reflection of Hallie Flanagan's own artistic standards; they were an integral part of her entire plan. If the Federal Theatre were to become more than a relief enterprise supplying busywork for needy actors, its planners realized that each theatrical center must so insinuate itself into the life of the community that local patronage would take over when federal subsidies ceased. To merit such patronage, the Federal Theatre would have to create new audiences vastly unlike the first-nighters described by *Stage* as "the people who possess . . . all the appurtenances of fine living around which the smart world of the theatre revolves."[66] And it would have to build these audiences and win their loyalty and support, not by competing with the commercial theatre, but by supplementing it—by specializing in plays of unknown dramatists, emphasizing regional and local material, experimenting with a "rapid, simplified, vivid form of stage expression," with new techniques and ideas.[67] Above all, Hallie Flanagan believed, the Federal Theatre must offer to the people of America "free, adult, uncensored theatre" relevant to the world in which they lived—a theatre experimenting with art forms, reflecting the economic and social forces of modern life, uniting the worker on the stage and in the audience

[65] *Ibid.*

[66] Quoted in Flanagan, "Report of the Director," the *New York Times*, May 17, 1936, Sec. 9, p. 2.

[67] "Spirit of New York Workers Praised by National Director," *Federal Theatre*, I, No. 1 (November 25, 1935), 2; Hallie Flanagan, "A Report of the First Six Months," *Federal Theatre*, I, No. 4 (March 1936), 8-9. Pierre de Rohan, editor of *Federal Theatre*, widely publicized these ideas in his own editorials. See Pierre de Rohan, untitled editorial, *Federal Theatre*, I, No. 2 (December 1935), n.p.; Pierre de Rohan, untitled editorial, *Federal Theatre*, I, No. 3 (1936), n.p.

A THEATRE IS BORN

in common belief.[68] Whether such a theatre could remain free and uncensored, when subsidized by congressmen concerned with relief and politics, not art, remained to be seen.

Indeed, by early March, Theatre Project officials had already had a taste of what could happen when a theatre that was also part of a governmental relief program tried to use some of its many actors in experimental productions relevant to a world of Fascist challenge abroad, and poverty and depression at home. Six months before, when no one had known whether the government could even pay royalties, Elmer Rice had wondered where he would ever get enough plays for a ready-made cast of five thousand whose talents varied from exceptional to nonexistent. Hallie Flanagan recalled the Vassar production of *Can You Hear Their Voices?*, with its use of factual material, charts, statistics, loud-speakers, and blackouts. These same techniques, she suggested, could be used on a grand scale in Living Newspapers: "We could dramatize the news without expensive scenery—just living actors, light, music, movement."[69]

Rice, always inclined to the experimental, was quick to see the practical advantages of a production with a wealth of crowd scenes and bit parts. As director of the New York Project, he promptly secured the sponsorship of the Newspaper Guild, whose members were also suffering from unemployment, putting its vice president, Morris Watson, in charge of a staff of newspaper men and playwrights from relief rolls. Watson soon realized, however, that by the time the newsmen had completed their research, the dramatists worked out a play, and the cast

[68] Hutchins, "Vassar's Hallie Flanagan," the *New York Times*, September 22, 1935, Sec. 10, p. 1; Flanagan, "Federal Theatre Project," *Theatre Arts Monthly*, XIX (November 1935), 868; Hallie Flanagan, "Federal Theatre: Tomorrow," *Federal Theatre*, II, No. 1 (1936), 26.

[69] Flanagan, *Arena*, p. 65; Hallie Flanagan, "Introduction," *Federal Theatre Plays: Triple-A Plowed Under, Power, Spirochete*, ed. Pierre de Rohan (New York: Random House, 1938), p. vii. For a discussion of the Living Newspaper as a theatrical form and as social drama, see Marjorie Louise Platt Dycke, "The Living Newspaper: A Study of the Nature of the Form and its Place in Modern Social Drama," (unpublished Ph.D. dissertation, New York University, 1947).

62

finished rehearsing, the news item would be dated and worthless. The logical solution—and certainly one compatible with Rice and Mrs. Flanagan's firm belief in the theatre as a social and educative force—was to choose topics which were either controversial or of continuing interest.[70] The New York staff, which had fallen heir to a stranded African opera troupe unable to speak English, appropriately agreed to dramatize the Ethiopian crisis—the Africans could beat drums and sing in the courtyard of Haile Selassie.[71]

When Morris Watson wrote to the White House in early January for permission to use a radio broadcast made by the President along with speeches of Haile Selassie and Mussolini, a second Ethiopian crisis broke. Roosevelt's longtime secretary, hard-boiled, efficient Steve Early, immediately fired off a memorandum to Jacob Baker asking about the Living Newspaper. "If this is a government production," he warned, "we are skating on thin ice when dealing with international affairs."[72] Summoned to Baker's office for an explanation, Hallie Flanagan, who only the day before had been assured that the closing of a Chicago Project production was not censorship but an "exception," recalled for Baker previous discussions of the Living Newspaper during which both he and Hopkins had applauded the whole idea. Reminding the Relief Administrator that she had acceded to the mayor's closing of *Model Tenement* in Chicago only because she felt it was not a strong play, she insisted that *Ethiopia* contained carefully documented factual material compiled by members of the New York Newspaper Guild, that it caricatured no one, and that it was free from political bias of any sort. The two finally agreed that she would state these facts in a brief

[70] Morris Watson, "Living Newspaper," *Scholastic*, xxvi (October 31, 1936), 8-9.

[71] The *New York Times*, January 5, 1936, Sec. 9, p. 4; Flanagan, *Arena*, p. 54.

[72] Watson to Stephen Early, January 9, 1936; Memorandum, Early to Baker, January 11, 1936, Flanagan Papers. The Early Memorandum as well as subsequent communications concerning *Ethiopia* are also located in Roosevelt MSS, Official File 80.

explanation of the Living Newspaper, which Baker would then send over to Early along with the script of *Ethiopia* and a request that the White House secretary discuss the entire matter with the Federal Theatre Director that afternoon.[73] The material had scarcely been delivered when Early sent word that he was much too busy either to read the script or to talk with Mrs. Flanagan, and that, no matter how carefully the material had been prepared, any play dealing with foreign relations was "dangerous" and the impersonation of foreign dignitaries, "particularly dangerous." The WPA, he predicted, was apt to get itself into trouble if such a play were permitted.[74]

To the exhausted Hallie Flanagan, Early's reply was a sickening blow. Having returned only two days before from a grueling stay in New York, she had been subjected to a speech from Baker and Hopkins about the necessity of making the Arts Projects politically valuable to the Administration, a pep talk about the importance of putting Democrats on the Project, orders to accede to the closing of *Model Tenements*, and finally, a crisis over *Ethiopia* that threatened to end not only the play itself but the Living Newspaper as well. Despairing over the "political censorship" that seemed to be "settling down" about her, she poured out her anxieties in a letter to Philip Davis: "It [all] means that I have stuck through this incredible agonizing business only to find that there is a joker at the bottom of the pile— that even if we *do* get these units set up, we are never going to be able to operate anything worth doing."[75] But until the final decision had been made, she refused to accept defeat. Carrying her case to the White House, she explained to Mrs. Roosevelt her reluctance to close the play and urged the First Lady to read the script and intercede for the Federal Theatre. The President's wife agreed and managed to persuade Early to withdraw his ob-

[73] Flanagan to Philip Davis, January 16, 1936; Baker to Early, January 16, 1936, Flanagan Papers.

[74] Mary Cox to Baker, January 16, 1936, Flanagan Papers.

[75] Flanagan to Philip Davis, January 16, 1936, Flanagan Papers.

jections.[76] Confident that *Ethiopia* would open after all, Mrs. Flanagan returned to New York to face the embattled delegations of Project workers, whose frequent demonstrations and threats of demonstrations pained this sensitive woman who had long sympathized with workers everywhere far more than she now dared betray.

Despite her efforts, the Ethiopian crisis proved no easier resolved in the theatrical arena than in the diplomatic. On January 18 the Federal Theatre Director received an order from Baker forbidding, in effect, the representation of the head of any foreign state, his minister, or his cabinet.[77] To her frantic protests, the Relief Administrator replied that Early had telephoned after his talk with Mrs. Roosevelt, reiterating his feeling that the play should be dropped.[78] When Mrs. Flanagan appealed once again to Mrs. Roosevelt, the First Lady assured her that she had discussed the entire matter with the President, who thought that the production should be allowed to open so long as foreign statesmen were not represented in person.[79] The reluctant Baker, however, needed much convincing. Confident that the play's excellence, originality, and objectivity would save it if the Relief Administrator would only see a performance, Hallie Flanagan finally persuaded him to come to New York.[80] Six days before the scheduled opening, Baker arrived, attended a rehearsal, and sent the Federal Theatre Director a second note permitting the use of quotations so long as the ruler or cabinet official did not actually appear on stage.[81]

[76] Flanagan, Notes on Conference with Mrs. Roosevelt at the White House, January 17, 1936, Flanagan Papers.

[77] Memorandum, Baker to Flanagan, January 18, 1936, Roosevelt MSS, Official File 80.

[78] Telephone Conversation, Flanagan and Mrs. Roosevelt, January 21, 1936, Flanagan Papers.

[79] *Ibid.*

[80] Flanagan to Regional Directors, January 26, 1936, RG 69, FTP Records, NOC-Reg. V.

[81] Memorandum, Baker to Flanagan, January 23, 1936, Flanagan Papers.

It was a reasonable alternative. But to the enraged Rice, who had endured red tape, union negotiations, theatre rentals, and countless delegations only to have his first play curtailed, Baker's ruling was proof that Washington never intended to permit the curtain to go up on anything but "pap for babes and octogenarians."[82] As Mrs. Flanagan hurried with Rice to Baker's office for a final appeal, she tried to persuade the irate playwright not to resign—the very fear that a play might involve the United States in international complications was, after all, a tribute to the power of the Living Newspaper.[83] Nevertheless, Rice was adamant; Baker, unmoved. When, after much discussion, the New York director again threatened to resign, the WPA administrator calmly pulled out a typed letter addressed to Rice and read:

> When difficulties have arisen in the past in connection with the operation of the Federal Theatre Project, within the framework of government structure, you have proposed either to resign or take the difficulties to the press. Now that a problem has arisen in connection with a dramatization that may affect our international relations, you renew your proposal of resignation in a telegram to Mr. Hopkins. This time I accept it, effective upon your receipt of this letter.

Baker signed the letter and rose, as did Rice and Mrs. Flanagan.[84]

When critics and reporters arrived the following day for a private showing of *Ethiopia*, they found the characteristically caustic, highly indignant Mr. Rice eager to comment on the

[82] Flanagan, *Arena*, p. 66.

[83] *Ibid.* Rice had already notified Hopkins that he would resign if the production were closed. See Telegram, Rice to Hopkins, January 21, 1936, Flanagan Papers.

[84] Baker to Rice, January 23, 1936, Flanagan Papers; the *New York Times*, January 24, 1936, p. 5; Flanagan, *Arena*, p. 66. According to Mrs. Flanagan, Rice did not really intend to resign, believing, when he submitted his resignation, that it would not be accepted. Interview with Hallie Flanagan, November 13, 1961.

theatre which he had so often assured them would be allowed to develop "uncensored politically or morally."[85] Rice had previously implied that there were those in "relatively high places" who were "more interested in the future of the Democratic Party than in the future of the theatre," and now he frankly stated that fear of international complications was only a pretext for censorship. The decision to stop *Ethiopia* was not made until after he had outlined some of the Living Newspaper's future productions—plays dealing with unemployment, the handling of relief, and conditions in the South. Admitting that in the play on the South there would be impersonations of some Southern congressmen protesting against an anti-lynching bill, Rice insisted that the real reason for censorship was the fear of alienating powerful Democratic supporters in the South—"in other words, hitting the Democratic party where it lives."[86]

Reactions to the incident were widespread. William Randolph Hearst's *New York Mirror* devoted two full pages of its Sunday magazine section to photographs of *Ethiopia* topped by the huge black headline, HOW THE ALPHABET GOVERNMENT LAID A MILLION-DOLLAR BROADWAY EGG. The bad showmanship of the WPA has resulted in costs running "into the millions—eventually to be paid by the taxpayers," cried the *Mirror*.[87] Neither denying nor substantiating the barrage of charges coming from both left and right, WPA administrators maintained an official silence; but Aubrey Williams sent the following letter to Eleanor Roosevelt at Hopkins' request:

> Mr. Baker is in New York today and it developed that with the presentation of *Ethiopia*, they have in mind producing Soviet Russia, the Scottsboro Case, Sharecroppers, etc. You can see from this that they intend to present only those things which are highly controversial and which immediately bring

[85] The *New York Times*, October 12, 1935, p. 19; January 5, 1936, Sec. 9, p. 4.

[86] *Ibid.*, January 25, 1936, Sec. 1, p. 7; *Variety*, February 5, 1936, p. 52.

[87] Clipping located in Flanagan Papers. For a contrary reaction, see "Mr. Rice Resigns," *The Nation*, CXLII (February 12, 1936), 174.

to the fore opponents and contra-opponents of this sort of activity on the part of the Federal Government.

Mr. Hopkins has decided that in view of this, it is not wise to go ahead with this project and instructed Mr. Baker to so inform Mr. Rice through Miss [sic] Flanagan. Undoubtedly, this will result in the resignation of Mr. Rice, but it is our opinion that this would have to come inevitably and that it was best to have it occur in connection with a subject which involves neutrality as we would be stronger in this position than in others.[88]

Two years—perhaps even one year—before, Hopkins' own liberal inclination could have led him to decide differently. But the indifference to politics and the impatience with politicians so evident in 1933-34 was gradually giving way to a growing appreciation of political realities. The reason was simple enough. This onetime social worker had become increasingly aware that he could put into operation and maintain a work relief program in which he fervently believed, only if he could secure funds from Capitol Hill where politicians, many of them Southerners, held congressional purse strings securely in their grasp. As a responsible administrator, he could not risk the possible jeopardizing of relief appropriations by a small number of socially conscious theatre people. As a member of the Democratic administration and as one who was especially sensitive to charges that the WPA would prove a political liability to that administration, he was no less likely to risk the alienation of Italian or Southern voters in an election year fraught with political passions. On the contrary, his assistant, Jacob Baker, quietly assured disturbed Southern senators and their constituents that the WPA had no plans for a theatrical production of sharecroppers, that the Federal Theatre was giving the "standard plays the public wants," and that a traveling company was shortly to leave for the South with a play called *Jefferson Davis*.[89]

[88] Williams to Mrs. Roosevelt, January 23, 1936, Flanagan Papers.
[89] Baker to Park Trammell, February 21, 1936, RG 69, FTP Records, NOC-State.

Others, whose first concern was neither relief nor politics, but theatre, did not remain silent. Admitting that international repercussions could conceivably occur if the Italian government should regard this "unbiased, dramatic account" of the Ethiopian crisis as "American animosity subsidized by the government," Brooks Atkinson complained that the theatre is invariably reduced to "innocuous commonplace" when it has to conform to "diplomatic manners." The episode, observed the *New York Times* critic, silly in itself, shows how utterly futile it is to expect the theatre to be anything more than a "sideshow" under government supervision.[90]

Hallie Flanagan did not wholly agree. Still convinced of the sincerity of Hopkins' promise of an uncensored theatre, she, too, chose to regard the entire matter as an episode rather than a precedent. Never once mentioning whether she knew of or approved of the highly controversial topics Rice had suggested for subsequent productions, she assured her regional directors that, in spite of the difficulty with *Ethiopia* and *Model Tenement*, their job was "to put on good plays some of which will obviously be controversial." In fact, she explained, "we are not dropping 'the Living Newspaper,' but are going on at once to the next bill in which we will not run into the same difficulties, though only time will tell whether we will run into others." In any event, she continued, "let us, in spite of these two unfortunate episodes, proceed on the assumption that they were *episodes*, and that by exercising care we can do the sort of plays we want to do as we want to do them." It is important to continue, she insisted:

> . . . first, because we are finding out something about the relationship of the government to the theatre, and second, because the comment by such people as Brooks Atkinson on the closing of *Ethiopia*, together with the serious consideration of a script of ours by Washington officials indicate a serious consideration of the theatre as an active force in life.[91]

[90] The *New York Times*, January 25, 1936, p. 18.
[91] Flanagan to Glenn Hughes, January 26, 1936, RG 69, FTP Records, NOC-Reg. V.

To go ahead with plays, some of which, however good, would be controversial, was a crucial decision when those plays were to be presented by a theatre that was also a relief project. Even if Hallie Flanagan had realized just how crucial the decision was, she would not have decided differently. Convinced that only a theatre relevant to contemporary art and society possessed the vitality that would make it "an active force in life," she firmly believed that the Federal Theatre must achieve this relevance and vitality if it were to play a part in the remaking of America and, more important, if it were to become a permanent part of a new, more just society.

Confident that Rice's resignation called attention to the importance of keeping the Federal Theatre close to Mr. Hopkins' "free, adult, and uncensored theatre," Hallie Flanagan turned the New York Project over to thirty-three-year-old Philip Barber who had served as Rice's assistant.[92] In full agreement with both his predecessor and the National Director on the philosophy of the Federal Theatre, Barber promptly announced plans for a second Living Newspaper. This timely presentation, which was to be a history of the economic difficulties of the farmer, received impetus from the recent Supreme Court decision invalidating the New Deal's Agricultural Adjustment Act. Assuring reporters that the Court would be treated in a dignified manner, Barber promised that the play would be a "factual, unbiased presentation" showing the AAA in a "favorable way."[93]

In true Federal Theatre fashion, the curtain did not go up without difficulty. Actors, long out of work, were suspicious of so unconventional a play. This kaleidoscopic document was not drama, they insisted, and furthermore, no one in New York was interested in farmers. Explaining that the Federal Theatre had to experiment with new forms if it were to succeed, Mrs. Flanagan and Barber promised that the show would be dropped

[92] Flanagan, *Arena*, p. 67; Flanagan, "Introduction," *Federal Theatre Plays: Triple-A Plowed Under, Power, Spirochete*, pp. viii-ix.

[93] The *New York Times*, January 28, 1936, p. 15; February 14, 1936, p. 22.

immediately if it proved unsuccessful. The cast agreed to continue rehearsals—only to become distraught over a new crisis. With opening night just a few days away, rumors swept through the theatre that a Federal Theatre Veterans League, organized for the self-appointed task of combating Communism on the Project, considered the production unpatriotic, and planned to have it closed and the performers hauled off the stage into patrol wagons. While such headaches gave Barber cause to remember Rice's parting remark—"Christ, too, was just thirty-three when he was crucified"—he somehow managed to keep rehearsals going.[94]

When the curtain went up on March 14, the "actors were full of misgivings, the audience full of tension, and the lobby full of police."[95] But, despite interruptions and the occasional ejection of troublemakers, the show did go on. In a rapid succession of short "takes"—pantomimes, skits, and radio broadcasts—the audience saw the history of the farm problem unfold throughout the 'twenties and early 'thirties. They watched as mortgages were foreclosed, farms auctioned, and crops deliberately destroyed. They saw the devastating effects of drought, the organization of farmer-consumer cooperatives, and the creation of the AAA. They heard the Supreme Court declare the Act unconstitutional, administration leaders planning a new Soil Conservation Act, and finally, they heard the news that farmers and workers were joining to combat speculation and excessive profits by the middleman.

These stylized vignettes, flashing on and off like scenes on a newsreel, were made exciting by all the theatrical devices at the stage technicians' command. Thus, the terrible helplessness of the drought-stricken farmer is conveyed in a brief scene beginning as the Voice of the Living Newspaper announces over a

[94] Interview with Philip Barber, November 14, 1961. An account of the various problems involved prior to opening night is contained in Flanagan, "Introduction," *Federal Theatre Plays: Triple-A Plowed Under, Power, Spirochete*, pp. ix-x.

[95] *Ibid.*, p. x; the *New York Times*, March 15, 1936, p. 27.

loudspeaker: "Summer, 1934: Drought sears the Midwest, West, and Southwest." A light swings in on a farmer kneeling in his parched field. Two voices are heard alternately over the loudspeaker; the first announcing in a "crisp, sharp, staccato" voice: "May first, Midwest weather report"; the second replying in "sinister foreboding" tones: "Fair and warmer." As the forecast is repeated for May second, third, and fourth, the music grows in intensity and leaps to a climax of "shrill despair," as the farmer who is examining the soil straightens up, "slowly lets a handful of dry dust sift through his fingers"—and cries, "Dust!"[96]

For all its documentation, these visual headlines bore the added and potent ingredient of emotion. Theatregoers, critics, and politicians were quick to respond—sometimes with equal passion. Indeed, the very size of the crowds which poured into the theatre night after night were a source of dismay to those who resented the use of Secretary of Agriculture Wallace's characterization of the Supreme Court decision as the "greatest legalized steal in American history," or the brief speech by Earl Browder sandwiched in between remarks attributed to Al Smith and Thomas Jefferson.[97] According to the Republican representative from Long Island, Robert L. Bacon, the play was "pure and unadulterated politics." The administration, he told reporters, was carrying its open warfare against the Supreme Court to the stage of the WPA Theatre. Subsidized political drama represented "the flower of American Brain Trust Communism."[98]

Although drama critics from the *Times, Tribune, Post*, and *News* reviewed the play respectfully, the *Times* suggested editorially that to choose a play which "carries a definite propaganda message" showed rather poor judgment when the bill for the Federal Theatre was paid by people regardless of party lines.[99] *Variety* agreed that the play, "obviously propaganda for

[96] Living Newspaper Staff, *Triple-A Plowed Under* in *Federal Theatre Plays*, pp. 34-35.

[97] *Ibid.*, pp. 46-48.

[98] The *New York Times*, March 15, 1936, p. 27.

[99] *Ibid.*, March 17, 1936, p. 20.

72

the AAA," was an unfortunate choice.[100] The *Herald Tribune* was somewhat less restrained. Headlines boldly proclaimed Veterans League charges that the WPA Theatre was RED.[101] The Hearst Press, which, along with the Republican National Committee, had complained about "US Dollars" for "Pink Plays" long before a single play was in rehearsal, now assailed *Triple-A* as "the most outrageous misuse of the taxpayers' money that the Roosevelt administration has yet been guilty of."[102] Another longtime critic, *The Saturday Evening Post*, went even further, pointing out the similarity between *Triple-A*'s call to the farmer and laborer to unite, and the American Communist Party's plea for the formation of a farm-labor party.[103] Although the play had only mentioned that farmers and laborers were forming a new organization in Minnesota and elsewhere, Party members and sympathizers were scarcely more discriminating than their opponents. Embracing the play with open arms, they applauded its "plain statement of the need for a Farm-Labor Party."[104] They expressed pleasure at the inclusion of a brief speech by Earl Browder, even though it was only an argument for the supremacy of Congress over the judiciary.[105] Delighted with the play's collective composition, they extolled the virtues of subsidized theatre until one writer felt obliged to warn his comrades that neither "this show, or a hundred like it spread throughout the country, will be a short-cut to the revolution."[106]

[100] *Variety*, March 18, 1936, p. 62.

[101] *New York Herald Tribune*, March 21, 1936, p. 13.

[102] *New York Evening Journal*, October 24, 1935, p. 32; March 18, 1936, p. 34. The Republicans' attack on the Project was contained in a pamphlet entitled "Roosevelt, the Waster." See Flanagan to Lester Lang, December 19, 1935, RG 69, GSS-211.2.

[103] Garet Garrett, "Federal Theatre for the Masses." *The Saturday Evening Post*, CCVII (June 20, 1936), 8-9. Quotations from the *Daily Worker* of March 7, 1936 and Earl Browder's CBS broadcast of March 5.

[104] Charles E. Dexter, "Introducing PUDC Newcomers to the Living Newspaper Cast," *Daily Worker*, March 22, 1936, p. 7.

[105] The *New York Times*, March 15, 1936, p. 27.

[106] John Mullen, "A Worker Looks at Broadway," *New Theatre*, III (May 1936), 27.

73

Distressed by this barrage of unwelcome plaudits and frantic headlines, Bruce McClure rushed up from WPA headquarters in Washington to do something. Instead of finding a Communist under the proverbial bed, he learned from Hallie Flanagan and New York City administrator, Victor Ridder, that WPA investigators had just discovered rightists on the Project selling Federal Theatre scripts to the Hearst press. A mail department employee, Hazel Huffman, had apparently also received a substantial sum for an affidavit claiming that she had opened Mrs. Flanagan's mail for three months and found it "incendiary, revolutionary, and seditious."[107] Rather than provide a martyr for the rightists and more fuel for the press, WPA officials concluded that the best strategy was to ignore the whole affair publicly, while keeping a private check on Project malcontents. As for the play itself, McClure joined playgoers in eight minutes of final applause and insisted that Mrs. Roosevelt be invited to a performance.[108] Although other less sanguine individuals were frankly surprised that the controversial Living Newspaper had been allowed to remain open with all the "contending forces" at work, Hallie Flanagan was delighted.[109]

Triple-A's victory over censorship was combined with an increasing number of new productions, all of which indicated that this relief project was fast becoming a theatre to be reckoned with. *Chalk Dust*, an attack on abuses in the big city public schools, earned the sponsorship of John Dewey and the interest of Hollywood producers who eventually bought the script.[110] *Murder in the Cathedral*, interpreted under Halsted Welles' direction as a call for religious submission, brought forgiveness for less distinguished productions and lyrical praise from the press. Brooks Atkinson called T. S. Eliot's poetic drama of Thomas à Becket's martyrdom, "a severely beautiful production worthy of

[107] Flanagan to Philip Davis, March 17, 1936, Flanagan Papers.
[108] *Ibid.*
[109] Rosamond Gilder, "The Federal Theatre," *Theatre Arts Monthly*, XX (June 1936), 435.
[110] *Variety*, April 15, 1936, p. 1.

the stinging verse its author has written." There is only "spirit and perception to lay hold of" in this difficult play, Atkinson observed, but Halsted Welles with his federal actors has "conjured out of the choral chants and violent imagery a moving and triumphant performance."[111] It was a verdict widely shared by New York critics. At the end of a special matinee, "a hard-boiled audience of Broadway professionals stood up and cheered," wrote *Billboard*'s Eugene Burr, "literally stood and cheered as this reporter has seldom if ever heard an audience cheer in a theatre." It was, he concluded, an "eye-clouding, heart-warming, thrilling and entirely deserved tribute. . . ."[112] Eleanor Roosevelt paid her tribute too. At the end of an evening performance, the deeply moved First Lady hurried backstage to congratulate the cast. And New Yorkers, save for a minority who lamented this right-wing deviation on the part of the Federal Theatre, filled the theatre night after night.

Even the Harlem unit seemed to be abandoning the crusading appeal of Frank Willson's *Walk Together Chillun* for a spectacular and hugely successful *Macbeth*. An imaginative adaptation of the Shakespearean tragedy, this tour de force was the brain child of two extremely talented young men determined to do what amused them in the theatrical world. Produced by John Houseman and directed by twenty-year-old Orson Welles, it was, in Brooks Atkinson's words, "a voodoo show suggested by the Macbeth legend."[113] On opening night ten thousand people lined up for tickets, while the Negro Elks' eighty-piece brass

[111] Brooks Atkinson, "Meditation of a Martyr in T. S. Eliot's *Murder in the Cathedral*," the *New York Times*, March 21, 1936, p. 13. See also "Strange Images of Death," the *New York Times*, March 29, 1936, Sec. 9, p. 1.

[112] Eugene Burr, "From Out Front," *The Billboard*, XLVIII (May 2, 1936), 18. As another example of critical praise, see Dorothy Dunbar Bromley, "A Play of Rich Beauty Under Aegis of WPA," *New York World Telegram*, Sec. 6, p. 8.

[113] Brooks Atkinson, "*Macbeth* or Harlem Boy Goes Wrong, Under Auspices of Federal Theatre Project," the *New York Times*, April 15, 1936, p. 25.

band paraded past the Lafayette Theatre in scarlet and gold. When the curtain rose, every major drama critic in the city was either present or about to be. Then, under the "unearthly" lights of the Federal Theatre's talented Abe Feder, Macbeth, in foot-wide epaulets of red cord, and pink and purple clad ladies moved about in a castle set in Haiti during the Napoleonic era, while Ethiopians dressed as witches brewed black magic to the beat of voodoo drums.

Shakespeare was probably turning over in his grave, said Robert Garland to *World Telegram* readers the following day, but, he added, "by all means" see the show. Burns Mantle of the *Daily News* agreed with his colleague on the *Times* that it was indeed "a spectacular theatrical experience." Even Gilbert Gabriel, critic for Hearst's *New York American*, dropped his customary coolness and admitted that "all that smites the eye in this particular 'Macbeth' is quite magnificent." Although John Mason Brown of the *Post* thought the play should have been rewritten in order to bring both the plot and language closer to its Haitian setting, the audiences who packed the Lafayette night after night were completely satisfied. Indeed, the production achieved such international fame that readers of the *Spectator* soon discovered that "everybody knew this Mr. Shakespeare had always intended his plays to be acted by Negroes," according to a buxom black lady in a red and yellow dress who watched the show for the fifth time alongside the London reporter.[114]

With four big productions on the boards by the end of March, the New York Project seemed to be making a place for itself. As if to proclaim the improved state of affairs, Burns Mantle wrote in bold black type: UNCLE SAM FINDS SHOW BUSINESS

[114] Robert Garland, "Jazzed-Up *Macbeth* at the Lafayette," *New York World Telegram*, April 15, 1936, p. 28; Burns Mantle, "WPA *Macbeth* in Fancy Dress," *New York Daily News*, April 15, 1936, p. 49; Gilbert Gabriel, "Ladies Luck and Macbeth," *New York American*, April 17, 1936, p. 19; Interview with John Mason Brown, November 10, 1961; Martha Gellhorn, "Federal Theatre," *Spectator* (London), CLVII (July 10, 1936), 51.

EXCITING; MOST OF THE OFF-STAGE NOISES AND BRIGHT RED
FLARES HAVE BEEN HANDLED. . . .[115]

Despite the general enthusiasm a handful of congressmen on
Capitol Hill were beginning to wonder if "exciting" theatre was
exactly what was needed on a relief project. When Hopkins
appeared before the House Committee on Appropriations in
early April, the Relief Administrator found Committee members
especially interested in the alleged political activities of the WPA
and, incidentally, the Federal Theatre. Representative Bacon,
who had previously denounced *Triple-A* as "pure, unadulterated
politics," explained that he had received complaints from a
group of veterans in New York City about a play called "The
AAA Plowed Under." This brings up a serious question, the Long
Island Republican continued, as to whether federal funds should
be used to put plays on the stage that are the subject of propaganda. Hopkins, whose cardinal rule in dealing with a congressional committee was never to apologize, quickly pointed out
that *Triple-A* was neither propaganda against the Supreme
Court, as Bacon had suggested, nor "a sort of Gridiron Club
proposition," as the Virginia Democratic representative, Clifton
Woodrum, seemed to think. On the contrary, it was a dramatic
version of the news: "something like the March of Time in the
movies," he assured them. Insisting that the Living Newspaper
production was an excellent play drawing huge crowds, as was
Murder in the Cathedral, he urged the Committee to see both.
Hopkins went on to explain in his inimitable manner that plays,
of course, were subject to many opinions. "The question is," he
continued, "is it good theatre, is it artistic, is it well done?" When
Bacon persisted in his argument that in an election year it was
especially important that the taxpayers' money, meant for relief,
not be used for political propaganda by a Theatre Project, Hopkins persisted in his assurances:

If you knew the kind of people that are administering this
for us, you would know that they would not tolerate for a

[115] Burns Mantle, "Uncle Sam Finds Show Business Exciting," *New
York Daily News*, March 29, 1936, p. 84.

moment identification with any kind of enterprise that was of a partisan propaganda nature, and nothing like that will be permitted to happen *in terms of the type of propaganda that you are thinking of. . . .*[116]

Hopkins, like many other convinced New Dealers, seemed to feel that any propaganda coming from the Federal Theatre was propaganda arising from the conviction that America should provide a better life for more of its people. But such sentiments, to many Republicans and conservative Democrats, smacked strongly of New Deal political thinking, if not worse.

Only a few days after the Relief Administrator had testified before the House Appropriations Committee, James J. Davis took the floor of the Senate to inform his colleagues that the Administration, either wittingly or unwittingly, was permitting money meant for relief to be spent by a woman infatuated both by the Russian theatre and the U.S.S.R. Launching into what he described as a "sordid chapter in American history," the Pennsylvania Republican read from letters sent to him by the Federal Theatre Veterans League and by an Equity member complaining of Communist infiltration on the New York Project; he read from *Shifting Scenes*, from *Can You Hear Their Voices?* and from other of Mrs. Flanagan's writings. Nowhere, he concluded, does that woman have "a good word to say about the United States, this government, American institutions, or the economic system which makes possible relief money for the WPA." Turning from Mrs. Flanagan to the administration, Davis questioned why someone who in 1929 wrote, "I became absorbed by the drama outside the theatre; the strange and glorious drama that is Russia," was appointed to administer over $7 million of American money:

If the administration appointed her without knowing her point of view it reveals unbelievable irresponsibility. If the adminis-

[116] Hearings before the House Committee in Charge of Deficiency Appropriations. *First Deficiency Appropriation Bill for 1936, Part 2, Emergency Relief*, 74th Cong., 2nd Sess. (1936), pp. 206-210. (Italics mine in quoted passage.)

tration appointed her as a mark of approval and sanction for her absorption in the "great drama that is Russia," it should now explain to the taxpayers of this country the use of relief money intended to feed the hungry for such alien purposes.[117]

The press, of course, was quick to pick up Davis' speech.[118] In the days that followed, Senator Robert Wagner of New York read to his fellow senators telegrams from officials in the New York Project and from the president of Equity repudiating charges contained in the letters to Davis.[119] Mrs. Flanagan issued a statement denying that she was interested only in Russian theatre and Russian methods of production, and then let the matter drop, confident that the Project's production record could speak for itself.[120] But charges of Communism, she would eventually discover, could not be easily silenced.

In fact, the Federal Theatre's critics may have been more effective than they realized, for by mid-April Hallie Flanagan was uncertain that the Project would even be continued on a national basis after the current appropriation ran out on June 30. Alerted to the possibility that the entire program might be turned over to the states, Frank Gillmore of Actors' Equity promised the Federal Theatre Director that he would use all his influence to prevent what both believed would be a disastrous decision.[121] Following up that promise, Gillmore immediately sent fifty telegrams to New York senators and representatives

---

[117] *Congressional Record*, 74th Cong., 2nd Sess. (1936), pp. 5,696-5,699. For earlier charges of the Veterans' League, see the *New York Times*, March 1, 1936, p. 12; March 15, Sec. 10, p. 1; March 22, Sec. 9, p. 10.

[118] The *New York Times*, April 27, 1936, p. 19; *New York Herald Tribune*, April 21, 1936, p. 15.

[119] *Cong. Rec.*, pp. 6,074-6,075.

[120] The *New York Times*, April 28, 1936, p. 17. Apparently Mrs. Flanagan also prepared a speech for Senator Wagner. A draft containing her penciled corrections is contained in RG 69, FTP Records, NOGSF.

[121] Gillmore to Flanagan, April 18, 1936, RG 69, GSS-211.2. This account of Gillmore's activities on the Federal Theatre's behalf is based on that contained in the Equity magazine unless otherwise indicated. See "Project to Continue on National Basis," *Equity*, XXI (May 1936), 8, 10.

and instructed the union's Los Angeles and Chicago offices to protest to their own congressmen. Officials in other theatrical unions needed few words from the Equity president to convince them that no more than a half-dozen states would be likely to maintain their own theatre projects, if national control were ended. Within days, protests to Washington had gone out from the national and local offices of the American Federation of Musicians and the International Alliance of Theatrical Stage Employees.[122] To the gentlemen of the press, the embattled Equity leader expounded at length on the untold confusion and suffering which would result if the Federal Theatre became a local rather than a national institution. Whether his efforts were responsible for what followed he did not know; but on April 21 he learned from Hallie Flanagan that the "situation we feared has probably been completely averted."[123]

Variety, which attributed the change to union pressure, warned, however, that the fight would not be won until attempts to earmark the relief appropriation had been defeated.[124] The fight was a hard one; Republicans and anti-administration Democrats charged the WPA with boondoggling, extravagance, and radicalism. Hopeful that these charges would be outweighed by glowing press reports of the Federal Theatre's increasing efficiency and successes,[125] Hallie Flanagan awaited the news that finally came on May 11—the appropriation bill had passed the House without the much feared earmarking of funds.[126] To her California director, Howard Miller, she wrote: "We are much more optimistic than we were a month ago. . . . Now there is

[122] Each of the seven hundred stagehands' locals sent telegrams according to *Variety* in its April 29, 1936 issue.

[123] Gillmore to Flanagan, April 23, 1936, RG 69, GSS-211.2.

[124] *Variety*, April 29, 1936, p. 54.

[125] Typical of these reports was *The Literary Digest* article which commented: "The greatest producer of hits is the federal government. It has four smashing successes in New York at one time, a record unequaled by anyone except Florenz Ziegfeld." See "Smart Uncle Sam," *The Literary Digest*, CXXI (May 9, 1936), 25.

[126] The *New York Times*, May 12, 1936, p. 8.

every indication, due, at least to some extent, to the pressure from the public, that we may continue another year." New York, she added, is going "very well indeed." *Triple-A, Chalk Dust, Macbeth,* and *Murder in the Cathedral,* all still playing to packed houses, boosted the morale of the Project immeasurably. Even more encouraging was the number of new productions ready to open: *1935,* another Living Newspaper; Michael Gold and Michael Blankfort's *Battle Hymn,* the life story of abolitionist agitator, John Brown; *Class of '29,* a new play about four college graduates' confrontation with a depression-stricken world; and two new dance productions.[127] New York was indeed doing very well.

On projects elsewhere, however, art and relief not only clashed, but often seemed mutually exclusive as directors tried to make actors of middle-age men and women, many of whom had lacked the ability and drive to push on to the twin meccas of show business in palmier days. From firsthand surveys squeezed in between crises in New York and Washington, and from the numerous reports and letters that poured into the national office, Hallie Flanagan was convinced that productions of merit simply were not being realized. In fact, all too frequently the sighs of relief which directors everywhere had breathed when those eligible were at last on Project rolls had turned to groans at the sight of the " 'artists' at work." In a moment of discouragement K. Elmo Lowe poured out the dilemma he faced in the Ohio region:

> I have reached an impasse. What should my standards be? Am I doing the workers an injustice to allow them to function in a profession for which they are unfitted? Are they unfitted for work in a provincial theatre? How much consideration should I give to the laudatory letters from high schools and clubs who get entertainment free of charge? What is the standard Rice, Stephens [*sic*] and Brown have set for themselves?

[127] Flanagan to Miller, May 13, 1936, RG 69, FTP Records, NOC-Reg. V.

Are their people and productions only relatively better than ours? Does the fact that the majority of my people could not get a job in New York prove that they cannot help to develop a theatre that is indigenous to their particular locale? . . . Have I any justification for burdening the capables with the incapables? Should I make a perceptible cut in personnel immediately . . . ? *Is this social work, or theatre?*[128]

Everywhere the questions were the same.

There were no simple answers. When directors decided to make cuts, they sometimes found the decision easier made than carried out. In Massachusetts the Federal Theatre had fallen heir to a number of vaudeville people, originally hired by the FERA on the basis of need rather than professional ability. "Subdued, shabby, hungry, and old," they qualified for relief assistance, but not for a work program.[129] Yet when New England director Hiram Motherwell attempted to prune the Springfield Project, Harry Hopkins was besieged by frantic letters from local Democrats who were afraid that those dismissed would never be transferred to other projects, since Republican officials in Springfield might refuse to cooperate with the federal government.[130] When directors chose not to cut, they faced the task of rehabilitating those they kept. The monologist who substituted Roosevelt's name in lyrics composed for President Wilson, and the vaudevillian who clung to his prohibition gags typified performers on the Pennsylvania Project. At least 80 per cent of them seemed to be out of touch with the world in which they lived.[131] In New Orleans and Washington, as well as in Pittsburgh, the problem of what to do with one-time vaudeville people, now "old, resigned and passé," confounded directors

[128] Lowe to Flanagan, January 18, 1936, RG 69, FTP Records, Narr. Reports.

[129] Report to Jacob Baker on FERA Drama Projects in Massachusetts, n.d., RG 69, FTP Records, NOC-Reg. I.

[130] Edward B. Cooley to Hopkins, January 25, 193[6], RG 69, FTP Records, NOC.

[131] Jasper Deeter to Lester Lang, December 13, 1935, RG 69, FTP Records, NOC-Reg. II.

unaccustomed to social as well as artistic problems of such formidable proportions.[132]

On larger projects the situation was only slightly better. In California, Gilmor Brown confessed that he was appalled at the task involved in rousing the majority of his actors from the "old, routine, lifeless methods" to which they had become accustomed.[133] Of the Los Angeles Project, director George Gerwing wrote: "If I were a commercial producer employing a cast, front-of-the-house help, backstage help, and similar personnel for theatrical activity, I would employ approximately thirty per cent of those on the FTP payroll."[134] Even the relatively few young people on the Project did not always possess the professional experience and training to be expected of Equity members, for one had only to have had a part in one professional production within a two-year period to qualify for union membership.[135] Moreover, after months, even years, of insecurity and anxiety scarcely conducive to creativity, young and old alike often carried with them the psychological scars of breadlines and relief rolls.

To rehabilitate and retrain these broken people, to create from their miscellaneous talents and backgrounds the kind of artistic productions desired by Hallie Flanagan, required not only hard work, but also considerable skill, originality, and sheer ingenuity on the part of the director. Theatrical leaders with such qualities were not plentiful on a poorly paying relief proj-

[132] Lester Scharff to Hallie Flanagan, April 28, 1936, RG 69, FTP Records, NOC-Reg. II; Tony Merrill to Esther Porter, March 16, 1936, RG 69, FTP Records, NOC; Howard Miller to William Everson, n.d., RG 69, FTP Records, NOC-Reg. V.

[133] Brown to Flanagan, March 12, 1936, RG 69, FTP Records, NOC-Reg. V.

[134] Memorandum, Gerwing to J. Howard Miller, February 15, 1936, NOC-Reg. V.

[135] In March 1936, the Equity Council attempted to tighten up membership requirements by insisting that within the two-year probationary period an actor must have performed work for which he was paid during at least fifty weeks. See "One Part Plus Two Years Does Not Make an Actor," *Equity*, XXI (April 1936), 3.

ect. Nor were those with imagination always equally endowed with the patience and perseverance necessary to convert old actors to new methods. Directors discovered, for example, that even the most tactfully worded suggestion to an old vaudeville performer about his "would-be funny speech" could elicit an impassioned discourse on art and the noble heights of unicycle riding.[136] Understandably, those individuals who resented the "general grubbiness" of what seemed to be "merely a relief job" soon resigned.[137] In areas where talent was more promising, they often held on; but more than one regional director found himself echoing the plaint of Gilmor Brown, "Oh Lord, if I could only find more directors to raise the standard of acting"; or wondering, as did Indiana's Lee Norvelle, how a sturdy foundation for a permanent theatre could ever be built from such "frail reeds."[138]

The artistic frailty of these old vaudeville and variety people was perhaps to be expected, but the warm response which their performances met was not. In Washington a small group of musicians borrowed from the local music project and a dozen "actors" of sorts gave free performances in foundling homes, settlement houses, old soldiers' homes, hospitals, and CCC camps throughout the area. "Ham from start to finish" was the candid evaluation of a Federal Theatre official who regarded the unit as one of the weakest; but, to his surprise, audiences loved every act.[139] Directors everywhere, realizing that this entertainment was hardly good theatre, shared the same experience.[140] From mis-

[136] Memorandum, Tony Merrill to Esther Porter, March 16, 1936, RG 69, FTP Records, NOC.

[137] Flanagan to Jasper Deeter, April 21, 1936, RG 69, FTP Records, NOC-Reg. II.

[138] Brown to Flanagan, March 12, 1936, RG 69, FTP Records, NOC-Reg. V; Norvelle to William P. Farnsworth, March 20, 1936, RG 69, FTP Records, NOC-Reg. II.

[139] Anthony Merrill to Flanagan [July 1, 1936], RG 69, FTP Records, Narr. Reports.

[140] The expressions of sheer enjoyment on the faces of various under-privileged groups was often a real revelation for Federal Theatre directors. See, for example, Hiram Motherwell to Flanagan, February 22, 1936, RG 69, FTP Records, NOC.

sion schools in South Dakota, park officials in Chicago, and CCC camps spread out across the Nebraska plains came enthusiastic letters of appreciation. Catholic foundling asylums and widows' homes in Normandy, Missouri and Lewiston, Maine sent word that variety acts had delighted children of seven and old ladies of seventy-seven. Ailing veterans in hospitals in southern California and eastern Massachusetts watched vaudeville acts with such obvious pleasure that hospital aides and American Legion officials were prompted to write letters of appreciation. From state schools for boys in Portland and Los Angeles came messages that the boys had been thrilled by Federal Theatre performances; the Maine youngsters even sent Hallie Flanagan their own crudely printed, deeply felt "Thank-you's."[141]

Dramatic productions met with responses that pleased Harry Hopkins and local players alike. Although in Plymouth, Massachusetts super-patriots decried the history depicted in Maxwell Anderson's *Valley Forge*—despite reassurances from the president of the Massachusetts Historical Society and the Harvard historian, Arthur M. Schlesinger[142]—such scruples were not shared by most Federal Theatregoers. In Missouri, where a traveling troupe was performing *Ladies of the Jury*, a small-town barber wrote to Federal Theatre officials expressing his approval of the entire Project, while a local doctor noted that the players had conducted themselves like ladies and gentlemen and people coming from twenty miles around had stood to see the performance.[143] Nebraskans were no less drama starved. When an Omaha group arrived in the town of Valley, eight hundred of that community's one thousand citizens crowded in to see the

[141] The above information, unless otherwise indicated, is based upon random samples of the hundreds upon hundreds of letters to Federal Theatre officials contained in RG 69, FTP Records, National Office Testimonial Letters (NOTL).

[142] A. M. Schlesinger to Hiram Motherwell, March 3, 1936; Stewart Mitchell to Hiram Motherwell, February 27, 1936, RG 69, FTP Records, NOC.

[143] Eliza Walker to W. B. Stone, June 12, 1936; G. F. Kling to W. B. Stone, June 17, 1936, RG 69, FTP Records, NOTL.

show.[144] In Concord, New Hampshire and Cincinnati, Ohio people were turned away.[145] By the end of May, Buffalo's marionette units had entertained nearly a half-million citizens of the Empire State, most of them children, while in New Orleans nearly ten thousand youngsters and adults had watched marionette shows, minstrels, tap dancers, and magicians surrounded by pink acacia and parakeets.[146] In New York City, where Federal Theatre employees were often people of unusual talent and their productions good theatre, children, parents, and grandparents alike flocked to parks where actors performed from the portable stages of the Suitcase Theatre; and they overflowed Brooklyn's Armory when the WPA circus arrived. Into the city's downtown theatres crowded thousands of young, lively, impecunious New Yorkers eager to be entertained, but still more eager to hear something said. The WPA, wrote Burns Mantle in the summer of 1936, has turned the theatre "back to the public to whom it rightfully belongs." The "Peoples' Theatre [is] grow-[ing] stronger"—and so it was.[147]

Pleased by the appellation, Hallie Flanagan had every reason to take pride in this growth. Within one year a plan for a theatre had been worked out, an institution created and made to function, and an audience discovered—an audience which included thousands who were seeing live performers for the first time. Harry Hopkins was also gratified by the Federal Theatre's ac-

[144] Flanagan, "Report of the Director," the *New York Times*, May 17, 1936, Sec. 9, p. 2.
[145] *Concord Monitor*, April 18, 1936; *Cincinnati Inquirer*, April 17, 1936, RG 69, FTP Records, Federal Theatre Project Press Clippings (FTP-PC).
[146] "Marionettes in the Federal Theatre" [press release], May 24, 1936, RG 69, FTP Records, National Office Publicity Material (NOPM); *New Orleans Tribune*, April 26, 1936, RG 69, FTP Records, FTP-PC; Hallie Flanagan, Personal Notes on the Federal Theatre Project, March 29, 1936, Flanagan Papers. Mrs. Flanagan's Notes are cited hereafter as Personal Notes on FTP.
[147] Burns Mantle, "Too Many Actors! What to Do?," *New York Daily News*, May 3, 1936, p. 80; Burns Mantle, "The People's Theatre Grows Stronger," *New York Daily News*, May 24, 1936, p. 78.

complishments. Apologizing for his virtual inaccessibility during recent months, the Relief Administrator promised that the Arts Projects would not be turned back to the states as Baker had apparently wished. Instead, Baker would be transferred and the Project placed under more sympathtetic supervision in the Washington office during the coming year. As for the Federal Theatre, Hopkins promised that he personally would be on hand to discuss plans for the season ahead.[148]

Yet neither progress nor promises could change the fact that this "People's Theatre" was also a welfare project. The inherent contradictions between the two had affected the form this institution had taken and the way it functioned. The form and the idea never seemed to coincide exactly as planned. Although Hallie Flanagan and her directors had tried to create a decentralized national theatre, enough state administrators frustrated national theatre and too many regulations thwarted regional theatre. Mrs. Flanagan wanted socially relevant plays; government officials wanted safe plays. Directors planned challenging productions, but with actors from relief roles. In short, men who thought they would be creating new theatre found themselves running a relief project; and everything had to be done under the unsympathetic eye of their congressional "angels." The tensions were simply too great. Thus, within a year after she had first discussed the possibilities of this new venture with her regional directors, not only Mabie and Rice, but also Frederick Koch, Gilmor Brown, Frederick McConnell, Thomas Wood Stevens, K. Elmo Lowe, Jasper Deeter, Rosamond Gilder, and Eddie Dowling had wearily returned to their old jobs. In the exodus, the Federal Theatre Director had lost a few who had contributed little; many more who had given unsparingly of themselves—their time, talent, and experience.

[148] Flanagan, Personal Notes on FTP, April 20, 1936, May 28, 1936; Flanagan to Philip Davis, April 20, 1936, May 28, 1936, Flanagan Papers; Flanagan to Howard Miller, May 27, 1936, RG 69, FTP Records, NOC-Reg. v. According to Florence Kerr a rift between Hopkins and Baker had occurred prior to the latter's transfer. Interview with Florence Kerr, February 2, 1962.

Her determination and energy still unimpaired, Hallie Flanagan turned to such competent young men as William Farnsworth, Howard Miller, and John McGee. Still in their twenties or early thirties, they soon became thoroughly capable administrators, well able to work within the bureaucratic confines of the WPA and completely devoted to the Federal Theatre and its National Director. To these, especially, as well as to all those on the Project who were alive to its theatrical possibilities and willing to work to see them realized, Hallie Flanagan returned that devotion. In like measure, she gave them a kind of charismatic inspiration born of unfailing confidence in the institution they were creating. With will enough and imagination enough, the limitations of relief would be overcome. The hardship and suffering of unemployed men and women would be so utilized as to give their art a sense of being rooted in social and economic reality.[149] And out of this theatre would come productions of such quality in the season ahead that the hopes of all who saw in the Project the beginning of a "People's Theatre" in America would be fulfilled. If, in the future, such fulfillment were realized, it would indeed be a triumph of will and vision over the basic contradictions inherent in an institution which had to combine relief and theatre to the eventual detriment of both.

[149] For a characteristic expression of this belief that the relief status of Federal Theatre workers could become an advantage, see Hallie Flanagan, "A Theatre for the People," *American Magazine of Art* (August 1936), p. 494.

CHAPTER THREE

Relevant Theatre in a Bureaucratic Framework

IN SPITE of the growing acceptance by public and press, the Federal Theatre Project was a none-too-secure foundation on which to build a national theatre. This was Hallie Flanagan's goal, but neither devotion to the Project nor utter absorption in it obscured the dimensions of the job ahead. "Our most urgent task," she told Federal Theatre workers, "is to make our theatre worthy of its audience. It is of no value whatever to stimulate theatre-going unless, once inside our doors, our audience sees something which has some vital connection with their own lives and their own immediate problems."[1] To study the American social and economic scene, past and present, to dramatize it with authority, wit, and power, and to rethink the American theatre "in terms of the economics, the human beings, and the art forms" of 1936-37 would prove a major endeavor under the very best circumstances;[2] and circumstances for the Federal Theatre were hardly favorable.

A hastily organized relief project, it was administratively flabby and artistically weak. Units throughout the country needed to be trimmed and tightened. New audiences had to be found with new dramas like the socially probing *It Can't Happen Here.* In short, theatre had to be produced within the inhospitable context of governmental bureaucracy. Because of that context, this second season became a painstakingly tedious exercise in administrative adjustment. Time and time again artistic efforts were interrupted by wholesale cuts of personnel and constant reorganizations. Yet plays were somehow produced in the midst of this enervating bureaucratic flux, as Hallie Flanagan and her

[1] Flanagan, "The People's Theatre Grows Stronger," *Federal Theatre*, I, No. 6 (May 1936), 6.

[2] Flanagan, Address to the Civitas Club of New York City, May 1936, RG 69, FTP Records, NOGSF.

directors struggled to turn a temporary relief measure into a professionally respectable theatre.

· I ·

The first requirement for theatrical progress was good administration. Federal Theatre officials had become convinced during the summer of 1936 that artistically sound productions were simply out of the question unless the units themselves were better organized and better run. A two-week tour of Michigan, Wisconsin, and Illinois had left Mrs. Flanagan appalled at the state of things in the Midwest. The Chicago director, Thomas Wood Stevens, had returned to his Globe Theatre, leaving the third largest Project in the country without a single "distinguished" production.[3] Nor did such productions appear likely in the several Texas projects unless the best of each could be combined in a single traveling group. Boston, still under the finger of the Massachusetts state administrator, needed considerable attention, as did Pennsylvania and New Jersey. In California Howard Miller frankly admitted that "some things" were done in ways that "still nauseate me," even though he claimed, with considerable justification, that the West Coast Project was the best in the country.[4] In short, Federal Theatre directors never doubted that the institution they had created could function, but they did know that many units had to operate with greater efficiency or not at all.

With their appropriation secured, they began work in earnest. Since all projects had to be "rewritten" on new forms at the beginning of the fiscal year, those without enough qualified actors were simply shut down. Thus, projects were discontinued

[3] Flanagan to J. Howard Miller, May 13, 1936, RG 69, FTP Records, NOC-Reg. V.

[4] Miller to Mary Virginia Farmer, July 30, 1936, RG 69, FTP Records, NOC. For information on the Texas and Boston Projects, see Charles Meredith to Richard B. Slaughter, July 23, 1936, RG 69, FTP Records, NOC-Reg. III; Blanche M. Ralston to Ellen Woodward, August 26, 1936; Flanagan to Leonard Gallagher, May 29, 1936, RG 69, FTP Records, NOC; George Gatts to William P. Farnsworth, June 10, 1936, RG 69, FTP Records, NOC-Reg. II.

in Asheville, Oakland, Little Rock, Cleveland, Toledo, Dayton, and in Virginia. When possible, capable actors were transferred to nearby theatre projects; less capable ones, to WPA-sponsored recreational activities. On the whole, however, closings were few.

The real work of reorganization was yet to be done with the many units remaining.[5] To rebuild these units into strong producing centers was a demanding task, requiring the constant supervision of men and women with a gift for administration as well as a sound artistic sense. To be truly effective, they had to possess the sensitivity of diplomats and the toughness of top sergeants. Perhaps no one displayed these qualities to better advantage than Lois Fletcher. As a Federal Theatre field agent working out of the South, she was thoroughly familiar with the administrative and financial side of the Project. More important, she understood the problem of liaison between Federal Theatre directors and various WPA officials in charge of Women's and Professional Projects. Under the close supervision of John McGee, who now had the entire South in his charge, she set out in July 1936 as a traveling troubleshooter, administrator, and director. Moving from Alabama to New Orleans, to Texas, and then to Oklahoma, she gradually worked northward in McGee's ever expanding "Southern" region.

By December she had reached Detroit to repeat what was now a familiar performance. Although it at first appeared that the former director had "upset things beyond repair," Miss Fletcher managed to persuade the state director of Women's and Professional Projects to let her take over. With a vigor that matched her imposing size, she promptly brought in a new director; borrowed a small group of actors from New York to supplement the Detroit company; got rid of an expensive theatre

[5] John McGee to Mary Dirnberger, July 15, 1936, RG 69, FTP Records, NOC; E. C. Lindeman to J. L. Bond, September 30, 1936, RG 69, FTP Records, NOC-Reg. III; Flanagan to Margaret Cameron, September 22, 1936, RG 69, FTP Records, NOC-Reg. II; William P. Farnsworth to Charles Hopkins, June 30, 1936, RG 69, FTP Records, NOC-State.

so as to reduce operating expenses; and enlisted local sponsors who would be willing to help with the cost of the Project. After a month of the usual "whip cracking," threats of reassignment to sewing rooms or manual labor projects, and frequent conferences with WPA officials, Miss Fletcher could point to another job well done. A competent director was in control of the Project, a reinforcement of actors had arrived from New York, and a group which had given nothing but free performances— "missionary work . . . for underprivileged people"—was rehearsing its first paying production.[6]

Such measures, wherever undertaken, offered hope for more efficient projects and more imaginative productions; but how successfully they were carried out depended on many things. Inevitably, Hallie Flanagan and her directors found themselves engaged in a continual accommodation between desirable standards and less desirable reality. In places where projects had gained little support from either the public or from local WPA administrators, Federal Theatre directors always had to win the confidence of local officials, and often, to obtain their permission to bring in out-of-state directors and actors. Men and women had to be found who could whip projects into shape and turn them over to directors capable of producing good theatre, while working with WPA officials and within bureaucratic restrictions. Such directors were indispensable to a smoothly functioning project, yet always few in number. In more than one instance Federal Theatre officials continued to tolerate an obviously inadequate individual lest, in replacing him, they merely "swap a jackass for a donkey."[7] On occasion, however, they had no

[6] McGee to Fletcher, July 6, 1936, July 29, 1936, RG 69, GSS-211.2; Fletcher to McGee, September 10, 1936, October 17, 1936, October 31, 1936; McGee to Florence Kerr, December 24, 1936; McGee to Blanche Ralston, December 24, 1936, RG 69, FTP Records, NOC-Reg. III; Memorandum, McGee to Flanagan, November 25, 1936, RG 69, FTP Records, NOC-Reg. IV.

[7] Joseph Lentz to John McGee, November 20, 1936, RG 69, FTP Records, NOC-Reg. V. The difficulty of finding the right directors was a constant complaint heard throughout the Project's existence. See Thomas

choice but to dismiss people with theatrical ability who simply lacked either the inclination or the capacity to cooperate with WPA officials.[8]

For those able to work within the rules and regulations of a relief project, Hallie Flanagan had every reason to hope that bureaucratic structure would be less confining in the year ahead. In a top level shake-up Harry Hopkins had dismissed Jacob Baker and named the former director of Women's Work, Ellen Woodward, as Assistant Administrator of Women's and Professional Projects, a position comparable to the other posts of assistant administrator held by David Niles and Corrington Gill. Responsible now for all white-collar work, Ellen Woodward would handle administrative matters for the four Arts Projects. Whether this Mississippi judge's daughter and former state senator would be more sympathetic to the arts than Jacob Baker, none of the Arts Projects directors knew. In any event, the Federal Theatre Director had Hopkins' promise that she could report directly to him on all theatrical decisions, such as choice of plays, methods of production, and appointment of directors.[9] With this assurance of support in Washington, the Project would have to function efficiently in the framework of the WPA. Hallie Flanagan aimed to see that it did. To regional directors she sent orders to develop the most cordial relations possible between the Federal Theatre and the division of Women's and Professional Work. Local projects supervisors and state directors were urged to hold frequent conferences on administrative matters

---

Wood Stevens to Howard Southgate, November 6, 1935, RG 69, FTP Records, NOC-Reg. IV; McGee to Flanagan, October 14, 1936, RG 69, GSS-211.2.

[8] This problem is well illustrated in a letter of dismissal written to the supervisor of the Cleveland Project. Wrote McGee: "Please believe that this is no reflection on your theatrical ability, but as you well know by this time, it requires a special combination of theatrical and diplomatic skill to do this kind of job." McGee to Theodore Viehman, November 18, 1936, RG 69, FTP Records, NOC-Reg. II.

[9] William P. Farnsworth, Address to the Chicago Congress of Federal Theatre Supervisors, August 26, 1936, RG 69, FTP Records, NOGSF.

with the district and state directors of Women's and Professional Projects. Copies of reports covering each project's finances, production activities, plans, and policy changes were to be sent to WPA officials. Even appointments were to be mutually discussed, although final approval rested with Federal Theatre directors alone. Mrs. Flanagan further insisted that WPA procedure had to be followed without fail, unless special rulings from Washington directed otherwise. In short, neither the complications of relief nor bureaucratic misunderstandings could be permitted to interfere with theatrical achievement.[10]

To make the kind of progress its National Director envisioned, the Federal Theatre needed a well-balanced program as well as efficient administration. Since May, when Hopkins had announced that the Theatre Project would be continued for another year, Hallie Flanagan had mulled over production plans and possibilities. By early October, when directors and supervisors from throughout the South gathered in Birmingham, possibilities had hardened into proposals. Describing the second chance that awaited the arts in America, she reminded her audience that out of economic necessity had come the opportunity to create a "new pattern of American culture." "For the first time in American theatrical history, directors and designers from coast to coast can sit around tables, pool their ideas, and be concerned not with . . . money or personal prestige, but with making an American theatre." With this advantage, there must be no falling back on the formulas of the past, no reproducing the kind of theatre that had landed 12,542 men and women on relief rolls. Instead, the Federal Theatre had to give its new audience something people could not get from any other form of entertainment, and at prices they could afford to pay.

Elaborating on this theme, Hallie Flanagan suggested that the Project give its audience cycles of plays. First, plays dealing with contemporary problems in American life should be launched in

[10] Flanagan to State Directors and Project Supervisors, July 17, 1936, RG 69, GSS-211.2; McGee to Dorothea Thomas Lynch, July 30, 1936. McGee's directive went to all state directors in Region III.

several cities simultaneously—plays like Sinclair Lewis' anti-Fascist *It Can't Happen Here*. There should also be plays about war, such as Euripides' *Trojan Women*; Living Newspaper productions written objectively with no adherence to any party line; and plays emphasizing regional themes. Second, the Federal Theatre could experiment in the field of entertainment: musical comedy, vaudeville, variety, and circus. This entire field, she argued, had to be completely rethought if the people in it were to be returned to private employment. Third, a potential audience could be developed with a theatre for children, perhaps by beginning with special holiday productions for different age groups or with marionette shows done in cooperation with schools and other institutions. In conclusion, she urged that the Federal Theatre not neglect religious drama.

To succeed with this four-pronged program, Hallie Flanagan reminded her directors once again that they had to learn to work through the WPA, particularly the directors of Women's and Professional Projects. "You cannot be of any use to the Federal Theatre," she admonished, "unless you understand the WPA and your part in it." "I think it is up to you . . . to become an asset of this organization and not a liability." To be a part of a relief organization, moreover, had certain advantages. "The fact that our production costs are low—and must be kept low—is an asset and not a liability, for it means that plays must be planned a long time in advance and that imagination and ingenuity must be used in the place of money."

Directors, Mrs. Flanagan went on, should also study their workers, retraining them and using whatever talents they had. Among the many who were old, tired, discouraged, and embittered, a sense of pride must be renewed—"pride that the government values their talents enough to conserve them by act of Congress, pride that into their hands the President of the United States has put the building of an American theatre." She urged other goals as well. By finding out what plays were most appropriate to children in school, patients in hospitals and insane asylums, and inmates of prisons and reformatories, the Federal

Theatre might discover new ways of making the theatre so vital a part of community life that the actors involved might become necessary to all sorts of civic and educational bodies. In fact, she concluded, "we need to study everything" because "our Federal Theatre has got to be contemporaneous, dynamic, funny, beautiful, accurate, direct, and daring in order to create a place for itself and its workers with the great new Twentieth Century American audience that awaits it."[11]

This bold vision revealed Hallie Flanagan at her best—as an imaginative disseminator of new ideas. But the Federal Theatre Director was also acquiring a capacity for putting ideas to work. Tightening her control, she now insisted that production plans be made three months in advance and that each play be submitted to her for approval. This new policy was a major departure from the old procedure of allowing each director complete freedom to select whatever plays he chose. Motivated in part by Hopkins' promise to support the National Director's final decision on any script so long as it had her prior approval, it was also designed to insure that local directors would produce the best plays available in an effective nationwide program. To facilitate this new procedure, Hallie Flanagan announced that a Play Policy Board would consider scripts recommended for each region and send the most promising to her for final approval.[12]

Greater control over choice of plays was a step in the right

[11] Flanagan, Address at Federal Theatre Conference in Birmingham, Alabama, October 7, 1936, RG 69, FTP Records, NOGSF.

[12] Memorandum, Flanagan to Philip Barber, November 9, 1936, RG 69, GSS-211.2; Flanagan to Howard Miller, January 14, 1937, RG 69, FTP Records, NOGSF. The Play Policy Board was composed of both the national and deputy directors, representatives from New York City, Chicago, the Eastern, Western, and Southern regions. To insure that some of the scripts approved by the Board would emphasize the Federal Theatre's regional character, regional play bureaus were also created in Los Angeles and Chicago. Patterned after Birmingham's Southern Bureau, they would collect, prepare, and recommend for production manuscripts and published plays dealing with regional themes or written by regional authors. See Susan Glaspell, George Kondolf, and John McGee to Flanagan, November 6, 1936, RG 69, FTP Records, NOC-Reg. IV.

direction, but the first real test of theatrical progress was the nationwide production of *It Can't Happen Here*. With the thesis that Fascism could happen even in America, and with characters modeled on Father Charles Coughlin and Huey Long, this play could not have been more timely. Such a production, opening on the Federal Theatre's first anniversary in twenty theatres in seventeen states, would demonstrate conclusively, Mrs. Flanagan believed, that the Project's administrative problems had been solved and that a theatre—national and thoroughly American—was emerging.[13]

But in true Federal Theatre style, *It Can't Happen Here* did not reach the public without considerable difficulty. To begin with, the play had not even been put into script form, much less translated into Spanish and Yiddish as had been planned. Since Sinclair Lewis was not on speaking terms with John Moffitt, who was to help adapt the novel to the stage, Mrs. Flanagan had to serve as go-between. During what she would later recall as the "funniest, craziest, and most exciting days" of her life, Mrs. Flanagan spent frantic hours in New York City's Essex House, running back and forth between the two men with numerous messages, generous supplies of ice water, black coffee, and Fannie Farmer candy.[14] Meanwhile her desk became yellow with telegrams from local directors, who passionately insisted that they could never meet the opening night deadline if any more revisions were made in the script. When New York directors complained that simultaneous openings were impossible, and promised to do the play only after successful "tryouts" in smaller towns, Hallie Flanagan's temper boiled. Furious at their provincialism and inability to grasp the national character of the Federal Theatre, she was quoted by *Variety* as grimly replying that the show would open on time in every single theatre, "even if the actors have to walk around the stage reading their parts

---

[13] Lewis reportedly claimed that W. H. Hays, "Czar" of the motion picture industry, refused to let MGM touch the story. The *New York Times*, August 22, 1936, p. 1.

[14] Flanagan to Sinclair Lewis, May 17, 1937, RG 69, FTP Records, NOC.

off a script in their hands and wearing signs identifying themselves."[15] She did agree, however, that it was best to cancel the production in New Orleans, where local WPA officials argued that the spirit of Huey Long was still marching on.[16]

Compounding these difficulties were a spate of contradictory news stories and editorials: the play was election propaganda for Roosevelt, it was anti-Roosevelt, it was pro-New Deal; the Federal Theatre was pro-Communist, it was subconsciously Fascist. All in all, some 78,000 lines of confusing print were lavished on *It Can't Happen Here* prior to opening night. Although this free publicity prompted New Yorkers alone to buy enough tickets to keep the play solidly booked for three months before it was even ready to open, Washington officials regarded it less favorably. Reportedly fearing that criticism from conservatives might stop the play entirely, they ordered local directors to "soft-pedal" publicity,[17] despite the fact that promotion men on all projects had already received strict orders to:

> . . . avoid all controversial issues—political angles of any degree—special appeals—racial or group appeals—or inferences in any of those directions, since Federal Theatre is interested only in presenting good theatre, neither adapting nor assuming any viewpoint beyond presenting a new and vital drama of our times, emerging from the social and economic forces of the day. . . .
>
> Also forbidden in most positive terms are any references to any foreign power, any policy of a foreign power, the personalities of any foreign power . . . ; any comparison between the United States and any specific foreign power, system, personality, etc. Our business is with a play of our time and country . . . and our job is wholly a job of theatre.[18]

[15] Flanagan, *Arena*, p. 119; *Variety*, October 28, 1936, p. 55.

[16] Flanagan to J. H. Crutcher, October 15, 1936, RG 69, FTP Records, NOC-Reg. III.

[17] The *New York Times*, September 29, 1936, p. 25.

[18] Quoted in Flanagan, *Arena*, p. 121. Information in this and the preceding paragraph, unless otherwise indicated, is based on *Arena*,

Finally, on the night of October 27, Hallie Flanagan watched the curtain go up at the Adelphi Theatre in New York on a stage which she, herself, had worked frantically to repaint and re-arrange and redress only the day before. That same night curtains went up from coast to coast. Commenting on the New York production, Brooks Atkinson admitted that although the play was not distinguished by Broadway standards, "thousands of Americans who do not know what Fascist dictatorship would mean now have an opportunity to find out, thanks to Mr. Lewis' energetic public spirit and the Federal Theatre's wide facilities."[19] In the days that followed, reviews poured into Hallie Flanagan's office from critics across the United States. The best analysis of the experiment, she believed, was that offered by Burns Mantle in a syndicated column in the *Chicago Tribune*.[20] The production, wrote Mantle:

> indicated rather revealingly . . . what could happen here if the social body should ever become theatre minded in a serious way. . . .
>
> Denver, though the audience was small, liked it. Boston was quite excited by it, 1,000 being present and 300 turned away. Cleveland's capacity audience shuddered a bit, but re-covered and gave the actors nine curtain calls. Tacoma ac-cepted the production as an "important and significant event." Omaha reports a capacity crowd and a lot of excitement. Seattle, with 1,500 present, gave the play a "tremendous ovation." Miami liked the play in English, and Tampa was strong for a Spanish translation. Birmingham approved, New-

pp. 115-129. Much of the controversy in the press was simply part of the preelection furor. Sympathetic reporters on the Hearst-owned *Los Angeles Examiner* told Federal Theatre officials that the paper had orders to launch an offensive against the Project and its National Di-rector during October. See Memorandum, Chandler Bullard to J. Howard Miller, October 12, 1936; Miller to William P. Farnsworth, October 15, 1936, RG 69, FTP Records, NOC.

[19] The *New York Times*, November 8, 1936, Sec. 10, p. 1.
[20] Flanagan, *Arena*, p. 126.

ark cheered, Bridgeport was a little stunned, San Francisco divided. Los Angeles found it pretty bald as drama and not very interesting as propaganda. Detroit thought it dignified and worthwhile and Chicago, we hear, took it in its critical stride, but reported audience reaction as being definitely and noisily in the play's favor.[21]

Indeed, audience reaction continued to be favorable for months to come. In New York City alone, the Yiddish version played eighty-six performances to 25,160 people; the Adelphi version, ninety-five performances to 110,518; and the borough-touring Suitcase Theatre version, one hundred and thirty-three performances to 179,209 people. In addition, the Boston company toured Pittsfield, Holyoke, North Hempstead, Worcester, Fitchburg, Brockton, Springfield, and Lowell. The Newark company traveled to nearby Bayonne, Princeton, Montclair, and Camden. The Detroit company played at Ann Arbor, Flint, Lansing, Saginaw, Kalamazoo, and Grand Rapids. Meanwhile similar tours were launched from Los Angeles, Miami, and Tacoma. After a four months run, *It Can't Happen Here* could boast an audience of 275,000 people and an admissions intake of $80,000, despite the fact that the average price theatre ticket was only thirty cents. By the time the last curtain was brought down, performances had reached the grand total of two hundred and sixty weeks, or the equivalent of five years.[22]

The production underlined not only the national character of the Project but also the nature of its growing audience. Like the sun-bronzed men in the Birmingham audience, suspected by a local critic of being construction workers, many of those who saw *It Can't Happen Here* were attending a legitimate theatre for the first time.[23] People such as they, Hallie Flanagan be-

[21] Burns Mantle, "Lewis Drama in Eighteen U. S. Theatres," *Chicago Sunday Tribune*, November 8, 1936, Sec. 7, p. 13.

[22] Flanagan, *Arena*, pp. 127-129; "Unemployed Arts," *Fortune*, xv (May 1937), 110.

[23] *Variety*, November 4, 1936, pp. 53-54. Commenting on reports received from various cities throughout the nation about this "new kind"

lieved, were the audience upon which the Federal Theatre must depend for its future. She also realized that this audience would have to be studied carefully before the Federal Theatre could appeal to its members, either as individuals or as participants in civic, educational, church, and labor groups. Initial steps in this direction had already been taken by officials in the Children's Theatre in New York, who worked with an Advisory Committee of educators to study the children's response to past productions and to select new scripts.[24] Not until the establishment of an Audience Research Department in October, however, did Federal Theatre officials make a serious attempt to learn something about the men and women filling their theatres. Audiences in New York and surrounding towns were then surveyed to determine the occupation of their members, the frequency with which they attended both the commercial and the Federal Theatre, the kinds of plays they preferred, and their reaction to the evening's performance. Thus, while designed to help in choosing more appropriate future plays, these surveys could also contribute to the improved productions which Hallie Flanagan was convinced were necessary to bind the Federal Theatre to its new audience.[25]

· II ·

To measures that would fuse this union, Federal Theatre officials had devoted their energy for four months. They had reorganized projects, worked out new programs, and engineered simultaneous openings of a theatrical tour de force that would

---

of audience, *Variety* stated that even in New York City critics were impressed by the number of people in the audience who apparently had never before been inside a legitimate house.

[24] Memorandum, Flanagan to Ellen Woodward, December 11, 1936, RG 69, FTP Records, NOGSF.

[25] Memorandum, Francis Bosworth to Regional and State Directors, March 15, 1937, RG 69, FTP Records, National Service Bureau-Audience Survey Reports (NSB-Aud. Survey Reports). Numerous Audience Survey Reports and Analyses are also contained in the National Office General Service Files (NOGSF).

herald the accomplishments of a second season.[26] Ready at last to produce the plays they had planned, these same directors found their efforts suddenly diverted to such unartistic matters as relief and bureaucracy. In the midst of the Presidential campaign, orders had come from Washington calling for dismissals. The special allowance of 25 per cent non-relief personnel, which Hopkins had given to all the Arts Projects to help them get started, was to be reduced to the usual 10 per cent effective in other WPA projects.[27] As soon as the Project grapevine picked up the news, workers in New York City began to make frantic protests. Finally Washington officials relented and promised not to cut anyone found in need by the Emergency Relief Bureau. Since the Board qualified all but 10 per cent as eligible for relief, WPA officials resolved their dilemma by simply dropping the entire matter until after the election.[28]

The period of grace was only temporary. The morning after Roosevelt's smashing electoral victory over Kansas Governor Alf Landon, directors of the Arts Projects were assembled in Hopkins' office to discuss impending cuts forced by the drought of the previous summer. Aid supplied by the WPA to drought victims had considerably depleted the relief agency's funds, Hopkins explained. He was forced, therefore, to reduce the number of WPA employees immediately, however inauspicious such a decision might seem in the wake of the election. Arts Project directors protested that over eight thousand workers would lose their jobs just as they were beginning to produce results that

[26] Mrs. Flanagan's insistence that the Federal Theatre justify itself in artistic as well as humanitarian terms is repeated without let up in letters, speeches, and articles throughout the autumn of 1936. See, for example, Flanagan to John McGee, August 3, 1936, RG 69, FTP Records, NOC-Reg. II; Flanagan, "Federal Theatre Tomorrow," *Federal Theatre* II, No. 1 (1936), 56ff.; "Highlights of the First Production Conference of the New York City Unit of the Federal Theatre, Called by Hallie Flanagan, National Director, and Philip W. Barber, New York Director" (New York: Play Bureau of the Federal Theatre Project, 1936).

[27] The *New York Times*, September 12, 1936, p. 15.

[28] *Ibid.*, September 17, 1936, p. 26; Flanagan, *Arena*, pp. 188-189.

Hopkins himself had termed phenomenal; but protests were futile. Orders went out in late November to reduce all personnel by 20 per cent, dismissing first all "unessential" non-relief cases and, second, those on relief who were least useful.[29]

Production activities ground to a halt, as workers began a series of demonstrations that rocked the Arts Projects throughout November, December, and January. The pleas and protests that filled numerous wastebaskets in WPA offices in New York and Washington were but the quieter manifestations of dissatisfaction. When eleven members of the ever-embattled Dance Project were arrested for disturbing the peace while picketing, labor unions announced a boycott of Federal Theatre shows until workers dismissed for striking were reinstated. Although Equity managed to prevent its members from taking part, three thousand workers demonstrated in front of local WPA headquarters. Mayor Fiorello La Guardia and WPA administrator Brehon Somervell, their offices besieged by delegations, finally decided to fly to Washington to discuss cuts. Apparently the talks brought about a change in policy, for a week later Colonel Somervell announced that the fixed quota of 20 per cent would be abandoned, and that "future layoffs would consist of non-relief workers and workers not in need of current assistance." Thus many of those receiving the pink dismissal slips had only to apply to the Emergency Relief Bureau for certification of need in order to be reinstated. Conflict over these "future layoffs," over reinstatement, and over professional experience continued, however. In mid-January the Colonel disgustedly announced that, in spite of all the sound and fury, dismissals had not taken

[29] Sherwood, *Roosevelt and Hopkins*, pp. 80 *passim* 87; Flanagan, Arena, pp. 181-182; the *New York Times*, November 26, 1936, p. 29. As Hopkins had foreseen, critics charged that men had been put on WPA rolls prior to the election and dismissed thereafter solely for political reasons. Although Hopkins was not averse to having the WPA help the Democratic Party, Charles points out that, when farmers placed on WPA projects from July through December are subtracted from the total number on WPA rolls, the regularly employed number of workers followed the usual seasonal increases. *Minister of Relief*, p. 167.

103

place on the Arts Projects, nor would they occur unless he were given complete control.[30]

For the local WPA administrator to have the Arts Projects completely under his jurisdiction was, for Hallie Flanagan at least, no solution at all. Under Somervell and his predecessors, Hugh Johnson and Victor Ridder, all of whom had been responsible for administrative matters, the New York Project had undergone five major reorganizations, each of which she believed made its operation as a theatre more difficult.[31] Reluctant to elaborate on these difficulties with the local administration, she was, nonetheless, familiar with the long background of misunderstanding, strife, and struggle for control which had existed from the Project's beginnings. Although the intricacies of this bureaucratic power struggle are obscure, it had, by late February, reached such proportions that Hopkins decided to intervene. In order to end what *Variety* called the "contest between the army and the artists," he removed administration of the New York Project from Somervell's jurisdiction and turned it over completely to the National Director with the assurance that no more cuts would be made for at least six months.[32]

[30] The *New York Times*, November 28, 1936, p. 29; December 1, 1936, p. 6; December 2, 1936, p. 16; December 3, 1936, p. 4; December 4, 1936, p. 24; December 10, 1936, p. 5; December 12, 1936, p. 10; December 15, 1936, p. 13; *Variety*, December 16, 1936, p. 61; December 30, 1936, p. 48; January 20, 1937, p. 57; January 27, 1937, p. 52; Flanagan, *Arena*, p. 189.

[31] Flanagan, *Arena*, p. 188. That problems developed between Federal Theatre officials and the New York administrators is hardly surprising. Fully aware of how difficult and politically unaware the former could be, Florence Kerr, who took over as director of Women's and Professional Projects in 1939, notes that Johnson was on "the rebound" following the NRA's dismantling, was "going to pieces personally" and "drank heavily" during his tenure as New York WPA administrator. Somervell, she considered "bright" but "a martinet of the first order." See Florence Kerr, tape recording, October 18, 1963, Archives of American Art.

[32] *Variety*, March 3, 1937, p. 54. Further indication of the ill will existing between Somervell and Federal Theatre officials is contained in a subsequent letter from Ellen Woodward to Hallie Flanagan. Somervell had refused to furnish WPA porters to clean up borough parks after

The decision had been made in favor of artists, but a winter filled with demonstrations and disturbances had done little to encourage art. The New York Project, which was to have led in the struggle for professional excellence during this crucial second season, emerged from four months of conflict with the morale of its workers shattered, and the attention of its directors long since deflected from theatre to the dismissal of relief workers and the jurisdiction of relief administrators. Until the Project could be consolidated under a harmonious and efficient administration and the morale of its members restored, theatre would continue to suffer. Hallie Flanagan was determined that it should suffer no longer than was absolutely necessary. Responsible now for the administrative as well as the technical functions of a Project which embraced nearly half of the people in the entire Federal Theatre, she and her deputy director, William Farnsworth, went immediately to New York.

Overhauling so huge and unwieldy a theatrical enterprise was no simple matter, but Farnsworth did his best. Keen, relaxed, humorous, and enormously capable, he proceeded to take charge of administrative matters with his usual disregard for bureaucratic absurdities and the morass of plots, counterplots, personal antagonisms, and jealousies exacerbated by recent disturbances. Days of intense effort were required to bring the twelve hitherto autonomous production units under Philip Barber's jurisdiction. The most difficult were those known as the "Big Four," a designation conferred by the other eight producers on Broadway-oriented Edward Goodman, poetic Virgil Geddes, nervously militant Morris Watson, and imaginative John Houseman. Reluctant to relinquish complete control of their respective proj-

the New York Project's caravan theatres had made their rounds. The matter became so serious that the Park Commission threatened to forbid further performances. When Mrs. Woodward went to Hopkins about the matter, the latter would only suggest that Mrs. Flanagan use theatre people to do the cleaning up "for the present," since technically Somervell did not have to have anything to do with the Arts Projects. See Woodward to Flanagan, July 2, 1937, RG 69, FTP Records, NOGSF.

ects—the popular price, experimental, living newspaper, and 891 (the classical unit)—they complained that they must each continue to have their own designers, press representatives, and lighting and costume people if they were to continue producing such hits as *Macbeth, Murder in the Cathedral, Triple-A Plowed Under, Chalk Dust, Class of '29,* and *Battle Hymn.*

Mrs. Flanagan, in turn, explained that there were simply not enough talented designers and technicians to service the entire Project, unless these people were placed in one central workshop and lent out as they were needed. Undeterred by protests, she proceeded with plans to consolidate all production services under Walter Hart, Barber's assistant. To Hart she also assigned responsibility for a new casting and retraining bureau under Madalyn O'Shea, whose course in the fundamentals of acting at the old Provincetown Playhouse was the pride of the National Director and the despair of workers who thought they had found a soft relief job. The technical division, including shops and warehouses, were put under separate supervision, as was information, promotion, house management, and booking.[33]

Encouraged by such progress, Hallie Flanagan dashed off a "thank-you" to Hopkins, assuring him that the reorganization was coming along splendidly. The Project's morale was soaring; the decision to separate the Theatre Project from the city WPA had indeed been the right one.[34] By the end of March the once scattered New York Project was consolidated into one large workshop in the Chanin Building at Forty-Second Street and Lexington Avenue. With Project officials, directors, actors, and research workers under the same roof and her watchful eye, Hallie Flanagan was determined to see the operation run

[33] The problems and progress of reorganization are contained in Mrs. Flanagan's frequent reports to Ellen Woodward. See Memorandum, Flanagan to Woodward, March 3, 1937, RG 69, GSS-211.2; Memorandum, Flanagan to Woodward, March 4, 1937, RG 69, FTP Records, NOGSF; Flanagan to Woodward and David Niles, March 27, 1937, RG 69, FTP Records, NOC; Flanagan, *Arena,* pp. 190-199.

[34] Memorandum, Flanagan to Hopkins, March 11, 1937, Flanagan Papers.

smoothly as an integrated whole and, above all, settled down to the business of theatre in the months remaining. By stationing her trusted executive secretary, Mary McFarland, in her hotel room to relay instructions to appropriate local and national officials, Mrs. Flanagan reserved the hours from lunch to midnight for planning and production.[35] It was an impossible schedule, but she had little choice. Time and time again the production schedule of the New York Project had been jeopardized by the disorders accompanying threats of dismissal and by the upheaval of reorganization. Such interruptions were unavoidable, but for this theatre, as for any other, "the play" was still "the thing."

· III ·

Actually, for the Federal Theatre the play was many things—the index of the Federal Theatre's ability to supplement the commercial stage through intelligent pioneering; the cord that would bind together actors and audience; and, in this second season, a further test of the relationship between government and the arts. But the handful of "socially conscious" plays that would put to test that relationship were not immediately forthcoming. Those productions which had somehow managed to open during the chaos of past months were praised or damned for different reasons. Although Virgil Geddes' *Native Ground* failed to captivate the reviewers, audience and critics alike responded enthusiastically to *The Sun and I*; Douglas Gilbert called it a "fine production," a "surprise and delight."[36] A well-written, elaborately mounted satire of the Biblical story of Joseph, the play combined potshots at dictators with the "splendors" of ancient Egypt. Indeed, *The Sun and I* had everything—a trifle too much to suit the discriminating Hallie Flanagan. So, too, did *Bassa Moona*, a production of the African troupe that

[35] Explaining how she was managing her schedule, Mrs. Flanagan wrote: "I dictate in the car going to my appointments, in bed, and while I am eating breakfast." Memorandum, Flanagan to Woodward, March 3, 1937, RG 69, GSS-211.2.

[36] Douglas Gilbert, "*The Sun and I*—Racy Satire on Biblical Story of Joseph," *New York World Telegram*, February 27, 1937, p. 6.

brought the Nigerian jungle to Harlem and thence to Broadway in a riot of sound and color.[37]

No less spectacular was an adaptation of a nineteenth century French farce, *Un chapeau de paille d'Italie* (or *Horse Eats Hat*), a riotous, ridiculous, and risqué account of the escapades of a young gallant, who had to find a hat similar to one eaten by a horse in order to restore proof of a young lady's honor. Produced by John Houseman, translated, directed, and acted by Orson Welles, this bit of theatrical lunacy unfolded at a furious pace against a background of Nat Karson's "lavishly eccentric decor" and Virgil Thompson's skillfully orchestrated music. Greeted with roars of laughter from an audience that included playwright-producer Marc Connelly and author John Dos Passos, it was, according to *Cue*, "perilously close to being a work of genuine theatre art"—a "feast for the True Classicist," said the *World Telegram*. But what was food for some was New Deal poison for others. The Federal Theatre's perennial castigator, Harrison Grey Fiske of *The Saturday Evening Post*, greeted the production with horrified stares. From Hearst's *Journal American* came a tirade about spending the nation's money on "an outmoded farce . . . garnished with sewage" and expressions of sympathy for the "young men and women . . . compelled by distress of circumstances . . . to participate in the offensive play." For a cast that included Orson Welles, Joseph Cotten, and Arlene Francis it was misplaced sympathy indeed.[38]

Undaunted by the slings and arrows of outraged moralists, Welles and Houseman turned next to Marlowe's play, *The Tragical History of Dr. Faustus*. Welles would undertake his first major acting role, as Faustus; Jack Carter, the Negro actor, would play Mephisto; and Abe Feder would do the lighting.

[37] Flanagan, *Arena*, p. 186.

[38] *Ibid.*, pp. 77-78; Interview with Marc Connelly, November 10, 1961; *New York World Telegram*, September 28, 1936, p. 12; *New York American*, October 6, 1936, RG 69, FTP Records, FTP-PC. For Fiske's earlier criticisms of the Project see Harrison Grey Fiske, "The Federal Theatre Doom-Boggle," *The Saturday Evening Post*, CCIX (August 1, 1936), 23ff.

Giving this sixteenth-century classic no more than a two-week run, New York officials decided to use it as a filler.[39] Although members of the City Projects Council—the white-collar affiliate of Workers' Alliance—cancelled their seats, decrying the lack of any "social slant,"[40] most New Yorkers were bothered by no such scruples. The crowds—fascinated by a stage of eerie blackness broken only by quick stabs of light, and black curtains opening in strange forms—watched spellbound night after night, as Faustus signed his pact with the somber Mephisto, pled with the masked Helen of Troy to make him "immortal with a kiss," and finally, begged in vain for his release. The critics, although divided on Welles' acting ability, regarded the production as an unqualified triumph—"creative and imminently successful."[41] Harry Hopkins was equally enthusiastic. Rushing backstage to congratulate the cast, he inquired of Houseman and Welles whether they were "having a good time on this job."[42] It was a question all three could answer with an unqualified "Yes."

Although Hopkins enjoyed *Faustus*, his favorite was a new Living Newspaper, *Power*. At one point it had seemed that the play might never reach the stage—not because of its faults, but because of those of its predecessor, *Injunction Granted*. The latter, written by the living newspaper staff under the supervision of Arthur Arent, and staged by Joseph Losey, was supposedly an objective account of labor's treatment in the courts, but had been turned by Young Turks on the Project into a

[39] Report of the Play Policy Board Conference, New York City, January 22-24, 1937, RG 69, FTP Records, NOGSF.

[40] To this news, Mrs. Flanagan, who "liked the production inordinately," sarcastically remarked, "I suppose they wanted Lenin's blood streaming from the firmament." Flanagan to Philip Davis, January 15, 1937, Flanagan Papers.

[41] See, for example, Edith J. R. Isaacs, "*Doctor Faustus*—Broadway in Review," *Theatre Arts Monthly*, XXI (March 1937), 184-185. *Newsweek* which was equally enthusiastic about the production and far more complimentary about Welles, suggested that the play be toured throughout the nation. See "Federal Project and the Devil Receive Their Due," *Newsweek*, IX (January 23, 1937), 30-31.

[42] Flanagan to Ellen Woodward, January 12, 1937, RG 69, GSS-211.2.

militantly pro-labor account of the working man's fight for liberation through unionization.[43] A run-through of the play was enough to convince Barber and Farnsworth that *Injunction Granted* should not be allowed to open, despite several highly theatrical scenes and the superb acting of a newcomer to the Project, Norman Lloyd.[44]

Hallie Flanagan disagreed. Confident that Losey and Living Newspaper supervisor Morris Watson would "clean up the script and make it more objective," she permitted rehearsals to continue.[45] Barber subsequently reminded the two of the National Director's many criticisms and suggestions, but to no avail.[46] Shocked by the opening night performance, she sat down at two thirty A.M. in Poughkeepsie and wrote to Watson and Losey:

In spite of my keen interest in *Injunction Granted*, I must make several points about it.

1) The production seems to me special pleading, biased, an editorial, not a news issue. (Witness the one-sided treat-

[43] Interview with Arthur Arent, November 11, 1961. Losey, blacklisted in Hollywood during the 1950's, is now one of the leading directors in the British film industry. One of his more recent films, *The Servant*, was a much discussed entry in the 1963 New York Film Festival. Returning to the U. S. in March 1964 for a visit, he discussed his career with Eugene Archer of the *New York Times*. According to Archer's account, the Wisconsin-born Losey attended both Dartmouth and Harvard, came to New York City in 1930 where he worked with Charles Laughton and the Theatre Guild, visited the U.S.S.R. to study the theatre in 1933 before joining the Federal Theatre. Of his work with the Living Newspaper, Losey told Archer, "like most intellectuals I was engaged in the thirties. After the war, I became less so." For a fuller account of Losey's career as director, see Eugene Archer, "Expatriate Retraces His Steps," the *New York Times*, March 15, 1964, Sec. 2, p. 9.

[44] Flanagan to Watson and Losey, August 20, 1936, RG 69, FTP Records, NOGSF.

[45] *Ibid.*

[46] *Ibid.* Hallie Flanagan had previously insisted that all portions of the script must be verified, a reminder which Barber passed on to Watson as early as June 30. See Memorandum, Barber to Watson, June 30, 1936, RG 69, FTP Records, Correspondence of Philip Barber, Director of the New York City Project (Barber Correspondence).

ment of the C.I.O. rally; the voice reading Hoover; the scene showing judges asleep, etc., etc.) Whatever my personal sympathies are I cannot, as custodian of federal funds, have such funds used as a party tool. That goes for the communist party as well as for the democratic party. To show the history of labor in the courts is appropriate; to load that document at every turn with insinuation is not appropriate.

2) The production, in my opinion, lacks a proper climax, falling back on the old cliché of calling labor to unite in the approved agit-prop manner. If the struggle now going on within the ranks of labor itself were made clear; if the three decisions best understood by the public—AAA, NRA, and the Coal Act were clearly shows [sic], the end could possibly show the Republicans pledging to turn labor questions back to the States; the Democrats to the Federal Government. Perhaps the standard of each political party on labor could be given. There would then be a question mark end, the only true end.

3) I do not see what the scene in the New Jersey legislature has to do with labor legislature [sic].

4) . . . [The] production uses too many devices, too much hysteria of acting. . . .

5) The production is historical drama and hence, by reason of compression, is open to the charge of superficiality. I think we should consider whether history should not rather be used, as it is in *Triple-A*, to illuminate the present, not lead up to it in the chronological manner.[47]

Watson, a veteran labor leader as well as a newspaper man, replied that the play was drawing crowds, and made no changes. In the barrage of publicity which followed, drama critics de-

[47] Flanagan to Watson and Losey, July 24, 1936, RG 69, FTP Records, NOGSF. Four days later Mrs. Flanagan recorded in her journal the following statement: "Had a fierce fight with Watson and Joe Losey and told them that as far as I was concerned they were both through." See Hallie Flanagan, Personal Notes on FTP, July 28, 1936, Flanagan Papers.

nounced the production and Communists complained that it offered unionization rather than revolution as a solution.[48] Although WPA officials were apparently undisturbed by the furor, Federal Theatre directors were not. On August 20 Hallie Flanagan issued an ultimatum. She reminded Watson and Losey that she had consented to let rehearsals continue only because she believed that they would make the necessary changes; but the changes had not been made. Recalling her earlier letter, she added:

> The point now is that Bill Farnsworth, as well as Phil Barber, together with many of our advisers and friends in New York are unanimously against any continuation of the Living Newspaper.
>
> The fact that *Injunction Granted* is drawing crowds does not help. Everyone knows that those crowds are being sent by their Unions. And let me say that I am informed that . . .[49] is being hawked in the lobby. *Will you please give orders that this be stopped at once?*
>
> Morris, I want you and Joe to be clear about this. As I have repeatedly said, I will not have the Federal Theatre Project used politically. I will not have it used to further the ends of the Democratic Party, the Republican Party or the Communist Party. I took your word and Joe Losey's word that it would not be so used and I think you both let me down. As you very well know the avalanche of unfavorable publicity on it is all ammunition against the project, to say nothing of being added ammunition against me personally.[50]

[48] "The Theatre," *New Masses*, August 4, 1936, p. 29. In *The Commonweal*, Granville Vernon wrote of the play: *Injunction Granted* is "inexcusable artistically, socially, morally; an exhibit of badly written badly produced, badly thought out special pleading. As propaganda it has no place in a taxpayer's theatre, and as art it has no place in the theatre at all." See "*Injunction Granted*: Latest Edition of the Living Newspaper is Out and Out Propaganda of the Left," *The Commonweal*, XXIV (August 21, 1936), 407.

[49] The title of the pamphlet (?) referred to is illegibly written.

[50] Flanagan to Watson and Losey, August 20, 1936, RG 69, FTP Rec-

The objectionable scenes were somewhat toned down and the play closed in September.[51]

Its successor, *Power*, was about the relation of consumers and the electrical industries. It was hardly the uncontroversial subject which Hallie Flanagan had requested for the next Living Newspaper, but Watson assured her that the play had been prepared with "scrupulous care so as to present merely a truthful version . . . without holding any class, interest, or individual up to ridicule."[52] He also agreed to send Hopkins a fully annotated copy of the script.[53] By the time Arent and several of his fellow workers had readied some thirty-three scenes, spotlights, movies, stereoptican slides, eighty-eight actors, and assorted microphones, sixty thousand New Yorkers, wise in the ways of the Living Newspaper, had already purchased tickets.[54] When the curtain went up on February 23, a packed house heard a torchlight procession of workers waving flags and singing:

> My name is William Edwards.
> I live down Cove Creek way;

---

ords, NOGSF. Apparently the pamphlets referred to were merely moved outside. In a letter to Steve Early, Ed Roddan, a member of the Democratic National Campaign Committee from New York, enclosed pamphlets which he said he bought outside the theatre. According to Roddan, the pamphlets were spread out on the sidewalk. During intermission "a chap shouts his wares for the crowd out for air, although he does not enter the theatre." The pamphlets "are all on Communism." See Roddan to Early, September 10, 1936, Roosevelt MSS, Official File 80.

[51] Although she subsequently defended the play to Mrs. Woodward, insisting that it was not Communist, Hallie Flanagan had to admit that it continued to be "too biased" in favor of labor. See Flanagan to Woodward, September 11, 1936, Roosevelt MSS, Official File 80. For a published version of the play, see that put out by the Play Bureau (Federal Theatre Playscript No. 9).

[52] Flanagan to Watson and Losey, August 20, 1936, RG 69, FTP Records, NOGSF; Memorandum, Watson to Flanagan and Barber, November 13, 1936, RG 69, FTP Records, Barber Correspondence.

[53] Watson to Hopkins, March 12, 1937, RG 69, GSS-211.2.

[54] Brooks Atkinson, "*Power* Produced by the Living Newspaper Under Federal Theatre Auspices," the *New York Times*, February 24, 1937, p. 18.

I'm working on a project
They call the T.V.A. . . .[55]

It was exuberant theatre—melodramatic and exciting. It was also propaganda. "After burrowing into history, court records, and newspaper files," wrote Brooks Atkinson, the "aggressive and versatile lads" of the Living Newspaper staff have "come out impartially against the electric light and power industry, and for the TVA, practically defying the Supreme Court in the last scene to sustain the injunction against TVA's construction of new power lines for new customers." Despite a long list of accredited sources, it was "the most indignant and militant proletarian drama of the season . . . staged with government funds."[56] *Life* called it "WPA public ownership propaganda . . . exciting and unique"; *The Nation*, a "unique piece of art." Its theme, said the editors, is "the search of Everyman (the consumer) for cheap electric power with which to make a better life. . . . Each fact is accurate; and the author of the play, Arthur Arent, proves what journalists have always maintained—that an accurate fact carefully aimed may be as deadly as a bullet."[57]

Both Harry Hopkins and Ellen Woodward were delighted. They agreed that the production should be brought to Washington along with *Faustus*, and then toured throughout the country.[58] Speaking to the cast after the opening night production, the Relief Administrator said:

I want to tell you this is a great show. It's fast and funny, it makes you laugh and it makes you cry and it makes you think—I don't know what more anyone can ask of a show.

[55] Arthur Arent, *Power* in *Federal Theatre Plays: Triple-A Plowed Under, Power, Spirochete*, pp. 68-69.

[56] Atkinson, "*Power* Produced by the Living Newspaper Under Federal Auspices," the *New York Times*, February 24, 1937, p. 18.

[57] "Power is WPA Ownership Propaganda," *Life*, II (March 22, 1937), 22; "Newspaper into Theatre," *The Nation*, CXXXXIV (March 6, 1937), 256.

[58] Woodward to Flanagan, March 18, 1937, RG 69, FTP Records, NOC.

114

I want this play and plays like it done from one end of the country to the other. . . . People will say it's propaganda. Well, I say what of it? It's propaganda to educate the consumer who's paying for power. It's about time someone had some propaganda for him. The big power companies have spent millions on propaganda for the utilities. It's about time the consumer had a mouthpiece. I say more plays like *Power* and more power to you.[59]

Although he admitted to Hallie Flanagan that he had stuck his neck out, neither was apparently very concerned, since they went to supper with Langdon Post, the Housing Commissioner, and immediately began planning a new Living Newspaper on the housing problem.[60]

Although *Power* continued to play well into the summer, so upset was the New York production schedule by the winter's reorganizational disorders that not until May was it joined by a number of new productions. Among the more outstanding was *Professor Mamlock*, a portrayal of the plight of an eminent Jewish surgeon in Germany, which brought forth respectable reviews from critics who considered it the best of the anti-Nazi dramas to reach the United States. *How Long Brethren*, Tamaris' impressive dramatization in dance of Negro songs of protest, won the acclaim of critics and an award for the best group choreography of the season. And *Unto Such Glory* and *Hymn to the Rising Sun*, two Negro plays by Paul Green, stirred Brooks Atkinson to the most "clamorous" review he could write.[61]

[59] Hopkins' speech is quoted in Flanagan, *Arena*, p. 185 and in part by Atkinson in the *New York Times*, February 24, 1937, p. 18.

[60] Flanagan, *Arena*, p. 185.

[61] Richard Watts, Jr., "Brown Terror," *New York Herald Tribune*, April 14, 1937, p. 14; Burns Mantle, "Federals Stage *Professor Mamlock*," *New York Daily News*, April 14, 1937, p. 53; Jerome D. Bohm, "Dance Dramas Are Presented Under WPA," *New York Herald Tribune*, May 7, 1937, p. 23; John Martin, "Dances Are Given by WPA Theatre," the *New York Times*, May 7, 1937, p. 29; Brooks Atkinson, "Paul Green's *Unto Such Glory* and *Hymn to the Rising Sun* Put on by the Federal Theatre," the *New York Times*, May 7, 1937, p. 28; also Flanagan, *Arena*, pp. 198-200.

Pride in these new achievements was somewhat dampened, however, when New York critics attended the Children's Theatre presentation, *The Revolt of the Beavers*. The play, a socially significant fairy tale by Oscar Saul and Lou Lantz, was about the adventures of two children in Beaverland—a country ruled by a cruel beaver chief who owned a "busy wheel" on which bark was turned into food, clothing, and shelter. When Boss Chief not only refused the working beavers their share of the bark, but threatened to replace them with the jobless, barkless beavers, Oakleaf came to the rescue. Returning from exile—he had tried previously to organize a club for "sad beavers to get glad"—Oakleaf disguised himself as a polar bear, organized both the working beavers and the barkless beavers, and led them in revolt. The cruel beaver chief and his henchmen were sent into exile, and the beavers worked, shared, and lived happily ever after.[62]

"Marxism à la Mother Goose," charged the distressed Brooks Atkinson.[63] Robert Coleman agreed, although a conversation with a five-year-old playgoer led the *Mirror*'s critic to suspect that the audience was far more interested in the beavers' games of hopscotch and skating than in revolution.[64] His suspicions were verified by a report from the New York University psychologist in charge of audience research. The youngsters interviewed, she explained, saw none of the play's social or political implications—only a fairy tale about good and bad beavers.[65]

But the damage had been done. Shortly after the play opened, copies of the *Times* review appeared on the desk of every congressman in Washington. Citing Atkinson's comments, Deputy

[62] Oscar Saul and Lou Lantz, *The Revolt of the Beavers* (1936). Typewritten copy in the Theatre Collection, New York Public Library.

[63] Brooks Atkinson, "*The Revolt of the Beavers*, or Mother Goose Marx, Under WPA Auspices," the *New York Times*, May 21, 1937, p. 19.

[64] Robert Coleman, "*Revolt of the Beavers*: Forest Fantasy," *New York Daily Mirror*, May 22, 1937, p. 22.

[65] Beryl Parker, Report of Audience Analysis Research Department, Children's Theatre, on *The Revolt of the Beavers*, RG 69, FTP Records, NSB-Aud. Survey Reports.

116

Macbeth, La Fayette Theatre

Eleanor Roosevelt, Harry Hopkins,
Fiorello LaGuardia

Hallie Flanagan and Harry Hopkins

Nativity Players in New York

Inventiveness of *Power*

Orson Welles as Dr. Faustus

St. Mary's Park, the Bronx

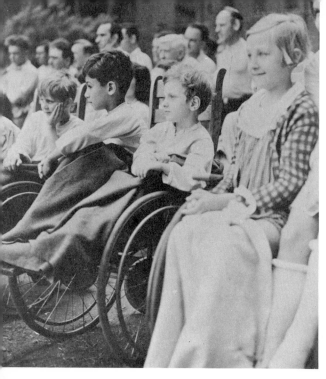

Audience at Bellevue Hospital

Pinocchio

One Third of a Nation

Androcles and the Lion

Power in New York

Joseph Cotton in *Horse Eats Hat*

Lobby of Adelphi Theatre

Revolt of the Beavers

Murder in the Cathedral

Harlem's *Swing Mikado*

Commissioner Brynes MacDonald announced that he was returning one thousand four hundred free tickets available to youthful members of the Police Athletic League. The play, he charged, was intended to educate New York boys and girls in the techniques of revolution.[66] The *Saturday Evening Post* editorialized that the Federal Theatre was teaching poor children to murder rich children.[67] Actually, the fears of the *Post*'s editors were no more warranted than the optimism of the *Daily Worker*'s reviewer, who was equally certain that five- and six-year-olds understood the play as a revolutionary allegory.[68] But the fact remained that the play was ill chosen and its production, ill timed.

Although Hallie Flanagan would subsequently cite audience research reports to those who feared the play's Marxist overtones, such implications had not been lost on her, when she had read the play the previous autumn. "It is for the Children's Theatre," she had hurriedly written to Philip Davis, "and very human and amusing and tragic and very class conscious."[69] What made her approval of the script particularly remarkable was her simultaneous decision to veto unequivocally the Living Newspaper script, *Money*, with the statement: "It is just an adolescent, anti-capitalist scream of hate, and I will not have such nonsense done on our stage."[70] Her failure to anticipate the reaction to *The Revolt of the Beavers* is even more surprising in light of her recent fight with the Living Newspaper staff over *Injunction Granted* and the still more recent furor over *It Can't Happen Here*. Perhaps she expected Marxian overtones to

[66] *Variety*, May 26, 1937, p. 55.

[67] "Once Upon a Time," *The Saturday Evening Post*, ccix (June 26, 1937), 22.

[68] Mary Morrow, "*Revolt of the Beavers* Makes Theatre History," *Daily Worker*, May 24, 1937, p. 9. Morgan Y. Himmelstein makes the same point in *Drama Was a Weapon: The Left-Wing Theatre in New York, 1929-1941* (New Brunswick: Rutgers University Press, 1963), p. 103.

[69] Flanagan to Philip Davis, November 8, 1936, Flanagan Papers.

[70] Flanagan, Personal Notes on FTP, November 8, 1937, Flanagan Papers.

go unnoticed. The play, she may have reasoned, was, after all, for the Children's Theatre, not the much praised, much damned, and very much publicized Living Newspaper. Whatever her reasons, the choice was a highly inappropriate one—particularly since the play opened at a time when the future of the entire WPA was once again up for debate. In short, *The Revolt of the Beavers* was a blot on the Federal Theatre's record, but in the context of two seasons of productions it seemed a rather small one.

Fortune, in its May issue, proudly summarized that record in its account of the cultural revolution being wrought by the Arts Projects throughout America:

> More spectacularly successful than either the Painters' Project or the Music Project or the Writers' Project is the Theatre Project. From any point of view save that of the old-line box-office critics to whom nothing is theatre unless it has Broadway stars and Broadway varnish, the Federal Theatre Project is a roaring success. Approximately sixteen million people had seen its productions down to midseason. . . . *It Can't Happen Here* . . . played to a total of 275,000 people in the first four months, and took in, over the same period, $80,000 at an average admission price of thirty cents. . . . *Macbeth* played for 144 performances, was seen by 120,000 people, grossed $40,000 and broke a nine-year attendance record. . . . *Murder in the Cathedral* ran to crowded houses for the full term permitted by the contract and was seen by a total of over 40,000 people. . . . The Children's Theatre in New York piled up a total attendance of over a quarter of a million in its first eight months, the New York Marionette Theatre reached 1,500,000 in its first two years. . . . *Doctor Faustus* has admirers as intelligent and as devoted as any collected by the various Shakespearean revivals of the last New York season. And the Living Newspaper, applying to the stage the technique developed in the air and on the screen by the March of Time, has created as much excitement among

118

playwrights as among Republicans who see its *Triple A Plowed Under* and its *Power* as government subsidized propaganda.[71]

It was indeed an impressive record—with one qualification: of the major plays mentioned by *Fortune*, those presented in the Federal Theatre's second season were no greater in number than those produced in the Project's first shaky months of operation, nor were they opened under any less duress. There was always the hope that the list might be expanded during the summer months, providing the Federal Theatre with the kind of artistic results that would help to insure institutional permanence; but in May 1937, the prospects were hardly encouraging.

· IV ·

In an atmosphere made hostile by the Supreme Court fight, Harry Hopkins had begun his testimony before congressional appropriation committees. Although the Arts Projects, remarkably enough, did not prove to be a subject for extensive discussion, the WPA came in for a real drubbing from administration critics.[72] Hopkins did his best to defend his program, but his best was not enough. Southern Democrats were tired of appropriating relief money over which they had little control, antagonized by Hopkins' espousal of a minimum wage, and anxious about political activities, including his possible candidacy for the nomination in 1940. Consequently, they joined Republicans in a second attempt to cut relief appropriations.[73] This time they succeeded. In what the *Baltimore Sun* described as a "childish" expression of hatred and resentment, the House even voted to cut the WPA chieftain's own salary from $12,000 to $10,000.[74]

[71] "Unemployed Arts," *Fortune*, xv (May 1937), 109-117ff.
[72] Hearings before the House Committee on Appropriations. *Emergency Relief Appropriation Act of 1937*, 75th Cong., 2nd Sess. (1937); Hearings before the Senate Appropriations Committee on H. J. Res. 361. *Emergency Relief Appropriation*, 75th Cong., 1st Sess. (1937).
[73] Sherwood, *Roosevelt and Hopkins*, p. 90.
[74] *Ibid.*

119

While the reduction in the appropriation was still being debated in Washington, rumors of impending cuts circulated wildly in New York. Although no orders had yet been given, the mere suggestion of cuts was enough to set off protests and demonstrations. After a performance of *Candide* and *How Long Brethren*, the audience joined the ever-embattled dancers in an all night sit-down strike in the theatre. Although Equity and other theatrical unions, believing that this was no time to risk antagonizing Washington, warned their members not to demonstrate, some were less cautious.[75] On May 27, various unions— among them the leftist Workers' Alliance, its white-collar affiliate, the City Projects Council, and the American Federation of Musicians—called a one-day work stoppage on all wpa Projects that left every Federal Theatre in New York City dark. "Whatever we think of their methods, we must inquire into the reasons for their protest," said Hallie Flanagan the following day in a speech before the convention of the American Theatre Council.[76] She had hoped the speech would prompt the convention to exert pressure in Washington on behalf of the entire Project.

It did not. The much reduced appropriation was passed. With one-fourth of the Theatre Project's funds gone, its ranks had to be reduced accordingly. Once again production activities had to be put aside, as theatre officials coped with non-theatrical demands. After three days of almost continuous conferences, Hallie Flanagan, William Farnsworth, and various department heads concluded that, if centers were to be continued throughout the rest of the nation, the New York Project, which had escaped previous cuts, would have to bear the brunt of the dismissals. Thus they decided to cut the New York Project by 30 per cent, abolish entirely the weakest of the smaller units elsewhere, and continue without reduction those which had already been pared

[75] *Variety*, June 2, 1937, p. 55.
[76] Flanagan, Address to the American Theatre Council Congress in New York City, May 27, 1937, RG 69, FTP Records, NOGSF; the *New York Times*, May 28, 1937, p. 16; *Variety*, June 9, 1937, p. 48.

to the core.[77] Mrs. Flanagan, on June 10, notified Project officials to prepare to cut non-relief workers first, then relief workers, depending on their actual value to the Project.[78] Although union leaders vehemently insisted that professional experience be the only criterion, Mrs. Flanagan remained convinced that other factors must be considered. The needs of the Project as a whole were her first concern.[79]

Cuts were accompanied by the inevitable wave of pickets and protests. In New York, where nearly two thousand workers were being dismissed, delegations and grievance committees constantly filled the offices of Mrs. Flanagan and Farnsworth. However rushed, both tried conscientiously to hear complaints. Other Federal Theatre officials did the same. Charles Ryan, the Project personnel officer, stayed in his office throughout the night after dismissal notices had been given out, listening to the stories and pleas of those who felt they had been discriminated against.[80] Although the demonstrations and protests continued, Hallie Flanagan was convinced that this sympathetic attitude did much to avert the hunger strikes, riots, attempted suicides, and other events—such as the fifteen-hour imprisonment of Arts Project administrator Harold Stein—which were turning the other New York Arts Projects into scenes of unmitigated chaos.[81] The

[77] Memorandum, Mary McFarland to Howard Miller, June 9, 10, 1937, RG 69, FTP Records, NOC-State; Flanagan to Herman Shumlin, June 25, 1937, RG 69, FTP Records, NOGSF.

[78] The *New York Times*, June 12, 1937, p. 8.

[79] Frank Gillmore to Flanagan, June 17, 1937; Flanagan to Gillmore, June 18, 1937, quoted in "Future of Federal Theatre Still Uncertain," *Equity*, XXII (July 1937), 6. See also *Variety*, June 16, 1937, p. 55; June 27, 1937, p. 55; July 14, 1937, p. 62. Equity officials were on solid ground in arguing that "professionals" should be given priority over "amateurs" since the Project had been set up to aid the former.

[80] Flanagan, *Arena*, p. 314.

[81] *Ibid.* For accounts of the upheavals taking place on the other Arts Projects, see the *New York Times*, June 20, 1937, p. 13; June 22, 1937, p. 4; June 23, 1937, p. 6; June 24, 1937, p. 6; June 25, 1937, p. 10; June 26, 1937, p. 1; June 27, 1937, p. 1. Quite disturbed about this much publicized furor, Aubrey Williams was inclined to feel that Ryan's willingness to listen to dismissed workers might be interpreted by the

personal price for this sympathetic involvement was not small, however. "Being so close to the cuts has so completely upset me," wrote Howard Miller to John McGee, "that I am experiencing a sensation of exhaustion such as I have never known before. I am completely nauseated when I think of the tragedy which is going to hit many whom we are separating. And the fact that Project standards will be considerably lower than those maintained during the past six months certainly doesn't act as a bromide. . . . This whole tremendous pressure . . . is an unwholesome thing for those of us attempting to run a job and do it well."[82] The impersonal figures and mathematical abstractions of bureaucratic necessity were painful wounds to Theatre officials; but there seemed to be no way to resolve the differences.

As if the inherent disparity between relief and theatre were not bad enough, the New York Project's officials found themselves beset by yet another difficulty: censorship. The "problem child" this time was *The Cradle Will Rock*. Hallie Flanagan first heard this controversial work one night when its author, Marc Blitzstein, sat down at a piano to play and sing his first opera. A talented composer with a gift for characterization, this slender young man of thirty-one had transformed a steel strike into a bitterly sarcastic, wittily derisive opera. Complete with bloated capitalists, sadistic "cops," heroic union organizers, and the proverbial prostitute with a heart of gold, it fairly burst with moral fervor and contemporaneity. *The Cradle Will Rock*, however, was no mere *New Masses* cartoon set to music. It was the first serious musical drama written in America which provided a new vernacular for the man in the street—an achievement, according to Aaron Copland, that made truly indigenous opera possible. Artistically brilliant and politically explosive, it was, above all, superb theatre. Hallie Flanagan had promptly agreed

---

latter as encouragement of their protests. See Telephone Conversation, Williams and Charles Ryan, June 26, 1937, Aubrey Williams Papers, Franklin D. Roosevelt Library, Hyde Park, N. Y.

[82] Miller to McGee, June 26, 1937, RG 69, FTP Records, NOC.

that the Federal Theatre would do the show with John Houseman as producer and Orson Welles as director.[83]

By June, when *The Cradle* was ready to rock, WPA officials
began to have second thoughts. The *New York Times* described
the opera as a pro-union account of a steel strike, and there
were rumors in Washington that it was dangerous. Both subject
matter and opening date coincided with the bitter struggle being
waged between CIO organizers and "Little Steel."[84] Whatever
the considerations, Lawrence Morris, Ellen Woodward's assistant, flew up for a preview and pronounced it magnificent.[85] Then,
with fourteen thousand seats sold and *The Cradle* about to open,
Hallie Flanagan received the following communication: "This
is to inform you that, effective immediately, no openings of new
productions shall take place until after the beginning of the
coming fiscal year, that is, July 1, 1937."[86] The official explanation stated that cuts must first be completed and the project
reorganized before openings could take place. Suspecting censorship in disguise, Mrs. Flanagan, Farnsworth, Houseman,
Archibald MacLeish, Virgil Thompson, and others interested in
Cradle tried vainly to get an exception to the ruling. Orson
Welles flew to Washington to talk with Ellen Woodward and

[83] Flanagan, *Arena*, p. 201; the *New York Times*, January 24, 1964,
p. 1; Ross Parmenter, "Gift of Characterization," the *New York Times*,
January 24, 1964, p. 35; Aaron Copland et al., "Marc Blitzstein Remembered," *Program for the Marc Blitzstein Memorial Concert, Philharmonic Hall, Lincoln Center for the Performing Arts* (New York:
Saturday Review, Inc., 1964), pp. F ff. Blitzstein was killed in January
1964 while at work on *Sacco and Vanzetti*, an opera commisssioned by
the Metropolitan Opera Company and the Ford Foundation.

[84] In February 1937, the CIO successfully organized General Motors
and in March U. S. Steel capitulated; however, "Little Steel" proved more
difficult. Throughout May and June, Bethlehem, Youngstown Sheet and
Tube, Republic, National, and Inland Steel waged an intense struggle
against the union which resulted in pitched battles between police and
strikers, loss of life, and great ill feeling on both sides. Hence *Cradle*
proved to be even more timely than perhaps its supporters had initially
realized.

[85] The *New York Times*, June 17, 1937, p. 1; Flanagan, *Arena*, p. 202.

[86] Woodward to Flanagan, June 11, 1937, RG 69, GSS-211.2.

123

David Niles, WPA director of information. Insisting throughout that the play was "not a political protest but an artistic one," Welles finally threatened to launch the production independently. Niles replied that, in that case, the WPA would no longer be interested in it.[87]

Welles rushed back to New York, where an opening-night audience had already assembled at the Maxine Elliot Theatre. He announced that the show would go on, the federal government notwithstanding. After several frantic phone calls, he reappeared to say that the old Venice Theatre had just been rented and asked that actors and audience proceed twenty blocks north to Fifty-Eighth Street and Seventh Avenue. While over six hundred spectators embarked on a march that made theatrical history, Welles, Houseman, and Blitzstein rushed about looking for a piano. They frantically negotiated with actors and musicians unions, not even knowing whether the cast would defy the government's orders—perhaps Blitzstein would have to sing the parts as well as play the score. When the audience was finally seated at the Venice Theatre, actors scattered themselves throughout the audience, so as not to violate an Equity order forbidding participation in an unauthorized presentation. Then Blitzstein, seated in front of an old upright piano at center stage, began playing and singing the first song. Suddenly a woman's voice was heard from the lower left box; Feder's brilliant spotlight swung down on the Moll. Moments later it moved to Reverend Salvation, as Hiram Sherman rose, his hands nervously grasping pieces of paper folded to look like the Bible. Soon Will Geer, as Steeltown owner, Mr. Mister, stood up, and then Howard Da Silva, as the husky, heroic union organizer, Larry Foreman. For actors and audience alike, it was one of those rare evenings of theatrical excitement they would recall a quarter of a century later with an enthusiasm tempered only by nostalgia.[88] For

[87] The *New York Times*, June 17, 1937, p. 1; Flanagan, *Arena*, p. 203.
[88] *Ibid.*; *Variety*, June 23, 1937, p. 62; Interview with Hiram Sherman, November 15, 1961; Interview with Howard Da Silva, November 14, 1961. Blitzstein's version of the opening night difficulties is recorded by

124

Blitzstein, it was a night of triumph. Audacious, witty, and in-spired, *The Cradle Will Rock* would one day become to America what Kurt Weil's *Dreigroschenoper* is to Germany.[89] But for many middle-class Americans—appalled at the sight of sit-down strikers, flying squadrons of union organizers, and a red-bereted Woman's Emergency Brigade—the production was further evidence of federal folly.[90]

Caught in the immediate problems of the entire Theatre Project, Mrs. Flanagan had no time to ponder the implications of events surrounding New York City's *The Cradle Will Rock*. In spite of protests and disturbances, Hopkins insisted that plans for the summer had to be carried out. Although Mrs. Flanagan had managed to launch a summer caravan program, she despaired of ever getting enough instructors from strife-torn New York to conduct classes at the Federal Theatre summer workshop for talented young people from across the entire country; but Hopkins was adamant. Convinced that the summer workshop (which the Rockefeller Foundation had agreed to sponsor

Spoken Arts (No. 717). The record is entitled "Marc Blitzstein Discusses His Theater Compositions."

Variety, which ordinarily had little patience with plays of social protest, reported that the production, owing to the circumstances surrounding its opening, should have been chaotic and mistake-ridden; but it was not. Despite its militantly one-sided characterization, *Cradle* was "strangely moving and affecting." The verdict still holds, judging from the response of those who attended the Marc Blitzstein Memorial Concert on April 14, 1964 at Philharmonic Hall, Lincoln Center. Leonard Bernstein played the score on an upright piano in center stage as had Blitzstein at the original performance. Hiram Sherman, Will Geer, and Howard Da Silva sang their original parts. Da Silva subsequently revived the production at Theatre Four in New York City in November 1964. For a discussion of the work's continued appeal, see John O. Hunter, "Marc Blitzstein's *The Cradle Will Rock* as a Document of America, 1937," *American Quarterly*, XVIII (Summer 1966), 227-233.

[89] Harold C. Schonberg, "Music: Marc Blitzstein," the *New York Times*, April 20, 1964, p. 35.

[90] See Leuchtenburg, *Franklin D. Roosevelt and the New Deal*, pp. 242-243 for a discussion of the reaction of the middle class to the CIO's unionization efforts.

at Vassar) was potentially the most important thing being done in any of the Arts Projects, he flatly refused to see it abandoned. By dividing her time between Poughkeepsie, New York City, and Washington, Mrs. Flanagan could get the Workshop under way, he insisted, and still oversee projects elsewhere.[91] Unfortunately for the Federal Theatre, Hopkins' high hopes for the Arts Projects were not shared with equal enthusiasm by all of his subordinates. While actors, directors, and designers signed up for classes in Poughkeepsie, tension between Federal Theatre officials and WPA administrators continued to mount.

· V ·

The most recent object of contention was the magazine, *Federal Theatre*. Begun in November 1935 as a mimeographed leaflet, it had become, with the help of over $6,000 worth of multilith equipment from the Rockefeller Foundation, a substantial periodical with a circulation of twelve thousand. Sent free to Federal Theatre units and tax-supported institutions, the two thousand copies which were sold in America and in Europe contributed most of the cost of publication, save for the labor of the ten people who put out the magazine. As an appraisal as well as a record of Federal Theatre activities throughout the United States, it was welcomed by universities, colleges, little theatres, and high schools. For the Federal Theatre's own units, Hallie Flanagan considered the magazine indispensable because of its unrelenting emphasis on both high standards of performance and the national character of the Federal Theatre.[92]

[91] Flanagan to George Kondolf, June 17, 1937, RG 69, FTP Records, NOC-State. Hopkins proved to be right about the importance of the Summer Theatre. After six weeks of study under some of the Federal Theatre's best directors, designers, and actors, many of those attending the workshop left Vassar with new ideas for productions and new plans to improve local projects. For a survey of the program, see Pierre de Rohan, *First Federal Summer Theatre . . . A Report* (New York: Federal Theatre National Publications 1937).

[92] Memorandum, Flanagan to Woodward, May 13, 1937, RG 69, FTP Records, NOGSF.

The first bureaucratic attacks on the magazine had been temperate—merely questions about its necessity. Then came word of an impending order ending all publications by the WPA. Mrs. Flanagan, given permission to present a statement explaining the value of the magazine and why it should be exempt from such an order, drew up a forceful plea for its continuance which she urged Ellen Woodward to press upon Hopkins and Aubrey Williams. Apparently she pleaded to no effect, for June slipped into July and August with still no assurance that the magazine would continue. With the advantage of hindsight, Mrs. Flanagan thought she perceived why WPA officials opposed continued publication. Thinking back, she recalled the pointed character of their questions. Was the magazine on sale at a worker's bookshop in California? Yes, but also at one hundred and twenty-one other newsstands across the country. Was its editor, Pierre de Rohan, a Communist? On the contrary, he was a Democrat and a World War I veteran, and he came to the Project with the recommendation of Vice President John Nance Garner. Wasn't there too much emphasis on the poverty of Federal Theatre audiences, too many pictures of shirt-sleeved crowds in city parks? Hadn't they used a quotation from Marx? Although she had read thoroughly the copy for each issue of the magazine before publication, Mrs. Flanagan had to rack her memory before she finally recalled a quotation that might have been construed as Marxist. It was a bit from W. H. Auden, included in the hope that it might encourage young actors, directors, and designers on the Project:

> Your knowledge and your powers are capable
>   of infinite extension;
> Act . . .
>   To each his need; from each his power.[93]

When her own arguments seemed to accomplish nothing, Hallie Flanagan turned once again to outside pressure. To people

---

[93] *Ibid.*; Memorandum, Flanagan to Woodward, September 16, 1937, RG 69, FTP Records, NOGSF; Flanagan, *Arena*, p. 204.

such as Brooks Atkinson, letters were sent containing a copy of the order stopping publication, excerpts from some of the more than eighteen hundred commendatory letters received by the magazine's editor, and a diplomatic request for help in putting "our case before Hopkins and the public."[94] To Gilmor Brown, President of the National Theatre Conference, she suggested that NTC might ask the Rockefeller Foundation to finance the current issue, which could be devoted to the Federal Theatre's educational experiments. If the forthcoming issue were taken care of, "it might give us an opportunity to consider what our next step should be."[95] In the meantime, messages from universities, theatre groups, movie-makers, and foreign embassies protesting against *Federal Theatre*'s demise were turned over to Ellen Woodward—but all to no avail.[96]

A far more serious indication of the changing position of the Federal Theatre in the bureaucratic constellation of WPA was the decision of the Washington office to turn over administration of all the New York Arts Projects to Paul Edwards, who was being brought up from the finance division of the national office. The reduced appropriations, it was explained, made impossible the continuation of two business offices—one for the Federal Theatre under Farnsworth, and one for the other Arts Projects under Harold Stein.[97] Whatever the official explanation, the change came as a complete surprise to the national directors, not one of whom had been consulted.[98] Hallie Flanagan was particularly upset. With Edwards instead of Farnsworth in charge of such matters as employment, finances, labor, and supply, she would lose the administrative control of the Project so recently won from Hopkins. Even the best-intentioned administrators, she

[94] Pierre de Rohan to Atkinson, June 1, 1937, RG 69, FTP Records, General Correspondence Regarding the Federal Theatre Magazine (Gen. Correspondence-FT Mag.).

[95] Flanagan to Brown, June 19, 1937, RG 69, FTP Records, NOGSF.

[96] See list of 300 individuals and groups expressing interest in the continuance of *Federal Theatre* in RG 69, FTP Records, NOGSF.

[97] *Variety*, July 28, 1937, p. 54; August 18, 1937, p. 69.

[98] Flanagan, *Arena*, p. 315.

believed, had little understanding of theatre. Hardly less encouraging was the realization that the most satisfactory working arrangement which had ever been devised for the New York Project would be completely upset.[99] Her misgivings counted for little, however. The decision had already been made, and Mrs. Flanagan found herself thrust once again into the throes of reorganization.

The reorganization was a major one. Once again the Project's administrative functions had to be transferred, its technical and artistic activities overhauled to fit its drastically reduced quota. Coming in the wake of a wholesale reorganization only a few months before and the disturbing cuts of the early summer, this new upheaval aroused little enthusiasm among those whose first concern was theatre. Although many hung on, they undoubtedly shared the sentiments of Walter Hart who did not. Recounting for Hallie Flanagan how, in January 1936, he had plunged into the Project's activities "with great enthusiasm for the idea of the Federal Theatre and for its promise toward the future of the American theatre in general," he continued:

Although my work in the theatre is primarily that of a director, when you asked me to become one of the executives of the project I did so and gladly performed the thankless task of working out organizational puzzles that were impeding the progress of the Federal Theatre. As you are aware, I established a system of supply for the entire project, and I organized the only completely successful method of purchasing the Federal Theatre has ever had. And what is more important, for at least a year, I fought to maintain theatrical standards in every department of the Federal Theatre to enable it to function, not as a road building project, but as a theatre. Only ceaseless, sleepless vigilance has saved the Federal Theatre from becoming a shambles under the barrage of constantly changing WPA rules and regulations and procedures in sextuplicate. The best theatrical talent on the project has to spend

[99] *Ibid.*, p. 190.

four-fifths of its time, not in theatre work, but in preventing
people and orders completely alien to theatrical practice from
preventing the exercise of that talent.

Every time a play is produced by the Federal Theatre a
major miracle has been passed. After passing ninety-five such
miracles one begins to tire. No theatre, even if it isn't the
Federal Theatre, has room for anyone who is tired. Now as
the Federal Theatre goes into its ninth reorganization within
eighteen months, I realize that I am tired—tired of the constant reorganizations, tired of the constant changes in rules
and regulations, in orders and counterorders. Most of all I am
tired of passing miracles. . . .

Although my enthusiasm for the ideal you have set for the
Federal Theatre remains undampened, I feel that this is the
time for me to pass this work on to others.[100]

Hart's resignation was a blow. This new loss, coming just after
the WPA had refused to exempt the gifted John Houseman from
the new congressional rule barring aliens from work-relief programs, left the production staff of the New York Project considerably weakened.

For Hallie Flanagan, the directorship of that Project proved
to be one of the most frustrating aspects of the entire reorganization—and one that left her again at odds with Washington. Over
a year before, when she had been uncertain as to whether she
could continue as National Director, Mrs. Flanagan had suggested as a thoroughly capable substitute, William Farnsworth,
lawyer-producer and formerly deputy administrator of the NRA
Amusement Code.[101] Freed now of his administrative duties on
the New York Project, he was Mrs. Flanagan's immediate choice
as its director.[102] Considered a "professional" in Broadway cir-

[100] Hart to Flanagan, August 13, 1937, RG 69, FTP Records, NOC; the
New York Times, August 16, 1937, p. 15.

[101] Flanagan to John McGee, May 14, 1936, RG 69, FTP Records,
NOGSF; Flanagan to Lester Lang, May 14, 1936, RG 69, FTP Records,
NOC-Reg. II.

[102] Memorandum, Howard Miller to Lawrence Morris, July 30, 1937,
RG 69, GSS-211.2.

cles, he was also approved for the job by Equity.[103] "Washington"—that much used synonym for the bureaucratic power structure in the headquarters of the WPA—thought otherwise. Who objected to Farnsworth and why is unclear;[104] that there were sufficient objections to prevent his getting the job is quite clear.[105]

Indeed, by August, the growing rift between the Director of the Federal Theatre Project and WPA officials in Washington was no secret. Commenting on the "lessening of the Flanagan influence," *Variety* noted that, whereas the National Director had been "doing business directly with Hopkins," with Ellen Woodward only technically in control, now all routine had to "filter through Mrs. Woodward's sieve with her executive assistants in a position to approve or reject all plans."[106] Potential directors for the New York Project were even more outspoken. Men such as Sidney Howard, president of the Dramatist Guild and Lawrence Langner, a director of the Theatre Guild, talked frankly to Mrs. Flanagan about "interference from Washington" and the fact that control of the entire Federal Theatre seemed to be gradually slipping into other hands.[107] Her interview with

[103] Flanagan to Lawrence Morris, July 27, 1937, RG 69, FTP Records, NOC.

[104] Reporting on a meeting between Hopkins and theatrical union officials, *Variety* commented that the WPA was known to be "touchy, at long last, under criticism that left-wingers are running the show" and that a "purge" of Federal Theatre officials was "predicted in political circles." See *Variety*, July 14, 1937, p. 62, Mrs. Flanagan subsequently claimed that the WPA would have been delighted to see all the national directors resign and the Arts Projects turned over to the states. See *Arena*, p. 315.

[105] Farnsworth subsequently resigned from the Federal Theatre claiming "private affairs" as the explanation. The *New York Times*, August 22, 1937, p. 22. In a letter to her husband, Mrs. Flanagan noted that she had tried to get Mrs. Woodward to ratify Farnsworth's appointment, but that the director of Women's and Professional Projects had declined, saying that she had to have the approval of Hopkins who was on vacation. Flanagan to Philip Davis, August 17, 1937, Flanagan Papers.

[106] *Variety*, August 18, 1937, p. 69.

[107] Flanagan, Comments on Possibilities for New York City Director, RG 69, FTP Records, NOGSF.

George Kondolf was no less revealing. Refusing to accept the New York directorship without assurances that he would be firmly supported in Washington, Kondolf explained that, as head of the Federal Theatre in Chicago, he had the backing of the WPA field representative, Howard Hunter; of the regional director of Women's and Professional Projects, Florence Kerr; and of the Illinois state administrator, Charles A. Miner. He added, "it looks more and more as if that was the backing that counted. What I mean to say is I do not believe even you could fire me, Hallie, in Chicago because I have the backing of Mrs. Kerr, Howard Hunter, and Miner and they go straight through to Hopkins."[108]

That the Federal Theatre and its National Director were caught in a bureaucratic contest for control was a fact of life that could no longer be obscured. Looking back over the summer, Mrs. Flanagan had to admit that Hopkins and Mrs. Woodward were increasingly making decisions concerning the Arts Project "on the advice of their own people," rather than in conjunction with the national directors. Not since May had she had any real support from Washington. Neither consulted nor allowed to choose her own personnel, she had been forced to stand by while the entire program was "practically wrecked." Convinced that the Federal Theatre was headed for "chaos" and further "loss of professional respect" unless something were done, Hallie Flanagan resolved to confront Hopkins' second-in-command, Aubrey Williams, with the whole "impossible situation." After much thought as to how to present her case, she decided to begin with a report of her interview with potential directors for New York, and then work into a list of questions:

1. Who gave the order that no plays should open during July, and was this aimed at *The Cradle Will Rock*?
2. Why was I not consulted before this order was given?
3. Why was the *Cradle* not allowed to open after July?

[108] *Ibid.*

132

RELEVANT THEATRE

4. Why was I not consulted re[garding] P[aul] E[dwards] until after the event?

5. Why was I not allowed to name W. P. F[arnsworth] as N[ew] Y[ork] C[ity] Dir[ector]?

6. Why was Houseman singled out and why was I told he must go?

7. Why was I told by [Lawrence] Morris that the F[ederal] T[heatre] m[agazine] could never be reinstated under [Pierre] de Rohan?

8. Have I or have I not still basic control of the F[ederal] T[heatre]? The above points challenge it. . . .

She would tell Williams, moreover, that until these questions were answered and until "certain assurances" were given, she would make no appointment to the New York post.[109]

It is unlikely that Hallie Flanagan's questions were answered to her complete satisfaction. In any event, she did agree to name George Kondolf to the New York directorship. An energetic young producer, Kondolf had taken over the thoroughly unsuccessful Chicago Project in the autumn of 1936 and made it respected by public and press alike. Along with the obvious advantage of this experience, Kondolf could boast the support of theatrical unions, acceptance in Broadway circles, a knowledge of WPA procedure, a relatively conservative political outlook, and at least nominal ties with the Roman Catholic Church. A host of WPA officials agreed that Kondolf was an appropriate choice. Describing the appointment as "a conservative one," Mrs. Flanagan ventured that its conservative character was "probably a good thing," as it might "counteract the charge of radicalism on the Project."[110] Apparently Hopkins was sure that it was a "good thing." He expected that the New York Director's Catholicism would help to offset charges of Communism

[109] Ibid.; Notes for interview with Aubrey Williams [August (?), 1937], RG 69, FTP Records, NOGSF.

[110] Memorandum, Flanagan to Hopkins, September 2, 1937, Flanagan Papers; Flanagan, Comments on the Possibilities for New York City Director, RG 69, FTP Records, NOGSF.

133

which were giving the entire Federal Theatre Project a bad reputation.[111]

Hopkins was unable to enjoy the anticipated benefits of this appointment, however, for both he and his wife were ill with cancer. Shortly after her death in October, he would leave for Mayo Clinic not to return to Washington until April 1938. In the months to follow, Mrs. Flanagan would feel keenly the loss created by Hopkins' absence, for the WPA chieftain in his war against poverty inspired in his fellow workers the same unswerving loyalty and devotion which she herself infused in those around her. A crusader herself, she recognized in this hardworking, wisecracking, and deliberately unsuave Iowan a kindred spirit. What she may not have recognized was that the crusader had tasted power during his years as Relief Administrator, and that his political instincts had been sharpened and his ambitions stirred.

Considered in 1937 as a possible successor by the President himself, Hopkins had, in effect, been absent long before he left for Minnesota—at least as far as the Federal Theatre was concerned. Throughout the critical summer months, he apparently had done nothing to help restore the Project to Hallie Flanagan's control. Distracted by illness, engrossed in the exhausting task of running a much-criticized relief program employing over two million people, it is understandable that he may have had neither time nor energy to devote to one small and controversial project. Since, however, he had managed in months past to confer with its National Director about problems, plans, and productions—managed even to attend performances while in New York City—Hopkins' withdrawal may have been motivated not so much by time and health as by political factors.

Hopkins' political education began when he learned that the best way to continue a program in which he fervently believed was to have Roosevelt continue in power. At the request of the President himself, Hopkins asked his field representatives and

111 Interview with George Kondolf, November 7, 1961.

others to report to him during 1936 on political conditions throughout the country. When he learned from these reports the extent to which the WPA was an issue in the campaign, he shed his previous disdain for politics and politicians, and set off on a campaign junket of his own to convince voters that the relief program was not the *bête noire* Landon and his supporters claimed. Convinced by election results that the President and his program had the support of most Americans, the Relief Administrator threw himself into political activity with new vigor after the election, supporting Roosevelt's attempts to enlarge the Supreme Court and liberalize the Senate leadership. Hopkins was drawn into a still closer relationship with the master politician in the White House upon the death of presidential advisor Louis Howe. By the summer of 1936, his own ambitions began to soar.[112]

Further stimulus was unwittingly provided by Hopkins' congressional opponents. It had become increasingly evident during the long wrangle over the Court reform bill that the coalition which had elected Roosevelt was in shambles, and that the President and his program were under heavy attack. In the course of that attack, Hopkins' requested appropriation for relief had been rejected, his funds reduced, his own salary slashed by a hostile, apparently vindictive, House of Representatives eager to earmark relief money. The effect of this congressional slap, according to Hopkins' biographer, was simply to further his determination to "possess himself of the Big Stick with which to smite the venal politicians hip and thigh."[113] But in order to get the Big Stick, Hopkins may well have reasoned that he would have to walk softly. Perhaps his calculations were influenced by presidential ambitions; perhaps, by a newly acquired political sensitivity to a Congress, determined to check the powerful, far-flung institution that had grown out of a device to solve the unemployment problem. In either case, he seems to have decided

[112] Sherwood, *Roosevelt and Hopkins*, pp. 80 *passim* 92; Charles, *Minister of Relief*, pp. 206-213.
[113] Sherwood, *Roosevelt and Hopkins*, p. 92.

135

that the political situation demanded some accommodation—possibly by whitewashing over any pinkish tinge he and his organization might have acquired.

Whatever the nature of that accommodation, the Arts Projects were naturally involved. By far the most controversial of the WPA projects, they were commonly regarded as a "kind of curious idea of Hopkins" benefiting people, most of whom could never hope to make a living as actors, writers, or musicians.[114] A summer of widely publicized demonstrations had done nothing to lessen the belief that this "four arts business . . . was a mistake to start with," a threat to the continued existence of the entire work program.[115] The largest and most controversial of these projects, Hallie Flanagan's "radical" theatre stood most in need of whitewashing. Thus the controversial and challenging Project which Hopkins, the Crusader, had permitted, and even encouraged, had to be discouraged by Hopkins, the Politician and Bureaucrat. The task fell to his lieutenants, some of whom were understandably more interested in perfecting an efficient, centralized, relief operation than in fostering a theatre. Moreover, as Ellen Woodward well knew, she, not Hallie Flanagan, had to justify the Federal Theatre's actions to unsympathetic congressmen. Thus it was Mrs. Woodward and David Niles who prevented *The Cradle* from rocking; and it was Aubrey Williams, not Hopkins, for whom the Theatre Project's National Director drew up her list of grievances. Devoted to her fellow Iowan throughout, Mrs. Flanagan placed the blame on "Washington"—probably meaning Hopkins' assistants—for what she believed to be an "impossible situation."[116]

Indeed it was common knowledge that the man described as Hopkins' "chief political adviser and campaign strategist," assistant administrator David K. Niles, was considerably less

[114] Telephone Conversation, Aubrey Williams and Charles Ryan, June 26, 1937, Aubrey Williams Papers, Franklin D. Roosevelt Library, Hyde Park, N. Y.

[115] *Ibid.*

[116] Flanagan, Comments on Possibilities for New York City Director, RG 69, FTP Records, NOGSF.

enthusiastic about the Federal Theatre than his superior.[117] It is equally probable, however, that these assistants were acting in concurrence with the wishes of the Relief Administrator himself. Even Hallie Flanagan had to admit that Hopkins and Mrs. Woodward were making decisions concerning the Arts Projects "on the advice of their own people" rather than after consultation with the national directors.[118] What she did not admit was that she was in part responsible because, as an artist interested in maintaining a creative atmosphere, she had been reluctant to stop productions which, as an administrator, she should have known better than to permit.

With the appointment of George Kondolf as director of the New York Project, Hopkins' intentions became even less a matter of conjecture. Not only did the Relief Administrator consider Kondolf's Catholicism a strong point in his favor, but, according to Kondolf himself, the WPA chieftain personally urged him to "tighten up" the New York Project and "get rid" of the Communist element. Since Kondolf, by his own admission, was involved in the Federal Theatre solely to gain experience, Hopkins and, undoubtedly, Niles were confident that the right man had been found for the job.[119]

That the Federal Theatre and the New York Project in particular had become politically embarrassing to the Relief Administrator was a possibility which Hallie Flanagan could neither understand nor accept. Sharing Hopkins' crusading but not his political instincts, she failed to recognize that the idealistic social worker had to be a politician if his program were to survive. Although she obviously displayed considerable political adroitness in getting her own conception of the Federal Theatre accepted by other members of the Project, her basic loyalty was always to the idea—the idea of a theatre *necessary* to the Ameri-

[117] Sherwood, *Roosevelt and Hopkins*, p. 111; *Variety*, August 18, 1937, p. 79.

[118] Flanagan, Comments on Possibilities for New York City Director, RG 69, FTP Records, NOGSF.

[119] Interview with George Kondolf, November 7, 1961.

137

can people because it was relevant to the changing world in which they lived. That such a theatre, in its efforts to be relevant, might sometimes be controversial, even radical, she would admit. But that Hopkins, who had pledged a "free, adult, uncensored" theatre, should temporize, because it seemed not only politically expedient but administratively responsible *not* to be controversial, was a fact completely alien to Hallie Flanagan's mental and emotional make-up. She could only regard such action as tantamount to a rejection of the Federal Theatre and the relief workers who comprised it. Thus, of the decision to stop publication of the *Federal Theatre* she later wrote: "Its economic, racial, and social point of view, in line with administration and WPA policies in 1935, was considered inimical in 1937. Washington no longer wanted our plays or our magazine to be the mouthpiece of the people on the project."[120] Like many thoroughly dedicated individuals, she had to pursue that to which she was committed wholeheartedly; anything less would have seemed almost a violation of her own integrity, a threat to the kind of theatre she was laboring to build. Her zeal—neither politic, bureaucratic, nor "safe"—was the kind of zeal that turned a relief project into a theatre. It was also the kind of zeal that made bureaucrats shudder.

· VI ·

By the autumn of 1937, many of those laboring with Hallie Flanagan to build her kind of theatre were indeed wondering if they had labored in vain. They had been told that the Federal Theatre could become necessary to the American people only if it gave them plays created out of the stuff of a changing world, soundly produced, and competently played. They had struggled to offer such productions in this second season. To some degree they had succeeded: *It Can't Happen Here* was clearly a tour de force; *Faustus*, a brilliantly original production; *Power*, melodramatic, but dynamic, theatre. For the most part, however,

[120] Flanagan, *Arena*, pp. 204-205.

those for whom the Project was first and foremost a theatre had seen their efforts interrupted and their plans thwarted with alarming frequency.

As part of a work-relief program, the Theatre Project was unavoidably subject to cuts in membership. Yet dismissals and rumors of dismissals meant disruption of theatrical activities. Workers, ever conscious of the tenuousness of their employment, struggled desperately to hold on to what little security they possessed, oblivious to the future consequences of their frenzied demonstrations. Directors forsook rehearsals in order to determine how many would remain and how many would be dismissed. The very fact that the first to go were those of least professional value served to accentuate the human tragedy involved. For the thousands remaining, the ordeal was a debilitating one which, at best, left the Project temporarily weakened; its production activities upset; the morale of its members shattered. Then, in the wake of dismissals came inevitable reorganizations because, with quotas slashed, the various activities of each project had to be reduced correspondingly.

In New York this revamping had occurred with what seemed to Federal Theatre directors disturbing frequency. Aside from the consolidation of the Project in the Chanin Building, Hallie Flanagan was convinced that previous reorganization, carried out under local WPA administrators, had made it increasingly more difficult for the Project to function as a theatre. The prospect of another overhaul, this time involving the surrender of their newly won administrative control, filled both the National Director and her coworkers with dismay. Artists rather than organization experts, they had long ago learned that the utmost resourcefulness was required to operate as a theatre a relief program which was part of a centralized governmental agency.

The most talented people on the Project—according to Walter Hart, a director turned administrator—had had to spend four-fifths of their time not in theatre work, but in preventing people and orders completely alien to theatrical practice from hindering the exercise of that talent. What professional results they had

139

achieved had been accomplished, according to Hart, in spite of control by people whose knowledge of the theatre was "zero," whose orders were "peremptory," and whose interest in making the theatre function was "the most perverse possible."[121] Nor had the situation been improved by the constant changes in rules, regulations, and procedures which accompanied successive reorganizations. On the contrary, recalled Philip Barber, "we could almost feel the long, bureaucratic arm of Washington reaching in ever closer."[122] To those attempting to administer a noncontroversial, smoothly operating federal relief agency, this extension of control no doubt seemed desirable. But to those whose first concern was theatre, it signified a further invasion of bureaucracy—timid, oppressive, confining. As thoughtful men, they had cause to wonder whether Hallie Flanagan's idea of a vital, relevant theatre could be realized in an organization created primarily for purposes of relief—an organization increasingly concerned with bureaucratic and political considerations. How long, they wondered, could miracles continue?

[121] Walter Hart, "Proposals for the FTP," the *New York Times*, September 19, 1937, Sec. 10, p. 1.
[122] Interview with Philip Barber, November 14, 1961.

CHAPTER FOUR

Regional Theatre in a Bureaucratic Framework

THE FEDERAL THEATRE embarked on its third and perhaps most crucial season in the early autumn of 1937. For two years, Federal Theatre actors had given plays not only in city theatres, but in Catholic convents and Baptist churches, circus tents and university halls, police stations, showboats, and CCC camps. In the parks of New York City alone, two million youngsters and adults had gathered on the grass each summer to watch caravans of traveling players perform *Jack and the Beanstalk, The Emperor's New Clothes, Midsummer Night's Dream, It Can't Happen Here*, John Howard Lawson's *Processional*, and Gilbert and Sullivan.[1] Even the less ardent supporters of this "People's Theatre" agreed that it would be difficult indeed to compute in dollars and cents the social and cultural gains from caravan performances alone.[2] Yet these were the terms in which the Federal Theatre would increasingly be called upon to justify itself in the year ahead.

Pressed to economize by greatly reduced appropriations, Hallie Flanagan now insisted that theatrical centers become inextricably bound up with the life of the communities in which they were located, not to achieve institutional permanence, but to insure greater local contributions to non-labor costs.[3] Thus the production of bold, imaginative plays that would enlarge the Federal Theatre's new audiences and transform them into lasting patrons became in 1937-38 no longer an ultimate goal, but rather a present necessity, not merely in New York, Los

[1] "Caravan Repertoire for 1937" [press release], RG 69, FTP Records, NOGSF.

[2] Dorothy Bromley, "WPA Building Culture," *New York World Telegram*, September 7, 1937, p. 22.

[3] Hallie Flanagan, Address entitled "Federal Theatre-1937," no audience designated, n.d., RG 69, FTP Records, NOGSF.

141

Angeles, and Chicago but in the smaller units which had sur-
vived cuts and closings. To create a theatre that would affect
the life of its audience in places where Federal Theatre units
already existed and, more especially, to bring such a theatre into
regions where units did not exist, would require a bold concerted
effort on the part of both Federal Theatre directors and WPA
officials. Whether the latter were prepared to make such efforts
for Harry Hopkins' "free, adult, uncensored"—and controversial—theatre was very much open to question.

· I ·

In September 1937, the Federal Theatre, battered by cuts
and reorganizations, seemed neither strongly regional nor particularly relevant. In Texas, where good actors were few, the
public indifferent, and the state administrator uncooperative,
projects had been closed, leaving John McGee's huge Southern
region with producing centers in only three states and a small
recreation and research project in North Carolina and Oklahoma
respectively. So many projects had been shut down in the theatrically barren Midwest that there remained only the director-
less Chicago Project, a Children's Theatre in Gary, and small
production units in Detroit, Des Moines, Cleveland, Cincinnati,
Springfield, and Peoria. In the East, the demise of centers in
Rhode Island and Delaware, and the resignation of the regional
director left that region further weakened. Cuts in Los Angeles
and particularly in New York meant a comparable curtailment
in the production activities of the Federal Theatre's two most
important projects.[4]

While George Kondolf proceeded to reorganize the New York
enterprise, Hallie Flanagan, thrusting aside the disappointments
of the past year, began work on production plans, confident that

[4] Memorandum, John McGee to Ellen Woodward, June 19, 1937;
Lawrence Morris to Ellen Woodward, September 22, 1937, RG 69, GSS-
211.2. State administrators in Rhode Island and Delaware were very
reluctant to see projects in these states closed. See McGee to Woodward,
July 7, 1937, RG 69, GSS-211.2.

a new season would bring new gains. Although productions would be fewer—the New York Project, for example, could handle only half of the eighty shows it had staged the previous season—the goals of the Federal Theatre's Director were unchanged. In May she had told the American Federation of Arts: "Human achievement is the basic necessity of our project . . . but it is not enough. With increasing insistence we must ask ourselves, 'What are these projects contributing to the arts fields in which they were set up? What bounds are being exceeded? What patterns changed, what challenges flung down?' " Reminding her listeners that "of all the arts the theatre has remained most impervious to the changing world," she insisted once again that the Federal Theatre had to respond if it were to endure:

In an age when the loud speaker blares forth astounding individual achievements, group movements, mass miseries, the theatre continues to tell in polite whispers its tales of small triangular love stories in small rectangular settings. Federal Theatre, particularly in its Living Newspapers, is trying to create theatre on other terms, to make it out of every day factual material, to dramatize the struggle not of two men for one woman, not of one psychological trait against another psychological trait in a man's soul, not of one social class against another social class. All of these struggles are important for the theatre, but the Living Newspapers seek to dramatize a new struggle—the search of the average American today for knowledge about his country and his world; to dramatize his struggle to turn the great natural and economic and social forces of our time toward a better life for more people.

Convinced that the Federal Theatre must be regional as well as relevant, she insisted that forthcoming productions take geography into account. Since both Eugene O'Neill and George Bernard Shaw had recently turned over their works to the Project as an expression of faith in its role as a "People's Theatre," an O'Neill cycle would include the production of *The Fountain*

143

at its original site, St. Augustine, Florida, while the sea plays and *Anna Christie* would be produced on the east coast and *Marco Millions* in an oriental setting on the West Coast.[5]

By September, plans were more specific. In addition to nation-wide cycles of Shaw and O'Neill, the Federal Theatre would continue to explore the American scene with new plays like *Prologue to Glory*, the story of young Abe Lincoln, and Boston's historical pageant, *Created Equal*. As part of that exploration, Living Newspapers would persist in their probe of local and contemporary problems: New York City would see *One-Third of a Nation*, a dramatic exposé of housing conditions in America's largest city; New Orleans and Cincinnati would have their own version of the play; Oregon's flax growers would see *Flax*; Denver would have a Living Newspaper on sugar and Iowa one on corn. At Christmas each project would combine both classical and religious drama with medieval shepherd plays. Of course, she added, "we must have our circuses, our ballets, our musical comedies, our flying carpets," in order to bring to the millions of Americans in theatrical centers and "in as many other towns and cities as we can reach by touring, a varied exciting, and substantial dramatic program of plays."[6]

Plays would be no better than their production. With tickets to downtown New York theatres now selling for as much as one dollar, the Federal Theatre had an added obligation to achieve professional excellence.[7] Once again Hallie Flanagan renewed her pleas for artistic advances in the months ahead. To Federal Theatre directors she sent requests to devote as much time as possible to the Shaw and O'Neill plays. "The excellence of these

[5] Hallie Flanagan, Address to the American Federation of Arts Meeting in Washington, D. C., May 12, 1937, RG 69, FTP Records, NOGSF.

[6] Hallie Flanagan, "Prologue to a Season," the *New York Times*, September 12, 1937, Sec. 11, p. 1.

[7] The decision to raise admissions was made in response to WPA demands that the Federal Theatre pay all expenses other than labor costs as soon as possible. See Hallie Flanagan, Notes on the Meeting of the Federal Theatre Advisory Board, August 3, 1937, RG 69, FTP Records, NOGSF.

144

productions," she insisted, "will have an important bearing on the plays available . . . for next year."[8] Actors, designers, stage-hands, and other theatrical employees were told that as professional workers it was to their interest that the words "Federal Theatre" on the marquee should come to be the "same guarantee of excellence afforded by the government stamp affixed by the Bureau of Standards."[9]

To union leaders Hallie Flanagan directed a similar message. At their first meeting together since the recent cuts, the Federal Theatre Director warned that the time had come to stop talking about the reinstatement of professional workers and start thinking about professional standards. Tossing aside diplomatic niceties of expression, she recalled for her audience their initial skepticism toward a relief venture, their subsequent fears of competition from a government-sponsored theatre, and finally, their suggestion that the Theatre "do something safe, something unnoticeable." Setting forth her own views with equal frankness, she persisted:

> I have not taken this advice because I do not believe it is good advice, even from your point of view—that of keeping your own people on a government payroll. If the Federal Theatre had played safe we would now be sorry. It is only because we have launched boldly with new plays and new techniques that we are now engaged in setting up our third season instead of closing up shop for good.

Muttering about competition, she insisted, was equally short-sighted. By building new audiences, introducing new dramatic forms such as the Living Newspaper, and stimulating new dramatists through the production of their plays, the Federal Thea-

[8] Flanagan to George Kondolf, October 9, 1937, RG 69, GSS-211.2. Shaw had always maintained tight control over his plays. Hence his decision to release them for the regular rental rate of $50.00 weekly was a great boon for the Project, as was O'Neill's similar decision.

[9] Flanagan, "Prologue to a Season," the *New York Times*, September 12, 1937, Sec. 11, p. 1.

145

tre afforded "the commercial theatre a form of competition which is the life and not the death of the trade."

Turning next to the oft-repeated charges that the Project favored "amateurs" at the expense of "professionals," Hallie Flanagan agreed that this had been true, particularly in regions outside New York. "Originally," she explained, "we planned to set up theatre projects only where twenty-five or more professionals were available on relief rolls. In some cases we were persuaded, for the benefit of ten or twelve professionals, or for the value to the community, to set up a project which then had to be supplemented by too many non-professionals." Such projects were now either closed or supplemented by qualified workers brought in from other cities. In New York and other large cities, where great numbers of people had to be enrolled in the Project in a short time, she admitted that people had been taken on who should not have been. "Some of these have been eliminated and all should be." Insisting that a small portion of the Federal Theatre's quota should be reserved for young people with talent but without theatrical experience, she nevertheless agreed that the remaining 80 to 90 per cent should all be people of professional background and achievement.

To the second criticism so often leveled at the Project—that it harbored Communists and permitted Communist activity—she replied:

We have access to no party records and we show favoritism to no party. . . . One of the fundamental principles on which this Project is set up is that there shall be no discrimination as to race, religion or politics and it is so stated in the Appropriation Act itself.

Another fundamental principle is the right of the worker to organize, either along the lines of unions here represented or along any other lines he chooses. A project set up to improve this situation of unemployed workers should meet in a spirit of complete cooperation with any duly appointed representative of those workers. However, the use of project

146

time, equipment, or money for any organization's purpose . . .
will not be tolerated. Proof of such activity, however, instead
of vague mutterings, must be brought.

Hallie Flanagan's major concern, however, was with professional standards, and to this she returned with blunt forcefulness:

> Up to now you have been, as union heads, chiefly concerned
> with getting professional rates, or an hourly adjustment
> amounting to professional rates for your people. I think your
> chief concern from now on should be *insisting on professional
> work of a calibre to merit these professional rates.* It should
> be your concern as well as mine, to see that the stagehands
> drawing $104 for 12 days work are able to give value re-
> ceived. It should be your disgrace as well as mine if we have
> musicians who can't play in our orchestra pits.
>
> To sum it all up, members of various theatrical unions have
> drawn in wages . . . many millions of dollars. Is it or is it not
> worth while to keep such a plan afoot, even if it is necessary
> for your unions to modify certain rules as to hours and
> wages . . . ?
>
> The future of the Project rests to some extent in the hands
> of these union members and in the advice you give them. If
> by your own attitude, you teach them to regard the Federal
> Theatre as a cow to be milked, I assure you that the cow will
> soon go dry. . . .[10]

In other words, professional workers receiving professional pay
had to meet professional standards. Readily admitting that this
was her "main point of insistence" as the Federal Theatre en-
tered a third season, its National Director would hammer home
her thesis from Boston to San Diego in the months ahead.[11]

The area between the coasts needed more than pep talks,
however. Many of the smaller projects lacked not only profes-

[10] Hallie Flanagan, Address to Meeting of Union Representatives and
Regional Directors, August 20, 1937, RG 69, FTP Records, NOGSF.
[11] Flanagan, "Prologue to a Season," the *New York Times*, September
12, 1937, Sec. 11, p. 1.

sional standards, but also the resources to attain them. Thus, to
the newly created National Service Bureau headed by John
McGee, Mrs. Flanagan assigned the crucial task of strengthening
smaller projects through loans of talent and equipment. The
Bureau, a kind of organizational umbrella covering such national agencies as Loan, Travel, and Publication, would make
available its personnel and services on a much expanded scale.[12]
At the request of the local director, McGee's staff would send
Detroit a leading man; Atlanta, an ingenue; Los Angeles could
get a musical score for *Caesar and Cleopatra*; Boston would receive costumes used in the New York production of *The Sun
and I*; and San Francisco, a production record of *Battle Hymn*.
And projects everywhere could get plays. Once the scripts were
approved, the Bureau, now the sole negotiating agency for the
entire Federal Theatre, would draw up a contract to be signed
by the playwright or his agent. If the latter could be persuaded
to accept the Federal Theatre's low royalty rates, the play would
be cleared for production with none of the legal tangle that had
ensued in previous years, when individual directors had made
their own arrangements.[13] A further advantage resulting from
the Bureau's activities would be a larger constituency who benefited from its varied and improved services: community and
university theatre personnel who used the Bureau's theatrical

[12] Flanagan to all Federal Theatre Employees, August 5, 1937, RG 69,
FTP Records, NOGSF. The National Service Bureau was inspired by a report of the Planning Committee of the Federal Theatre Summer Session
at Poughkeepsie in 1937. The functions of the Bureau as outlined in the
report were much more extensive, however, than those actually carried
out by the Bureau. See "A Report of the Planning Committee of the
Federal Theatre Summer Session of 1937," RG 69, FTP Records, NOGSF.
[13] Royalty terms were revised in the fall of 1937 so that playwrights
would receive $50.00 for the first three weeks, $75.00 for the next three,
and $100.00 thereafter (The *New York Times*, October 16, 1937, p. 24).
But despite this upward revision, royalties remained lower than those
paid by community theatres or little theatres, thus restricting the plays,
particularly musical comedies, available to the Federal Theatre. The
Project did have one advantage, however. It could sometimes guarantee
productions in several cities which, of course, meant more attractive
terms for the playwright. Flanagan, *Arena*, p. 263.

148

library of five thousand volumes; and commercial theatre people who had access to the most recent technical developments of its research staff.[14] In short, this new agency could become a powerhouse of ideas, personnel, and property. Confident that McGee would make it such, Mrs. Flanagan returned to Washington.

At national headquarters, she examined the new administrative system which Howard Miller, her new deputy director, promised would enable him to keep his fingers on the pulse of projects throughout the nation.[15] Obviously this statistical "pulse-taking" could tell much about the administrative soundness of a project; but Hallie Flanagan realized that the reports which inundated her office were inadequate substitutes for firsthand appraisals of artistic achievement. Eager to see how the entire national program might be strengthened, she set out on October 14 for a two-month inspection tour.

Beginning with the East, Mrs. Flanagan conferred first with George Gerwing, whom she had borrowed from his California post until a regional director could be found for the New England-Middle States area. Units in this area, Gerwing reminded her, varied as greatly in artistic quality as did the coast line of the states which housed them. The small Connecticut Project was making "tremendous artistic achievement while maintaining low costs." But, despite good reviews from the press, it did not seem to be winning public support. Valiant little vaudeville

[14] *Ibid.*, pp. 265-266. The activities in which the research department was engaged included: the study of mobile projections (projections of objects instead of slides); the development of a remote control switchboard; the development, in cooperation with European designers, of a technical and stage lexicon; studies to make a uniform set of drafting symbols so as to simplify details of stage drawings; and the development of a new transparent heat-resistant bakelite. See Flanagan, Address to the American Federation of Arts Meeting in Washington, D. C., May 12, 1937, RG 69, FTP Records, NOGSF.

[15] For the kinds of material coming into the National Office and for evidence of Miller's interest in working out more simplified reports, see Memorandum, Flanagan to State Directors, June 3, 1937; Memorandum, Miller to State Directors, August 3, 1937, RG 69, FTP Records, NOGSF; Miller to Flanagan, June 8, 1937, RG 69, GSS-211.2.

REGIONAL THEATRE

groups in both Connecticut and Maine continued to delight children in reformatories, youths in CCC camps, patients in hospitals, as well as lodge members, Grange members and town councilmen. The tiny New Hampshire Project, she was told, lacked first-rate talent and would need loans if it were to give productions of merit. New York State, whose Buffalo marionette units had long been the pride of the Federal Theatre, needed not talent, but rather a thoroughgoing reorganization and a capable executive assistant to supplement the skills of its director. If the best of the state's theatrical talent could be brought together under suitable direction, Hallie Flanagan was convinced, New York could build up an excellent repertory company. The Pennsylvania Project, badly organized and poorly guided in the past, was rapidly emerging from chaos, according to Gerwing. If the Negro unit's production of *Jericho*, under the directorship of James Light, proved successful, Philadelphia might indeed be on its way up. Reports from Massachusetts, however, were less encouraging. The Boston Project, consisting of some six hundred members, over half of whom were elderly vaudevillians, was purely a relief affair. Unless this group could be persuaded to try good plays, both Mrs. Flanagan and Gerwing were well aware that its shows would never make enough to cover non-labor costs, much less win the support of Bostonians.[16]

Like the New England projects, Federal Theatre units in the Midwestern region were generally small, though of less varying professional quality. In Detroit, Mrs. Flanagan found the federal unit, with its handful of veterans from tent shows and traveling road companies, still lacking vitality and real professional quality. Although productions had improved vastly with the addition of New York actors and a new director, more time and money, stronger direction, and better choice of plays would be needed

[16] Memorandum, Lawrence Morris to Ellen Woodward, September 22, 1937; Flanagan to Woodward and Morris, October 21, 1937; Memorandum, Gerwing to Flanagan, October 29, 1937, RG 69, GSS-211.2. See also Flanagan, *Arena*, pp. 223ff.

150

if this disparate group were to win a place for itself in the big, dingy, automotive capital.[17]

Ohio's Federal Theatre had no such problem, for the spring floods that had swept down through the river valley had brought the Project and a hitherto indifferent public together for the first time. In fourteen days, federal troupers had played forty engagements to over fourteen thousand flood victims. Traveling by car, truck, and boat, they had laughed, danced, clowned, performed magic tricks, and persuaded cold and homeless people to join them in song. When the flood waters had subsided, the Ohio Project, still subject to fluctuation, had more ups than downs. According to the regional director, Herbert Ashton, Cleveland's Theatre for Youth had arranged to play Dickens' *Christmas Carol* and other plays in the public schools, using a share of the admissions to pay for scenery, royalties, costumes, and other expenses. In Cincinnati, Ashton reported, the light opera group continued to delight eager audiences with its new production of *The Chocolate Soldier*, while the dramatic company worked to retain the audience first discovered with *It Can't Happen Here.*[18]

Indiana, the National Director was reminded, now had only one unit, a community Children's Theatre run by ten persons. Here, in the shadow of the Gary steel mills, children of many different nationalities sat raptly through free performances of such classics as *Robinson Crusoe* done with puppets and folk dances from Croatia or Greece. Active as they were, this little band of players was in desperate need of equipment which had been used by the now defunct Indianapolis Project. So far, Ashton reported, his request to transfer the equipment had been ignored by WPA officials.[19]

Iowans were enjoying the touring production of O'Neill's delightful comedy, *Ah, Wilderness*—all except one minister who insisted that the barroom scene be cut. Nevertheless, Both Hallie

[17] Memorandum, Flanagan to Woodward and Morris, October 28-29, November 1, 1937, RG 69, GSS-211.2; Flanagan, *Arena*, pp. 159-163.
[18] *Ibid.*, pp. 166-169.   [19] *Ibid.*, pp. 152-153.

Flanagan and her regional director knew that the position of this small unit was still precarious. Set up nine months before, the Project had the support of a state WPA administrator far more friendly than the one with whom E. C. Mabie had negotiated; but its talent was none too good. Unless productions were strengthened enormously, the Federal Theatre could count on scant public support in this Republican stronghold.[20]

Chicago was more encouraging. The citizens of that city had given the Federal Theatre increasing support as its productions improved. *O Say Can You Sing*, George Kondolf's loud, lavish revue which satirized the Federal Theatre far more effectively than any anti-administration newspaper, had enjoyed a record-breaking run of seven months.[21] More to the critics' liking was Howard Koch's new drama of Lincoln, *The Lonely Man*, which they called the "most ambitious and literate of the WPA dramas yet attempted."[22] Although neither was still playing when Mrs. Flanagan arrived in Chicago, a likely successor, *The Straw*, had just opened. Beautifully directed, staged, and acted, the O'Neill play was receiving good reviews and the applause of sellout crowds. The Federal Theatre Director was most pleased by the professional quality of the production, which she considered "probably the most finished thing yet done on the project." Anxious that such efforts be repeated, she talked plays, produc-

[20] *Ibid.*, pp. 164-165. The Iowa Project was closed in December 1937, although it received full cooperation from both the state administrator and the director of Women's and Professional Projects. See Flanagan to George Keller, December 9, 1937; Flanagan to Jessica Hanthron, December 9, 1937, RG 69, FTP Records, NOC.

[21] Mrs. Flanagan agreed with the critics that the revue was a bit too loud, lavish, and, in places, vulgar but Hopkins enjoyed it thoroughly and wanted to move it to New York. *Arena*, p. 140.

[22] Lloyd Lewis, "A Labor Lincoln," the *Chicago Daily News*, May 17, 1937, p. 21. *Variety*'s Chicago critic was also full of praise. See *The Lonely Man*, *Variety*, May 26, 1937, p. 54. The public was equally enthusiastic, judging from the reaction of the Superintendent of the Winnetka Public Schools who urged his faculty to see the production. See Carleton Washburn to Faculty of Winnetka Public Schools, June 8, 1937, RG 69, FTP Records, NOTL.

152

tions, and production standards with Chicago officials until she finally boarded the Pullman for Seattle.[23]

Refreshed by the solitude and quiet of a long train trip, Hallie Flanagan arrived on the West Coast for a month-long tour which would be occasionally discouraging, frequently exhilarating, and consistently demanding. Seattle had both its unique and discouraging aspects. Bequeathed a number of skilled woodcarvers, Seattle's Federal Theatre boasted a series of carefully crafted, accurately scaled models of historic theatres made under the direction of the University of Washington. The Project itself, however, had never really recovered from its production of *Power*. Produced with the cooperation of the mayor and the municipal power company, the play earned $4,000 in five nights of performance—and the concern of the state administrator. Resolved to do noncontroversial things henceforth, directors had allowed the audience created by *Power* to slip away. The Project, which consisted of white, Negro, and vaudeville units, had been cut to the bone; its supervisors, directors, and technicians had been reduced from thirty-three to seven. Lacking both a theatre and the money to rent one, the federal company had leased a little, old, out-of-the-way movie house much in need of repair. The building was far from the homes of patrons on his invitation list, the director explained; consequently, audiences were small. When Hallie Flanagan suggested that there had to be people in Seattle—housewives, lumberjacks, farmers, and sailors—who would like to see Federal Theatre shows, she was told that it was better not to try to appeal to a class of people other than "the usual type of theatregoers," because an audience that "looks poor" was apt "to give the impression of being radical." Poor or not, Mrs. Flanagan replied, audiences and actors deserved an evening together. She was even more convinced after attending a rehearsal of *Androcles and the Lion*. Although the play needed designers and "hard, firm direction,"

[23] Flanagan to Philip Davis, October 28, 1937, Flanagan Papers.

Seattle's Negro unit had a production worth seeing. Hopeful that loans from regional headquarters in Los Angeles might be arranged, she paid her customary call at state WPA offices, only to learn that Washington officials, despite their hospitality, did not share the sympathetic interest displayed by Oregon's state administrator.[24]

Upon arriving in Portland, Mrs. Flanagan was joined by Ole Ness who had taken over as regional director during Gerwing's absence. The two were promptly rushed off to dinner by local officials, and then to what she privately considered a woefully bad rehearsal of *The Taming of the Shrew*. But these one-time vaudeville, stock, and circus people who had labored hard and excitedly with the works of the English bard in their bare, old hall soon redeemed themselves with *Flax*. Perhaps prompted by Hallie Flanagan's unceasing injunctions to work out new ways of using available talent and local themes, the Portland director, Mrs. Bess Whitcomb, had decided to try a musical Living Newspaper on the Oregon flax industry. Using choreography worked out at the Federal Theatre summer session and actors, directors, and designers brought up from California, the Oregon group produced *Flax*, and then went on to do a dance drama celebrating the building of the Bonneville Dam. Delighted with their accomplishments, Hallie Flanagan sent immediately for Yasha Frank of the Los Angeles Project, in hopes that this man who had used California vaudevillians to such advantage might work out something for their Portland counterparts. After looking at Oregon's talent, Frank promised to begin with a production of *Pinocchio*, complete with real acrobats in the circus scenes. With plans finally under way for children's plays, more regional dramas, and conventional plays using outside talent, Mrs. Flanagan bade good-bye to these old Oregon troupers confident that, if the Federal Theatre's varying talent could be used with equal

[24] Flanagan, Personal Notes on FTP, November 2, 1937, Flanagan Papers; Hallie Flanagan, "Work in Progress" [speech or press release], fall 1937, RG 69, FTP Records, NOGSF.

154

effectiveness elsewhere, this temporary institution might yet create a lasting place for itself.[25]

As the train rolled southward to San Francisco, Mrs. Flanagan recalled her first visit there, with a group of frightened, insecure actors huddled in the dingy, old hall that had housed the San Francisco Project. Since then things had changed in ways that weekly reports could only suggest. When the train pulled to a stop, the National Director, her deputy director, and her acting regional director were rushed to the flag-flying Alcazar Theatre. Moving along with the crowds which streamed past the box office and into the gold and red plush interior, the visitors were ushered to their seats by handsomely clad attendants. Although the play, *The Warrior's Husband*, was hardly her favorite, nothing could dampen Hallie Flanagan's enthusiasm for the thoroughly professional manner in which it was done. The next day—with its official conferences, visits to shops, laboratories, classes, and rehearsals—only confirmed her initial judgment. A rehearsal of Galsworthy's great classic, *Justice*, and a run-through of three marionette shows provided additional evidence of the actors' stability and professionalism. A long visit with Eugene O'Neill, who wanted to hear about the progress of the Federal Theatre's nationwide O'Neill cycle, was a fitting climax to an exciting, encouraging visit.[26]

Los Angeles, which housed the regional headquarters of the Federal Theatre as well as its second largest project, was further proof that out of this theatre could come thoroughly professional productions of new plays and classics. Ushered about by Ness and the indefatigable Miller, Hallie Flanagan discovered a theatrical plant which was adequate testimony to both the executive and the theatrical ability of the various men who had served her as regional directors. Its administrative "set-up"—efficient and tightly organized—was the "very best" anywhere. Smoothly

[25] Flanagan to Philip Davis, November 6, 1937, Flanagan Papers; Flanagan, "Work in Progress," RG 69; Flanagan, *Arena*, pp. 298-299.

[26] Flanagan to Philip Davis, November 9, 1937, November 13, 1937, Flanagan Papers.

run shops designed, staged, and built shows; printed posters, throw aways, and programs; and lent actors, directors, dancers, costumes, properties, and even sets to projects all along the west coast. And each operated with "clockwork" efficiency.[27]

Productions were no less impressive. *Ready! Aim! Fire!*, a musical satire on dictatorship, was the creation of two Project members who had worked out a revue suitable for former vaude-villians. Less sophisticated and subtle than a Broadway musical, the show was tremendously funny, "expertly done," and break-ing all box-office records. The dance group, answering the National Director's pleas for native material in *American Exo-dus*, Hallie Flanagan found to be one of the best anywhere. For *The Weavers*, the opening play in a new International Cycle, the only adjective was "magnificent." Here, too, were Shaw and O'Neill plays: *Caesar and Cleopatra* with its excellent score written by Project members; the Negro *Androcles and the Lion*; and *Emperor Jones*, a production of the marionette unit. Nativity plays celebrating Advent were being performed in Los Angeles churches. And in his Theatre for Youth, which boasted seventy thousand members, Yasha Frank delighted huge audiences with a repertoire of children's plays that included *Pinocchio, Hansel and Gretel, Alice in Wonderland, Rip Van Winkle,* and *Twelfth Night*. Produced with warmth, gaiety, and professional excel-lence, they brought praise from both the National Director and Walt Disney who predicted many more successes if present standards were maintained.[28]

Yet California, for all its successes, was no trouble-free the-atrical fairyland. Upon emerging from performances of *Hansel and Gretel* and *Pinocchio*, Mrs. Flanagan was abruptly stopped

[27] Flanagan, "Work in Progress," RG 69; Flanagan, *Arena*, p. 282. Mrs. Flanagan's judgment about the Los Angeles Project is borne out by people not connected with the Federal Theatre. See Paul Gerard Smith, "Back-stage of the Federal Theatre," *Robert Wagner's Script*, XXI (May 6, 1939), 16-17.

[28] Flanagan, Personal Notes on FTP, November 19, 1937; Flanagan, "Work in Progress," RG 69; Flanagan, *Arena*, pp. 281-283; Walt Disney to Yasha Frank, December 30, 1937, RG 69, FTP Records, NOTL.

by a delegation protesting against so-called Communist plays and the alleged immoral behavior of the players. When she finally managed to pin down these accusations, she explained that *The Weavers*, Gerhardt Hauptman's dramatization of the Silesian Weavers' strike of the 1840's, was a classic, and that the play in which a girl was unrolled from a carpet was Shaw's *Caesar and Cleopatra*. She was sure that the self-appointed censors would enjoy both. After ordering that these charges, like all such complaints, be investigated, Mrs. Flanagan dismissed the incident as only a small "cloud in the horizon." Neither delegations nor the never-ending telephone calls, telegrams, and letters complaining of "labor troubles in Hartford, censorship in Boston, script troubles in Jacksonville, troubles plain and fancy in New York" could overshadow her pride in the superb professional productions and administrative efficiency of the Los Angeles Project.[29]

Troubles in Washington, however, could not be so easily dismissed. In the midst of inspecting the small San Diego Project, Mrs. Flanagan received word to return immediately to Washington. There was no explanation—only a telegram bearing the message: OFFICE MOVING TO THE OURAY BUILDING. Uncertain about the import of this announcement, she hurried back to Los Angeles where, after a heartwarming send-off from twelve hundred Project workers, she and Miller boarded the train for Denver loaded down with violets, roses, and a "wooly dog tied to a big bouquet from the Children's Theatre," a gift for her own children. Her elation over the past achievements and future prospects of the Los Angeles Project soon gave way to fear that projects everywhere might be denied the opportunity to achieve professional standards. Mindful of the frustrations and disappointments of the previous season, she wondered if once again theatrical progress was to be interrupted. Perhaps developments at WPA headquarters pointed to the Federal Theatre's eventual demise rather than to its continued growth. She recalled only

[29] Flanagan, Personal Notes on FTP, November 19, 1937; Flanagan, *Arena*, pp. 284-285.

too clearly that "Washington," in spite of promises, had not yet raised Howard Miller's salary upon his promotion to deputy director. Miller was sought after by the German producer, Max Reinhardt, and she feared that he would be the next to go. To Philip Davis, always a source of support, she wrote: ". . . having lost Bill [Farnsworth], Houseman and Welles, I simply can't go on if they continue to refuse to back me in trying to hang on to the few good people I have." Miller did not leave, but Mrs. Flanagan found little else to assuage her fears when she at last returned to the bleak December greyness of the nation's capital.[30]

· II ·

The Arts Project had indeed been moved from the "decayed splendor" of the McLean Mansion to the "shabby respectability" of the Ouray Building. With its "small dull offices, dull tan walls, and dull brown woodwork," the building itself seemed to Hallie Flanagan somehow symbolic of a dispassionate, unimaginative bureaucracy which conspired to make her think "dull brown thoughts" and threatened to turn her Theatre into a dull, colorless, bureaucratic concern. No longer warmed by California's sun and successes, she battled with David Niles over censorship. But the very fact that the Federal Theatre's National Director and the head of the WPA's Labor and Information Service should do battle over *The Cradle Will Rock* rather than some new production seemed to her to reveal the bankruptcy of bureaucratic control. During the four months when she and Farnsworth administered the New York City Federal Theatre, they had reorganized and consolidated the Project in new headquarters, "opened seven reputable shows, three of which were really good, and fired two thousand people." In the four months since "Washington" had turned over the administration of the Project to Paul Edwards, Federal Theatre officials had been "unable to open shows, to solve . . . labor problems or even to demote, to say nothing of

---

[30] Flanagan, *Arena*, p. 285; Flanagan to Philip Davis, November 23, 1937, Flanagan Papers.

158

firing, a single person."[31] What Hallie Flanagan did not mention was that "Washington"—Aubrey Williams, Niles, and the other administrators responsible for the relief agency in Hopkins' absence—was deeply disturbed over more important problems. In December 1937, the future of the entire WPA hung in the balance.

Eight months before, Roosevelt had decided to cut spending. The nation seemed to be on the road to recovery and inflation, he believed, was a real danger. Accordingly, relief funds were reduced and WPA building projects were discontinued—at the same time that $2 billion was being collected in social security taxes.[32] With pump-priming stopped and some of the water drained out of the spout, the economy promptly began a downward slide. The President, however, did nothing. Persuaded by conservative advisors that business should be given a chance to try to stand alone, Roosevelt agreed to balance the budget and sit tight.[33] Economic indices did not: between August and December stock prices fell 30 to 40 per cent; the *New York Times* Business Index plummeted from 112.2, the year's high, to 85, reflecting the eradication of two years of industrial gains. In that same three-month period, millions of workers lost their jobs and, in New York City alone, applications for home relief more than doubled after having declined for nearly a year and a half.[34] That portion of the nation which Roosevelt had described over a year before as ill fed, ill clothed, and ill housed was now considerably greater than one-third. Yet a surge of radical discontent commensurate with their size and strength never materialized. The recession served instead to strengthen conservatives.[35]

[31] Flanagan, Personal Notes on FTP, December 2, 1937, Flanagan Papers.

[32] Leuchtenburg, *Franklin D. Roosevelt and the New Deal*, p. 244.

[33] James A. Farley, *Jim Farley's Story: The Roosevelt Years* (New York: McGraw-Hill, 1948), p. 101. Secretary of the Treasury, Henry Morgenthau, eager to see the budget balanced, was particularly influential in persuading the President to adopt this policy. See John Morton Blum, *From the Morgenthau Diaries: Years of Crisis, 1928-1938* (Boston: Houghton Mifflin Co., 1959), pp. 383-387.

[34] The *New York Times*, December 12, 1937, Sec. 4, p. 1; *ibid.*

[35] Leuchtenburg, *Franklin D. Roosevelt and the New Deal*, p. 254.

On Capitol Hill, Democratic members of a bipartisan anti-New Deal coalition were determined to gain control of the party in 1940 by defeating the President's legislative program, and they had pursued their strategy with considerable success. With only two weeks to go before the Christmas recess, a special session of Congress had failed to pass a single piece of "must" legislation requested by the President. Even those observers who attributed this inaction to "lethargy" rather than open revolt admitted that cleavages in both houses boded ill for the next session.[36] In the Senate, conservatives were secretly circulating a manifesto which called for a balanced budget, respect for state rights, and the usual conservative rallying points. Although a few were willing to sponsor the manifesto, many more were sympathetic to the National Association of Manufacturers' claim that the recession had been caused by uncertainty about the government's plans and labor troubles, not the least of which was a summer of sit-down strikes unchecked by the President.[37] Some congressmen also shared the conservatives' distrust of New Deal administrators, whom they suspected of promoting humanitarian programs as a means to power. Hopkins, in particular, was thought to be building a permanent army of relief workers in order to perpetuate a bureaucracy: Vice President John Nance Garner, leader of the conservative coalition, pointedly told the Relief Administrator that he did not like the implication in the description of relief workers as "clients."[38] And even the *New York Times*, dismayed by the unrestrained demonstrations of

[36] Turner Catledge, "F.D.R. Program Stalled in Special Session," the *New York Times*, December 12, 1937, Sec. 4, p. 6; Arthur Krock, "Congress Clears Way for Recovery March," the *New York Times*, December 26, 1937, Sec. 4, p. 3. New Dealers were even more worried. New York's Mayor Fiorello La Guardia frankly doubted that F.D.R. could name his successor, so great was conservative strength. Harold Ickes was only slightly less dubious. See Harold L. Ickes, *The Secret Diary of Harold L. Ickes: The Inside Struggle, 1936-1939*, II (New York: Simon and Schuster, 1954), 252, 260.

[37] Leuchtenburg, *Franklin D. Roosevelt and the New Deal*, p. 254.

[38] Bascom N. Timmons, *Garner of Texas: A Personal History* (New York: Harper and Bros., 1948), p. 220.

the Workers' Alliance, editorialized about WPA employees who acted as if they regarded their jobs as a vested right.[39]

Although Hopkins had never been a congressional favorite, heretofore he had enjoyed the President's full support. By December, however, the old Roosevelt "magic" seemed to be waning: the President had been repudiated in the Supreme Court fight, frustrated in his recent legislative attempts, and discredited by the recession. Perhaps more important, he persisted in his apparently genuine efforts to economize. The new budget for the fiscal year 1938-39 reportedly represented a reduction of $800 million under the current budget—a cut of one-half billion dollars in relief funds alone.[40]

Relief officials, already engaged in a policy of "rigid retrenchment," were ill equipped to meet this latest crisis. In order to keep within their present budget, they had already abandoned long-term construction projects in favor of "light work" which could be taken over and completed by local authorities or, if necessary, halted altogether. At the President's behest, they had also launched a drive the previous July to increase local contributions—and with good results: the portion of the total cost borne by local sponsors had risen from 5 per cent to 28 per cent by the end of October. But no amount of economizing could compensate for a proposed one-half billion dollar cut in funds. Unless the rising number of unemployed forced the President to scrap his budget-balancing plans, the WPA was on its way out. At best, WPA officials could expect a gradual curtailment of federal work-relief in favor of state programs; at worst, the substitution of cash relief on the local level. In the meantime, there was nothing to do but continue belt-tightening measures, even if state guidebooks, months in preparation, never reached the press, or struggling theatres, on the verge of winning a place for them-

[39] The *New York Times*, October 27, 1937, p. 24.

[40] Delbert Clark, "Budget Debate Revived: To Balance or Not To?," the *New York Times*, December 12, 1937, Sec. 4, p. 7; Delbert Clark, "Future of Whole WPA is Now in Balance," *ibid.*, December 19, 1937, Sec. 4, p. 6.

selves in their communities, were denied the physical and human resources necessary for good productions.[41]

In New York City's much beleaguered Theatre Project, this problem had already arisen: the particular issue was one of reducing the salaries of supervisory personnel. If the reductions were made, Hallie Flanagan realized only too clearly, capable supervisors would become even fewer and professional standards, lower rather than higher. If they were not made, Paul Edwards argued, Congress would close the Arts Projects because of their higher "man-month" cost. On the other hand, he predicted, salary cuts would result in the usual strikes and demonstrations. Hopkins himself resolved the argument, but he did not dispel Hallie Flanagan's concern for the future of the theatre.[42]

During a brief stopover in Washington, the WPA chieftain proposed that, instead of cutting salaries, New York officials reduce the number of people in higher brackets whenever feasible, move to cheaper headquarters, and economize in every possible way. Nevertheless, there was little rejoicing among those gathered in Ellen Woodward's office to discuss this latest economy measure, for Hopkins also sent word that the President had just ordered an additional three hundred and fifty thousand people put on the payroll. While WPA officials complained that more workers could not possibly be added without further funds, the Federal Theatre Director was summoned to Hopkins' office. Because she had not seen the Relief Administrator since the death of his wife two months before, Hallie Flanagan was shocked at the "haggard" appearance of the always lanky Iowan who turned from the window to greet her. Frightened about his illness and anxious to unburden himself, Hopkins confessed that he was leaving that night for the Mayo Brothers Clinic to have "some damn thing" which he guessed was cancer cut out. Admitting that this was a "devil of a time" to have to go, he explained that the news of his departure would appear in the papers in a

41 *Ibid.*
42 Flanagan, Personal Notes on FTP, December 9, 1937, Flanagan Papers.

162

few hours. "Anyway," he added, "I sent for you to say good-bye, and to say I am sorry about the mistake of not seeing you oftener. You have done a big job—nobody knows how big—and I'm grateful. I wanted you to know it and if you can possibly stand it, I want you to keep on during the hard days coming. We mustn't lose what ground we've gained." Deeply disturbed about both Hopkins and the Project, Hallie Flanagan soon discovered that the Relief Administrator's prediction of hard days ahead was well founded.[43]

The bureaucratic pressure which she had sensed upon her return to Washington as something vague, yet ominously impending, began in 1938 to assume a definite, almost characteristic, form. Hoping to relieve the depressing dullness of her new quarters, Mrs. Flanagan asked for rugs and venetian blinds made on WPA projects. Her request was refused. Announcements of plays, which had formerly appeared under the name of the National Director of the Federal Theatre, suddenly began coming out in the name of WPA administrators. Then, on January 12, Ellen Woodward announced that all the Arts Projects in California were being turned over to Lieutenant Colonel Donald H. Connolly, state WPA administrator. By way of explaining the change, Mrs. Woodward alluded to charges of Communism and immorality in the California projects. Although the WPA had investigated the charges and found them invalid, the decision was final. She apparently made no mention of economy as a factor in the decision, nor did *Variety*, which also spoke of a "general housecleaning."[44]

Hallie Flanagan proceeded to adjust to the new order. In a firm yet thoroughly gracious letter to Connolly, she assured him of her full cooperation. Explaining the operation of the California Federal Theatre in some detail, she took great care to describe to the Colonel the manner in which plays were chosen; the excel-

[43] *Ibid.* Hopkins' appearance and state of mind are corroborated by Ickes. See *Diary*, II, 240, 260. Those close to Hopkins were aware that his wife's death had been a severe blow to him.

[44] *Variety*, January 12, 1938, p. 54; Flanagan, *Arena*, pp. 245-286.

lent critical reputation which the Project had acquired; and the pride with which Hopkins regarded the extensive program then underway. With only a reminder that Hopkins entrusted to her "all decisions as to policy and program," she pledged her full support to the state administrator, promised to rely on him for administrative matters, and enclosed letters to her regional and state directors urging them to do the same. Two weeks elapsed during which Connolly did not bother to reply.[45]

In the meantime, the distraught California directors, George Gerwing and Ole Ness, received warnings that all Arts Projects appointees who valued their jobs would henceforth communicate to the Washington office only through Colonel Connolly. All incoming letters from national directors were opened. Gilmor Brown, who had been associated with the Project since its inception, was suddenly dismissed. All scripts were called in. The productions of *Stevedore* and Elmer Rice's anti-Fascist drama, *Judgment Day*, were canceled.[46]

Hallie Flanagan's reaction was swift when she learned from Brown that Connolly was violating every understanding which Mrs. Woodward had promised would be observed. She immediately reported the entire situation to the former's assistant, Lawrence Morris, who assured her of his concern, but explained that he could do nothing without the authorization of Mrs. Woodward, who could not be reached because of illness.[47] Mrs. Flanagan was forced to stand by while the California press denounced censorship of Federal Theatre productions, and Actors' Equity, Screen Actors' Guild, the Arts Union Conference, the American Civil Liberties Union, and the National Council on Freedom from Censorship clamored for action.[48] When she heard both the Federal Theatre and its National Director ridiculed in a New York production (probably the ILGWU's *Pins and Needles*) as being too timid to produce anything controversial,

[45] Flanagan to Connolly, January 28, 1938, RG 69, FTP Records, NOC. The Colonel never replied according to Mrs. Flanagan. See *Arena*, p. 286.
[46] Flanagan to Hopkins, January 28, 1938, RG 69, FTP Records, NOC.
[47] *Ibid.*   [48] *Variety*, February 2, 1938, p. 55.

her sorely taxed patience evaporated. She decided to ignore bureaucratic procedure and write to Hopkins himself. Describing for the Relief Administrator the incident, which had been promptly picked up by *The Washington Post*, she pointed out that their critics objected to two things: the censorship of *The Cradle Will Rock*; and the censorship of *Judgment Day*. Of the first, she wrote:

> This I consider a tragic mistake. . . . I heard Marc Blitzstein play this score long before anybody knew who Marc Blitzstein was. I immediately felt it was the work of genius and secured it for the Project. We spent seven months and thousands of dollars on it and sold 25,000 seats in advance. Then, in spite of my protests, the whole thing was stopped.
>
> I pointed out that if it was stopped we would lose Houseman and Welles, my two most valuable assets, and that we would also lose *Julius Caesar* which was to be the opening gun of this year's program, and that we would also lose the *Duchess of Malfi* and other plays. In spite of that, the censorship went through.

Obviously it was too late for the Federal Theatre to reap the praise currently being heaped upon the new Mercury Theatre's production of *The Cradle* and *Julius Caesar*;[49] but it was not too late, she insisted, to stop the "censorship and intimidation" going on in California. After recounting Connolly's actions as well as her own initial efforts at cooperation, she made her final plea:

> Harry, I know you have been ill and I would not come to you except that I have reported all of this to Mr. Morris, and I presume through Mr. Morris to Mrs. Woodward, on Monday of this week. . . .
>
> Only you are powerful enough to end this sort of petty dictatorship of the arts. It is my honest belief that the Four

[49] The Mercury Theatre, founded by Orson Welles and John Houseman after leaving the Project, produced in its highly successful first season several shows originally slated for the Federal Theatre unit they had directed.

Arts Projects should be removed from Colonel Connolly and restored as an independent unit. . . . If this action is too drastic I believe that the only salvation of the arts, unless you want them to degenerate into hammy plays in schools, is to notify Colonel Connolly that the National Directors of the Federal Arts have always had the following rights:

1. to allocate funds
2. to hire and dismiss artistic personnel
3. to choose plays and methods of production
4. to communicate freely with their own appointees.

Harry, you know my devotion to you personally and you know that my very life is bound up with this project. I believe in you, in the project, and in the magnificent future of both. Please help me in carrying out your own order to create a "free, adult American theatre."

Apparently hesitant about sending so personal and impassioned an appeal, she left the letter unsealed, revising it slightly the following day. But even if subsequently mailed, it had no immediate effect.[50]

Not until they were prodded by a congressional hearing did WPA officials take action. Fearful of how Arts Projects directors might reply to questions about problems in California, David Niles had the four national directors assembled in Mrs. Woodward's office on February 8, the day that they were to testify before the Patents Committee. After announcing that their briefs had been approved, Niles delivered a long speech on "loyalty, cooperation, and standing together." In the event that they were

[50] Flanagan to Hopkins, January 28, 1938, RG 69, FTP Records, NOC. At the top of this letter the words "not sent" are penciled. A slightly different version of the letter—but not of the events transpiring in California—was written the following day and presumably mailed. See Flanagan to Hopkins, January 29, 1938, RG 69, FTP Records, NOC. Hopkins was also bombarded by telegrams from Burgess Meredith and Henry Fonda on behalf of Equity and the National Council of Freedom from Censorship. F.D.R. and Aubrey Williams received wires from the Arts Union Conference in New York City. See *Variety*, February 2, 1939, p. 55.

questioned by the Committee, "minor" irritations must be forgotten and all must speak for the good of the WPA, he counseled. When asked directly how she would reply to possible questions about the California incident, Mrs. Flanagan answered that she would say there was censorship of *Judgment Day*. While Niles insisted to unconvinced Arts directors that it was not censorship but "selection," and that the public must not learn of this "family difficulty," Ellen Woodward withdrew to another office to make a telephone call. Upon her return, she announced that she and Connolly had arrived at a complete understanding: national directors would be given artistic control of their Project and allowed to correspond freely with their own directors; and *Judgment Day* has been merely "postponed." It was then time to go before the Patents Committee.[51]

The Committee had been conducting hearings on a bill which would create a permanent Department of Science, Art, and Literature and a national theatre as well. Thus the four Arts directors and Ellen Woodward had been summoned for testimony, along with leading musicians, artists, and theatre people. Although the Federal Theatre won warm praise from the latter, its problems did not go unmentioned. Concerned as to whether artistic freedom could be maintained under WPA control, Burgess Meredith, acting president of Actors' Equity and the new chairman of the Federal Theatre Advisory Committee, denounced the "tendency in WPA administration at the present time to place people in charge of various theatre projects who have little sympathy with them." Morris Watson, the outspoken national vice president of the American Newspaper Guild and the former managing producer of the Living Newspaper, vigorously protested the "censorship and suppression" of plays in California by "regular Army officers who have been placed in charge of the WPA four arts program. . . ." Moreover, he continued, it was an "open scandal" in New York that the Project had been permitted to do only one major play in more than six months,

[51] Flanagan, *Arena*, pp. 287-288.

compared with the "series of hits" produced previously when "persons interested and sympathetic were in charge." when subsequently questioned about these charges, Ellen Woodward explained to the Committee that state administration was more economical because the same finance, employment, and procurement service could be used for the Arts Project, thereby reducing the number of clerical persons employed. Although Colonel Connolly did have administrative control of the Project, he was not responsible for technical supervision, she hastened to add. In the course of her own report about the origin of the Theatre Project and its varied activities, Mrs. Flanagan explained that *Judgment Day* had been postponed. "Despite local problems of censorship, this Federal Theatre has probably been one of the freest theatres ever subsidized by a government in the history of the world," she loyally declared.[52]

Outside the committee room "local problems of censorship" were not so easily minimized. In spite of Ellen Woodward's conversation with Connolly, and Aubrey Williams' subsequent assurances that Hopkins wanted artistic control completely restored to the national directors of the Arts Project, the California situation remained unchanged. One week after appearing before the Patents Committee, Hallie Flanagan learned from Howard Miller, now in California, that the state administrator still had complete control of communication, plays, and personnel. All correspondence was channeled through Connolly's office, and much of it was never delivered to the theatre people for whom it was intended. George Gerwing was still turning over mail sent to his home because he feared that one false step would mean dismissal. With Gerwing out of the way, Connolly, who was already hiring conductors for the Music Project, would be only too happy to put in his own man as regional director of the West Coast Theatre, Miller warned. Mrs. Flanagan tried to reassure her deputy director with the reminder that Aubrey Williams had

---

[52] Hearings Before the House Committee on Patents on H. J. Res. 29, *Department of Science, Art, and Literature*, 75th Cong., 3rd Sess. (1938), pp. 1 *passim* 110.

promised to get in touch with Connolly when the latter returned to Los Angeles the following day. Tomorrow was none too soon for Hallie Flanagan, who could recall a conversation with the Colonel two years before when he had expounded on military discipline and his conception of a good theatre project—"anything that keeps out of the papers."[53]

In New York, where the Project had been moved from the Chanin Building for reasons of economy, these local problems assumed a far more subtle guise. Plays were not censored; they simply were not being produced. Washington, observed Brooks Atkinson in the *New York Times*, was probably pleased when this Project, whose propensity for "treading on political toes" endangered the whole WPA, was as "relatively inactive" as it was now under the administration of Paul Edwards and George Kondolf.[54] There was, however, one major exception to this inactivity—*One-Third of a Nation*.

One-Third of a Nation, described as "the most sensational story on the New York stage at the moment," was the Living Newspaper polished to a new professional brilliance.[55] A dramatic indictment of the dirt, disease, and human misery of metropolitan slums, it was a forceful tribute to Hallie Flanagan's conviction that the theatre could quicken, start, and make things change, at a time when nine million unemployed Americans proved that America needed changing. Hopkins, having seen for himself what the theatre could do with an earlier Living Newspaper, *Power*, had encouraged Mrs. Flanagan to go ahead

[53] Telephone Conversation, Flanagan and Miller, February 16, 1938, RG 69, FTP Records, NOGSF. When Mrs. Flanagan had gone to California in 1935 at the time the Project was being set up, she and Connolly had met and discussed the Theatre as indicated above. The Colonel, loath to have any part of a project over which he did not have complete control, had told her that her regional director could be completely responsible for administrative as well as artistic matters. See *Arena*, p. 274.

[54] Brooks Atkinson, "Perpetuating the Federal Theatre," the *New York Times*, February 20, 1938, Sec. 11, p. 1.

[55] Brooks Atkinson, "Saga of the Slums," the *New York Times*, January 30, 1938, Sec. 10, p. 1.

169

with a play on housing.[56] Arthur Arent, avoiding the obvious bias that had marred several previous Living Newspapers, had written a trenchant exposé of tenement life, taking as his title Roosevelt's dramatic words at the second inaugural: "I see one-third of a nation ill-housed, ill-clad, ill-nourished. It is not in despair that I paint you that picture. I paint it for you in hope—because the Nation, seeing and understanding the injustice in it proposes to paint it out."[57] Produced first at Vassar College as the culminating work on the Federal Theatre's summer session, the history of New York housing had been portrayed in a variety of acting styles set against an expressionistic background of large objects suspended in space—a huge garbage can, a rickety iron bed, a wobbly staircase, and a broken commode seat. Delighted with the premier production, the New York Housing Commissioner, Langdon Post, had announced that the play could "do more to convert people" than all the speeches he had given in the past three years. Eleanor Roosevelt had been no less enthusiastic, predicting that the play would be a great contribution to the education of America.[58]

When *One-Third of a Nation* opened in New York in January 1938, the set had been transformed by its designer, the brilliant young Howard Bay, into a scrupulously realistic cross section of a four-story tenement complete with furniture and other dismal objects which Bay had rescued from demolition crews about the city.[59] But whether beat-up garbage cans were suspended in

[56] Flanagan, *Arena*, p. 185.

[57] The Second Inaugural Address. "I See One-Third of a Nation Ill-Housed, Ill-Clad, Ill-Nourished," January 20, 1937. *The Public Papers and Addresses of Franklin D. Roosevelt*, comp. Samuel I. Rosenman (New York: Macmillan, 1941), vi: *The Constitution Prevails* (1937), p. 5.

[58] Flanagan, *Arena*, pp. 212, 221-222. Only Act i was done at Vassar.

[59] The freedom and time to go poking about the city in search of debris was a luxury afforded only by the Federal Theatre and one much appreciated by young designers like Howard Bay. The set for *One-Third of a Nation*, incidentally, won Bay the job as set designer for Lillian Hellman's *Little Foxes*, starring Tallulah Bankhead. Interview with Howard Bay, November 16, 1961.

space or jammed into hallways, the impact was the same. Praising Lem Ward's direction and Bay's set, from which nothing was missing but "the smells," Burns Mantle of the *New York Daily News* lamented only that the play offered no real solution to housing problems save "the hope-inspired belief that the Wagner-Steagall Bill might be a beginning." If the play offered no solution, wrote John Anderson of the Hearst-owned *Journal and American*, it at least explained "brilliantly" and vividly why one-third of a nation was ill housed. "A vivid, coherent report, often deeply moving, and almost always forceful," declared Richard Lockridge in the *Sun*. "A swiftly paced, exciting pageant," declared the *Daily Mirror*'s critic, Robert Coleman. An "important piece of work . . . done with force, sincerity, and thought," said Sidney Whipple in the *World-Telegram*. "Seeing *One-Third of a Nation*," concluded John Mason Brown in the *New York Post*, was "every good citizen's duty," for "the facts upon which it is based are truths that can be verified at first-hand by walking no more than three blocks in any direction up and down this city." As Walter Winchell put it, the New York critics had "sprayed it with their best Sunday adjectives." Reviewers in such periodicals as *Theatre Arts Monthly, The Catholic World, The Commonweal, The Nation, The New Yorker, Life, Time,* and *The Literary Digest*, were quick to agree. Few were more perceptive in their analysis than Brooks Atkinson. Praising the "trenchantly acted scenes," the "vital functional stage setting" of this "colossal," the *New York Times'* critic described *One-Third of a Nation* as a "rabble rouser of uncommon eloquence . . . aggressively on the side of the New Deal . . . a painfully documented simplification of history and facts, and to that extent . . . a superb job of writing and staging." What it says is "sensational" because "no published report can be one-tenth so vivid and no tour of tenements one-fourth so comprehensive." It was, he concluded, "a caustic and vibrant piece of theatrical muckraking."[60]

[60] Burns Mantle, *"One-Third of a Nation* Reveals Sad Failure of

171

Muckraking, when carried on by what Atkinson considered to be "one of the most powerful mediums of expression in the country," was bound to have repercussions, particularly when a production supported by federal relief funds included in its cast of characters members of the United States Senate. The brief scene portraying the Senate debate over the Wagner-Steagall Housing Bill had occasioned no comments from the critics. On the contrary, the *Herald Tribune*'s Richard Watts had remarked on the Federal Theatre's obvious effort to be fair—even to slum lords who were tempting targets for vilification.[61] But word was soon relayed to Capitol Hill that Senators Harry Byrd, Millard Tydings, and Charles O. Andrews—all Southern Democrats who had expressed reservations about the bill—had been held

Housing Laws," *New York Daily News*, January 18, 1938, p. 43; John Anderson, "*One-Third of a Nation* Vividly Presented," *New York Journal and American*, January 18, 1938, p. 12; Richard Lockridge, "The Housing Problem is Considered by the Federal Theatre at the Adelphi," the *New York Sun*, January 18, 1938, p. 14; Robert Coleman, "*One-Third of a Nation* Offered at the Adelphi," *New York Daily Mirror*, January 19, 1938, p. 25; Sidney Whipple, "Problems of Slums Presented in Play," *New York World Telegram*, January 18, 1938, p. 16; John Mason Brown, "*One-Third of a Nation* at the Federal Theatre," *New York Post*, January 18, 1938, p. 6; Edith J. R. Isaacs, "Who Killed Cock Robin?—Broadway in Review," *Theatre Arts Monthly*, XXII (March 1938), 173-174. Euphemia Van Rensselaer Wyatt, "The Drama: *One-Third of a Nation*," *The Catholic World*, CXLVI (March 1938), 728-729; Granville Vernon, "The Theatre: *One-Third of a Nation*," *The Commonweal*, XXVII (February 4, 1938), 414; Joseph Wood Krutch, "The Living Newspaper," *The Nation*, CLXVI (January 29, 1938), 137-138; Otis Ferguson, "You've Got to Have a Place to Live," *The New Republic*, LXXXXIV (February 16, 1938), 46; Robert Benchley, "No Fights This Time," *The New Yorker*, XIII (January 29, 1938), 23; "The Federal Theatre Makes an Exciting Play of the Housing Problem," *Life*, IV (February 14, 1938), 24. ". . . 'one-third of a nation,'" *Time*, XXXI (January 31, 1938), 40. "WPA's New Show . . . one-third of a nation . . . ," *The Literary Digest*, CXXV (February 12, 1938), 21-22; Brooks Atkinson, "Living Newspaper of the Federal Theatre Reports the Housing Situation," the *New York Times*, January 18, 1938, p. 27; "Saga of the Slums," the *New York Times*, January 30, 1938, Sec. 10, p. 1.

[61] Richard Watts, "Housing Problem," *New York Herald Tribune*, January 18, 1938, p. 14.

up to "opprobrium." As the *Herald Tribune* pointed out in a front-page story, the senators did not claim they had actually been misquoted—their speeches had come right out of the *Congressional Record*—but they did claim that their "appearances," coming after scenes portraying the evils and miseries of slum life, were fitted in so as to make them villains by implication.[62] And they soon made their indignation felt at WPA headquarters.

Florida's Senator Charles O. Andrews promptly enclosed the *Herald Tribune* article in a letter to Hopkins and explained that he had, in fact, voted for the slum clearance bill as well as all

[62] *Ibid.*, February 7, 1938, p. 1. The *Herald Tribune* pointed out that the Senate debate had not been quoted in its entirety and that at one point in the script two separate sentences uttered by Byrd had been omitted and the preceding sentence joined with the one following. The changes had indeed been made but the meaning was not appreciably changed. The problem, of course, arises from the use of such material in a dramatic production. Obviously the impact of the following interchange becomes considerably greater in the context of a Living Newspaper on slums than in the comfort of the Senate chamber:

ANDREWS: Mr. President, I should like to ask the Senator from New York where the people who live in the slums come from.

WAGNER: A great many of them have been here a long time. . . . What does the Senator mean by where do they come from? Whether they come from some other country?

ANDREWS: I think we ought not to offer an inducement to people to come in from our country or foreign countries or anywhere else and take advantage of our government in supplying them with homes. For instance, if we examine the birth records in New York we find that most of the people there in the slums were not born in New York, but the bright lights have attracted them from everywhere, and that is one reason why there are so many millions in New York without homes. . . . If they could be induced to stay on the farms or in the foreign country whence they come there would not be any slums.

Had Arent wished to caricature the Senate he could easily have chosen the speech of other senators opposing the bill. For example, Senator Walter F. George of Georgia or Senator Robert Reynolds of North Carolina who declared ". . . if $700,000,000 of the people's money is to be expended, I want North Carolina—God bless her!—to have her part, although she does not need it particularly." See *Cong. Rec.*, 75th Cong., 1st Sess. (1937), pp. 7,977-7,978 (Andrews), p. 8,202 (Reynolds).

WPA appropriation bills. "Who is responsible for this play," he demanded, "and what action, if any, has been taken by your department to have these particular scenes eliminated from it?" The senator also asked that he be sent the names, addresses, and salaries paid each actor, actress, writer, and producer associated with the play, as well as an estimate of the total weekly salaries of all others associated with it.[63] A request for even more detailed financial information followed from Virginia's economy-minded Harry Byrd, who was also a member of the Senate Committee on Investigation of Executive Agencies of the Government.[64] By mid-February, a fellow Southerner and Democrat, Josiah W. Bailey of North Carolina, had seen to it that the entire Senate understood that "one-third of a nation" was not just a phrase from a presidential speech, but a play put on by the WPA in which his friend, Mr. Wagner, was the "hero," his other friend, Mr. Byrd, "the villain," and the senior senator from Florida, Mr. Andrews, a "sort of supernumerary."

Beginning with the play's bibliography, Bailey took one look at its length and remarked to his fellow senators that he imagined that the author was getting paid by the hour for reading all "this stuff," and that he should certainly "hate to have done it." Turning next to the play itself, Bailey regaled his colleagues with portions of the script interspersed with his own comments. Stage directions placing Idaho's distinguished Republican lawmaker, William S. Borah, "left of center" prompted the North Carolina Democrat to remark: "that is a new description of Senator Borah, but I judge it is right," whereupon his audience burst out laughing. After reading back into the *Congressional Record* portions of the debate on the housing bill, Bailey digressed for a moment on a list of National Service Bureau publications. Noting that the Bureau published lists of recommended anti-war plays, marionette plays, Catholic plays, and Jewish plays, the good senator from North Carolina declared: "I want them to have some Baptist, Methodist, Seven Day Ad-

---

[63] Andrews to Hopkins, February 10, 1938, RG 69, FTP Records, NOGSF.
[64] Byrd to Hopkins, February 10, 1938, RG 69, GSS-211.2.

ventist, and Mormon plays. We all pay taxes. I do not see why we cannot be put on the stage." Claiming that he was intrigued by the prospect of his fellow senators being "actors on the stage forever," Bailey waxed eloquent over the "immortality" that WPA playwrights could confer on the Senate. "Why," he proclaimed, "the play . . . will be reproduced longer than *Hamlet*, and people will be talking about the Senator from New York instead of the Prince of Denmark." Expanding on the possibilities before them, Bailey continued:

> When most of us die, we are forgotten . . . but with the National Service Theatre [*sic*] we may rest assured that down yonder at the WPA there are some playwrights who are putting us down in books, and that we may become a part of the permanent literature of the ages.
>
> Men will walk the stage a thousand, two thousand, three thousand years from now, representing us in our proper persons and our dignity. It is the first time, I think, that the Senate ever won immortality, and the first time Senators ever had a chance to do it. So I recommend this as a very worthy thing, and also present it to the Senate as an illustration of what is going on in this Government by way of taking money from the taxpayers in the name of helpless people, and then employing it in setting people down to read newspapers and books, and then write a play like that.
>
> Who ever thought of the Federal Government getting into anything like that? When Senators appeal to me to appropriate money in the name of the helpless and suffering millions, it reaches my heart . . . [but when] I see what is being done, I raise a very serious question about it.[65]

Whatever her private feelings about this impromptu burlesque, Hallie Flanagan immediately began some political fence-mend-

[65] *Cong. Rec.*, 75th Cong., 3rd Sess. (1938), pp. 2,304 *passim* 2,308. The *Herald Tribune* reported the incident under the headlines "*Third of a Nation* Gets Laugh in Senate; Bailey Acts out WPA Play, With Gestures as Senators Snicker." See the *Herald Tribune*, February 23, 1938, p. 13.

ing, no doubt with the encouragement of WPA officials who saw behind this senatorial "hamming" a clear indication that relief, not theatre, was the intention of those who held the nation's purse strings. A statement explaining that Senator Andrews had voted for the Wagner-Steagall Bill, despite his position during debate, was quickly inserted into the script of *One-Third*.[66] After trying unsuccessfully to get an interview with Andrews himself, Mrs. Flanagan wrote to the senator expressing her regrets that unfavorable reports of the play had reached him. Explaining that she had seen *One-Third of a Nation* three times and that, on no occasion had there been the "slightest evidence of any satire in the portrayal of any member of Congress," she urged the senator to attend the play as a guest of the Federal Theatre—an invitation previously extended to the members of the House Patents Committee.[67] But, unlike the Prince of Denmark to whom Bailey so eloquently referred, Hallie Flanagan had not managed to lay to rest the ghost of congressional criticism.

On February 27, when Aubrey Williams appeared before the Senate Appropriations Committee considering supplementary funds for work relief, Senator Richard R. Russell announced that he wanted "a little information" about the Theatre Project. Did plays originate with the states or were they selected in Washington? Did they charge admission for that play about the senators? Was it true that this particular play would become part of the World's Fair exhibit in New York? The Relief Administrator explained that he had indeed looked into *One-Third of a Nation*; but he did not explain what the Living Newspaper production was about, why, or in what context members of the Senate were included in the cast of characters. He did say, however, that the Federal Theatre Director insisted there was nothing in the play that the senators involved could object to. As

[66] Memorandum, Flanagan to Ellen Woodward and Lawrence Morris, March 5, 1938, RG 69, FTP Records, NOC.

[67] Flanagan to Andrews, March 7, 1938, RG 69, FTP Records, NOGSF; Flanagan to William I. Sirovich, February 10, 1938, RG 69, FTP Records, GSS-211.2.

for his own position, Williams held that "if a man feels he is ridiculed, that's the important thing. . . ." But the Georgia senator, explaining that he was "not at all sensitive," was after something more important. Some "very dangerous precedent[s]" were being set, he argued, when public figures were "exalted" or "minimize[d]" with funds from the public Treasury. Senators Townsend and Byrnes agreed.[68] When taxpayers' money was involved, argued Townsend, plays should be "very carefully censored" so as not to hold anyone up to ridicule.[69]

Confident in her own knowledge that members of the Senate were not being ridiculed in *One-Third of a Nation*, Hallie Flanagan was not overtly troubled about senators who *felt* they were. Freed from the task of selling an already controversial program to Congress, she could consider the play the artistic and social triumph that it was; the criticism against it, a tribute to the power of the theatre as reformer. The Federal Theatre, she still believed, would win the support—both present and permanent—of the American people by giving them professionally produced plays relevant to the world in which they lived—a world in which one-third of the richest nation was ill housed. To those who claimed that such plays gave them apoplexy, she would only reply: "Giving apoplexy to people who consider it radical for a government-sponsored theatre to produce plays on subjects vitally concerning the governed is one function of the theatre."[70]

She also realized that an equally important function of the Federal Theatre was to provide plays, whether they be Living Newspapers or traveling circuses, to those outside two or three large metropolitan areas.

[68] John G. Townsend, Jr. (Republican, Delaware); James F. Byrnes (Democrat, South Carolina).

[69] Hearings before the Senate Committee on Appropriations on H. J. Res. 596. *Supplemental Appropriation: Relief and Work Relief, Fiscal Year 1938*. 75th Cong., 3rd Sess. (1938), pp. 43-46.

[70] Hallie Flanagan, "Theatre and Geography," *American Magazine of Art*, xxxx (August 1938), 464.

· III ·

The plan submitted to Harry Hopkins two years earlier had called for a regionally centered national theatre which would win the support of the people because it would become an integral part of community life. The Project which emerged, however, was not the theatre that its planners intended. At Hopkins' urging, Hallie Flanagan took steps to recapture part of that regional aspect: touring companies were sent out of New York City and Los Angeles; directors, designers, and actors were lent to Detroit, Atlanta, and Portland. But the obstacles, particularly in the first years, had seemed almost overwhelming. Transfers, whether for touring groups or actors on loan, had to be arranged through the various state offices of the WPA—a procedure which officials from the Treasury Department, the WPA finance division, and the New York Project's business office insisted was "extremely dangerous business."[71] Detailed itineraries had to be worked out for touring companies, transportation arranged between station and theatre, and railroad tickets purchased in advance. Added to the expense of transportation and lodging, property bills, electrical bills, and theatre rentals made the cost of touring double that of regular operation.[72] With urging from Roosevelt down through Hopkins and Hallie Flanagan, local sponsoring groups were encouraged to help with touring costs.[73] But to persuade the businessmen's

[71] Memorandum, Flanagan to Ellen Woodward, January 14, 1937, RG 69, GSS-211.2.

[72] Flanagan to Francis Bosworth, May 12, 1936, RG 69, FTP Records, NOGSF.

[73] Hopkins constantly prodded Mrs. Flanagan about touring. In a characteristic expression of his own administrative methods, he suggested that if the Federal Theatre's financial staff could not figure out how to move people, they should be fired and men found who could. (Memorandum, Flanagan to Ellen Woodward, January 14, 1937, RG 69, GSS-211.2; William Stahl to Flanagan, June 18, 1937, RG 69, FTP Records, NOGSF.). Roosevelt was equally insistent and talked to Mrs. Woodward about encouraging touring and forming sponsoring committees to help with expenses. See Lawrence Morris to—— Mayforth, August 2, 1937, RG 69, GSS-210.13.

clubs and civic organizations of Burlington, Iowa to put up two hundred dollars for a touring production of O'Neill's *Ah, Wilderness* was no easy task. It was particularly difficult if these gentlemen, most of them lifelong Republicans, had read in the *Des Moines Register* or *The Saturday Evening Post* that the Federal Theatre was a mouthpiece of the administration or, worse still, of the Communist Party.[74] Yet, as Hopkins and Hallie Flanagan well knew, these were the very people who needed to be convinced for, as each project of dubious professional quality and achievement was shut down, state after state was left virtually untouched by Federal Theatre productions.

By February 1938, the Relief Administrator was clearly more concerned about whether touring companies were reaching into the smaller towns of the South and Midwest than whether Living Newspapers were "propagandizing" New Yorkers. When questioned about the Project during his long convalescence at Joseph P. Kennedy's Florida home, he told reporters that he considered the Federal Theatre a highly desirable enterprise. One mistake, however, was that, until now, the Project had been too highly concentrated in a few large cities. Hallie Flanagan agreed. Henceforth, she told New England directors, the Federal Theatre had to extend a bold, imaginative program into new areas and build up greater public support.[75]

In many parts of the country the two tasks were interdependent if not mutually inclusive. The Federal Theatre could strengthen support in communities where it had small projects only if the projects themselves were strengthened. Cut to the quick in the previous quota reductions, most needed a dozen qualified people, both actors and technicians. Reminding Mrs. Woodward's assistant, Lawrence Morris, of Hopkins' most recent statement about decentralization, the Federal Theatre Director suggested that any new increase in quota might consist

[74] Flanagan, *Arena*, p. 165.

[75] Heywood Broun, "It Seems to Me," *New York World Telegram*, February 17, 1938, p. 21; Hallie Flanagan, Notes for Address to New England Directors, March 3, 1938, RG 69, FTP Records, NOGSF.

of people hired in New York, Chicago, and Los Angeles with the understanding they would go to smaller communities.[76] If theatres and sponsors were available, an entire company might be set up in cities which had previously lacked sufficient local talent to form a Federal Theatre Project. By March, with the recession already in its seventh month, WPA officials felt confident enough of an increase in relief funds to talk about sending new companies to such cities as Minneapolis and St. Paul, Baltimore, Richmond, and Charleston; lending actors and technicians to projects in New Orleans, Tampa, Miami, Jacksonville, Atlanta, Newark, Hartford, Detroit, Seattle, and Portland —provided, of course, local authorities would cooperate.[77]

To build strong companies, however important, was not enough. Even if loans were made, the building process was a slow one involving theatres in only eight states. In the meantime, the Federal Theatre had to tour—and not just on the CCC circuit in New England or South Carolina. To develop the kind of widespread public support necessary to its future, the Project's best productions had to reach the towns and cities of the twenty-nine states where the Federal Theatre had no projects, sponsors, or public support. Obviously such an undertaking required careful preparation, and to this end Hallie Flanagan labored with Evan Roberts, who headed the Federal Theatre's rapidly growing radio division. According to their plan, touring companies would be sent out—three from New York, one from Chicago, and two from Los Angeles—with a varied repertory chosen with the help of local WPA representatives from the most successful plays produced in those cities. Five field agents—dividing the country

[76] Memorandum, Flanagan to Lawrence S. Morris, February 24, 1938, RG 69, FTP Records, NOGSF. Burgess Meredith of Equity approved the plan. Actors would be kept on the payroll of the city where they were hired, put under the jurisdiction of the National Service Bureau, and sent to smaller projects. Transportation would be paid, but no per diem allowance for living expenses. See Flanagan to Ellen Woodward and Lawrence Morris, March 5, 1938, RG 69, FTP Records, NOC.

[77] Memorandum, Lawrence Morris to David Niles, March 13, 1938; Robert C. Schnitzer to Jay du Von, March 22, 1938, RG 69, GSS-211.2.

between them and working closely with regional and state officials in both the WPA and the Federal Theatre—would arrange with local civic and educational agencies for performances in every city of every state which agreed to sponsor plays on a subscription basis, thus guaranteeing nonlabor costs. As part of a nationwide promotion drive, Roberts planned a series of radio programs to be broadcast simultaneously on the Mutual Broadcasting System. For thirteen weeks prominent actors appearing in a series of radio plays would appeal to listeners from coast to coast to sponsor the subscription plan.[78]

The program was extensive, bold, and very necessary. To succeed it had to have the backing of Washington officials, the cooperation of regional and state administrators, and the support of well-known theatrical people. Having secured the encouragement of Roosevelt and Hopkins, the approval of Ellen Woodward, and the support of Equity's Burgess Meredith, Hallie Flanagan was hopeful that the Federal Theatre might yet become the national theatre it was intended to be. Turning the plan over to Roberts, she left for an inspection tour of the South, on the lookout for new ways that this Theatre might serve the American people.

The Federal Theatre's Southern outposts, like many small units, needed strengthening. If local dramas and festivals were to be increasingly emphasized, projects in New Orleans and Atlanta would have to have personnel from New York. Although the production of *Altars of Steel* a year earlier by the small Atlanta group had prompted *Variety* to proclaim that the "spirit of Hallie Flanagan waves over Dixieland,"[79] neither strong theatre nor strong public support had developed in this fast growing metropolis of the New South. But if Atlanta was

[78] Memorandum, Flanagan to Lawrence Morris, March 26, 1938, RG 69, FTP Records, NOGSF. WPA field representatives would be consulted in the choice of plays for their particular area.

[79] *Variety*, March 17, 1937, p. 52. This play on the steel industry was written by a Birmingham author, Thomas Hall Rogers, and played in Birmingham before that project was closed and its more talented members moved to Atlanta. See Flanagan, *Arena*, pp. 88-91.

discouraging, Jacksonville was not. Here, a once mediocre stock company carried an animated history of the drama to schools and rural communities throughout Northern Florida—proof once again of what an imaginative director could do with the talent at his disposal.[80]

In North Carolina, the Federal Theatre followed a somewhat different pattern. During his years as director of the Playmakers at the University of North Carolina, Frederick Koch had built up a statewide interest in drama by developing community theatres. To eighteen such amateur groups, the North Carolina Project had supplied a director and sometimes an assistant in staging. By working to improve standards of production, during the eight months when they were not involved in the state's historical pageant, *The Lost Colony*,[81] these Federal Theatre workers had helped local theatrical groups attract broader audiences in a state which, like many others throughout the South and Midwest, had few professional theatres. Such a program, Hallie Flanagan realized, was of value both as entertainment for the communities it served and as a pattern to be expanded to other parts of the country where amateur groups needed professional direction and the Federal Theatre needed public support.[82]

By April, when directors gathered in Washington for the semi-annual meeting of the Play Policy Board, the Federal Theatre was committed to an all-out effort to expand its program and broaden its base of support. Projects across the country had been asked to explore the problems of enlisting organized public support in their particular communities, and to cooperate in developing a national subscription audience. Project officials

[80] Flanagan to Ellen Woodward and Lawrence Morris, March 11, 1938; Flanagan to Gay Shepperson, March 18, 1938, RG 69, FTP Records, NOGSF.

[81] Paul Green's historical pageant told the story of the first English settlement in the New World on Roanoke Island off the coast of North Carolina. Performed during the summer months, the production not only included WPA actors, but WPA labor also went into the reconstruction of buildings which became part of the set.

[82] Hallie Flanagan to Ellen Woodward and Lawrence Morris, April 17, 1938, RG 69, FTP Records, NOGSF.

whose approval was needed to carry out the touring programs, had agreed to meet with the Policy Board. Since both Hopkins' and the President's interest in touring was well known, Federal Theatre officials had every reason to hope for support. They were not disappointed. Ellen Woodward, assuring those present of her full cooperation, announced that the President was confident that the touring plan could be carried out, and that Aubrey Williams had promised full support. David Niles, envisioning the good will to be reaped in all those places yet untouched by the Theatre Project, enthusiastically urged its directors to "go to it" and get procedures worked out immediately. "It is the finest thing that has come out of the Federal Theatre," he declared. "As for trying to sell the idea to [state] administrators, I think you can build up your program in such a way . . . that it will sell itself. If any administrators cannot see it, stay out of their states and when they see how it works they will come on their knees to you." Corrington Gill of the Finance Division also pledged his support, but added that administrative policies would have to be revised and published, and new procedures worked out if private agencies were to be used in securing subscriptions. Lawrence Morris, though dubious as to whether the President and Hopkins knew what "kind of problems . . . they are asking us to solve," thoroughly approved. The fact that both Gill and Niles were present, he added, would help to dispel the notion expressed by one of their associates—that the only time he heard of the Arts Project was when they were doing "something different" and, no doubt, unbureaucratic.[83]

This same concern for a more extensive program and greater public support was no less evident when Federal Theatre directors moved to the National Service Bureau to make production plans for the coming months. Expanding on Hallie Flanagan's familiar admonition—"know your audience"—John McGee urged directors, before selecting individual plays, to determine for each project in their jurisdiction the kind of program most

[83] Report of Federal Theatre Policy Board Meeting, First Session, Washington, D. C., April 12, 1938, RG 69, FTP Records, NOGSF.

183

likely to capture a new audience. The personnel of each project should be similarly analyzed, he suggested. Less-gifted performers, who possessed a thorough knowledge of the theatre, had to be channeled into an expanded community drama program like those already functioning in North Carolina, Oklahoma, and New York. Expanding this program, he insisted, was "essential" to the "geographic spread of our influence." The remaining nucleus of qualified professionals should, with the help of loans if necessary, be made into competent producing units able to tour surrounding areas. At the same time, directors had to begin an intensive campaign to extend and organize audiences in their particular areas while also helping to develop a national subscription audience.[84]

With a plan to win that audience outlined, the next step was to work out the machinery. While McGee and Roberts returned to Washington in an effort to iron out "procedural snags" so that the touring program could get under way, regional directors set to work on a summer program that would include regional tours by local companies. They soon discovered, however, that the blessings of WPA officials in Washington did not necessarily insure the cooperation of local officials. In Michigan, where Herbert Ashton was planning a statewide tour, the state administrator agreed to reverse his previous stand and permit the Federal Theatre director to bring in as many as twenty actors to supplement the Detroit company.[85] But in Florida, where the entire relief program was apparently clouded by politics, the state administrator reportedly vetoed all requests for outside personnel. Federal Theatre officials and directors of Women's and Professional Projects explained that additional actors and technicians were needed to carry out a program that included a special summer workshop as well as statewide tours. Their explanations were to no avail: the state administrator refused to

[84] *Ibid.*, Second Session, New York City, April 13, 1938.
[85] Robert C. Schnitzer to Howard Miller, April 20, 1938, RG 69, FTP Records, NOC; Herbert Ashton to Flanagan, March 13, 1938; Ashton to Schnitzer, May 4, 1938, RG 69, GSS-211.2.

believe that there were not enough local people available to meet the Project's needs.[86] Whatever the pressures behind his decision, there was no denying that the whole business of lending could be a sticky one administratively. In New York, for example, an actor worked 96 hours a month at the same salary for which an actor from Florida or Michigan might work 124 hours.[87] Thus a state administrator, already submerged in red tape, could understandably feel that having a half-dozen extra actors on hand was simply not worth the problem involved, particularly if the actors on loan occasionally failed to arrive at the time promised or, worse still, failed to fill the needs of the local project.[88]

City directors proved no more exempt than regional directors from conflicts of authority. The line separating artistic and administrative responsibility was admittedly a thin one, and the best-intentioned administrator was apt to become involved in the hiring and firing of artistic personnel if, as in New York, he was in charge of labor matters.[89] Arts Project administrator Paul Edwards, it seemed to Federal Theatre officials, was "catching the Connolly disease"—a malady from which the California Project had by no means fully recovered.[90] What seemed even

[86] Joseph Lentz to Flanagan, May 16, 31, 1938; Lentz to J. Howard Miller, May 31, 1938, RG 69, GSS-211.2; Lentz to Miller, July 23, 1938; Memorandum, Robert C. Schnitzer to Flanagan, September 30, 1938, RG 69, FTP Records, NOC.

[87] Memorandum, Miller to Lawrence Morris, September 19, 1938, RG 69, GSS-210.13.

[88] Memorandum, Morris to John McGee, n.d., RG 69, GSS-210.13.

[89] This division of authority between administrative and technical (artistic) matters was a frequent source of controversy. Federal Theatre officials in California, for example, argued that the construction of scenery and, consequently, the purchase and use of the necessary tools was a technical matter. Connolly disagreed, arguing that the purchase of supplies came under his jurisdiction. See Memorandum, Robert C. Schnitzer to Lawrence Morris, March 31, 1938, RG 69, FTP Records, NOC.

[90] The delicate nature of the California situation is indicated by one of the compromises adopted. Hallie Flanagan and Ellen Woodward agreed that copies of all correspondence from the Federal Theatre's Washington headquarters would be sent to the assistant regional director of Women's and Professional Projects rather than directly to Theatre

more distressing was the relative inability of Washington officials to effect a cure in such cases. Ellen Woodward might press local directors of the Women's and Professional Projects to cooperate with Federal Theatre plans; she could even instruct them to intercede with state administrators on the Project's behalf. But in the last analysis she could do little more than persuade Colonel Connolly to postpone rather than censor a play, urge the Florida administrator to admit outside personnel, or request some other official to admit touring companies.

Persuasion, however, was simply not enough. If the Federal Theatre was to receive cooperation from local officials, Hallie Flanagan was convinced, orders to that effect would have to come from Hopkins himself. The Relief Administrator, however, had been caught up in the campaign to promote him to the Presidency upon his return to the capital. Not until mid-May, when the four Arts directors met to discuss plans for the coming year, did Mrs. Flanagan have an opportunity to talk with him privately. With her usual enthusiasm she outlined the details of what was the most far-reaching program proposed since the Project's inception: professionally produced plays of unmistakable quality in the big city project; more and better productions throughout the country; new advances in radio, cinema, publishing, and research. But the plan would remain on paper, she insisted, unless her position were strengthened. With painstaking clarity, she explained to Hopkins that the Federal Theatre could not win the support of a broad geographic area unless he personally emphasized to regional officials, and especially to state administrators, that this was a national program which demanded their cooperation. They must be made to see the importance of touring across state lines as well as the necessity for supplementing weaker units with loans of personnel from large centers in other parts of the country. Furthermore, if the entire program was to operate efficiently, she, like the other Arts directors, be-

Project people. See Robert C. Schnitzer to Mary McFarland, March 7, 1938, RG 69, FTP Records, NOC.

lieved that Hopkins himself would have to reiterate to local WPA administrators that, under the existing division of artistic and administrative authority, the choice of plays and the hiring and dismissal of all artistic personnel were the exclusive responsibilities of the National Director and her appointees. Unless Hopkins heeded their collective memorandum, unless her own position was thus strengthened, and unless she received financial backing and cooperation from the Washington office, the plan she had outlined would have to be scrapped. A probable result, she warned, would be "the gradual weakening of any national policy" and the transferal of the Project to local officials, "who by the very nature of things must be concerned with showing administrative gains rather than artistic achievement on a nationwide scale."[91]

Hopkins made public his assurance of support at a reception following interviews with the national directors. Before some two hundred actors, writers, artists, and musicians gathered at the Mayflower Hotel in Washington, he pledged that the Arts Project would remain under federal supervision as long as he was Relief Administrator.[92] Hallie Flanagan needed more than verbal reassurance, however, if the Federal Theatre was to achieve its grand design.

By the summer of 1938, individual projects had already begun responding to demands for a quality program and an expanded audience. The Cincinnati Project pioneered the use of lighting and no scenery in its own very effective production of *One-Third of a Nation*; while in Miami, Federal Theatre workers ventured forth with an experimental production of *Altars of Steel*.[93] With three hits still running, the New York Project launched its fourth caravan season with a send-off from Mrs.

[91] [Hallie Flanagan], Notes for Interview with Hopkins, May 19, 1938; Memorandum, National Directors of the Federal Arts Project to Harry L. Hopkins, May 19, 1938, Flanagan Papers.

[92] Flanagan to Ole Ness, May 25, 1938, RG 69, FTP Records, NOGSF.

[93] Herbert Ashton to Flanagan, May 13, 1938, RG 69, GSS-211.2; Memorandum, John McGee to Florence Kerr, Summer 1938, RG 69, FTP Records, NOGSF.

Roosevelt, and stories and reviews in every metropolitan daily and numerous national magazines. Meanwhile, directors were building up audiences for downtown theatres. A Children's Theatre Club, theatre parties,[94] free tickets to strategically chosen groups, and a speaker's bureau which provided exhibits and lecturers to civic and educational groups were all part of New York's drive for a large and loyal audience.[95]

Nevertheless, the real key to broad public support remained the nationwide touring program. By July, procedures for interstate tours had been sufficiently worked out so that regional directors could begin making concrete plans for their particular bailiwicks. In Chicago, John McGee, who had taken over as regional director for the Midwest, prepared a lengthy memorandum to be sent to all state administrators in his region. Carefully explaining why the Federal Theatre, if it was to serve "all America," had to be "an itinerant affair," McGee pointed out that the taxpayers and their representatives in Congress rightly expected that Project talent not be restricted to the three large metropolitan centers where it was originally located and where, despite persistent efforts, it had hitherto remained. After assuring state administrators that the Federal Theatre was in no way

[94] By April 11, 1938, over thirteen thousand organizations in the metropolitan area had arranged theatre parties. See Theodore Mauntz, Report on Promotion for George Kondolf, April 11, 1938, RG 69, FTP Records, NOC.

[95] Letters arranging theatre parties, correspondence with Children's Theatre Club members, and other promotional material are located in RG 69, FTP Records, NOPM. Indicative of Kondolf's promotional efforts are letters which went out to all Daily Vacation Bible School teachers on June 28 suggesting that with the close of Bible School, they might wish to recommend various Children's Theatre productions to their pupils. The New York director was also quick to arrange theatre parties for teachers attending summer sessions at nearby colleges. (Kondolf to Flanagan, July 21, 1938, RG 69, FTP Records, Narr. Reports.) Other efforts to interest teachers in Federal Theatre productions included free tickets to officers of the National Education Association who were attending a NEA convention in New York City, and a speech by Philip Barber at one of the sessions describing New York City's classical cycle, a joint venture of the Federal Theatre and the public schools. (Kondolf to Flanagan, July 5, 1938, RG 69, FTP Records, Narr. Reports.)

188

a "propagandistic theatre"—that, in fact, the relatively few plays dealing with controversial themes (less than 2 per cent) had usually espoused solutions less radical than those proposed by the administration—McGee explained how that theatre could be made to serve the entire Midwest. According to his plan, all properly qualified workers in the entire region who could be moved without family hardship would be assigned to a central Chicago Project, operating administratively through a single business office in Illinois. The best of these workers would be rehearsed under the most capable directors available and then sent out on extensive tours; those unable to move would work in a community drama program and help build audiences for touring productions. In short, Chicago would become the hub of a Midwestern wheel from which touring productions would extend in all directions.[96]

McGee, having served as director of the far-flung Southern region since the Project's inception and also as head of the National Service Bureau, was uniquely aware of the necessity for wider service and thoroughly familiar with the bureaucratic framework within which the Federal Theatre had to function. The administrative changes—or more precisely, the simplification of procedure—which he listed as essential to the operation of this regional plan in a separate memorandum to Florence Kerr, appeared simple enough.[97] Since Mrs. Kerr, as regional director of Women's and Professional Projects, and Howard Hunter, WPA field representative for the Midwest, had strongly urged his appointment, McGee had reason to believe that the plan which he outlined in conjunction with the national touring program could be implemented.[98] Hallie Flanagan, who had

[96] Memorandum, McGee to Florence Kerr, July 13, 1938, RG 69, FTP Records, NOGSF. The memorandum was to be sent to all state administrators; however, there is no indication that it was actually mailed.

[97] McGee's plan called for an administrative consolidation to coincide with regional organization of theatrical activity. *Ibid.* (attached memorandum).

[98] See Memorandum from Ellen Woodward in which she recommends McGee's appointment and explains his plans for the Midwest. Memorandum, Woodward to Hopkins, July 13, 1938, RG 69, GSS-211.2.

discussed the necessary reorganization with Mrs. Kerr and Hunter during a recent trip to Chicago, was no less confident;[99] but both counted on the support of WPA officials in Washington.

By early August, it looked as if that cooperation would not be forthcoming. Although David Niles, Ellen Woodward, and Corrington Gill had approved the touring and subscription plan at the Policy Board meeting in April, the appointment of the five field agents who would arrange for local sponsorship was repeatedly held up. Federal Theatre officials pled for permission to use people on the touring division of the New York City Project as field agents, in spite of their belief that no one presently on the Project had the necessary experience and ability for the job. But "Washington" objected that the cost of travel would be too great. When, despite Hopkins' and Mrs. Woodward's promises to insure full cooperation from state administrators and regional field representatives, WPA officials in the South and on the West Coast objected to having any outside theatre people brought into their respective areas, the frustrated Evan Roberts regretfully suggested to the Federal Theatre Director that her only alternative was to turn the touring program over to the regional officials.[100] It was an alternative that Hallie Flanagan was not yet ready to accept.

From the Play Policy Board meeting on August 12 came the announcement that nationwide tours would begin in October as part of an extensive program to carry Federal Theatre productions into new areas.[101] Two weeks later the Federal Theatre announced plans to send the New York production, *Prologue to Glory*, on the road in cooperation with the theatrical impresario, Lee Shubert. Shubert had agreed to make all arrangements and bear any losses and all non-labor costs in exchange

[99] Flanagan to Kerr, July 21, 1938; Flanagan to Hunter, July 21, 1938, RG 69, FTP Records, NOC-State.

[100] Memorandum, Roberts to Flanagan, August 3, 1938, RG 69, FTP Records, NOGSF.

[101] The *New York Times*, August 13, 1938, p. 16. See Kondolf's remarks on the meeting in his letter to Mrs. Flanagan, August 15, 1938, RG 69, FTP Records, Narr. Reports.

for a percentage of the box-office receipts; the Federal Theatre would continue to pay actors' salaries, plus an allowance of three dollars a day for living expenses. The announcement had no sooner reached the press than cries of unfair competition arose from Broadway managers; Equity and other theatrical unions joined in the protests. Such an arrangement would nullify special union-Federal Theatre working conditions, they claimed. Actors, stage managers, costume and lighting people could travel only under the usual union provisions for touring.[102] In the face of this onslaught, WPA officials made a predictable retreat. The Federal Theatre announced on September 29 that it had abandoned all plans for nationwide tours. Owing to the protests of unions and producers and to other "technical problems," there would be no contract with Shubert. In part because of costs, any future tours "would be handled by regional offices of the Federal Theatre and not made a separate project as planned."[103] But, as John McGee soon discovered, even regional tours were a virtual impossibility.

Two months after McGee had been sent to Chicago expressly to expand theatrical activities throughout the Midwest, he still had not received permission to begin work. "I can see no earthly excuse," he wrote to Howard Miller "[why it should] take more than two weeks for Mrs. Woodward to get Mr. Hopkins' signature on whatever documents are necessary to set up the administrative machinery out here following the meeting we had in Washington." Recalling that at the Washington meeting there had been a "complete meeting of minds," that a memorandum on the subject had been drawn up for Hopkins and approved by Florence Kerr, McGee added that Mrs. Kerr had subsequently told him that she had informally spoken to Hopkins, who seemed to agree with the entire proposal. "Will you be kind enough to inquire of somebody," requested the irate director, "how long I am expected to defer making plans for the rapidly approaching theatrical season, if I am to be hamstrung

[102] The *New York Times*, August 26, 1938, p. 19.
[103] *Ibid.*, September 29, 1938, p. 30.

by further waiting and ordered not to employ people or make plans for regional operations pending . . . [a] decision."[104] Exactly three weeks later Ellen Woodward informed Federal Theatre officials that Aubrey Williams had approved the Midwestern plan.[105] But when McGee examined newly imposed regulations from Washington, he began to wonder if the struggle had been worth the effort.

According to procedure worked out in July, companies would be permitted to tour, provided that permission had been obtained from the regional director of the Federal Theatre, the state administrator in whose state the touring company originated, the state administrator in whose state the company wished to play, and the regional administrator of the Women's and Professional Division. Now Ellen Woodward further insisted that each state administrator also be consulted about each specific playing date within his state and that his approval be telephoned or telegraphed to Washington.[106] To McGee it was utter nonsense. Furious over this "idiotic duplication of approvals," he notified Howard Miller that he would not move a single company out of Chicago until someone had enough "common sense" to cut through this crippling mass of red tape.[107] Miller could offer scant comfort. According to the deputy administrator, the whole problem of touring was so "confused" by the number of approvals required that Federal Theatre officials were enormously "slowed down in trying to send *any* company on the road."[108] One week later, Miller again replied— this time with more definite information. Mrs. Woodward had announced that the regional plan for the Midwest was being "postponed." Expressing his regret at the decision, Miller added, "I really think it [the regional touring plan] is the solution to

[104] McGee to Miller, September 8, 1938, RG 69, GSS-211.2.

[105] Memorandum, Ellen Woodward to Robert Schnitzer, September 29, 1938, GSS-210.13.

[106] Memorandum, McGee to Florence Kerr, October 10, 1938, RG 69, GSS-211.2.

[107] McGee to Miller, October 10, 1938, RG 69, GSS-211.2.

[108] Miller to McGee, October 18, 1938, RG 69, GSS-211.2.

our problem." Since Mrs. Kerr "still seems to be interested and wants the matter postponed and not disapproved," he continued, "I hope we can raise the question again in the near future."[109]

Miller was right. A touring plan—regional, if not national—seemed the obvious solution to the Federal Theatre's most serious problem. But if Hallie Flanagan was to solve this problem and win broad-based support, she had to be able to put that plan into effect immediately, rather than in some vaguely defined "near future." To be sure, the Federal Theatre already had supporters, but they were relatively few in number and they wielded little political power save in New York and Southern California.

For the nature and small size of this support Hallie Flanagan was only partially responsible. Three years before, she had approached the task of building a theatre project out of an unknown number of unlocated relief workers. She had been armed only with courage, determination, and the belief that the theatre could become useful and relevant to millions of Americans. Wholly dedicated to this idea, she had tried to create the kind of regionally based theatre that would make permanent patrons of the American people—not necessarily their relief administrators or their representatives in Congress. Forced to work within the confines of a relief organization, she found herself in charge of a theatre which, as appropriations were reduced, cuts made, and projects closed, became increasingly and overwhelmingly metropolitan rather than regional. Attempting to be relevant to the social and economic realities of the troubled 'thirties, this theatre persistently, and sometimes irresponsibly, produced a small number of plays which, while often winning the praise of critics and the applause of large audiences, understandably frightened relief administrators in Washington and antagonized certain powerful legislators on Capitol Hill. Because she had begun to see the implications of this lack of support at WPA

[109] Miller to McGee, October 24, 1938, RG 69, GSS-211.2.

headquarters, and because she was as determined as ever that this government venture make its mark as a theatre, Hallie Flanagan, in the fall of 1937, had renewed her struggle to wrest from projects everywhere professionally sound productions of plays that would win the support of the people for whom they were intended. Under pressure to pay an increased share of expenses, the Federal Theatre had henceforth to win a large and loyal audience, not just out of hope for permanent patrons, but out of need for paying customers.

As part of a relief project, however, the Federal Theatre had to carry out this drive for audience support during a period of retrenchment for the WPA as a whole. In a sense the two organizations were moving in opposite directions and friction was bound to occur. Forced to economize by vastly reduced appropriations, Washington officials placed the second largest and most productive project in the nation under the administrative control of state officials more interested in order and discipline than in theatre and audiences. When Connolly attempted to take over the Arts Projects in California, WPA officials were slow to act. Perhaps they were merely marking time to see whether the entire relief program would be turned back to the states; perhaps they were not eager to rush to the defense of a theatre that was making the entire WPA a target for senatorial indignation; or perhaps they were simply reluctant to take on a state administrator who had already made clear his reluctance to be saddled with Arts Projects he could not control completely. Whatever the combination of factors involved, the California situation revealed once again the difficulty of maintaining, much less expanding, a nationally directed Theatre Project in a bureaucracy more disposed to avoiding conflict and publicity than in promoting theatre.

As the recession deepened and Roosevelt again embarked on a huge relief-recovery program, relief officials appeared willing enough to see theatrical activities expanded to embrace a broader portion of the American public. Her drive for audience support given new impetus, Hallie Flanagan was quick to respond with an imaginative program that would rebuild the foundation for a regionally centered national theatre. But WPA officials failed to permit the implementation of plans they had previously encouraged with apparent sincerity and even enthusiasm. To ascribe that failure to a deliberate attempt to kill a project which had proved politically embarrassing and administratively troublesome would be an oversimplification. The pressures on Ellen Woodward and her associates, while eluding precise documentation, were nonetheless numerous and compelling.

As administrators of a federally financed relief program, WPA officials were both aware of and affected by the changing political climate on Capitol Hill. In April 1938, when they endorsed plans for a nationwide touring program, a reinvigorated Roosevelt had committed himself to a relief-recovery bill which Congress passed virtually intact. But this most recent bit of pump priming produced no economic miracles. It gave the economy a nudge rather than a hard shove, antagonized business, and added to the public debt. Although conditions began to show a slight improvement during the summer months, the sluggishness of the economy robbed New Dealers of much of their self-confidence. Congressional conservatives on the other hand were as determined as ever to obstruct further Presidential reforms. They tasted victory when the President's executive reorganization bill went down to defeat in the House. Although the administration's federal wages-and-hours law managed to squeak by, the strength of the opposition was such that Roosevelt agreed to work openly with Hopkins and other administration liberals in an attempt to purge the party of ultraconservatives in the impending primary elections.[110]

His decision, however, was a misguided one. Administration candidates were trounced by conservatives in every state but Florida and New York, and Hopkins was charged with using the WPA to build a national machine. Although the accusations

[110] Leuchtenburg, *Franklin D. Roosevelt and the New Deal*, pp. 257 *passim* 267; the *New York Times*, April 15-August 31, 1938.

were largely untrue,[111] charges of corruption in Kentucky provided ample ammunition for congressmen demanding a probe into the political activities of the WPA. In the meantime, however, congressional inquiries had already been launched in other quarters. Senator James F. Byrnes headed a Special Committee to Investigate Unemployment, and by August the Federal Theatre had come under the purview of the House Un-American Activities Committee led by Martin Dies of Texas, who had sworn to rid the government of such subversives as Harry Hopkins, Frances Perkins, Harold Ickes, and other "communists and fellow travelers."[112] According to Dies' fellow committeeman, New Jersey's Republican Representative J. Parnell Thomas, the Federal Theatre was not only a "link in the vast and unparalleled New Deal propaganda machine," but a branch of the Communist Party as well.[113] In short, New Dealers in general and WPA officials in particular had little reason to look to Capitol Hill with any degree of confidence.

For the latter the future was doubly tenuous, as their current appropriations would run out in February 1939.[114] Distressed by the probable scrutiny of three congressional committees, they feared possible curtailment from Congress as a whole. Without the prodding of Hopkins—now far more interested in presidential politics than in nationwide tours—his more cautious associates were subject to second thoughts about this whole touring scheme. Rather than face the criticism of congressmen, WPA officials concluded that it was safer not to carry out the original touring and subscription plan. Highly sensitive to accusations

[111] Donald S. Howard, *The WPA and Federal Relief Policy* (New York: Russell Sage Foundation, 1943), pp. 587-594; Charles, *Minister of Relief*, pp. 195-197, 202; Leuchtenburg, *Franklin D. Roosevelt and the New Deal*, pp. 267-270; Farley, *Jim Farley's Story*, pp. 120-150.

[112] Sherwood, *Roosevelt and Hopkins*, p. 104.

[113] The *New York Times*, July 27, 1938, p. 19.

[114] Roosevelt originally requested for the WPA $1,250,000,000 for the first seven months of the 1938-39 fiscal year. Congress changed the sum to $1,425,000,000 and added an extra month so that the appropriation would last until February 1939. See the *New York Times*, April 15, June 4, June 22, 1938, p. 1.

196

of competition with private industry that had arisen in connection with the Federal Theatre's drive to get a paying audience,[115] these same officials beat a hasty retreat when theatrical managers denounced the New York Project's touring arrangement with Shubert. Eager to avoid conflicts with state administrators, they imposed an elaborate system of approvals for interstate tours. When the Federal Theatre's veteran directors complained that this proliferation of red tape tied the regional touring plan in knots, Ellen Woodward declared the plan "postponed." For administrators committed to preserving a relief program, such decisions, under the circumstances, were understandable, reasonable, and safe. For those whose first interest was theatre, they were disastrous.[116]

Hereafter, Hallie Flanagan would find her time and attention devoted increasingly to defense of the Federal Theatre, rather than to its expansion. Postponement was tantamount to a veto: the time for launching a bold program that would thrust the Federal Theatre into communities across the nation, winning for that institution an expanded audience and new constituents, had passed. In its flight for survival, the Federal Theatre would have to depend upon supporters already won.

[115] When, for example, Federal Theatre officials acquired greater space for advertising—they had originally had only small weekly announcements—Broadway producers let out cries of "encroachment." The *New York Times*, May 4, 1938, p. 53.

[116] The differing outlook of WPA and Federal Theatre personnel is consistent with the analysis of behavior contained in "Bureaucratic Structure and Personality" and "Role of the Intellectual in Public Bureaucracy," two chapters in Robert K. Merton's *Social Theory and Social Structure* (Glencoe, Ill.; The Free Press, 1949).

CHAPTER FIVE

Politics Versus Theatre: The Dies
Committee Investigation

THE AUTUMN of 1938 saw Hallie Flanagan's hopes for new
sorties into the hinterland deferred and her troubles compounded
by a long investigation of the Federal Theatre by the House
Committee on Un-American Activities. The Committee, which
consisted of one quasi-New Dealer, one dedicated New Dealer,
two conservative Democrats, and two staunch Republicans, was
headed by Martin Dies of Texas.[1] A large, powerfully built
young man, Dies combined a Populist penchant for inflationary
schemes with isolationism and extreme nationalism. Elected
to Congress in 1931, he had wasted no time launching his campaign for immigration restrictions to prevent the United States
from being the "dumping ground" of Europe.[2] But the zealous
Texan was known principally as the self-appointed president of
the Demagogues Club, an informal group of House members
"addicted to flamboyant speeches saturated with hokum."[3]
Nevertheless, he appeared to take seriously his new duties as
chairman of the House Un-American Committee and promptly
announced that there would be no "star-chamber proceedings,"
"no shooting in the dark."[4] This resolve to eschew excessive
publicity in favor of responsible inquiry was not shared, how-

[1] Members listed in the order of the above description are: John J.
Dempsey (Democrat, New Mexico), Arthur D. Healey (Democrat,
Massachusetts), Joseph Starnes (Democrat, Alabama), Harold G. Mosier
(Democrat, Ohio), J. Parnell Thomas (Republican, New Jersey), and
Noah M. Mason (Republican, Illinois). See Raymond P. Brandt, "The
Dies Committee: An Appraisal," *The Atlantic Monthly*, CLXV (Feb-
ruary 1940), 232.

[2] *Ibid.* For a statement of Dies' views on monetary legislation, labor,
foreign affairs, etc., see William Gellerman, *Martin Dies* (New York:
John Dey Co., 1944), pp. 31-57.

[3] Brandt, "The Dies Committee: An Appraisal," *The Atlantic Monthly*,
CLXV (February 1940), 232.

[4] The *New York Times*, June 19, 1938, p. 26.

198

ever, by at least one member of the Committee, J. Parnell
Thomas.

Thomas announced on July 26, 1938, that he would have the
Federal Theatre and Writers' Projects investigated as soon as
the Committee began hearings. "It is apparent from the startling
evidence received thus far," said Thomas, "that the Federal
Theatre Project not only is serving as a branch of the communistic organization but is also one more link in the vast and
unparalleled New Deal propaganda machine." According to the
New Jersey Republican, Hallie Flanagan would be asked to explain why applicants for jobs on the Project had first to join the
Workers' Alliance, a Communist organization, and why the only
plays authorized were those with "communist leanings," such as
Prologue to Glory, *Haiti* and *One-Third of a Nation*.[5]

Hallie Flanagan was aghast—despite the fact that for three
years charges of communism had been intermittently hurled at
the Federal Theatre by veterans' groups and by conservatives
both within and outside of Congress. Denying any knowledge of
the informal hearings Thomas was supposed to have held, she
indignantly added: "Some of the statements reported to have
been made by him are obviously absurd." *Prologue to Glory*, E.
P. Conkle's tender dramatization of young Abe Lincoln's ro-
mance with Anne Rutledge, was no more Communist than was
the Harlem group's swashbuckling *Haiti*. And *One-Third of a
Nation*, for all its indignation at the miseries of slum life, sounded no call to mount the barricades on Pennsylvania Avenue. Nor
had she written and produced a Communist play in Soviet Russia, as Thomas erroneously charged. Yet she realized that such
charges, however irresponsible, could not be ignored when made
by a member of the House Un-American Activities Committee.

Assuming that she would indeed be subpoenaed, Mrs. Flanagan drafted for David Niles' approval a letter to Dies saying that
she would be available to testify on August 11. Noting that the
date coincided with the meeting of the National Policy Board,

[5] The *New York Times*, July 27, 1938, p. 19. Thomas was subsequently
imprisoned for defrauding the United States government.

she explained that the six regional directors would be present should the Committee care to question them about projects throughout the nation.[6] But Dies, who had now tasted the honey of headlines, replied that the Committee had not yet subpoenaed her, although apparently Thomas intended to do so. "If your presence is required," he added, "it will be several weeks after August 11, as we [already] have a heavy schedule of witnesses."[7]

Her offer rejected, Mrs. Flanagan opened the Policy Board meeting with a speech that fairly sparkled with ideas for expanding and decentralizing Federal Theatre activities. As part of this drive to build up regional centers, she urged that projects concentrate on plays dealing with regional life, as well as those classics which would have special significance for a particular area. Federal Theatre directors responded by approving plans for a series of French plays for New Orleans, an historical cycle for California, an outdoor pageant commemorating the four hundredth anniversary of De Soto's arrival in Florida, and new community drama and research projects for towns and cities everywhere.[8]

Meanwhile Thomas had launched a new attack, and he had witnesses to support his charges.[9] On August 19, these opponents of un-American activity assembled in the Committee's chandelier-lit chamber on Capitol Hill to denounce the Federal Theatre. First to testify was Hazel Huffman, a former employee of the mail division of the WPA, who claimed to have been hired by the office of the New York City WPA administrator, Victor

[6] Flanagan to Dies, August 5, 1938, RG 69, FTP Records, NOGSF. Word of Niles' approval was telegraphed to Mrs. Flanagan in Poughkeepsie. See Telegram, J. Howard Miller to Flanagan, August 5, 1938, RG 69, GSS-211.2.

[7] Dies to Flanagan, August 9, 1938, RG 69, FTP Records, NOGSF.

[8] Hallie Flanagan, Address to the Play Policy Board, First Session, Washington, D. C., August 11, 1938; Memorandum, Flanagan to Ellen Woodward, August 16, 1938, RG 69, FTP Records, NOGSF.

[9] New York Herald Tribune, August 11, 1938, p. 10. Thomas' charges were also carried in the Daily News and the Sun. See George Kondolf to Hallie Flanagan, August 15, 1938, RG 69, FTP Records, Narr. Reports.

Ridder, as an investigator to read Federal Theatre mail.[10] Subsequently dismissed when her dubious activities were uncovered, Miss Huffman now claimed to represent the so-called Committee of Relief Status Professional Theatrical Employees of New York City, an organization which Equity officials regarded as a fly-by-night affair conducive to dual unionism.[11] The witness' credentials were of scant concern to Dies and his associates, however. After an initial admonition to stick to un-American activities, Miss Huffman was granted the same latitude in discussion and immunity from cross-examination accorded previous witnesses, who had made sweeping allegations of Communist influence in everything from the CIO to the Camp Fire Girls.[12]

The Federal Theatre was dominated by Communists, Miss Huffman said, because the Workers' Alliance, an organization "closely allied" with the Communist Party, had been permitted by Aubrey Williams and Hallie Flanagan to gain control of the Project. Mrs. Flanagan, she continued, had been known "as far back as 1927 for her communistic sympathy, if not membership." She had devoted 137 out of 280 pages of her study of the European theatre, *Shifting Scenes*, to "eulogizing Soviet Russia and the Russian Theatre." And in an article on workers' theatres, written for a 1931 issue of *Theatre Arts Monthly*, she had acknowledged her "presence and participation in the meeting at which predominated the 'red' banner—'Workers of the World, Unite.' " As further evidence of Mrs. Flanagan's "active participation and interest in things communist," Miss Huffman sub-

[10] Hearings before a Special House Committee on Un-American Activity on H. Res. 282, *Investigation of Un-American Propaganda Activities in the U.S.*, 75th Cong., 3rd Sess. (1938), Vol. I, 775, 796. (House Un-American Activities Committee Hearings).

[11] See p. 74 of text. For Equity's views on Miss Huffman and her organization, see "Notice to H. Huffman & Co. 'Keep Out!,' " *Equity*, XXII (December 1937), 12; "Authorized Spokesman," *Equity*, XXIII (October 1938), 15.

[12] For an analysis of prior testimony, see August Raymond Ogden, *The Dies Committee: A Study of the Special House Committee for the Investigation of Un-American Activities, 1938-1944* (Washington: The Catholic University of America Press, 1945), pp. 50-60.

mitted a copy of *Can You Hear Their Voices?* along with a laud-
atory review of the play in the *New Masses*. The play, she and
Thomas agreed, clearly "implied contempt for the Government."
Lest the congressmen before her retain any illusions, Miss Huffman explained that, in connection with dismissals from the Project, the National Director had frequently declared: "The foremost consideration must be the needs of the Federal Theatre
Project." This, to Miss Huffman and Representative Starnes,
clearly meant that Mrs. Flanagan held "relief for human beings
in want . . . to be secondary"—a position that was patently un-
American.

Naturally, Communist plays had been "the rule" under Mrs.
Flanagan, Miss Huffman continued. Among some twenty-eight
plays alleged to be nothing more than Communist propaganda,
Thomas' star witness included the Living Newspapers, *The Case
of Philip Lawrence*, *Professor Mamlock*, George Bernard Shaw's
On the Rocks, Sinclair Lewis' *It Can't Happen Here, The
Cradle Will Rock*, Paul Green's *Hymn to the Rising Sun*, and
the children's play, *The Revolt of the Beavers*. Elaborating on
each, the loquacious Miss Huffman informed her listeners that
The Case of Philip Lawrence dealt with Negro discrimination;
One-Third of a Nation, with "social housing"; *Professor Mamlock* (which she persisted in calling *Professor Hamlock*), with
"unmasking ugly fascism"; *Hymn to the Rising Sun*, with "so-
called legalized torture of the chain gang"; *On the Rocks*, with
"fascism and communism." This last was "designed to set up
some new political system," while *One-Third of a Nation* was
"in opposition to the Episcopal Church." In *Woman of Destiny*,
she continued, a woman who was "very ardent for peace . . .
threw the country into war." "That," Mr. Starnes asked, "is the
idealistic communistic method of peace anyway, is it not?" Miss
Huffman agreed and rambled on.

Project supervisors "worked hand-in-glove" with the Com-
munist-dominated Workers' Alliance and its white-collar division, the City Projects Council (CPC), she charged. These officials permitted such Communist literature as the *Daily Worker*

and the *Red Spot Light*, along with various petitions, to be distributed on government property by Federal Theatre employees. They also allowed professional agitators with no theatrical experience to be put on the Project, but seldom hired bona fide theatrical people who did not belong to the Workers' Alliance. Those managing to get on the Project who were not Alliance members lived in constant fear of demotion or dismissal.

As if charges of Communist control were not damaging enough, Miss Huffman accused Project officials of poor administration. Rehearsals continued for an unreasonable period because too much time was spent discarding the cast—"they choose people and then reject them." The placement system was poor: people with neither theatrical experience nor Alliance affiliations were brought in from the outside; Samuel Goldstein, a Bowery peddler, was hired because of his long sideburns. Concluding finally with the hope that the Committee would "clear out the communism on the Federal project," . . . and place it in the hands of a "good all-around American . . . interested in obeying the law," the Committee's principal witness stepped down.[13]

William Harrison Humphrey, who for six weeks had played Earl Browder in *Triple-A Plowed Under*, was then sworn in. When pressed for facts by Representative Starnes, Humphrey admitted that he had none. He had just come by to testify because he thought they might be "interested." At the insistence of Ohio's Republican congressman, Harold Mosier, the Committee commended Humphrey for offering his assistance "as a good American," and then adjourned.[14]

When Dies opened the hearings the following day, he reminded witnesses that the Committee was interested solely in un-American activities, not mismanagement and inefficiency. Then employees and former employees of the Federal Theatre Project filed forward to testify. Francis M. Verdi told the Committee that he had been asked by both Equity and Mrs.

[13] *House Un-American Activities Committee Hearings*, I, 775-829.
[14] *Ibid.*, 829-832.

203

Flanagan to conduct an investigation to determine the validity of complaints that less experienced members of the Workers' Alliance had managed to hold on to their jobs during the June and July cuts in 1937, while members of Equity and other professional theatrical unions were being fired. Just before he was to have given his report, which was damaging to the Workers' Alliance, Verdi explained, he had been told by one of Kondolf's assistants that the report was "no longer desired." Explaining that Mrs. Flanagan, who by this time no longer had jurisdiction over the New York Project, had never "by implication or by word, encouraged the Workers' Alliance and its communistic tendencies," Verdi added that he would continue his crusade against the Alliance despite warnings of further professional persecution. Cut off in the midst of his chronicle of previous demotions, Verdi was thanked and asked to step down.[15]

The witnesses who followed added testimony that seemed to substantiate Miss Huffman's charges about the Workers' Alliance and the CPC. Members of the Alliance were given preference when plays were being cast, according to Charles Walton, a former stage manager. The CPC did create "an un-American atmosphere" by keeping people continually stirred up, agreed Garland Kerr, who had been with the original CWA drama group in New York City. Many of the Alliance members on the Project were nonprofessionals who lived in "garrets" below Fourteenth Street and had been brought into the Federal Theatre from the city drama projects and classified as professional actors. Amateurs, they spent most of their time "fighting for their jobs rather than working at them." Miss Huffman's husband, Seymour Revzin, who was presently working on the New York Project as a community drama coach, agreed that members of the CPC and Workers' Alliance circulated petitions, sold Communist propaganda, solicited funds for the Spanish Loyalists on Project time, and sat around comparing the "bounties of Russia" with the "very bad conditions" existing in the United

[15] *Ibid.*, 833-839.

States. A further transgression on the part of that "most vicious" organization was implied by a small, blonde, Viennese-born actress who told the Committee that she had been asked for a "date" by a Negro on the Project and that members of the Workers' Alliance hobnobbed "indiscriminately" with Negroes as part of the Communist program for "social equality and race merging."[16]

By the time the last witness, a messenger boy, finished an account of a memorial service held at Carnegie Hall by Loyalist sympathizers,[17] Dies and his fellow representatives had countenanced what a careful and judicious student of the Committee regards as "one of the most curious aberrations . . . ever permitted to figure in its hearings."[18] For the better part of two days, witnesses had touched on everything from Communist tactics to a Bowery peddler with sideburns, despite the chairman's belated protestations that the Committee was only interested in un-American activities. Their accusations, rarely checked, were an amazing mixture of truths, half-truths, and outright untruths—"one of the weirdest collections of evidence ever permitted before the Committee."[19] But permitted it was and, for the reporters who had the run of the committee room, it furnished headlines that would hearten the most hardboiled tabloid editor.

Witnesses returning to New York were greeted with reports of their testimony from every newsstand in the city. WPA THEATRE FACES PROBE AS "HOTBED" OF REDS, FLANAGAN A WPA "RED," SECRETARY OF N. Y. ACTORS' RELIEF GROUP TELLS HOUSE "HALLIE IS COMMUNISTIC," REDS URGED "MIXED DATE" BLONDE TELLS DIES PROBERS—and so the headlines ran.[20] In the days that followed, the metropolitan papers deluged

[16] *Ibid.*, 839-860.   [17] *Ibid.*, 860-868.
[18] Ogden, *Dies Committee*, p. 63.   [19] *Ibid.*, pp. 62-63.
[20] *New York Daily News*, August 20, 1938, p. 29; the *New York Times*, August 20, 1938, p. 1, August 21, 1938, p. 2; *New York World Telegram*, August 20, 1938, p. 92; the *New York Sun*, August 19, 1938, p. 19; *New York Journal and American*, August 21, 1938, p. 36. The New York Project's Publicity Department figured that 154 inches of

their readers with accounts of testimony, pictures of witnesses, and editorials vigorously supporting the Committee or denouncing its investigations as another of the hysterical "Red hunts" in which Congress so frequently indulged.[21] Nowhere was there a single column directly refuting testimony against the Federal Theatre. On "no account," WPA officials had cautioned Hallie Flanagan, was she to reply to such accusations.[22]

However, the WPA had not dismissed charges against the Federal Theatre as lightly as it appeared. By August 25, Paul Edwards, at the request of his superiors, was funneling into the Washington office employment records of the men and women who had appeared before the Committee, lists of nationally prominent persons who had agreed to express their approval of the Federal Theatre either in newspapers or by telegrams to Dies and his fellow representatives, and copies of letters of endorsement from public officials. A survey of personnel records alone, suggested the New York administrator, was sufficient reason to question the reliability of many of the witnesses. "In almost every instance," Edwards concluded, "the[se] people . . . are disgruntled employees . . . who have at some time or other been refused promotions because of lack of ability by either the Director of the Federal Theatre Project or myself." Hazel Huffman, he recalled, had visited his office on numerous occasions attempting to have her husband, Seymour Revzin, reclassified for a better position. Another example was Francis

---

adverse publicity had appeared in the metropolitan dailies during the week of August 14-21. George Kondolf to Hallie Flanagan, August 31, 1938, RG 69, FTP Records, Narr. Reports.

[21] *St. Louis Post-Dispatch*, August 17, 1938, p. 26.

[22] Flanagan, *Arena*, p. 335. When charges of Communist infiltration had been made in the past, denials had been issued by Federal Theatre and WPA officials, the matter dropped, and positive assessments of Project activities and plans released to the press. Note, for example, the charges carried in the *New York Times* on July 19, 1937, p. 1; the denial on July 20, 1937, p. 8; and the letter from the New York Project's publicity director, Ted Mauntz, to David Niles urging that the charges not be dignified by further rebuttal. See Mauntz to Niles, August 25, 1937, RG 69, GSS-211.2.

M. Verdi, who testified that his investigation of employees dismissed during the 1937 cuts had been stopped when Kondolf's executive assistant learned that the report would be unfavorable to the Workers' Alliance. In fact, Verdi's services had been terminated at a meeting in Edwards' office only after Burgess Meredith, acting president of Equity, had informed Verdi of his displeasure at the inefficient way the survey was being carried out, refused on behalf of Equity to accept the final report, and announced that his organization no longer wanted Verdi as its liaison man with the Federal Theatre. Obviously, Edwards concluded, there was no reason to permit Verdi to continue with his survey if the report would not be acceptable to the most important actors' association in the nation. As for charges that the Workers' Alliance controlled appointments to all available jobs, the New York Arts Projects administrator enclosed affidavits from employment officials declaring that they had neither furnished the Alliance with lists of available jobs nor consulted with its representatives about filling openings on the Project. Here was sufficient ammunition for an effective counter blast; but the Washington office continued to maintain a cautious silence, perhaps out of a desire to avoid further publicity, or perhaps in order to make further investigations.[23]

Thomas soon renewed his attack. Repeating charges that the Communist Party had gained "complete control" of the Federal Theatre, he claimed that Project employees who had testified before the Dies Committee had had their pay docked in way of retaliation.[24] Still unable to reply publicly, Hallie Flanagan once again wrote to Dies, reminding him of her offer to testify and citing Thomas' charges of financial reprisals as an example of the "inaccurate and misleading statements" made about the Project. Employees, she hastened to explain, could be paid only for time spent at work; witnesses would receive their full pay

[23] Edwards to Truman Felt, August 25, 1938, RG 69, FTP Records, NOGSF. In early August, Edwards began his own inquiry into charges of Communist activity. The *New York Times*, August 5, 1938, p. 4.

[24] The *New York Times*, September 1, 1938, p. 4.

if and when they made up time spent in Washington.[25] Much to the concern of fellow Theatre officials, her explanation, unlike Thomas' accusations, never made headline news.

Emmet Lavery, a lawyer and playwright as well as director of the National Service Bureau, was frankly upset with such "official inaction." "I feel that I must protest promptly and vigorously against an anaesthetic of silence which will in the end sabotage not only the project but the professional reputation of the executive identified with it," he declared in an impassioned letter to Hallie Flanagan.

> Day after day hearsay testimony floods the newspapers of the country, so that slander and libel thrive on the simple fact of their constant repetition and our administrative control does nothing, does nothing so consistently that any impartial lawyer might think we were all getting ready to plead guilty and throw ourselves on the mercy of the court!

Unable to understand why the WPA had refused to work out a coordinated program of defense or counterattack, Lavery reiterated his belief that the Federal Theatre should have countered each press release given out by the Committee with one of its own, once Dies had tabled the National Director's request to testify along with the regional directors. "What," he asked, "is the WPA going to do?"[26]

Mrs. Flanagan immediately forwarded Lavery's letter to Lawrence Morris, adding, "I think you should see this reaction to . . . silencing all our people on the Dies matter."[27] WPA officials were not convinced, but Hallie Flanagan was not yet defeated. If she could not reply directly to charges against the Project, then she would reply indirectly. A glowingly optimistic account of the Federal Theatre's production plans for the new

[25] Flanagan to Dies, September 1, 1938, RG 69, FTP Records, NOGSF. Mrs. Flanagan's letter was printed in the *New York Times*, September 2, 1938, p. 21.

[26] Lavery to Flanagan, September 2, 1938, RG 69, FTP Records, NOGSF.

[27] Memorandum, Flanagan to Morris, September 9, 1938, RG 69, FTP Records, NOGSF.

208

season would serve as a vehicle for some straight talk about the kind of productions done in the past. Covering a large portion of the front page of the theatre section, it could hardly be missed by that fraternity of readers who faithfully devoted their Sundays to the *New York Times*.[28] Similarly, the National Director's annual report to Hopkins on past achievements and future plans became—with Niles' permission—"a dignified way of answering lies" which had to be scotched.[29] It was mailed to mayors and WPA officials in every city which had a theatre project, to members of the Federal Theatre Advisory Committee, officers in Actors' Equity Association, drama critics, newspaper editors, columnists from Vermont to California, playwrights, actors, and other "persons of standing" in the theatrical and literary world.[30]

Almost as if he anticipated this pathetically cautious and circuitous counterattack, Thomas renewed his assault. In a radio address, he inveighed against "shameful and invidious condition[s]" in the Federal Theatre. Describing the Project as a "veritable hotbed of un-American activities," the New Jersey congressman accused its Director of having Communist sympathies and its plays, of ridiculing American ideals and suggesting rebellion against the government.[31] Once again the whole cycle of attack and silence repeated itself. Thomas' remarks would have gone unchallenged had not New York's Democratic congressman, Emanuel Celler, raised his voice in defense of the

[28] The *New York Times*, September 4, 1938, Sec. 10, p. 1.

[29] Flanagan to Niles, September 12, 1938, RG 69, FTP Records, NOC.

[30] Memorandum, Lawrence Morris to Ellen Woodward, September 22, 1938, RG 69, GSS-211.2. The Federal Theatre's third anniversary constituted another occasion for positive publicity. Responding to a tactful reminder from the New York Project's publicity director, leading Broadway actors and critics congratulated the Federal Theatre on a job well done. See letters and telegrams contained in RG 69, FTP Records, NOGSF and also columns by Richard Lockridge in the *New York Sun*, November 12, 1938, p. 12, and Burns Mantle, in the *New York Daily News*, October 28, 1938, p. 57.

[31] J. Parnell Thomas, Radio Address made over Station WQXR at 6:30 Monday evening, September 12, 1938, RG 69, FTP Records, NOGSF.

Project at a meeting of the American Theatre Council.[32] Not until mid-September, when Thomas and his fellow Committee member, Joseph Starnes, heard witnesses describe Communist activity on the Writers' Project, did WPA officials urge the Committee to hear the two national directors whose Projects were under attack.[33]

Hallie Flanagan, hoping that Dies might be moved by Mrs. Woodward's pleas for a hearing, began at once the grueling task of marshaling evidence that would refute the charges which had battered her theatre with such monotonous regularity during the past two months.[34] Transcripts of hearings were studied and analyzed; production records, playscripts, sponsors' lists, personnel records, administrative orders, and notarized statements were examined and reexamined. But these findings, however convincing, would be made public only if the Federal Theatre Director was granted a hearing before the Committee.[35] For the sake of that theatre, she could ill afford to wait in silence.

However "incredible the whole thing" seemed,[36] Hallie Flanagan realized that this was no red-tinged nightmare that would disappear upon awakening. Somehow she had to persuade the WPA to step into the public arena, and step in soon, for it was there that the whole matter of the objectives and procedures of the Dies Committee was being fought out. Accordingly, Federal Theatre officials requested that a qualified public relations

[32] Flanagan to Celler, September 14, 1938, RG 69, FTP Records, NOGSF.

[33] The Dies Committee began hearing testimony against the Writers' Project on September 16, 1938. The following day Mrs. Woodward wrote to Dies urging him to hear the national directors of both Projects and protesting his failure to call on WPA officials for testimony. See the *New York Times*, September 17, 1938, p. 18.

[34] Memorandum, Mary McFarland to Leslie Roberts, September 19, 1938; Memorandum, McFarland to Irwin Rubenstein, September 19, 1938; Memorandum, McFarland to George Kondolf, September 19, 1938, RG 69, FTP Records, NOGSF.

[35] Flanagan to Eleanor Bodine Fisher, September 22, 1938, RG 69, FTP Records, NOGSF.

[36] *Ibid.*

man be assigned to the WPA's apparently understaffed Department of Information. Able to write authoritatively about the theatre, he would whip the wealth of material on the Project into articles and feature stories for routine release to the wire services and issue "calm," "factual" replies when "public misstatements" were made about the Project.[37] An even more effective apologist for the Federal Theatre than any press release would be one of its own first-rate productions. If only *Prologue to Glory*, the Lincoln play which had won applause from New York audiences and a four-star rating from critic Burns Mantle, could be brought to the capital, Washington would realize that the Federal Theatre was neither ridiculing American ideals nor advocating revolution. But to this request, as to all previous requests for a performance in Washington, Hallie Flanagan received a familiar reply: such an expensive venture would have to be "postponed for the present."[38] Forbidden to reply directly with information refuting specific charges, and frustrated in her attempts to reply indirectly with proof of positive accomplishments, she could only wait.

By early October, it looked as if the waiting might be over. After a new flurry of correspondence with Dies, who claimed to have interpreted previous letters as an expression of willingness to testify rather than as an actual request to do so, the Federal Theatre Director was finally promised a hearing along

[37] Robert C. Schnitzer to Lawrence Morris, September 23, 1938; Flanagan to Schnitzer, September 29, 1938, RG 69, FTP Records, NOC.

[38] Ellen Woodward to Flanagan, September 26, 1938, RG 69, FTP Records, NOC. Fear of criticism about the cost of bringing a production to Washington seems to have acted as a powerful deterrent against doing so. In a letter to Emmet Lavery, Hallie Flanagan explained that in 1936 arrangements had been made for local sponsorship and even for theatre rentals in the belief that the Federal Theatre would bring *Power*, *Dr. Faustus* and the Chicago revue, *O Say Can You Sing*, to Washington. At the last minute, Hopkins had canceled all plans on the grounds that the expense of bringing even one play would be seized upon by congressional critics. In the fall of 1937, arrangements had again been made only to be subsequently vetoed by Niles. See Memorandum Flanagan to Lavery, March 8, 1938, RG 69, FTP Records, NOC.

211

with Ellen Woodward.[39] When she could testify, Dies would not say. All she could do was to stand by silently, while headlines proclaimed Dies' warning that workers in the Federal Theatre and Writers' Projects were "doing more to spread Communist propaganda than the Communist Party itself."[40] Although Mrs. Roosevelt had previously assured her anxious friend that she and the President "never worried much" about such charges,[41] even the chief executive grew concerned as the Committee pushed on with its probe in the midst of the 1938 campaign, attacking first, Michigan's governor, Frank Murphy, then implicating California's Democratic gubernatorial candidate, Culbert Olson.[42] Not until early November, shortly after the President had delivered a scathing condemnation of the Committee and its methods, was the date for the Federal Theatre Director's appearance actually set and the waiting brought to an end.[43]

In a final burst of preparation, Lavery and Theodore Mauntz of the New York Project's Publicity Department rushed down from New York to help members of the WPA's legal division wind up a two-hundred-page brief analyzing and answering every charge "specific enough to admit investigation." The completed document—including work records, copies of administrative orders and memoranda, excerpts from play reviews, lists of organizations sponsoring theatre parties, as well as numerous affidavits—was a clear, concise, and, in many respects, convinc-

[39] Dies to Flanagan, September 26, 1938; Woodward to Dies, September 29, 1938; Flanagan to Dies, October 1, 1938; Dies to Flanagan, October 6, 1938, RG 69, FTP Records, NOGSF.

[40] *New York Journal and American*, October 19, 1938, p. 33.

[41] Mrs. Roosevelt to Flanagan, September 28, 1938, RG 69, FTP Records, NOGSF. Mrs. Roosevelt continued to regard Dies' charges as another of the many attacks made against the President and his program which neither of them could afford to take seriously. Interview with Eleanor Roosevelt, November 8, 1961.

[42] Ogden, *Dies Committee*, pp. 74-81.

[43] For Roosevelt's statement denouncing the Committee, see "A Statement on the Sit-Down Strikes in Michigan and Governor Murphy," *The Public Papers and Addresses of Franklin D. Roosevelt*, comp. Samuel I. Rosenman (New York: Macmillan, 1941), VII: *The Continuing Struggle for Liberalism* (1938), pp. 559-561.

ing answer to charges and inferences that the Project, its plays, audiences, and important executives were Communist.[44]

In her own much-revised opening statement, Hallie Flanagan tried to answer briefly these same charges by pointing out that Federal Theatre audiences, for example, were hardly the card-carrying cadres the Committee seemed to think. On the contrary, they consisted in large part of theatre parties representing the Knights of Pythias, Knights of Columbus, Odd Fellows, Elks, Moose, Shriners, Masons, Eagles, Rotary, Kiwanis, Eastern Star, Hadassah, Orders of Amaranth, Girl Scouts, Boy Scouts, Camp Fire Girls, Veterans of Foreign Wars, American Legion, Jewish War Veterans, Army and Navy Clubs, YMCA, YWCA, and the Daughters of the American Revolution. She was also determined to acquaint the Committee with a list of the Project's accomplishments. Was it un-American, she would ask Martin Dies, to have provided relief for unemployed theatrical people and to have returned two thousand professionals to jobs in private industry, while winning critical acclaim from the leading dramatic critics in America? Was it un-American to have produced 924 plays—including classics, Americana, children's plays, dance plays, musical comedies, Living Newspapers, marionette shows, historical dramas—and to have carried thousands of these plays to schools, hospitals, camps, playgrounds, prisons, and reformatories?[45]

The effectiveness of Mrs. Flanagan's rebuttal was played up in straightforward, aggressively written press releases which also cited the Project's accomplishments;[46] but at the last minute it

[44] Hallie Flanagan, Draft of Statement to the Dies Committee, November 16, 1938; "Brief Containing Detailed Answers to Charges Made by Witnesses Who Appeared before the Special Committee to Investigate Un-American Activities, House of Representatives," RG 69, FTP Records, NOGSF.

[45] Hallie Flanagan, Draft of Statement to the Dies Committee, November 16, 1938; also subsequent undated Drafts, RG 69, FTP Records, NOGSF.

[46] Untitled press releases accompanying Drafts of Mrs. Flanagan's Statement, RG 69, FTP Records, NOGSF.

213

looked as if these press releases would have to be revised. The director of Women's and Professional Projects, Hopkins ruled, would present the brief of both national directors. Bitterly disappointed, Hallie Flanagan consoled herself with the reminder that what mattered most was that the information in the brief reach the public so that "misapprehensions" could be cleared up.[47]

Ellen Woodward had little reason to expect gentle handling when she appeared before the Un-American Activities Committee on December 5. Less than two weeks before, its chairman had demanded the resignation of Harold Ickes, Harry Hopkins, and Frances Perkins, and denounced their associates as Socialists, Communists, and "crack pots" whose position in the government impeded the nation's economic recovery.[48] More important, Dies had demonstrated in recent Committee hearings a hitherto hidden ability to conduct searching cross-examinations—a talent which he was about to use with devastating effect.

The witness was sworn in and the questioning began. Why had she, rather than the directors of the Writers' and Theatre Projects, come to testify? Defending her right to appear before the Committee as the "responsible official" in charge of her division, the Mississippi-born Mrs. Woodward began reading a prepared statement in her Southern drawl. She was permitted a few moments of grace while she briefly described the projects under attack; but with the first denial of un-American activity, questions followed furiously. Pressed to explain her statements, prove her assertions, qualify her generalizations, describe and defend her sources of information, she had to yield ground over and over again. When she insisted that most of the witnesses who testified against the Theatre Project were "disqualified to testify on the subject matter under investigation," she was forced to admit that artistic training was not necessary for the recognition of un-American activities. When she repeatedly asserted

[47] Flanagan to Frank Gillmore, December 2, 1938, RG 69, FTP Records, NOGSF.
[48] The *New York Times*, November 25, 1938, p. 3.

that she knew of no Communist activity in either the Theatre Project or the Writers' Project, she was pushed to admit that her statement was based not on her own personal knowledge, but rather on the reports of subordinates. When she tried to refute accusations that audiences attending Federal Theatre plays were composed almost entirely of Communist or radical groups, she was criticized for making a "broad, sweeping declaration . . . not backed up by a reading of the testimony of the [previous] witness." Miss Huffman, Dies insisted, had made no such accusation. She had simply said:

> We felt that the play was put on because they [Federal Theatre directors] could not get any audience for anything except communistic plays. They sell block tickets to organizations, and the majority of these organizations which buy these block tickets are the Workers' Alliance, and what we call the 'Below Fourteenth Street' group . . . the communist party, various little locals, and that sort of thing.

Mrs. Woodward retorted that she had originally prefaced her own statement by saying that she would answer accusations "made directly or by inference." She had made her point.

She should have followed it up with evidence showing that the majority of the organizations buying block tickets were not those listed by Hazel Huffman. Instead, the apparently shaken witness began discussing charges that the operation of the Project was dominated by alleged front organizations of the Communist Party. Minutes later she was involved in a similar plight. This time she was forced to concede that witnesses had called only some of the Project's plays un-American—twenty-six, to be exact. When she doggedly persisted in reading reviews of those plays, she was told that she was not answering charges of communism. A favorable review, Dies insisted, "simply means that the dramatic critic believes that this play, from a dramatic standpoint, is a good play; he is not charged with the duty of deciding whether or not the play spreads propaganda or Communist doctrine." Questioned as to whether she was familiar with the contents of the twenty-six plays under attack, Mrs. Woodward was again compelled to admit that she had read or seen only about half. Asked whether she could offer from her "personal knowledge" anything about the background of the authors, she had to confess that she could not. At last, Dies announced that the Committee would adjourn until the following morning when Hallie Flanagan would be asked to testify. Still insisting that she was the "responsible head" of her division, the exhausted witness stepped down with parts of her much-interrupted statement still unread. In a brief appearance on the following day, Mrs. Woodward declared that she would terminate her statement so that Mrs. Flanagan could testify on "certain details" with which the National Director would be "more familiar." Her own statement, Dies assured her, would be included in the record, but the Committee would have to determine later whether the large briefs on the Theatre and Writers' Projects would be published. Obviously—and with good reason—Ellen Woodward was none too pleased with her day in the court of Martin Dies.[49]

As an assistant administrator of the WPA Mrs. Woodward had come before the Dies Committee prepared to read a statement which refuted charges of Communism on two of the projects under her jurisdiction—a statement based in large part on reports of subordinates. Because she was willing to stand by these reports and the people who had made them, she assumed that her statement would be accepted with no less credence than Dies gave to the findings of his subcommittee headed by Starnes in New York City. It was an understandable, but naïve, assumption. Dies would accept testimony taken by his subcommittee for the same reason that he permitted previous witnesses to read a prepared statement accusing anyone and everyone, with merely "perfunctory or confirmatory interruptions" from the

<hr/>

[49] *House Un-American Activities Committee Hearings*, IV, 2,729-2,830, 2,837-2,838.

Committee: such accusations furnished new ammunition for his quarrel with the President. Martin Dies was neither foolish enough nor fair enough to permit a pro-administration witness the same latitude. For over six hours he, Starnes, and Thomas had conducted a vigorous, stimulating interrogation which, if applied to Hazel Huffman, would have revealed her testimony for what it was—a collection of frequently inaccurate, uninformed statements in support of flimsily based accusations containing some degree of truth. Every statement that the WPA administrator made had to be proved, "every word that she uttered had to be explained; the sources of her charges were explored in detail and her fitness to testify was thoroughly discussed." In short, the cross-examination of Ellen Woodward was a "model of what might have been done" with all the testimony heard by the Committee. Dutifully reported in the *New York Times*, it made no headlines. In the *Washington Star*, it was buried in the middle of a column headlined: JAMES ROOSEVELT GAVE NOTHING TO CHURCH, MINISTER SAYS— "President's Son Criticized at Dies Hearing by Washington Pastor."[50]

On the following day Hallie Flanagan was sworn in by Dies, whom she later described as a huge, "rangy Texan with a cowboy drawl and a big black cigar."[51] He, in turn, would probably have recalled a tiny, soft-spoken redhead who looked "as if the first mild breeze would blow her back to Vassar College."[52] They were not ill matched. Mrs. Flanagan was determined to talk about the Federal Theatre and its accomplishments, even if it meant interjecting information between questions. Dies and at least two of his colleagues were equally determined to talk about Mrs. Flanagan, even if it meant constantly interrupting each other as well as the witness. Asked about her official

[50] Ogden, *Dies Committee*, pp. 94-95; the *New York Times*, December 6, 1938, p. 17; *Washington Star*, December 6, 1938, RG 69, FTP Records, FTP-PC.

[51] Flanagan, *Arena*, p. 340.

[52] Interview with James Ullman, November 17, 1961.

217

duties, Mrs. Flanagan replied: "Since August 29, 1935, I have been . . . combatting un-American inactivity." Realizing that the subtlety was lost on the representatives, she immediately launched into a description of the kind of inactivity she had been trying to combat; but the Committee would not be put off. What, Starnes asked, was the primary purpose of the Federal Theatre? Was it not true that she considered the welfare of the Project more important than relief of the needy? In making that accusation, the National Director replied, Miss Huffman had quoted only a portion of an order dealing with dismissals which, if examined in its entirety, would reveal that all of those involved were relief personnel. Under such circumstances, value to the Project was surely a legitimate consideration. Had she appeared before a congressional committee and urged the establishment of a National Theatre? No, at the request of her superiors she had merely appeared before the Patents Committee to discuss the Federal Theatre. Had she been to Russia? Yes, along with twelve other countries when she was studying European theatres on a Guggenheim grant. Did she spend more time in Russia than in any other country? Yes, there were more theatres in Russia than in any other country. Did she write a book about her trip? Yes, *Shifting Scenes*; and when the book came out in 1927, not one reviewer had considered it subversive. Why did she go back to Russia in 1931? Was she a delegate to anything? No. Did she meet Elmer Rice in Russia at this Russian Theatre Festival she was attending? No. Had she been a member of a Russian organization? No.

The Committee then shifted to Communist activity on the Federal Theatre Project. What about the dissemination of Communist literature on the Project? Skirting around Ellen Woodward's unequivocal denial, Mrs. Flanagan replied that she had never seen Communist literature distributed. If such action had taken place, it was done against her express orders forbidding such improper use of Project time or property. Persons found guilty would, of course, be dismissed immediately.

218

Starnes returned to a discussion of the theatre, only to have the witness meet his query about the use of the theatre as a weapon with a discussion of the theatre as "a great educational force," as "entertainment" and "excitement." In short, she replied, the theatre could be "all things to all men." This tack failing, the Alabama Democrat began reading quotations from the two sources which Hazel Huffman had cited as proof of the author's Communist sympathies: *Shifting Scenes* and an article in *Theatre Arts Monthly* on the amateur agitprop companies springing up in New York and elsewhere in the early 'thirties.[53] Asked about each quotation, Mrs. Flanagan replied that she had indeed written these statements—in fact, they sounded rather better than she had remembered. In each instance, however, she had been reporting on what was happening in the Russian theatre in 1928 and in the American workers' theatres in 1931. Had she written the following? "Admittedly a weapon in the class struggle, this theatre is being forged in the factories and mines. Its mouthpiece is the *Workers' Theatre*, a magazine mimeographed monthly by the Workers' Laboratory Theatre of New York." Hallie Flanagan replied once again that she had been reporting, at the request of the editor of *Theatre Arts Monthly*, on a theatrical movement which had nothing whatsoever to do with the Federal Theatre. "But," Starnes protested, "this is a quotation from you. What I am quoting from is an article headed 'A Theatre is Born,' by Hallie Flanagan." "Exactly," replied the author. Disgusted by this apparent obtuseness, she added, "but the theatre was not born through me, Mr. Starnes."

[53] Hallie Flanagan, "A Theatre is Born," *Theatre Arts Monthly*, xv (November 1931), 908-915. The article is a sympathetic account of a meeting sponsored by the John Reed Club and the *New Masses* in New York City on June 13, 1931 for the purpose of organizing workers' theatres. In the article she is critical of the exclusive emphasis on revolt and predicts that the forthcoming plays will be "crude, violent, childish, and repetitious." "It is only in the event of the success of its [the workers' theatre] herculean aim—the reorganization of our social order—that we shall become an involuntary audience," she concludes.

Plays of "social significance" were the next point of attack. Did the Federal Theatre produce propaganda plays or plays that bred class consciousness? Insisting that they first define "propaganda," Mrs. Flanagan replied:

> Propaganda, after all, is education. It is education focused on certain things. For example, some of you gentlemen have doubtless seen *One-Third of a Nation*; and I certainly would not sit here and say that that was not a propaganda play. . . . I should like to say very truthfully that to the best of my knowledge we have never done a play which was propaganda for communism, but we have done plays which were propaganda for democracy, propaganda for better housing. . . .

Asked about specific plays, she readily admitted that *Injunction Granted* was "propaganda for fair labor relations and for fairness to labor in the courts"; but, she insisted, "I do not believe it fosters class hatred."

Starnes, changing the line of questioning, returned to the *Theatre Arts Monthly* article. Mrs. Flanagan insisted once again that the statements quoted were purely descriptive— descriptive, moreover, of the mood and beliefs of the people about whom she was writing, not her own. Although she tried to work in a discussion of Federal Theatre audiences, the Alabama representative could not be diverted by a listing of the religious, civic, and educational groups which supported the Theatre Project. Picking up the now familiar theatrical periodical, Starnes turned to a description of the sense of high purpose and dedication which characterized the workers' theatre movement. "They intend to remake a social structure without the help of money," he read, "and this ambition alone invests their undertaking with a certain Marlowesque madness." "You are quoting from this Marlowe. Is he a Communist?" Starnes asked. Mrs. Flanagan replied that she was referring to Christopher Marlowe. "Tell us who Marlowe is," Starnes insisted, "so we can get the proper reference, because that is all that we want to do." With a dramatist's full appreciation of irony, she replied: "Put in the record that he was the greatest dramatist in the period of Shakespeare, immediately preceding Shakespeare." Starnes tried to retrieve himself, but it was a blunder that would wind up in his obituary.[54]

Thomas, taking over from his embarrassed colleague, began questioning the witness about *The Revolt of the Beavers*. The play, Mrs. Flanagan insisted somewhat obliquely, had been written for neither critics nor commissioners, but for children. According to the surveys made by a psychologist at New York University, the children attending *The Revolt of the Beavers* believed that the play taught them "never to be selfish . . . that it is better to be good than bad. That beavers have manners just like children . . . [that] if you are unkind any time in your life, you will always regret it . . . ," and so on.

Turning next to the Living Newspaper production, *Injunction Granted*, Thomas read an episode in the play in which members of the Workers' Alliance criticized the New Jersey legislature for its failure to provide adequate relief for the unemployed. As a former member of that legislature, the New Jersey Republican demanded to know whether the witness thought it proper for an agency of the federal government "to put out this kind of propaganda against the elected legislature of a particular state." Hallie Flanagan replied that all information had been taken from newspaper accounts, and that it was perfectly proper for the Federal Theatre to produce a limited number of plays dealing with contemporary problems.

Dies, resuming his New Jersey colleague's line of inquiry, continued to press the National Director about the kind of plays which a federally subsidized theatre should produce. While both agreed that theatre could teach as well as entertain, each had his own opinion as to whether a government theatre was justified in using propaganda for purposes of education. For example:

[54] The *New York Times*, January 10, 1962, p. 47.

221

CHM. DIES: Do you think the Federal Theatre should be used for the purpose of conveying ideas along social, economic, or political lines?

MRS. FLANAGAN: I would hesitate on political. . . .

CHM. DIES: Eliminate political, upon social and economic lines.

MRS. FLANAGAN: I think it is one logical, reasonable, and I might say imperative thing for our theatre to do.

CHM. DIES: You think it is entirely proper that the Federal Theatre produce plays for the purpose of bringing out some social idea that is a heated issue at a particular time?

MRS. FLANAGAN: . . . it is one of the things that the theatre can do.

CHM. DIES: Do you not also think that since the Federal Theatre Project is an agency of the Government and that all of our people support it through their tax money, . . . that no play should ever be produced which undertakes to portray the interests of one class to the disadvantage of another class, even though that might be accurate, even though factually there may be justification normally for that, yet because of the very fact that we are using taxpayers' money to produce plays, do you not think it is questionable . . . ?

MRS. FLANAGAN: I think we strive for objectivity, but I think the whole history of plays in the theatre would indicate that any dramatist holds a passionate brief for the things he is saying.

The argument persisted, but Dies could not make his witness back down. Neither, in fact, was convincing the other—they simply were not speaking the same language. Finally, Mrs. Flanagan pointed out that she had appeared to refute specific charges of Communist activity. Dies, disregarding the huge amount of hearsay evidence that he had allowed in the past, replied that the fact that she personally knew of no such activity was hardly proof that it did not exist. Nor was he interested in affidavits from people on the Project denying charges made against them by previous witnesses. Upon learning that it was 1:15, the chairman announced that the Committee would

222

adjourn for an hour, and that the director of the Writers' Project would be heard next. Mrs. Flanagan interrupted to ask if this concluded her testimony; Dies promised to "see about it after lunch." Mrs. Flanagan then asked if she might be allowed to make a final statement. "We will see about it after lunch," Dies replied, and the gavel fell.[55]

Henry Alsberg was promptly sworn in as soon as hearings were resumed. When Mrs. Flanagan complained to the secretary that she had not completed her testimony, he promised to have her brief included in the transcript.[56] Somewhat reassured, she settled back while Alsberg frankly admitted that portions of several of the state guidebooks had to be "toned down" by his Washington staff before publication so as to avoid anything of a controversial or biased nature.[57] When Mrs. Flanagan approached David Niles about making the brief public, he, too, assured her that the Committee would not suppress evidence and promised to have mimeographed copies distributed to every member of Congress.[58] Mrs. Flanagan's office subsequently sent over five hundred copies to Niles' office. They were never distributed.[59] When printed records of the hearings appeared, the brief was not included. A small portion of the evidence she had waited so long to get before the public was, at best, dutifully reported in the *New York Times*; at worst, grossly distorted in the *Chicago Tribune*. "The Dies House Committee," the *Tribune* chortled, "received further evidence today that Communists in supervisory capacities on the Federal Theatre and Federal Writers' Projects of the WPA are using government funds for relief to disseminate revolutionary propaganda."[60]

[55] *House Un-American Activities Committee Hearings*, IV, 2,838-2,885.
[56] Flanagan, *Arena*, p. 346.
[57] *House Un-American Activities Committee Hearings*, IV, 2,886-2,908.
[58] Flanagan, *Arena*, p. 346.
[59] *Ibid.*
[60] The *New York Times*, December 7, 1938, p. 2; *Chicago Tribune*, December 7, 1938, p. 5. The *Tribune*'s report, written by Chesly Manly, appeared under the headlines BARE REDS' USE OF RELIEF CASH IN PROPAGANDA.

223

Even if her testimony had been accurately reported in its entirety, the more discerning reader would have been forced to conclude that Hallie Flanagan could not, as she claimed, positively refute "every charge" made against the Project.[61] She could demonstrate that Federal Theatre plays were not advocating overthrow of the government, that its audiences included a wide variety of thoroughly American groups, and that its Director had consistently forbidden the distribution of Communist literature on Project time by Project personnel. She could not, however, effectively deny that the distribution of such literature had taken place—albeit illegally—or that members of the Workers' Alliance, the CPC, or the Supervisors Council had exerted the subtle pressures of which they were accused. The less discerning reader, influenced by Dies' and Starnes' preoccupation with the witness' past writings and present conception of the theatre, might well have questioned the testimony of a woman whose ideas hardly seemed "safe."

Actually, the public never really had a chance to arrive at an honest assessment of the extent of Communist activity in the Federal Theatre. During the four months that had elapsed since J. Parnell Thomas first denounced the Project as a "hotbed of communism," press coverage of the Dies Committee was estimated to have exceeded more column inches of space than that given to any other single organization in the country— coverage which unbiased observers termed favorable and Dies himself called fair.[62] While newspapers throughout the nation splashed across their pages charges against the Federal Theatre, not one detailed denial was issued by the Project's Director in its defense. Unable to convince the WPA that failure to answer charges would be interpreted by the public as an admission of guilt, she had waited in silence until called before the Commit-

[61] Flanagan to Claude Pepper, January 13, 1939, RG 69, FTP Records, NOGSF.

[62] S. Henderson Britt and Seldon C. Menefee, "Did the Publicity of the Dies Committee in 1938 Influence Public Opinion?," *The Public Opinion Quarterly*, III (July 1939), 451; Ogden, *Dies Committee*, p. 102.

tee. Her belated reply, when finally made, was awarded scant notice in the press, except in those anti-administration newspapers which twisted her words with impunity.

When the Committee's chief witness, Hazel Huffman, returned for further testimony on December 8, Representatives Dempsey and Healey insisted that both she and the Committee distinguish between "what is un-American and what is propaganda."[63] But such distinctions, like Dempsey's observation that determining the propriety of federally subsidized propaganda plays was not "within the scope of this Committee," were far less newsworthy than the absent chairman's luncheon speech attacking Nazis.[64] The effectiveness of what was reported was revealed by a Gallup poll showing that three out of five voters were familiar with the work of the Dies Committee; and of these, 75 per cent favored continuing the investigations.[65]

On January 3, 1939, Dies, who had already begun campaigning for continuance of the Committee, promptly presented the new Congress with a report of his investigations. In the section dealing with the Federal Theatre, the Committee described its inquiry in a single paragraph:

> We heard some of the employees and former employees in the Federal Theatre Project in New York City. . . . From that testimony we conclude that a rather large number of employees of the . . . Project are either members of the communist party or sympathizers with the communist party. It is also clear that certain employees felt under the compulsion to join the Workers' Alliance in order to retain their jobs.

[63] *House Un-American Activities Committee Hearings*, IV, 2,987-2,998. Neither Dempsey nor Healey had attended many of the previous sessions. When Hazel Huffman returned to vindicate herself against Mrs. Woodward's assertion that she was not a qualified witness, Dempsey attempted to give her a taste of the kind of cross-examination to which Ellen Woodward had been subjected.

[64] The *New York Times*, December 9, 1938, p. 10.

[65] The *Washington Post*, December 11, 1938, Sec. 3, p. 1.

No mention was made of Hallie Flanagan's testimony, but Alsberg was quoted as not "denying" that there were a number of Communists on the Writers' Project.[66]

The statement was considerably more restrained than might have been expected—a tribute no doubt to the effectiveness with which Representatives Dempsey and Healey had wielded the threat of a minority report.[67] Charges or influences that the Federal Theatre's audiences and management consisted mainly of Communists were wisely dropped, as was any mention of Communist propaganda in Project productions. While the Committee had not seen fit to inhibit its witnesses with a definition of terms, it had described un-American propaganda in its report to the House as any teaching which embraces all or an essential part of the principles of Communism.[68] Conceivably, therefore, Dies could have cited a handful of plays such as John Howard Lawson's strike drama, *Processional*, as portraying class conflict—certainly an essential Communist principle—but, like other socially relevant plays produced by the Federal Theatre, the Lawson play was not manufactured in Moscow. Although the author had become a Party member in the 'thirties, the play itself was an expressionistic drama of 1925 vintage. Its characters—"striking miners, cruel vigilantes, warmongering newspapermen, cheating capitalists, foreign-born radicals, flaming youth and ridiculous Klansmen"—owed as much to Mencken as to Marx.[69] Even when Lawson revised parts of the play for the 1937 revival, he left his strikers rough, stupid miners rather

[66] Report of the Special House Committee on Un-American Activities—Pursuant H. Res. 282, *Investigation of Un-American Activities and Propaganda*, 75th Cong., 4th Sess. (1939), p. 31 (*House Un-American Activities Committee Report*).

[67] Healey and Dempsey were deterred from submitting a minority report only when Dies agreed to insert a paragraph disavowing responsibility for the credibility of Committee witnesses and admitting that much of their testimony had been "exaggerated" and "biased." See Brandt, "The Dies Committee: An Appraisal," *The Atlantic Monthly*, CLXV (February 1940), 237.

[68] *House Un-American Activities Committee Report*, p. 12.

[69] Himmelstein, *Drama Was A Weapon*, p. 104.

than ennobled representatives of the proletariat.[70] Thus, of the nearly one thousand plays produced by the Federal Theatre, only *The Revolt of the Beavers* could clearly have been labeled "un-American."[71] With the single exception of this Marxian fantasy for children, the songs of social significance sung by the Federal Theatre did not include the Internationale. Some plays, to be sure, exposed injustices; others called for reform; and still others proposed solutions. But the injustices, while often publicized by the Communist Party, were real enough to be seen by any sensitive American without the help of the Party. Their exposure, inspired by the words of the Second Inaugural —"I paint this picture [of one-third of a nation ill housed, ill clad, ill nourished] because the nation, seeing it and understanding the injustice in it, proposes to paint it out," was in the tradition of the muckrakers rather than Marx. Similarly, their solution, to the despair of critics from the *Daily Worker*, seldom correctly corresponded to the Party line. Obviously the political wisdom of producing plays which called for better housing for slum dwellers, union membership for workers, and cheap power for consumers was questionable. But, as Dies apparently realized, it was not a question to be answered by a Committee charged with investigating un-American activities.

Even on the question of Communist activity, the Committee moved gingerly, reporting only that "a rather large number" of employees on the Federal Theatre Project in New York City were either "members of the communist party or sympathizers with the communist party." Their conclusion was hardly surprising, in view of the congressional ruling explicitly forbidding discrimination against certified relief clients on the basis of political affiliation. Just how large this "rather large" number of Communists actually was, however, only Party lists would have revealed. Dies, himself, admitted that the Committee was never

[70] *Ibid.*

[71] For a careful analysis of other socially relevant plays produced by the New York Project, see Himmelstein, Ch. 6.

able to secure complete membership records.[72] "Sympathizers" belonging to the Workers' Alliance and its various affiliates, while probably more numerous than card-carrying Communists, never included more than a small minority of theatrical people, since most already belonged to the old established stage unions which vigorously discouraged dual membership.[73] According to an Alliance executive, "professionals" who had joined the relief union were primarily members of the Negro, Jewish, and dance groups, the Living Newspaper research staff, the radio division, and the National Service Bureau, with clerical and maintenance workers making up the greater portion of Theatre Project members.[74]

Whatever their actual number, the activities of these people, and not their presence on the Federal Theatre, was the proper subject for investigation. Among both Communists and fellow travelers who may, or more probably may not, have belonged to an Alliance affiliate, were a few, highly talented, creative individuals. Alienated from the strident, tawdry commercialism of the 'twenties and distressed by the evictions, breadlines, hunger marches, and Hoovervilles of the 'thirties, they sought commitment through a movement that promised to save mankind from poverty and war at a time when millions were on relief and the Third Reich threatened the peace of the Western world. Not necessarily simpleminded or maladjusted, they re-

[72] Martin Dies, *Martin Dies' Story* (New York: Bookmailer, 1963), p. 63.

[73] Investigators hired by the House Appropriations Committee to secure information on the Federal Theatre were told by Equity officials that the Actors' Union estimated that those on the Project who were either unaffiliated or affiliated with the Workers' Alliance amounted only to about 10 per cent. See Harold H. Buckles and H. Ralph Burton. Interview with Robert I. Haines, July 15, 1939. Record Group 233, Records of the House of Representatives, Appropriations Committee, Subcommittee on Work Projects Administration (RG 233, Approp. Comm. on WPA).

[74] John Rimassa to George Kondolf, April 5, 1938, RG 69, FTP Records, NOGSF. Rimassa was chairman of the Federal Theatre Executive Committee of the Workers' Alliance.

garded their commitment, to use Arthur Koestler's words, as the "logical extension of the progressive humanistic trend."[75]

Usually on the intellectual periphery of Communism rather than at the center of the party organization, they made a substantial contribution to the Federal Theatre without permitting political attachments to interfere with artistic efforts.[76] Others, also capable, were less willing or able to maintain this separation. And the rank and file of extreme leftists, especially those with little artistic ability and few professional qualifications, undoubtedly devoted more energy to furthering the fortunes of the Workers' Alliance, the CPC, the Supervisors Council, and the Communist Party, than those of the Federal Theatre. The Party, after all, had as its primary goal after 1935 the infiltration and control of labor unions, literary and theatrical groups, popular front organizations, and even the government itself.[77] The Federal Theatre, a far more wealthy and successful enterprise than the dramatic groups previously under Party command, rep-

[75] Arthur Koestler, *Arrow in the Blue* (London: Collins Press, 1952), p. 249.

[76] For an excellent study of writers and the nature of their attachment to Communism, see Daniel Aaron, *Writers on the Left: Episodes in American Literary Communism* (New York: Harcourt, Brace and World, 1961). Somewhat comparable studies of the theatre are Himmelstein, *Drama Was A Weapon* and Gerald Rabkin, *Drama and Commitment: Politics in the American Theatre of the Thirties* (Bloomington, Ind.: Indiana University Press, 1964). The general mood of some of the more talented and socially conscious actors and directors during this decade is well conveyed in Harold Clurman's history of the Group Theatre. See, *The Fervent Years: The Story of the Group Theatre and the Thirties* (New York: Hill and Wang, 1957). More general, but also worthwhile, are James Wechsler, *The Age of Suspicion* (New York: Random House, 1953), Murray Kempton, *Part of Our Time: Some Ruins and Monuments of the Thirties* (New York: Simon and Schuster, 1955), and Irving Howe and Lewis Coser, *The American Communist Party: A Critical History* (Boston: Beacon Press, 1957), Chs. 7-8. Brief but useful are portions of Daniel Bell's chapter on the development of Marxism in the U. S. contained in Donald Egbert and Stowe Persons' *Socialism and American Life* (Princeton, N. J.: Princeton University Press, 1952), Vol. I, 346-369.

[77] For a discussion of Party tactics and activities from 1935-39, see Howe and Coser, *The American Communist Party*, Ch. 8.

resented a potential weapon of no mean consequence in the revolutionary struggle.[78] Although Communists were never able to gain control of the management of the Federal Theatre, in the course of their attempts the Workers' Alliance and its affiliates were unquestionably guilty of some of the thoroughly undesirable, if seemingly minor, activities with which they were charged.[79] Although forbidden by Project officials, such activities were difficult enough to pin down and, in some cases, still more difficult to prove "un-American." In its final report,

[78] Despite all the hue and cry during the early 'thirties about the "new theatre movement," drama had not proved a very successful weapon in the Communist arsenal, according to Morgan Himmelstein. The amateur troupes which tried to win adherents to the cause, first with street corner agitprops and then with the realistic dramas of the Theatre Collective and the Theatre for Action, had spluttered out without kindling revolutionary fires in the New York populace. The League of Workers' Theatres, organized around 1932, not only failed to attract many amateur theatre groups in its fight for a Soviet America, but also failed to control those it did attract. Unable to supply its troupes with good Marxist scripts or to inspire professional performances of plays it could provide, the League had been saved only by the advent of the Popular Front. Reorganized as the New Theatre League, Party thespians promptly abandoned old revolutionary sectarianism in favor of the struggle against war, Fascism, and censorship. With its new program sufficiently vague, the New Theatre League managed to "discover" Clifford Odet's *Waiting for Lefty*. But its audiences, Himmelstein contends, were soon preempted by the far more popular Federal Theatre. See Himmelstein, *Drama Was A Weapon*, for a fuller discussion of left-wing theatre in New York during the 'thirties.

[79] For samples of the kind of literature the Alliance and its affiliates could legally distribute before work began at nine o'clock, see RG 69, FTP Records, NOGSF. Included in this material is "The Prompter," put out by the City Projects Council on June 9, 1937, containing an announcement of a fine of one day's pay for all employees not joining in the work stoppage to protest cuts. Also included are Workers' Alliance handbills concerned with strike notices and "Play Red," a publication of the Communist Party unit of the Play Bureau (a part of the National Service Bureau). Conferences between representatives of the CPC and Mrs. Flanagan concerning the distribution of literature were held in March 1937, with Hallie Flanagan insisting on the nine o'clock deadline. See Reports of Conferences between Representatives of the Federal Theatre and the City Projects Council, March 24, 1937, also others not dated, RG 69, FTP Records, NOGSF.

the Committee limited itself to the observation that "certain employees felt under compulsion to join the Workers' Alliance in order to retain their jobs."[80] Here Dies was on somewhat more solid ground. In one year alone, the joint appeals board of the New York City Arts Projects heard thirty-six cases in which Project supervisors were found guilty of discharging Federal Theatre employees for failing to join a union, almost invariably the Workers' Alliance.[81]

Hallie Flanagan, while refusing to acknowledge the Marxist overtones in *The Revolt of the Beavers*, was not unaware of what Walter Winchell called the New York Project's "Revolution-by-Wednesday boys." Informed in detail of the "doings of the Communists" in the experimental theatre unit less than a year after the Project's inception, she found the "whole thing . . . infuriating."[82] "Between the fascists and communists" the Federal Theatre "will not have much chance," she privately bemoaned.[83] Unable to act without some proof of activities contrary to Project orders, she could only wait until a reorganization of the New York Project, necessitated by cuts, provided an occasion to disband the experimental unit. Nor did she have much leeway in dealing with the Workers' Alliance. Although removed by both sex and geography from the kind of extreme pressures and harassment to which Kondolf was subjected,[84] both she and the New York director had officially to deal with the Alliance as one of many unions whose demands—in this case, strident and vociferous—were to be met whenever possible. In private, however, she repeatedly warned the heads of both the Workers' Alliance and the CPC against endangering the jobs of the entire Project; in lecture after lecture, she reminded members that the future lay in working for the Fed-

[80] Dies' assumption that the Workers' Alliance was dominated by the Communist Party was a sound one. See Howe and Coser, *The American Communist Party*, p. 197.

[81] The *New York Times*, February 14, 1938, p. 20.

[82] Flanagan to Philip Davis, July 30, 1936, Flanagan Papers.

[83] *Ibid*.

[84] Interview with George Kondolf, November 1, 1961.

eral Theatre, not for some faction or political creed.[85] But as long as workers could not be dismissed for organizational activities which were not conducted on Project time or with Project equipment, she was frankly at a loss as to what to do when admonitions and cajolery failed. Kondolf, despite his intense dislike of Alliance agitators, was able to do little more. Responsible for a theatre and theatrical productions, the overworked producer made every effort to fill new openings with bona fide Equity members.[86] But he well knew that even the most judicious "weeding" of undesirable elements would be met with cries of illegal discrimination, demands for a hearing, probably reinstatement of those fired, and, of course, the inevitable publicity.

Had the Federal Theatre Director explained these difficulties in the course of her testimony, her session before the Dies Committee might have been more pleasant. But, as Alsberg's experience proved, any admission was likely to be interpreted as a full confession by certain members of both the Committee and the press. At the time, Hallie Flanagan's immediate concern had been to get before the Committee and the public facts that would vigorously and convincingly refute the many erroneous accusations hurled month after month at the entire Federal Theatre. Yet she knew she had failed completely. "Eventually I assume that the material presented at this hearing will be printed," she wrote to Florida's new Democratic senator, Claude Pepper, "but how many people will ever read it or hear of it?" In the eyes of the public, she lamented, "the project and its director still stand falsely accused."[87]

In the eyes of the public, the Project and its Director did stand accused—and, in large part, falsely so. Although a minority of militant leftists on the New York Project were far from blameless, responsibility for the accusations which ulti-

[85] Memorandum, Flanagan to Emmet Lavery, March 8, 1938, RG 69, FTP Records, NOC.

[86] Interview with George Kondolf, November 1, 1961.

[87] Flanagan to Pepper, January 13, 1939, RG 69, FTP Records, NOGSF.

mately jeopardized the future of a nationwide theatre employing nine thousand needy workers rested heavily with the Dies Committee. Without regard for fairness of procedure or rules of evidence, the Committee had virtually opened its doors to anyone who cared to make charges against labor unions, public organizations, and departments and agencies of the federal government. The Theatre Project—with its leftist element, its reputation for "radical productions," and its tie-in with the New Deal—was an ideal target for enemies of the administration as well as disgruntled Project employees. Given a relatively free hand, Representative Thomas and his witnesses had blasted forth with frequently unsupported, widely publicized charges that went virtually unchecked. To be sure, publications such as *The Nation* and *The New Republic* had criticized the Committee's methods and procedures with equal fervor.[88] The President, soundly denouncing the one-sided nature of its investigations, had urged members to stop allowing the Committee to be used as a "forum" for headline seekers with "mere opinion evidence" inadmissible in any ordinary court.[89] And Hallie Flanagan had made a gallant effort to defend the Project—but to no avail. The Federal Theatre Director and the Committee

[88] Paul Y. Anderson, "Fascism Hits Washington," *The Nation*, CXLVII (August 27, 1937), 198-199; Paul Y. Anderson, "Investigate Mr. Dies!," *The Nation*, CXLVII (November 5, 1938), 471-472; Paul Y. Anderson, "Behind the Dies Intrigue," *The Nation*, CXLVI (November 12, 1938), 499-500; TRB, "Demagoguery on the Chesapeake," *The New Republic*, XCVI (August 31, 1938), 102; "The Dies Committee Mess," *The New Republic*, XCVI (August 31, 1938), 90; "Still a Mess," *The New Republic*, XCVI (September 28, 1938), 198; Heywood Broun, "Uriah Comes to Judgment: Dies Committee," *The New Republic*, XCVI (September 7, 1938), 129-130. The only defense of the Federal Theatre which was published in a periodical was that by Emmet Lavery. See "Communism and the Federal Theatre," *The Commonweal*, XXXVII (October 7, 1938), 610-612. *Collier's* probably best expressed the attitude of a greater number of Americans in its editorial "More Dollars for Dies," LIII (January 14, 1939), 50. Admitting that witnesses for the Committee had been "funny looking phonies," their "yarns about Fascism and Communist activities . . . fantastic," the editor nonetheless argued that it was a "good thing" to have the Committee spotlight on subversive groups.

[89] See p. 212, footnote 43.

chairman, in effect, spoke a different language, so dissimilar were their assumptions. The Vassar professor, with her ebullient faith in the ability of a democracy to tolerate honest difference and reform legitimate wrongs, was confident that a federally supported theatre could and should help men to understand the injustices that fed the ideologies which Dies had sworn to expose. The Texas Democrat, fearful for his particular concept of Americanism in a troubled era, tended to regard any expression of discontent with the "existing order" on the part of labor, the Negro, the farmer, the "intelligentsia," and indeed any segment of American society, as an expression of "class consciousness"— the first step toward communism.[90] However sincere in that belief, the fact remains that Dies, by permitting, even encouraging, the irresponsible charges that swirled around the Project for months on end, effectively stamped the Federal Theatre with the Communist label just as it was about to embark on a campaign for broad audience support.

The effect was disastrous. Relief officials, already hesitant about an extensive touring program that threatened to incur the opposition of a few state administrators, commercial managers, and possibly congressmen, hurriedly consigned the program to a state of indefinite postponement. Anxious to avoid the publicity —and the consequences—of a direct confrontation with Dies and Thomas, they cautiously refused to allow a counterattack in the press. But even a vigorous denial would not have spared the Federal Theatre. That the question of Communist control had been raised by a congressional investigating committee was itself insidious; whatever the answer, there was no defense against

[90] This near-obsession with "class consciousness" seems to have been shared by Dies' fellow congressmen. On May 31, 1939, the *Washington Post* reported a speech made by Virginia's Harry Byrd under these headlines: "Byrd Sees Class Hatreds As Nation's Chief Menace," p. 2.

For a discussion of Dies' particular concept of Americanism see Gellerman, *Martin Dies*, pp. 138-146. Dies' fourteen "means" by which "class consciousness" is promoted are contained in a speech he delivered in support of a bill to deport alien Communists. See *Cong. Rec.*, 72nd Cong., 1st Sess. (1932), p. 12,100.

234

the very fact of the question itself. Henceforth, the Federal Theatre would have to prove its innocence to the very communities whose support it sought—communities whose citizens, no longer so stirred by the old Roosevelt talk about a New Deal, were beginning to regard a work relief program as a tiresome and unwanted burden.

CHAPTER SIX

Politics Versus Theatre: Congress Kills Pinocchio

THE Dies Committee had concluded its investigations by the end of 1938. The Federal Theatre, restored by the press to its accustomed place in the theatrical section, was once again a subject for drama critics who were becoming increasingly respectful of federal plays and players. But officials of this beleaguered relief project could ill afford to bask in the warmth of critical favor. In order to survive, the Federal Theatre had to stretch its roots across the great American hinterland, sinking them deep into the soil of each region. However, in most areas the soil was never cultivated; the tours, community theatre projects, and plans to create larger and loyal audiences throughout the nation had, for the most part, been postponed if not actually abandoned. Eager to remedy this situation, Hallie Flanagan would try once again in the months ahead to translate those plans into action, but she would find her task increasingly difficult. By the spring of 1939, Washington's political climate had become too rough for the survival of all but the hardiest New Deal species.

· I ·

During the long months of the Dies Committee's investigation, the men and women of the Federal Theatre had sung, danced, and acted their way through a colorful array of marionette shows, musical extravaganzas, modern dramas, Living Newspapers, armory-housed circuses, and nativity plays. In Oklahoma, the cavorting of gaily clad puppets brought shouts of glee from orphans in Tipton and school children in a succession of Oklahoma towns—Maud, New Kirk, Kellyville, Kingfisher, Kiowa, Indianola, Luther, Hugo, Broken Bow, Fairview, Val-

iant, Idabel, and, finally, Tulsa.[1] Half a continent away "huge
hordes of hatless, drama-starved youngsters" swarmed down
from the Bronx and Brooklyn into the Adelphi Theatre to see
One-Third of a Nation.[2] In cities where Federal Theatre units
had been none too strong and audiences none too enthusiastic,
an elated cast heard Philadelphia's old Walnut Street Theatre re-
sound with applause for the Quaker City's own version of the
Living Newspaper slum drama.[3] Further north, Boston's production of *A Moral Entertainment* won over the hitherto un-
friendly *Evening Globe*, and a delighted state director pushed
ahead with plans for a classical cycle that would tour New
England colleges and universities.[4] But once again it was the
ubiquitous "Big Three" whose productions sent reviewers scurry-
ing for adjectives.

In Los Angeles, a young man, afire with Hallie Flanagan's
vision of what could be accomplished by imaginative use of
available talent, combined loudspeakers, motion pictures, "old-
time" sets and costumes, and a host of former vaudevillians in
Two-A-Day, a glorified variety show.[5] The result was a hit—
"colorful, spirited, and funny"—that had columnists predicting
a run of seventy weeks and Broadway producers talking about
production rights.[6] Nor was *Two-A-Day* California's only success. *Run Little Chillun*, a joint effort of the Music Project and
the Negro unit, brought out "first-string" critics from the

[1] See letters from school officials in the above-mentioned towns to
Oklahoma director, John Dunn, January and February 1939, RG 69, FTP
Records, NOTL.

[2] Walter Winchell, "On Broadway," *New York Daily Mirror*, October 21, 1938, p. 25.

[3] Flanagan to Hubert Humphrey, November 18, 1938, RG 69, FTP
Records, NOC.

[4] John Luce to Flanagan, December 30, 1938; Jon B. Mack to Flanagan, January 16, 1939, RG 69, FTP Records, NOC.

[5] Gene Stone to Flanagan, December 19, 1938, RG 69, FTP Records,
NOGSF.

[6] R[obert] W[agner], "*Two-A-Day* Twice," *Robert Wagner's Script*, XX
(December 17, 1938), 13; Flanagan to Jon B. Mack, December 25, 1938,
RG 69, FTP Records, NOGSF.

Times and *Examiner*, a long line of celebrity-filled limousines to the old Mayan Theatre, a monthly audience that numbered nearly thirty thousand, and that sure harbinger of success, the ticket scalper, who busily hawked the Federal Theatre's fifty-five-cent tickets for five dollars.[7]

In Chicago, as well, Negro troupers turned musical scores into theatrical magic. When the curtain went up on an original jazz version of Gilbert and Sullivan's *Mikado* in September 1938, the adjectives were as unrestrained as the show itself:

> startlingly good . . . gorgeous . . . a colored convulsion . . . razzmatazz that beats a white hot tempo . . . choice musicianship . . . sultry settings . . . Covarrubias out-of-Bali . . . a killer-diller bound to shake the foundations of Jackson Boulevard . . . bigger and better chorus than you ever listened to in a white man's show . . . colossal . . . superb . . . electrifying . . . the most delirious outlay of unbridled trucking and cake-walking the Chicago stage has ever seen. . . .[8]

It was a verdict widely shared by Chicagoans, who nightly packed the Blackstone Theatre to watch the Mikado, complete with grass skirt and top hat, make his entrance, not to the flutter of ladies' fans, but to the lapping of waves in a South Sea war canoe. When attendance figures climbed to two hundred and fifty thousand, that spectacular gentleman and his sarong-clad ladies swung over to New York, leaving behind the story of their rhythmic exploits in newsreels and the colored pages of *Life*, as well as in numerous articles and reviews. In short, they achieved a publicity record which any commercial producer might envy.[9]

New York, meanwhile, boasted records of its own. By the time that *Haiti, Prologue to Glory,* and *One-Third of a Nation*

[7] Richard Sheridan Ames, "Uncle Sam's Success Story," *Robert Wagner's Script,* xx (October 22, 1938), 6-7.

[8] Quoted in Flanagan, *Arena,* pp. 145-146.

[9] "*Mikado* in Twentieth Week," Press Release, February 6, 1939, RG 69, FTP Records, NOPM; Howard Miller to Harry Minturn, March 3, 1939, RG 69, FTP Records, NOGSF.

238

closed down to make way for new productions, the Lincoln saga had made Burns Mantle's list of the ten best plays of the 1937-38 season; the Living Newspaper drama had made Sidney Whipple's.[10] Although the first important entry of the new season, Theodore Pratt's *Big Blow*, never quite measured up to the illustrious trio it was replacing, this melodrama of life and death in Florida's "cracker county" was by most standards a "decided hit." Audiences crowded into the Maxine Elliot Theatre at the rate of over seven hundred nightly, and critics termed the play "one of the Federal Theatre's finest which, in these days, is saying a great deal."[11] While other major productions were undergoing Kondolf's last-minute scrutiny, the New York director authorized as a "filler" two marionette shows, *The Story of Ferdinand* and *String Fever*. To his surprise, the huge, fourteen-hundred-seat auditorium filled to capacity at virtually every performance, and at least one little girl was photographed in tears at the box office when told by her mother that no more tickets were available.[12]

By Christmas Eve 1938, New Yorkers, who has paused on blustery street corners to watch strolling WPA troupes of nativity players, could take their choice of three new productions—if they could get tickets.[13] At the Daly Theatre on Sixty-Third

[10] Flanagan, *Arena*, p. 320; Sidney Whipple, "Ten Best Plays of Year," *New York World Telegram*, December 31, 1938, Sec. 1, p. 1. Whipple also included *The Cradle Will Rock* in his list of top ten plays.

[11] Arthur Pollock, "The Federal Theater Presents Its First Play of the Season, *Big Blow* . . . ," *Brooklyn Eagle*, October 3, 1938, p. 6. The reviews of Burns Mantle, Robert Coleman, Sidney Whipple, John Mason Brown, Richard Lockridge, and John Anderson are found respectively in the *New York Daily News*, October 3, 1938, p. 33; *New York Daily Mirror*, October 3, 1938, p. 13; *New York World Telegram*, October 3, 1938, p. 10; *New York Post*, October 3, 1938, p. 10; the *New York Sun*, October 3, 1938, p. 15; *New York Journal and American*, October 5, 1938, p. 18.

[12] Memorandum, George Kondolf to Hallie Flanagan, January 3, 1939, RG 69, FTP Records, Narr. Reports; *New York Daily News*, December 29, 1938, p. 24.

[13] These strolling groups of players had become a regular part of the Federal Theatre's national program by December 1938. In New York,

239

Street, young Clifford Odet's story of a depression-stricken Jewish family may have lacked in the Yiddish version some of the bite of the original English; but, according to the *New York Times* reviewer, Lem Ward's production of *Awake and Sing* was "a more trenchant domestic drama than the Yiddish stage had witnessed in some time, measuring up to the good things the Federal Theatre ... [had done] before."[14] Further uptown, at Harlem's LaFayette Theatre, both Negro and white queued up nightly for Shaw's *Androcles and the Lion.* Gay, humorous, and competently done, the play won warm praise from critics, with Brooks Atkinson and John Mason Brown agreeing that the Negro production was better than the Theatre Guild's revival and thoroughly deserving of the playwright's "genial blessing."[15]

But the production which seemed to capture all the gaiety and happiness of the holiday season was Yasha Frank's *Pinocchio.* Displaying the same ingenuity he had lavished on his Los Angeles Children's Theatre, the resourceful Frank had combined a fairy tale with the talents of former vaudevillians in a musical extravaganza that won rave notices even from such critics as the *Journal and American*'s John Anderson.[16] Displaying a rare unanimity of opinion, the *Daily Worker* and the *Wall Street Journal* agreed that this imaginative, funny, and touching story of the puppet who came to life was a magnificent tribute to the potentiality of the Federal Theatre. In a final burst of praise, the Wall Street reviewer added: "As Pinocchio, Edwin Michaels turns in such a perfectly filled role that one can only wonder

---

both Negro and white companies reenacted with song the birth of Christ on the steps of the New York Public Library, the Cathedral of St. John the Divine, as well as on assorted street corners throughout the city.

[14] The *New York Times*, December 23, 1938, p. 16.

[15] Brooks Atkinson, "Shaw's *Androcles and the Lion* Acted by the Harlem Unit of the Federal Theatre," the *New York Times*, December 17, 1938, p. 10; John Mason Brown, "The Federal Theatre Does *Androcles and the Lion*," *New York Post*, December 17, 1938, p. 8.

[16] John Anderson, "*Pinocchio* at Ritz Has Real Charm," *New York Journal and American*, January 3, 1939, p. 12.

at the obtuseness of the theatre business which leaves men like this to find their outlet on WPA."[17]

The Federal Theatre had indeed made its mark! Small but telling evidence was again stamped on a pair of tickets—this time to *Pinocchio*. The speculator who sold them had charged $6.60 for two fifty-five-cent tickets to a WPA show.[18] The tickets, the reviews, the picture of the sobbing child snapped by a *Daily News* photographer—all were indisputable tokens of theatrical success.

With success had inevitably come new problems, revealing once again the basic incompatibility of relief and theatre. That a relief venture could become a professionally respectable production center had scarcely been a matter for conjecture even among more sanguine Broadway spokesmen in 1935. Yet in the three years since representatives of the commercial theatre had prophetically, if somewhat inconsistently, restricted Elmer Rice and his improvident band of actors to "off-Broadway" houses, cries of competition had proved to be a rough index of the Federal Theatre's professional excellence. When directors transferred old or incompetent actors to other white-collar jobs at reduced pay, Equity charged that the Project's primary purpose was relief, not excellence of presentation. When, in an effort to gain larger audiences and greater financial support, Federal Theatre officials acquired additional newspaper space for advertising, Broadway producers emitted cries of "encroachment" and demanded that the New York Project return to its weekly box. When the financially pressed Chicago Project charged an additional fifty cents for tickets to *Prologue to Glory*, local producers made no attempt to conceal their resentment. To bring to Chicago a play that should never have left New York, to spend federal funds advertising it, and then to charge as much as $1.65

---

[17] John Cambridge, "*Pinocchio*, A Delightful Show For Young And Old," *Daily Worker*, January 4, 1939, p. 7; *Wall Street Journal*, January 3, 1939, p. 59.

[18] John Chapman, "Mainly About Manhattan," *New York Daily News*, January 4, 1939, p. 35.

for admissions was, they declared, ample evidence that the Federal Theatre had forgotten its "relief nature." Even the fact that the Project made its own costumes and lent them free to churches and schools brought complaints to Washington about unfair competition with private industry.[19]

The objections of commercial costumers, however, were a mere ripple compared to the waves stirred up by the Mikado's war canoe. Commercial producers, attracted to a money-making musical, were eager to take over the Federal Theatre's much acclaimed hit. Economy-minded WPA officials, on the other hand, were loath to give it up without some guarantee that the original cast would be given employment when the production reopened under private auspices. After weeks of much publicized dickering, negotiations broke down. Relief officials promptly moved the play to New York for a gala opening attended by Mrs. Roosevelt, Mayor La Guardia, Secretary of Commerce Harry Hopkins, WPA officials from Chicago, New York, and Washington, and a host of theatrical celebrities. Marveling at the "completeness with which mere intonation and emphasis transformed the ballad of the dickey-bird into an unmistakable coon song," Joseph Wood Krutch and his fellow critics turned out enthusiastic reviews; radio networks vied for broadcast rights; and Michael Todd announced the production of his own *Hot Mikado*. In the weeks that followed Todd's announcement, cries of competition burst forth again—this time on the floor of Congress. Although even *Variety* admitted that it was the Chicago showman who was competing with the WPA, the revival of charges and countercharges hardly benefited the Federal Theatre, however much publicity accrued to the vociferous Todd's more expensive production.[20]

[19] *Variety*, March 30, 1938, p. 55; May 4, 1938, p. 53; November 16, 1938, p. 49; June 8, 1939, p. 49.

[20] Flanagan, *Arena*, pp. 146-148; Leonard Carlton, "*Swing Mikado* Praised on WOR," *New York Post*, February 2, 1939, p. 27; Joseph Wood Krutch, "The Swing Mikado," *The Nation*, CXLVIII (March 18, 1939), 329; *New York Post*, February 28, 1939, p. 54. Ill feeling between Federal Theatre officials and Todd was considerably intensified when Todd

As a way of avoiding this potentially explosive problem of competition, Harry Hopkins had always encouraged Federal Theatre officials to move caravans of traveling players out into the hundreds of cities and towns virtually untouched by the commercial theatre. But the extension of a federal dramatic program to the theatrically virgin territory of the South and Midwest was precisely what Hallie Flanagan had failed to accomplish. Pinocchio and Mikado, words that signified theatrical magic in New York and Chicago, were but titles of a children's book and an English operetta in Richmond, Charleston, Dallas, Little Rock, Indianapolis, Omaha, and Milwaukee.

To be sure, there had been plans to expand the Federal Theatre. On the same hot August day on which Dies had sworn in his first witness before the House Un-American Activities Committee, Hallie Flanagan had appealed to the Play Policy Board for additional programs tailored to the needs of communities remote from New York City. As yet unaware that the Federal Theatre's most important venture, the nationwide touring program, was fast becoming a pipe dream, Federal Theatre directors had worked out projects for research and community drama.[21] From Yasha Frank, creator of *Pinocchio*, came a blueprint for a nationwide Children's Theatre which he guaranteed would not only "infiltrate" the Federal Theatre into the cultural life of each community, but would also win for it the support of the National Education Association and the Parent-Teachers Association.[22] But plans, blueprints, and proposals, whether for

spent a week in Chicago "taking down dialogue in shorthand and otherwise helping himself to the WPA's production ideas." See *New York Daily News*, February 1, 1939, p. 25. Todd also had his director and general manager on hand for the New York premiere of the WPA production—action which understandably enraged New York officials. Interview with Sam Handelsman, November 16, 1961; the *New York Times*, March 2, 1939, p. 28.

[21] For details on both projects see Memorandum, Ellen Woodward to Regional Directors of Women's and Professional Projects, October 15, 1938, RG 69, GSS-211.2.

[22] Yasha Frank, "A Survey for a Proposed National Plan for a Chil-

joint Federal Theatre-high school Shakespeare festivals or for research in American theatrical history, were but the first tentative step.

To transform these ideas into reality required careful preparation. The approval and support of Ellen Woodward and various regional directors of Women's and Professional Projects had to be enlisted. Permission to hire a small but necessary number of supervisory personnel had to be obtained. Unenthusiastic state administrators needed to be persuaded of the importance of a Children's Theatre in areas where all theatre had long been regarded with suspicion, and where the Federal Theatre was vaguely associated by *Saturday Evening Post* readers with a play called *The Revolt of the Beavers*. Skeptical Equity officials had to be convinced that community drama projects would not be preparing stage-struck high school seniors or frustrated housewives for an already overcrowded profession. For these projects especially, qualified directors, stage designers, painters, carpenters, and seamstresses had to be found who would willingly cooperate with recreational programs sponsored by the TVA, CCC, and other federal agencies. Personally as well as professionally, those chosen had to be capable of insinuating both themselves and the Project they represented into communities remote from the marquee-filled world of Times Square. In short, to get even the community drama program under way required considerable time and concentrated effort. Caught in the furor aroused by the Dies Committee's investigation, engulfed in the day-to-day administration of a mercurial, problem-prone relief project, Hallie Flanagan and her associates had had neither.[23]

The prospect for implementing such plans in the new year was slight indeed. Despite a string of hits, problems of subtle censorship, weakening morale, resignations and reorganization

dren's Theatre," October 6, 1938; also Frank to Flanagan, October 3, 1938, RG 69, FTP Records, NOGSF.

[23] Flanagan to Edward Hall, July 29, 1938; Irma Ringe to Flanagan, August 2, 1938, RG 69, FTP Records, NOGSF.

continued to plague projects in Los Angeles, Chicago, and New York respectively.[24] Far more decisive, however, were orders from Washington in late December 1938: local administrators were told to reduce WPA rolls substantially. "Coming just at a time when we felt the necessity for expansion," the cut was a "great blow," Hallie Flanagan confessed to producer-director Cheryl Crawford.[25]

A blow it was, but hardly an unexpected one. Although WPA ranks had swollen steadily in recent months, so had the armies of the Nazi Reich. By January 1939, Hitler had moved into Austria and part of Czechoslovakia. Accordingly, those who attributed the reduction of work rolls to the need to free funds for rearmament were probably closer to the truth than Presidential critics, who saw election-time politicking in the rise and fall of WPA employment figures.[26] In fact, the hiring of additional workers throughout the summer and fall of 1938 seems to have been a natural, if delayed, response to the recession; the dis-

[24] In California friction between the Federal Theatre and Colonel Connolly resulted in director George Gerwing's resignation in November 1938. His replacement, James Ullman, found the Colonel still adamant about his right to approve all scripts, despite Mrs. Woodward's insistence that such decisions were the sole responsibility of the Federal Theatre directors. See Flanagan to Gilmor Brown, November 29, 1938; Ullman to Flanagan, December 10, 1938; Flanagan to Ullman, December 23, 1938, RG 69, FTP Records, NOGSF. In Chicago, McGee's resignation meant not only the official burial of plans for theatrical expansion in the Midwest but also the necessity for Mrs. Flanagan to find a replacement for one of her most loyal administrators. See Flanagan to Harry Minturn, December 8, 1938, RG 69, FTP Records, NOC-State. In New York, Kondolf's concentration on major productions had apparently led him to neglect completely the Children's Theatre, circus, marionette and variety units. Criticism of this and other aspects of Kondolf's administration resulted in another reorganization of the New York Project which required much of Mrs. Flanagan's time and attention. See Flanagan, Report of Conference with George Kondolf, Howard Miller, Paul Edwards, November 18, 1938, RG 69, FTP Records, NOGSF; The New York Times, November 25, 1938, p. 25.

[25] Flanagan to Crawford, December 27, 1938, RG 69, FTP Records, NOGSF.

[26] See, for example, "This is No Time for a Cut on the Project," Equity, XXIII (December 1938), 3.

missals, a no less natural curtailment in the economy's slow, but sustained, recovery.[27]

There was nothing natural, however, about discharging men and women on relief. With the news of dismissals, the Federal Theatre promptly became a scene of much publicized protests, disrupted activities, and stillborn plans. Recovery, as Equity was quick to point out, had not extended to the theatre business—in New York alone half of the city's forty houses were still dark. Mustering the support of fellow artists, organized labor, and the public, the actors' union protested against impending cuts with delegations to Washington, mass demonstrations, and parades in New York—but to no avail.[28] Federal Theatre officials would now have to devote the time and energy normally spent on production activities to scaling down the Project without drastically curtailing theatrical activities, antagonizing union officials, or alienating popular support.

It was an impossible assignment. To union leaders, the Federal Theatre Director sent a detailed explanation of the basis on which cuts would be made, as well as her personal assurances that past theatrical experience would be of prime importance in determining who should remain.[29] In New York, members of the Production Board met in closed session with various depart-

[27] Charles, *Minister of Relief*, pp. 167-168.

[28] "This is No Time for a Cut on the Project," *Equity*, XXIII (December 1938), 3; "Equity Fights WPA Cuts," *Equity*, XXIV (January 1939), 5-6; "Equity Faces Long, Hard Fight Over WPA," *Equity*, XXIV (February 1939), 3; the *New York Times*, December 23, 1938, p. 40.

[29] Flanagan to Arthur Bryon, January 2, 1939, RG 69, GSS-211.2. This same letter went out to the Wardrobe Attendants, United Scenic Artists, American Federation of Musicians, International Alliance Theatrical, Hebrew Actors Union, Association of Theatrical Agents and Managers, Associated Actors and Artists of America and the Workers' Alliance. Mrs. Flanagan's assurances were well received by Equity, and relations between union leaders and Federal Theatre officials appear to have been considerably better than during previous cuts. See Frank Gillmore to Flanagan, January 7, 1939; Ruth Richmond to Flanagan, January 7, 1939, RG 69, FTP Records, NOGSF.

246

ment heads to review each individual case.[30] But no amount of deliberation could avert the protests that invariably followed, when over one thousand actors and technicians found themselves without prospects for employment or help from already over-burdened theatrical relief agencies.

Artistic standards as well as human values were inevitably affected. The large metropolitan projects were primarily respon-sible for whatever artistic reputation the Project had achieved; yet, if these escaped with a superficial pruning, small units would have to be shut down in precisely those areas where the Federal Theatre needed to expand. By way of compromise, Project officials tried to distribute cuts so as to spare all except the clearly inferior smaller units. But, as California director James Ullman soon discovered, decisions that seemed clear in principle could become confused in practice. Sent West to pro-tect the Los Angeles Project from Colonel Connolly, Ullman surveyed the situation and chose finally to scrap the small, rather mediocre San Diego unit. When his decision became known, San Diego business and religious groups and over twenty thousand irate citizens bombarded Federal Theatre headquarters with petitions and telegrams charging discrimination. Con-fronted by the conflicting demands of public relations and theatrical excellence, Hallie Flanagan chose to keep the San Diego unit open and its newfound partisans, however mixed their motives, supporters of the Federal Theatre. It was a politic choice.[31]

The support of townspeople, as of union leaders, was not with-out its price, however. In order to keep small theatre groups going, large projects were slashed. Among those dismissed were often talented youngsters who lacked the experience of their

[30] Memorandum, George Kondolf to Flanagan, January 3, 1939, RG 69, FTP Records, Narr. Reports.
[31] Flanagan to Ullman, January 4, 1939; Flanagan to Ullman, Jan-uary 14, 1939; Flanagan to Mrs. L. J. Compton, January 11, 1939, RG 69, FTP Records, NOGSF.

longer-unionized elders. Moreover, large losses meant delays in production, when virtually the entire cast of a play had to be replaced. In New York, where the problem of recasting and revising was compounded by losses in that traditional bottleneck, the costume and scenery workshops, George Kondolf reluctantly postponed the opening date of *Sing for Your Supper*.[32] It was an understandable decision but one with disastrous consequences, for that much rehearsed revue soon became a prime target for congressmen quick to cry "boondoggle." Nor were repercussions confined to New York. Wherever sizable cuts were made, projects had to undergo the inevitable reorganizations as programs were adjusted to curtailed funds and personnel.

Hardest hit, of course, were plans for expansion. Postponed by the WPA because of expense and opposition from commercial managers, and neglected by the Federal Theatre during the Dies investigation, they had now to be virtually abandoned. A relief project subject to the ebb and flow of economic and political tides, the Federal Theatre simply lacked the money, personnel, and backing necessary to carry out the kind of far-flung campaign that both Roosevelt and Hopkins had originally envisioned. On the other hand, these unemployed players could not afford to forego the public support which they stood to gain through expansion. "The only way we have of combatting the false statements circulated by newspapers which chose to play up the garbled testimony . . . [given] before the Dies Committee" is "to develop a program which will meet community needs and sponsorship," Hallie Flanagan wrote to Eleanor Roosevelt.[33] In part, she was right. However, by the end of January, the Project's crucial need for community support had become distressingly apparent for reasons more important than those mentioned by the National Director.

[32] Memorandum, Kondolf to Flanagan, January 10, 1939, RG 69, FTP Records, Narr. Reports.
[33] Flanagan to Mrs. Roosevelt, January 25, 1939, RG 69, GSS-211.2.

248

· II ·

Roosevelt and the New Deal were in trouble. Although the President was still personally popular, public endorsements were becoming more and more restricted to the man himself, rather than to his program. The recently adjourned Congress had dealt the administration a succession of blows. After the failure of the purge, there was little reason to expect that congressmen would be more favorably disposed to the requests of a President now in the final months of his second term. In fact, all evidence pointed to the contrary. Republicans were newly strengthened and economy-conscious; conservative Democrats, eager to take over the Party before the 1940 election. Even many New Dealers were ready to disengage themselves from presidential coattails now that the election of 1938 was past history. Legislators, returning to the capital after the Christmas holidays, talked openly of a struggle to regain control over expenditures; and Washington's political prophets accordingly predicted a "tempestuous" session with the first contest coming over relief. They were not mistaken.[34]

On January 3, senators interrupted the opening rituals long enough to hear a special committee report on the alleged political activities of the WPA during the fall elections. Although many charges against the relief agency could not be substantiated upon investigation, said chairman Morris Sheppard, WPA funds had been used unjustifiably in several states. Senators whose anti-administration activities earned them a place on the presidential purge list were eager to substantiate committee findings. Something, they insisted, had to be done to prevent these occur-

[34] "The Fortune Survey: XIX," *Fortune*, XIX (March 1939), 66-67; Ernest K. Lindley, "The New Congress," *Current History*, XLIV (February 1939), 15; "Congress Looks Toward the 1940 Campaign," *The Congressional Digest*, XVIII (January 1939), 1-3. Setbacks suffered by the President included: the defeat of the Supreme Court bill; two defeats of the wages-and-hours bill before its final passage; defeat of the reorganization bill; failure of the attempted purge; and loss of seats in the 1938 elections. See Samuel I. Rosenman, *Working With Roosevelt* (New York: Harper and Bros., 1952), p. 181.

rences and, more important, to curb the President's discretionary powers in future relief appropriations as well. The implications of such sentiment were soon forthcoming.[35]

Only two days after the Dies and Sheppard reports had been filed, Roosevelt sent a special message to Congress requesting a supplemental appropriation of $875 million for relief. The timing for such a request could hardly have been less propitious. Conscious of this, Roosevelt had hoped to avert trouble by appointing a thoroughly nonpolitical figure to succeed Hopkins, whom he had recently named Secretary of Commerce. His choice was Colonel F. C. Harrington, the correct, able engineer who had served three years as assistant WPA administrator in charge of operations.[36] An army officer receiving army pay, Harrington would not have to have his appointment confirmed by the Senate, nor would he likely be "confused with communism" or politics.[37] But neither the appointment nor the White House proposal to place relief personnel under civil service sufficiently sweetened the President's request. Virginia's Clifton Woodrum, leading the attack for the conservative coalition in the House, announced that in order to cut deficit spending the Appropriations Committee was offering a joint resolution slashing the amount requested by $150 million. When New Dealer

[35] The *New York Times*, August 6, 1939, Sec. 4, p. 1; "The Sheppard Committee Reports on Use of WPA Funds in Politics," *The Congressional Digest*, XVIII (February 1939), 40; "Congress Moves to Control Relief," *The Congressional Digest*, XVIII (February 1939), 35.

[36] Having so thoroughly abstained from politics that he had never even voted, Harrington was totally removed from charges of political activity currently being leveled at the WPA. (The *New York Times*, December 25, 1938, p. 2.) An administrator with some thirty years of experience, Harrington was a man of unquestioned ability. Florence Kerr, herself a woman of considerable administrative ability, contends, however, that Harrington lacked imagination when it came to the WPA and its potentialities. The Colonel, according to Mrs. Kerr, believed that a really sound work program would include only four million people because there simply was not enough work to be done to occupy a larger number. Her own feeling is that he never really wanted to be connected with the work program. See Florence Kerr, tape recording, November 6, 1963, Archives of American Art.

[37] Sherwood, *Roosevelt and Hopkins*, p. 106.

Clarence Cannon of Missouri objected that the reduction was the result of a "preconceived notion to cut whatever figure was recommended," his fellow committeeman, John Taber, replied that the reduction had not been large enough. "Read the Dies Committee report," urged the New York Republican, "and learn about the un-American activity in which the WPA is engaged."[38]

On the following day, while the Senate Commerce Committee questioned Hopkins about the political activities of the WPA,[39] the House passed a Deficit Relief Bill appropriating only $725 million of the $875 million requested by Roosevelt. The *New York Times* called it "open rebellion against the Administration"; Woodrum, a "start on the road to lower appropriations."[40] One thing was certain: a coalition of Republicans and conservative Democrats had not only defeated all efforts of loyal New Dealers to restore the figure requested by the President but, with the "most deafening chorus of 'noes' the House Chamber . . . had heard in years," they had defeated an amendment calling for $22 million to be allotted to the Federal Arts Projects. Only a suggestion that the Projects were in some way connected with the Dies Committee investigation was enough to insure defeat. After a dramatic and bitter struggle between New Dealers and anti-New Dealers, the Senate voted forty-seven to forty-six to uphold the figure set by the House. A packed gallery applauded the result.[41]

Although a major revision of relief policy was postponed until appropriations were made for the fiscal year 1939-40, dissatisfaction with present policy was mounting both in and outside of Congress.[42] The Senate, avowing its intention to revamp the

[38] The *New York Times*, January 13, 1939, p. 6.

[39] Hopkins was appearing before the Committee in order to gain confirmation as Secretary of Commerce.

[40] The *New York Times*, January 14, 1939, p. 1.

[41] *Ibid.*, January 26, 1939, p. 1; January 27, 1939, p. 1; January 29, 1939, p. 1.

[42] For Congressional thinking on relief, see "Congress Moves to Control Relief," *The Congressional Digest*, XVIII (February 1939), 35.

entire program in the regular relief bill, continued its investigation of unemployment under a special committee headed by James F. Byrnes. Although generally regarded as an administration supporter, Byrnes' clear lack of enthusiasm for the President's relief program prompted Harold Ickes to label the South Carolina Democrat a New Dealer "gone sour."[43] Yet the senator, not the PWA administrator, seemed to reflect the nation's sentiments on relief. According to the Gallup and Roper polls, most Americans wanted politics taken out of relief, methods of administration changed, and appropriations reduced.[44] Reflecting this general discontent, the *Washington Post* sounded a call for a gradual reduction in relief funds. Given the will to economize, the WPA itself could reduce costs, suggested the editorial. "Frilly artistic projects entailing extremely high overhead costs in proportion to the number of jobs made available should be discontinued."[45]

The suggestion that "frilly artistic projects" be eliminated had been made before; the Federal Theatre, in particular, had been subjected to intermittent attacks since its inception. For the first time, however, a combination of factors—the controversy over relief, the trend toward economy, the President's waning influence on Capitol Hill, the readiness of many congressmen

[43] As early as 1937 Byrnes had led the economy bloc in a battle to cut down appropriations for work relief. The change in attitude in 1939 regarding WPA expenditures was made possible, Ickes says, by the fact that Byrnes had been reelected in 1936 and his tenure now outlasted the President's. (See Ickes, *Diary*, II, 63, 155.) According to *Newsweek*, however, Byrnes was never friendly to huge relief expenditures for black, nonvoting constituents, preferring instead to put money into "measures promising direct returns at the polls." See "Budget: The President and the Republicans Preach Thrift to Embarrassed Democratic Spenders," *Newsweek*, IX (May 1, 1937), 8.

[44] "Should Existing Methods of Administering Relief Funds Be Changed: The Gallup Poll," *The Congressional Digest*, XVIII (February 1939), 52; "The Fortune Survey: XIX," *Fortune*, XIX (March 1939), 66-69ff.

[45] "Should Existing Methods of Administering Relief Funds be Changed: the *Washington Post*," *The Congressional Digest*, XVIII (February 1939), 53.

to associate un-American activities with the Federal Theatre—made it impossible to assume that such suggestions would continue to be ignored.

Hallie Flanagan, her political instincts sharpened by three years in Washington, fell victim to no such assumptions. Although observers predicted that in the year before an election, Congress—for all its talk—would only "shave relief appropriations somewhat" while doing some "righteous cheeseparing," the Federal Theatre Director realized only too clearly that her actors might well wind up among the shavings and parings.[46] Somehow, in the weeks ahead, she had to find a large and articulate constituency willing to fight for this vulnerable Project's continued existence. Without money or personnel for an intensive expansion program, she could only work through units already existing by shoring up weaker ones with large-scale loans of actors, technicians, and equipment, and by securing nationally integrated programs and larger, better organized groups of sponsors.

To build a broad-based constituency in three short months for an institution which she had been unable to decentralize effectively in the course of three years was an impossible task. Yet Hallie Flanagan refused to admit impossibility. At a meeting of the New York Project's Production Board, she spoke in blunt, uncompromising language of the alternatives facing the Federal Theatre and the New York group in particular.[47] With a congressional investigation impending, she warned her listeners that "possibly four months" remained in which to strengthen the entire Project and win the necessary support of the American people. The New York Project, she readily admitted, had raised standards of production with a succession of good shows; but it had done little for its Children's Theatre, dance, caravan and circus units, and still less for the Federal Theatre as a whole.

[46] Lindley, "The New Congress," *Current History*, XLIX (February 1939), 17.

[47] Flanagan, Report of Meeting with the New York Production Staff, February 1, 1939, RG 69, FTP Records, NOGSF.

If the New York Project was ended, the reason would be its own "ostrich-like quality of refusing to see itself [as] part of a nation wide picture." She scolded members of the Production Board for failure to coordinate an *articulate audience* willing to fight for the Project," a "defeatist attitude" with regard to touring, lack of interest in a national program, failure to clear plays with the Play Policy Board, and reluctance to work with the National Service Bureau on concrete plans for loans of surplus scenery and costumes as well as personnel. "The greatest danger we face," she declared, "is the criticism from Congress that too much of our money is spent in New York City; that the rest of the country, particularly rural areas, does not receive the advantage of the large sums of money being spent by taxes from all over the country." The only way to answer this criticism, Mrs. Flanagan concluded, was for New York to "become aware of the national picture"—to facilitate touring and loans of personnel and equipment, and to begin planning a national program that would create the "articulate sponsorship of large groups of people."

Ostensibly simple and obviously necessary, these were nonetheless radical demands. Located in the theatrical capital of the United States, the New York Project was naturally susceptible to the myopia which afflicted the commercial theatre. Even those directors who shared the initial vision of a national theatre, when submerged in the operation of an enterprise embracing nearly half of the people employed in the entire Project, could easily forget that the half was not the whole. When they, in turn, were replaced by men from the commercial theatre whose chief concern was to produce shows comparable to those on Broadway, the "insularity" of which Hallie Flanagan complained had taken hold. Whether her pleas for change would be heeded in time, the Federal Theatre Director did not know. She did know that she, at least, must not neglect that other half. A few days later, she left the February chill of the capital for what was to be her final inspection tour.

254

The familiar trip westward was both heartening and discouraging: heartening, because she was convinced that for those
who cared about an American theatre, these relief projects were
the "foundation of something tremendous"; discouraging, because there was so little time to shore up the foundations and
make more people care.[48] Chicago, she realized, needed to turn
the people who lustily applauded the *Mikado* into patrons who
would loyally support the Federal Theatre.[49] California, described by *Variety* as "tied up by red tape . . . torn by strife . . .
and turmoil," required not only stepped-up efforts to win
audience support, but a director as well.[50]

James Ullman had arrived in Los Angeles to take over the
West Coast directorship only to be met with orders to reduce
Federal Theatre rolls by one-fourth. Drawing upon his experi-
ences in the stormy New York Project, the young producer
somehow managed to keep the Project going in the midst of
conferences with WPA officials, Project workers, union representatives, members of the Federal Theatre Advisory Committee, church leaders, American Legion officers, civic leaders,
and reporters. But after three months as administrator—three
months during which he had scarcely seen the inside of a theatre—Ullman had resigned.[51] Once again the demands of relief
theatre and bureaucracy had proved irreconcilable; and once
again the Federal Theatre's second largest project drifted rud-
derless. To find a theatrically competent replacement—one
familiar with the Project, acceptable to state WPA officials, and
willing to reconcile these disparate demands for a pitifully poor
salary—would prove a long and frustrating task.[52] In the mean-

[48] Flanagan to Marc Connelly, February 14, 1939; Hallie Flanagan to
Regional and State Directors, April 24, 1939, RG 69, FTP Records, NOGSF.

[49] Not only Chicago, Detroit, and the Western projects, but all Federal Theatre units were weak in getting information to the public about
"what we are doing and in building our federal theatres into the community," Mrs. Flanagan told her directors. See Flanagan to Regional
and State Directors, April 24, 1939, RG 69, FTP Records, NOGSF.

[50] *Variety*, March 1, 1939, p. 48.

[51] Interview with James R. Ullman, November 17, 1961.

[52] At this time the Federal Theatre also needed at least three other

time, Hallie Flanagan discovered that the San Francisco theatre at the International Exposition on Treasure Island was indeed at "sixes and sevens."[53] To postpone the opening of a theatre that could reach World's Fair visitors from congressional districts across the country was unthinkable; thus she set to work immediately.[54]

In Seattle two weeks later, the National Director found the same problems that she had encountered on small projects elsewhere. The Negro company needed more money for equipment, costumes, sets, and publicity—money that became less available with each cut. Actors, tough old troupers trained in vaudeville, needed work in diction, voice, and movement. Above all, the entire project needed to be integrated into the community. Yet, despite such handicaps, the choice of plays and standards of production were improving, as indeed they were everywhere. Ensconced in the old Metropolitan Theatre, Hallie Flanagan watched a run-through of *Spirochete*, a Living Newspaper which portrayed the effects of syphilis and man's efforts to find a cure. Delighted with the production, she was particularly impressed with the portrayal of Dr. Metchnikoff. The part, she was told, was played by Toby Leach, whose superb performance had made him the subject of a special story in the Sunday edition of the *Seattle Times*. Asked whether she had noticed that Toby always played beside a table or chair, the Federal Theatre Director replied that she had not. "Well," continued her host, "we do that as a precaution. You see, both of Toby's legs are broken. Broke 'em in a barrel act which he did in the big time twenty years ago." A middle-aged circus performer, his injuries skillfully disguised, playing in a Living Newspaper based on research supervised by the scientist, Paul deKruif, and the United

---

directors. Salary for each would be $175.00 per month. See Flanagan to Marc Connelly, February 14, 1939, RG 69, FTP Records, NOGSF.

[53] Flanagan to Lawrence Morris, February 9, 1939, RG 69, FTP Records, NOC-State.

[54] Flanagan to George Gerwing, February 10, 1939, RG 69, FTP Records, NOGSF.

256

States Surgeon General—that, Hallie Flanagan proudly confided to Howard Miller, is the "whole Federal Theatre in a nut-
shell, or shall we say, in a barrel?"[55]

But for hundreds of Tobys yet to be retrained and imagina-
tively directed in original productions, the prospects of a feature
story in the local newspaper were becoming slight indeed. Back
in San Francisco, Mrs. Flanagan picked up the *Examiner* two
months after she had testified before the House Un-American
Activities Committee only to see the headlines: "Federal Theatre Communist Trend Must be Eradicated." Still forbidden
to reply, she sent a copy of the article to Washington headquarters with a request for advice and the admonition: "I do
not want . . . [the article] dismissed on the ground that 'nobody
believes the Dies Committee,' as apparently out here everybody
believes it."[56] In Los Angeles, where she finally managed to get
the state WPA's tentative approval for the appointment of a new
regional director, she, in turn, was presented with an organization chart which removed from Federal Theatre jurisdiction
over 50 per cent of the employees paid out of Project funds. "Is
this in accord with your wishes?" she telegraphed Washington.[57]
Apparently it was. In any case, WPA officials subsequently refused to intervene when Connolly's successor, disregarding Mrs.
Flanagan's recommendations, appointed his own man to the
regional post. When the Federal Theatre Director objected that
this was the first time an appointment had ever been made to
her staff without her approval, she was told that California
was in a "special category"; the appointment would have to
stand. In the "housecleaning" that eventually followed, theatrical
activity came to a "dead stop" on what had once been the
Federal Theatre's prize project.[58] Thus, it was hardly coincidence
which led Ullman to conclude an assessment of that "huge,

[55] Flanagan to Miller, February 25, 1939, RG 69, GSS-211.2.
[56] Flanagan to George Gerwing, February 11, 1939, RG 69, FTP Records, NOGSF.
[57] Telegram, Flanagan to Florence E. Kerr, March 6, 1939, RG 69,
FTP Records, NOGSF.
[58] Flanagan, *Arena*, p. 293.

fantastic, embattled, much praised and much damned organization," the Federal Theatre, with these words:

> A year or so ago a great many people cherished the hope
> that the Federal Theatre might gradually develop into a true
> National Theatre, largely or entirely divorced from relief
> and operated on a permanent basis. That hope, I think, is
> considerably more remote now than it was then. . . . It is
> foolhardy to indulge in prophecy in regard to anything as
> unpredictable as the FTP, but the best guess at the moment
> is that it will gradually be cut in size and financial resources
> until it becomes purely a relief agency for the support and
> rehabilitation of indigent theatrical people.[59]

Ullman might have added as a final phrase, "under state control," could he have foreseen developments in California. Even
without the addition, it was an educated guess; if events in Washington were any indication, it was also an overly optimistic
one. Time, for the Federal Theatre, was running out.

What had heretofore been a defensive war against the expansion of the New Deal was fast becoming an all-out effort to
dismantle the WPA and other relief programs. In February 1939,
the President himself signaled the end of further reforms with
the announcement that he would press for no additional legislation. By March, the administration's waning prestige had observers predicting the candidacy of tough, red-faced, little
"Cactus Jack" Garner, rather than a third term for F.D.R. On
Capitol Hill, economy forces had seized the initiative with a
proposal from Senator James F. Byrnes to consolidate all relief
activities under a Department of Public Works. The bill which
had the backing of the Senate Committee on Unemployment
made no provision for continuing white-collar programs such
as the Arts Projects.[60]

[59] James R. Ullman, "Report on Democracy Versus the Theatre," the
New York Times, March 12, 1939, Sec. 11, pp. 1-2.

[60] Leuchtenburg, *Franklin D. Roosevelt and the New Deal*, p. 272;
Lindley, "The New Congress," *Current History*, XLIX (February 1939),

It was a "serious omission," Colonel Harrington told his congressional superiors in deferential tones so unlike the jaunty rejoinders characteristic of his more aggressive predecessor. Byrnes was not so sure. For the benefit of fellow committeemen, the South Carolina Democrat began questioning the Relief Administrator as to the real value of the Theatre Project. Was not the WPA directly competing with private enterprise by bringing the Negro *Mikado* to New York? Harrington carefully pointed out that no financially responsible producer had offered to take over the show with its present cast intact. But, if the *Mikado* were successful, might it not close down commercial plays whose people would then wind up on relief rolls? Harrington replied that if he understood the argument, it would mean the Federal Theatre should only continue those productions which proved unsuccessful. Byrnes was not deterred. The WPA was responsible for recent closings—the D'Oyle Carte Company for example—was it not? The Colonel explained that the opera company had come to this country for a limited engagement only. But was not the *Mikado* competing with the ILGWU's *Pins and Needles*? The beleaguered administrator finally replied that he had had far more complaints about competition afforded by WPA's construction program than by its drama projects. Senatorial critics, however, were little impressed; their counterparts at the opposite end of the capital would prove even less so.[61]

By mid-March, the House Subcommittee on Appropriations had begun preliminary hearings on a second deficiency bill that would grant an additional $150 million for relief—the exact sum slashed from the President's original request just

16; "Taxes and Neutrality," *The Congressional Digest*, XVIII (April 1939), 100; "Congress Applies the Brakes to the New Deal," *The Congressional Digest*, XVIII (March 1939), 67; The *New York Times*, March 10, 1939, p. 2.

[61] Hearings before the Special Senate Committee to Investigate Unemployment and Relief on S. 1265. *Department of Public Works* . . . , 76th Cong., 1st Sess. (1939), pp. 273-281 for Harrington's testimony.

two months before. WPA officials, called in to testify, encountered in virtually every question asked about the Federal Theatre an ill-disguised dissatisfaction with the Project. When Florence Kerr, who had succeeded Ellen Woodward as director of Women's and Professional Projects, appeared before the Committee, Woodrum let loose a barrage of now familiar questions. By bringing *Swing Mikado* to New York, was not the WPA competing with commercial producers, to say nothing of the New York City Project? Had there not been offers from private producers to take it over? Had Mrs. Kerr encouraged prospective buyers? Did they charge admission? Did not this charging of admission mean that the Federal Theatre was taking money from commercial theatre? Who was Ko-Ko? Was "she" on relief? Undeterred about a simple mistake of sex, Woodrum pressed on. Was "she" a colored girl? What was "her" salary? Who was Yum-Yum? Was she on relief? Was she a colored girl? What was her salary? Was it the object of the Federal Theatre to promote and revitalize theatre business or to furnish relief to unemployed actors? That the Virginia Democrat had made up his own mind on this last matter was evident from the line of questioning. "But have you not all the way through your theatrical program accentuated the question of publicity and propaganda rather than actually meeting the needs of people on relief?" Brushing aside Mrs. Kerr's denials, he made his position still more emphatic. Speaking "entirely for himself," Woodrum wished it "to be on the record" that he did not approve of the way the Federal Theatre Project was being conducted:

> My conception of a project of this type would be that it might operate where it was necessary to operate it to furnish relief assistance to unemployed theatrical people, but when you go beyond that field and enter into the field of amusement and entertainment, touring over the country, from place to place, charging admissions at cut rates in open competition with the theatre industry, which at best is languishing

and sick, you are going beyond what I think Congress intended. . . .

Colonel Harrington, at a loss as to how to defend this apparently benighted enterprise, ventured to point out that for three years the WPA had been criticized for substandard productions which did not entertain. "Now," he continued, "we come along with a production that the public, by patronizing it, indicates to be good entertainment, and we seem to be under criticism for having produced a good show."

While Woodrum criticized the Federal Theatre for charging admissions, he refused to admit that the Project might attract an audience willing to pay $1.10 or less but unable to pay the $3.00 or $4.00 price demanded by the commercial theatre. Congressman John Taber then shifted to a different tack. Why, the New York Republican asked, had eleven of the original thirty-two units been closed? Personnel cuts resulting from smaller appropriations was apparently not the answer Mr. Taber was after. Had these projects been financially successful? WPA officials could not answer offhand, but Florence Kerr remarked that, after all, the purpose of the Theatre had been to give employment rather than to make money. Her observation was not appreciated. When Taber requested that information on these units be submitted, Committee Chairman Edward Taylor, a Democrat from Colorado, sarcastically observed: "You will have to hire about two dozen clerks and stenographers to tabulate it, will you not?" William Ditter of Pennsylvania noted that the fact that the three largest units were in New York, Chicago, and Southern California did not "relieve those of us who reside in states that are helping to pay the bill."[62]

The criticism of the Committee had, in some instances, pointed up legitimate problems. Woodrum, with his observa-

[62] Hearings before the House Subcommittee of the Committee on Appropriations on H. J. Res. 209 and 246, *Further Additional Appropriations for Work Relief and Relief, Fiscal Year, 1939*, 76th Cong., 1st Sess. (1939), pp. 143 *passim* 209. (House Hearings on H. J. Res. 209 and 246, *Additional Relief Appropriations, 1939*.)

tions about the purpose of the Project, had touched on an un-resolved problem inherent in the dual nature of a work-relief program—the basic dichotomy between relief and theatre. Congressmen resolving that dichotomy in favor of relief would understandably have serious reservations about any enterprise aspiring to create a dynamic theatre with federal relief funds. That such a theatre, with its large units in New York, Chicago, and Los Angeles, was sufficiently decentralized to benefit much of the nation, was a source of concern to its Director, to Hopkins, and to the President of the United States, as well as to Representative Ditter. Criticism that was well-intentioned and well-founded, however, was infrequent.

The implications of this scarcely concealed antagonism were not lost upon Hallie Flanagan when she returned to Washington. Still much disturbed about the California Project, she privately admitted to a friend that she had felt like a swimmer being pulled down in water "almost too deep" during her last two days in Los Angeles. The situation had not improved: California was still without a regional director. She could not say why, unless the delay, like the plan to remove Federal Theatre employees from her jurisdiction, was part of an attempt "to separate the California Project from the national picture." Prospects for the entire Federal Theatre, she confessed, were even more discouraging:

> I came back here to find four major triumphs . . . : *Pinocchio* . . . and the *Swing Mikado* of Chicago playing to standing room; *Androcles and the Lion* bringing Shaw to Harlem, and *Big Blow* which opened in October, still running. George Sklar's *Life and Death of an American*; the interminable *Sing for your Supper* and a new, very powerful Living Newspaper, . . . *Medicine* [are] all slated for the next few months. If we go out it will be at least with a major conflagration lighting up the sky.
>
> However, I cannot say this consoles me much. Here we have the foundations of the thing many of us talked and

dreamed of for years—a people's theatre in America. I propose to stand by it until the last gun is fired but it certainly now looks as if that would be by June if not before.[63]

Hallie Flanagan would never completely understand why these guns were being fired or the men firing them. But after her harshly effective introduction to the realities of congressional politics at the hands of the Dies Committee, she no longer underestimated their marksmanship. Moreover, the stockpiling of ammunition had already begun.

In late March, the House gave its overwhelming endorsement to a sweeping investigation of the WPA preparatory to drawing up the new relief bill. And by mid-April, special investigators were on their way to New York, Chicago, and Los Angeles with instructions to "inquire fully" into the Arts Projects, "particularly the Theatre Project," as to types of plays produced, expenditures, personnel, and subversive activities.[64]

With a full-scale investigation underway, a bill already in the Senate which would withdraw all federal funds from white-collar projects, and one in the House which would virtually abolish all work relief projects in favor of direct aid to the States, the position of the Arts Projects appeared tenuous indeed.[65] Roosevelt was understandably concerned. In his April relief message to Congress, the President emphasized the prime importance of white-collar projects tailored to the needs of professional workers. Remarking on the House Investigating Committee, the Chief Executive expressed his belief that the in-

[63] Flanagan to Herbert Biberman, March 22, 1939, RG 69, FTP Records, NOGSF.

[64] Congressional Intelligence, *1939 Factual History of the Federal Government*, 76th Cong., 1st Sess. (1939), p. 9; "Taxes and Neutrality," *The Congressional Digest*, XVIII (April 1939), 100; The *New York Times*, April 27, 1939, p. 26; Hearings before the Subcommittee of the Committee on Appropriations on H. Res. 130. *Investigation and Study of the Works Progress Administration*, 76th Cong., 1st Sess. (1939), I, 180-181. (*Hearings on Investigation of the WPA*.)

[65] The Bills referred to are the so-called Byrnes bill (S.2202) and the Woodrum bill (H. J. Res. 151).

vestigation, "*if* guided along constructive lines," would demonstrate the wisdom of measures adopted to meet the needs
of the unemployed. There is a tendency, he warned, "to enlarge
upon the criticism of a few isolated projects to an extent which
obscures the real character and value of the program as a
whole."[66] But Committee members, with a few exceptions, did
not share the President's views.

On May 1, Investigator Ralph Burton was back in Washington
ready to testify. Although he admitted that three weeks had not
been time enough to obtain all the evidence needed, the Washington attorney could have had few doubts, after the following
exchange, as to the kind of additional information desired:

MR. TABER: Is it tremendously hard to find out what they are
doing with the money?

MR. BURTON: Very difficult.

MR. TABER: Did you get any idea of what they are doing with
the money they took in, as to whether they are putting it in
the Treasury, or putting it in their pockets?

MR. BURTON: I have called for that information, but that had
not been received at the time I left New York for this
hearing. . . .

MR. DITTER: I understand that some $40,000 was spent for
make-up creams and beauty greases; do your figures show that
broken down?

MR. BURTON: The breakdown of what is called other costs of
the project hasn't been submitted yet.

MR. DITTER: You are going to break that down?

MR. BURTON: I intend to.

MR. DITTER: *To see whether it conforms to the suggestions I
have made?*

MR. BURTON: I expect to get that information on the next trip.

[66] Roosevelt's letter to the Appropriations Subcommittee is printed in
Hearings before the Subcommittee of the House Committee on Appropriations on H. J. Res. 326, *Work Relief and Relief for Fiscal Year,
1940*, 76th Cong., 1st Sess. (1939), p. 2 (italics mine).

Burton did have information on the leases of the various theatres used by the New York Project and the plays being produced or rehearsed in each. He reported, mixing fact with fiction, that *Sing for Your Supper*, the Project's new revue, was playing at the Adelphi Theatre, which rented for $2,333.33 per month; that the play was a "flop"; that rehearsal time had been too long; and that Negroes and whites were "mixed" and "danced together." At this last bit of information, Woodrum immediately began asking about the racial character of other New York productions. Distressed by the questions of his Southern colleague, Clarence Cannon managed to interject the fact that little Shirley Temple danced with Negroes in her movies. There really is nothing "extraordinary" about mixed casts or Negroes dancing with whites, the Missouri Democrat insisted; nor should "special emphasis . . . have been laid on that fact. . . ."

The language of the plays, rather than their racial character, interested Indiana's Louis Ludlow. Burton agreed that *Sing for Your Supper* had "lewd lines"; but before the investigator could prove his point, Woodrum, Virginia gentleman that he was, suggested that the lines would be "rather embarrassing with ladies and gentlemen present." Burton, agreeing that they should be included in the record without being read, offered one example, a line from a song:

> I don't want to be intellectual
> I want to be sexual.

Nor was that all he had to offer. The former attorney for the Daughters of the American Revolution was prepared to submit testimony, written and oral, to show that employment in the New York Arts Projects was "largely controlled by the Workers' Alliance and its Communist affiliations." Before the *Daily Worker* and delegations from the Workers' Alliance had objected to his questionnaires, he had managed to get answers

265

from seventy-nine Project members; and, of the seventy-nine, fifty-two admitted membership in the Alliance.[67]

While Burton was testifying in Washington, investigators sent to look into the Illinois WPA compiled a preliminary report on the Chicago Federal Theatre. They found that older actors complained that favoritism was shown to young people who were supposedly using the Project as a means of gaining theatrical experience. After going over personnel records, however, E. W. Erickson concluded that the great majority of those on the Chicago Project had spent their entire lives in the acting profession. According to Erickson, production schedules indicated that rehearsals ran about two months, not an "unusual period." Types of plays produced varied. A played called *Power* had been criticized as fostering public ownership of utilities. There had been no opportunity to "go into the script" of these plays, "but it should be noted," Erickson continued, "that under WPA regulations a maximum royalty of fifty dollars per week was allowed." Hence, he concluded, it was not possible to obtain the rights for such popular plays as musical comedies. Virtually dismissing any suggestion of Communist activity, Erickson wrote perceptively, if awkwardly:

> With respect to subversive activities, that is questionable. That these people are more or less temperamental can easily be understood when one considers that in the past they have played before huge audiences and have earned in some instances up to $500 per week. In the opinion of your investigators, there is a field for a national theatre and the project is rehabilitating a great many people of unquestioned ability in the entertainment field.[68]

When Erickson and his fellow investigator, J. M. McTigue, subsequently appeared before the Committee they were questioned about personnel figures, theatre rentals, Project costs,

[67] *Hearings on Investigation of the WPA*, I, 192 *passim* 210.

[68] [E. W. Erickson], untitled report on the Federal Theatre in Chicago, April 30, 1938, RG 233, Approp. Comm. on WPA.

266

admission receipts, and rehearsal periods for the one hundred and fifteen plays produced by the Chicago company. Although no mention was made of subversive activities, Representative Ditter was anxious to leave no vices unexamined:

MR. DITTER: Just before you get away from those titles of plays, did you notice any of them that were of a salacious character? You said you had some seven and a half pages of them.

MR. ERICKSON: Here is one: *Saintly Hypocrites and Honest Sinners.*

MR. McTIGUE: Do you mean was there any criticism out there with regard to the type of play that was produced?

MR. DITTER: I would rather get my criticism from either yourself or Mr. Erickson. You both appear to me to be sensible men and pure minded. . . .

MR. ERICKSON: Thank you, Mr. Ditter. I saw one show in Chicago. That was *Big Blow.* . . . It dealt with a Nebraska man and his mother and aunt leaving the wind-swept Nebraska country for the north Florida country and establishing a home there, and it went into the trials and tribulations they had, how they had to make a living, and then the "big blow" came along, the hurricane—

MR. DITTER: That was a rather commendable show. I would like to know whether there were any salacious ones that . . . you gleaned from the list of them—not that you took your time to go to see them.

MR. ERICKSON: I am not an art critic to begin with, Mr. Ditter; in the second place, I do not think I am able to criticize a play as to whether it is salacious or not. . . .

MR. DITTER: If you are doubtful about that word 'salacious' I mean the kind of play that might raise your eyebrows [laughter] but not grow hair on your head. . . .

MR. JOHNSON: The *Big Blow* was a blow at Nebraska, was it not, and in favor of Florida—was it not, Mr. Witness?

MR. ERICKSON: What?

267

MR. JOHNSON: . . . it undertook to knock Nebraska, did it not?
MR. ERICKSON: No, it did not.

After a few more questions on finance, a brief exchange about
the Music and Art Projects, Erickson was excused. Statements
in his report favorable to the Federal Theatre were neither
questioned, repeated, nor included in the Committee's published
record. What did make its way into print was a lengthy cata-
logue of the Project's sins.[69]

Throughout the spring, Committee "findings" once again provided a ready topic for reporters and editorial writers from
New York to Georgia. The *Augusta Chronicle* waxed indignant
over the "wild extravagances in the expenditures of WPA funds,"
claiming that the New York Project spent $40,000 for "light-
ing alone."[70] The *Baltimore Sun* charged directors with hiring
"very few good actors," presenting plays "so bad they can't get
audiences," providing competition with the commercial theatre,
and confining production efforts "to a few metropolitan centers."[71] What the press omitted, radio provided. In "a few short
words about the Federal Theatre Project" subsequently distributed by the Republican National Committee, Missouri congressman, Dewey Short, recited for CBS listeners a long list of
the "suggestive or salacious titles" to plays produced by the
relief agency. Old stock company standbys such as *Bill of
Divorcement, The Bishop Misbehaves, Companionate Maggie,
Just a Love Nest, Love 'Em and Leave 'Em, Up in Mabel's
Room, Lend Me Your Husband, Old Capt'n Romeo's Four
Wives* were but a few of the titles cited by the Missouri Republican as proof of the "vulgar and villainous activities which the
people of the U. S. . . . [were] taxed for."[72] From Cincinnati
came word that a government investigator had uncovered productions with "mixed white and colored casts."[73]

[69] *Hearings on Investigation of the WPA*, I, 862-865.
[70] *Augusta Chronicle*, April 13, 1939 Clipping in Flanagan Papers.
[71] *Baltimore Sun*, May 2, 1939. Clipping in Flanagan Papers.
[72] *Variety*, May 17, 1939, p. 42.
[73] *Ibid.*

"I am afraid that unless the Gods are with us, the curtain falls on July 1 with a resounding bang," Hallie Flanagan wrote despairingly to Ole Ness of the California Project.[74] From bitter experience with the Dies Committee, the Federal Theatre Director had learned the difficulty of neutralizing adverse publicity without a full-scale counteroffensive. In the spring of 1939, as in the previous fall, the Federal Theatre was permitted no such offensive. In New York, to be sure, Arts Projects administrator Paul Edwards prepared a statement for the House Investigating Committee in which he repudiated charges of waste, inefficiency, and Communism; pointed out specific misstatements on the part of Committee investigators; and cited evidence of the economies effected during his tenure as administrator.[75] Actors Equity collected money to help defeat legislation withdrawing federal support from the arts.[76] And from the pages of the *New York Times*, Brooks Atkinson explained simply and logically the conditions that "scandalize Congressmen who happen to be looking for something to scandalize them."

Many Federal Theatre productions were not first-rate, wrote Atkinson, but they did provide entertainment for thousands who could not otherwise afford to attend the theatre. A case in point was *Swing Mikado*. Seen by more than 76,000 New Yorkers during the sixty-two weeks it played as a Federal Theatre production, the play had been turned over to private producers who promptly raised the price to $2.20. After twenty-four performances, the production had folded. Plays were in rehearsal a long time, Atkinson admitted, but what congressional critics failed to realize was that commercial timetables were simply not

[74] Flanagan to Ness, May 8, 1939, RG 69, FTP Records, NOC-State.

[75] Paul Edwards, Report Concerning Testimony Before the Committee of the House of Representatives Investigating the Works Progress Administration, May 20, 1939, RG 69, Records of the Works Projects Administration, Records of the Division of Investigation, Woodrum Committee, 1934-43 (WPA, DI Records, Woodrum Comm.).

[76] John Lorenz, "Arts Unions Offer Sincere Thanks," *Equity*, XXIV (May 1939), 4; "Equity's Twenty-Sixth Annual Meeting," *Equity*, XXIV (June 1939), 5.

applicable to the Federal Theatre. In a private production, cast and crew labored far into the early morning in order to meet the opening night deadline; in the Federal Theatre, they punched a clock and went home—thanks to governmental regulations and the demands of labor unions which made sensible operation almost impossible. Moreover, with actors working ninety-six hours, stagehands, sixty-eight, and musicians, forty-three, the task of getting them all together for a rehearsal at the same time assumed formidable proportions. As a result, rehearsal periods extended indefinitely, particularly when cuts made the training of new members of the cast necessary; and the cost of production inevitably rose. Although the Project was far from perfect, the *Times* critic concluded, its contributions were such that it thoroughly deserved to be "rescued from the partisan politics which, on the one hand are creeping into its administration, and on the other are threatening to put it out of business."[77]

The conclusions were sound; but Atkinson's efforts, like those of Edwards and Equity, hardly constituted the kind of large-scale rescue operation the situation demanded. On June 1, the *Washington Post* announced: "WPA THEATRE PROJECT MAY BE ABOLISHED." According to the *Post*, the House Appropriations Committee had decided to drop the Theatre Project completely, while continuing the other Arts Projects on a "strictly local basis."[78] Six days later, special investigator Ralph Burton was back in Washington with testimony designed to puncture any ground swell aimed at saving the Federal Theatre.

The New York Project, according to Burton, spent over $8,000 for rent and over $2,000 for telephone service in one month alone. No restrictions were placed on long-distance calls; excessive amounts of lighting equipment were purchased and then allowed to lie idle; and rentals on at least two theatres were, in the opinion of a Broadway producer of thirty years' experience, "preposterously high." Moreover, the Project was

[77] Brooks Atkinson, "FDR'S WPA FTP," the *New York Times*, May 28, 1939, Sec. 10, p. 1.
[78] The *Washington Post*, June 1, 1939, p. 3.

riddled with subversives. As evidence of their influence, Burton cited *Life and Death of an American*, a recent production praised by critics for the brilliant performance of young Arthur Kennedy and the complete lack of "shrill propaganda." Ignoring the verdict of the New York critics, and of John Mason Brown in particular,[79] Burton declared that propaganda in the play was "so pronounced one could not fail to rapidly detect it unless he should fall asleep." Even then, "wild applause" from the audience, which had the "appearance of an extremely radical type," was ample indication that the play had been written primarily for propaganda purposes. The Committee investigator found further evidence of Communist influence in the method of ticket sales, whereby "radical organizations" were permitted to buy a block of tickets at a discount and then sell them to their members at the regular price. Among the "radical" groups listed with the Young Communist League and the League of Industrial Democracy were the American Civil Liberties Union and the Sisterhood of the Sunnyside Jewish Center. Such groups had purchased over seven thousand tickets to *Life and Death of an American*, Burton reported, while other groups had bought only four thousand.[80]

Burton was followed by Charles St. Bernard Dinsmore Walton. In a repeat performance, the New York stage manager told Woodrum and his fellow representatives what he had already told the Dies Committee. The Workers' Alliance "absolutely dominated" the Federal Theatre; *One-Third of a Nation* was Communist propaganda; and, in short, the whole "set-up" was nothing more than a "clever fence to sow the seeds of Communism." When Cannon ordered the witness to substantiate his charges, Woodrum broke in to cut off a cross-examination. But the little Missouri Democrat, insisting that this was no kangaroo

[79] A synopsis of reviews by New York critics is contained in a report from George Kondolf to Hallie Flanagan, May 23, 1939, RG 69, FTP Records, Narr. Reports. See also: *Variety*, May 24, 1939, p. 42; Dewitt Bodeen, "New York Stage: *Life and Death of an American*," *Robert Wagner's Script*, XXI (June 10, 1939), 27.

[80] *Hearing on Investigation of the WPA*, I, 1,067 *passim* 1,081.

court, continued to press for proof, only to be met with the same reply: "This is my opinion. As an old theatre man I have a right to my opinion and this is my opinion. . . . I know Communism when I see it." Other witnesses repeated charges against the Writers' Project made nine months earlier. It was unimportant that the accusations were not new; they still provided sensational copy for even the most respectable newspapers.[81]

Thus, the *Washington Post* enlivened its front page with the headlines: COSTLY SPOTLIGHTS SUNBURN WPA ACTORS, INQUIRY TOLD. According to the *Post*, four $1,000 spotlights in *Sing For Your Supper* "sunburned the actors—all because the lighting man had a 'connection' with an electrical concern supplying the spotlights."[82] The following day all eight New York dailies brought out bold, black type for accounts of the hearings: WPA WITNESS SAYS SOVIETS TRAINED HIM IN STREET FIGHTING: WORKERS' ALLIANCE ORGANIZES "HUNGER MARCH" ON WASHINGTON: COMMITTEE HEARS OF STAY IN MOSCOW. . . .[83] With scrupulous fidelity to the facts, the *New York Times* also recounted Walton's charges and Cannon's attempts to get them substantiated. But, as the headlines so clearly indicated, the "real" story was made by the two former Dies Committee witnesses from the Writers' Project, whose testimony included everything from Communist promises of a "black belt" republic administered by a Moscow Commissar to a description of the Workers' Alliance as a "nursery" for the Communist Party. Alongside the prospect of a Communist-created Negro republic or Walton's claims that Voltaire wrote a play that "started the Revolution," Congressman Cannon's demands for concrete proof of subversive activities on the New York Federal Theatre paled into relative obscurity.[84]

In short, the same familiar cycle was repeating itself—Committee investigations, sensational charges, widespread and highly

[81] *Ibid.*, 1,081-1,094.
[82] The *Washington Post*, June 6, 1939, p. 1.
[83] Headlines quoted are from the *New York Times*, June 7, 1939, p. 1.
[84] *Ibid.*

damaging publicity. And once again WPA officials had to decide whether a discretionary silence was indeed the better part of valor. Paul Edwards thought not. As the official responsible for financial and administrative direction of all the New York Arts Projects, Edwards issued an emphatic denial of any irregularities in the purchase of electrical equipment within hours after tales of "sunburned" actors had escaped Committee chambers.[85] Six days later information explaining the purpose of theatre parties, procedures for theatre rentals, authorizations for long-distance telephone calls, and the circumstances of Walton's demotion was en route to WPA headquarters in Washington.[86]

For Hallie Flanagan, however, orders apparently had not changed. No doubt believing that, after her session with the Dies Committee, Mrs. Flanagan's denials would count for little, WPA officials continued to insist that any reply must come from Edwards. Charges had been leveled only at the New York Project, they pointed out, and not at the Federal Theatre as a whole.[87] With investigations already underway in Chicago and California as well as New York,[88] it was a tenuous distinction and, for Hallie Flanagan, an infuriating one. Unless something was done quickly, the Federal Theatre once again stood in grave danger of being convicted—first in a legislative investigation and then in the court of public opinion. Much disturbed, she pointed out in a letter to Woodrum (also made available to the press)

[85] Edwards' denial was reported on June 6, 1939 in the *Post*, p. 17, *Journal and American*, p. 12, *Sun*, p. 6, and *World Telegram*, p. 6.

[86] Paul Edwards to F. H. Dryden, June 12, 1936; Statement Replying to Charges Made Before the Subcommittee of the Appropriations Committee Investigating the Works Progress Administration, June 5 and 6, 1939, RG 69, WPA, DI Records, Woodrum Comm.

[87] Flanagan, *Arena*, pp. 35-53. Apparently WPA officials did agree to let the Federal Theatre answer unfavorable news stories provided the replies were cleared through proper channels. See Memorandum, Flanagan to Lawrence Morris and Florence Kerr, May 11, 1939, RG 69, GSS-211.2.

[88] See [E. W. Erickson], untitled report on the Federal Theatre in Chicago, April 30, 1938; F. H. Smith to Edward Taylor and Cedric F. Johnson, June 1, 1939 regarding the Committee's investigation of the California Project; RG 233, Approp. Comm. on WPA.

that no one in a "directional capacity" had been permitted to testify before the Committee; that charges against the Project were untrue; and that constant repetition of "so distorted a picture" presented a "false impression of the Federal Theatre to the people of the nation." Communists might well be among the forty million persons who attended Project plays, but so were representatives of every religious and political faith. As for Project employees, she could only reply that, according to congressional statutes, no inquiry could be made into a relief client's political loyalty.[89]

A few days later, Colonel Harrington appeared before the Committee with a thirty-nine-page statement, intended as a partial answer to criticism of the WPA. Emphasizing the importance of the Arts Projects, the Relief Administrator admitted that mistakes had been made in their operation. He was prepared, however, to make extensive changes, including a complete reorganization of the Theatre Project and the transfer of its directors to Washington where they would be under "close supervision." "I certainly hope," Harrington added, "that restrictions which would practically wreck this very valuable project will not be included in legislation." Upon completing his testimony, the Colonel invited questions from members of the Committee. There was a long moment of silence; then Woodrum closed the interview with a perfunctory "Thank you, Colonel, for your appearance." The incident was appropriately commemorated by *Time*. Under a photograph of the Relief Administrator were the words: "got the silent treatment."[90] Since the Virginia Democrat had already told reporters that two-thirds of those on the Federal Theatre had no right to relief, Harrington had had little reason to expect that his testimony would make a dif-

[89] The *New York Times*, June 12, 1939, p. 17.

[90] *Ibid.*, June 14, 1939, p. 1; Hearings Before the House Subcommittee of the Committee on Appropriations, *Work Relief and Relief For Fiscal Year 1940*, 76th Cong., 1st Sess. (1939), pp. 1-93; "Relief: For 1940," *Time*, XXXIII (June 26, 1939), 20.

ference. It did not. After a few last-minute technical changes, the new relief bill was sent to the printer.[91]

In New York, meanwhile, Paul Edwards renewed his criticism of the House investigation as he announced new cuts in Project ranks. Information given the Committee in its "one-sided investigation" as "unfair and misleading." Although the Workers' Alliance was "quite articulate," its members on the Theatre Project were few, its influence, no greater than that of any of the twenty-nine unions with which the Federal Theatre had to deal.[92] But the Committee was no more affected by the remarks of Edwards than it had been by those of Hallie Flanagan or Harrington. Tired of appropriating funds for unemployed millions who somehow seemed to remain jobless, fearful of the WPA's potentiality as a rival political machine, and suspicious of a relief enterprise with theatrical pretensions and a reformist rationale, Congress had indeed taken the stage. A controversial and constituentless protagonist, the Federal Theatre stood vulnerable at the denouement.

· III ·

The Relief Bill for 1939-40, described by the *New York Times* as "aimed at radicals," was reported to the House on June 15. While granting the full amount requested by the President, the bill called for sweeping changes in the relief program. With $125 million earmarked for PWA building projects, the WPA's appropriation was reduced, the post of administrator, abolished in favor of a three-man board, and payment of relief workers at prevailing wage rates, discontinued. Other restrictive provisions stipulated that relief personnel employed on WPA projects for eighteen months or more be dismissed, and that a loyalty oath be required of new workers. Writers', Music, and Art Projects were to be continued only if locally sponsored; the Theatre Project was to be abolished outright.[93]

[91] The *Washington Post*, June 14, 1939, p. 1.
[92] The *New York Times*, June 14, 1939, p. 19.
[93] *Ibid.*, June 13, 1939, p. 1; June 14, 1939, p. 1.

All attempts at amendment were immediately quashed by Woodrum who moved that the House adjourn shortly after four o'clock, thus enabling leaders of the economy bloc to rally their forces before the next day's session. In a press conference, the silver-haired Richmond Democrat revealed the strategy that had earned him a reputation as one of the ten ablest representatives on the Hill.[94] Noting that the full amount requested by the administration had been granted, he suggested that those attempting to make changes would be placed in the unenviable position of appearing to support such organizations as the Workers' Alliance and the Communist Party.[95]

It was a "nasty" situation, said Harrington, much disturbed about the Committee's provision for a three-man administrative board.[96] Hallie Flanagan agreed; but for her there was only one concern—the Federal Theatre. Little suspecting that the Committee would recommend "outright execution rather than slow strangulation," she learned of the ban from a newspaper handed her by a ticket seller as she walked out of a New York theatre. Shocked and dismayed, she made her way to a telephone. Dismissing any thought of talking to Harrington, with whom she had never once had an opportunity to discuss the Project, she called Hopkins' good friend, Howard Hunter, only to learn that the report was indeed true. No reason had been given as to why the theatre had been singled out. In Washington a short time later, she was told regretfully, but finally, that the WPA would not wage a fight to save the Federal Theatre. The relief agency's own position was precarious enough without jeopardizing it further. In that case, Mrs. Flanagan decided, she would fight alone.[97]

It was a gallant gesture made in the face of formidable odds. Congressional dissatisfaction with the administration and its relief program had not abated. However one-sided and incom-

[94] "Milestones," *Time*, LVI (October 16, 1950), 93.
[95] The *New York Times*, June 16, 1939, p. 2.
[96] *Ibid.*
[97] Flanagan, *Arena*, pp. 352-354.

plete Woodrum's investigation had been, he and his fellow committeemen had every reason to believe that a relief bill embodying their findings would receive support from many sources: administration opponents; economy advocates; politicians sensitive to the mounting public protest against relief costs and abuses; as well as those representatives sincerely desirous of improving WPA policies and procedures.[98] Even the bill's critics could be expected to concentrate their fire only on those provisions most directly affecting the WPA.[99] Thus, with a confidence born of an awareness of political realities, Clifton Woodrum informed the House on June 17 that henceforth no funds would go to the Federal Theatre. When the applause subsided, he continued:

> It has produced nothing of merit so far as national productions are concerned. . . . Every theatrical critic of any note expressed his disapproval of projects of this type. . . . I have here the manuscript for *Sing For Your Supper*. If there is a line in it or a passage in it that contributes to the cultural and educational benefit of America, I will eat the whole manuscript. . . . It is a small trashy kind of stuff. It has been a complete flop and it cost over $300,000 to produce. So we are going out of the theatre business.[100]

Biased and uninformed, Woodrum's statement did not go unchallenged. The following day, fiery little Vito Marcantonio, an American Laborite from New York, announced that he had received numerous letters from organizations such as the Federation of Arts Unions which the Committee investigating the

[98] Note the editorial response to the bill in the *Washington Post*, June 16, 1939, p. 12.

[99] The limitations placed on building projects, abolition of the prevailing wage scale, and the huge slash in the budget of the National Youth Administration were expected by some to be the main issues of conflict (the *New York Times*, June 15, 1939, p. 1). Others predicted that opposition would be concentrated on the proposed three-man administrative board. (The *Washington Post*, June 18, 1939, Sec. I, p. 2.)

[100] *Cong. Rec.*, 76th Cong., 1st Sess. (1939), p. 7,166.

277

Project had refused to hear. Woodrum interrupted, explaining that the investigations had not been completed. "But before you have finished your hearings," Marcantonio replied, "you have used testimonies which these people want to refute, and you have used it [sic] with absolute reliance on the witnesses who testified against these projects. . . . You condemn these projects before hearing their defenders. . . . What good will a hearing do after Congress has killed . . . [them]?"[101]

The Project's many opponents were in no mood to quibble over niceties. In vigorous attacks on the Federal Theatre and its so-called subversive activities, congressmen touched on everything from Mrs. Roosevelt's attendance at a convention of the Workers' Alliance to the Communists' advocacy of a third term for the President. Economy-conscious Republicans were no less outspoken. Rejoicing at the savings to be made by disbanding the Project, Massachusetts' Charles L. Gifford declared that the new bill brought a "ray of sunshine," and that he loved "that gentleman from Virginia (Mr. Woodrum) who at last sees the danger of furnishing the administration with a blank check."[102]

Federal Theatre supporters tried to stem the tide of criticism, but with little success. The House had heard nothing of the Arts Projects' positive accomplishments, declared Jerry Voorhis, an earnest young California Socialist turned Democrat. New Mexico's John Dempsey who, like Voorhis, had recently been named to the House Un-American Activities Committee in a last minute coup by the liberals, insisted that the Dies investigation showed that Mrs. Flanagan was "neither Communist nor a 'fellow traveler,' but a highly efficient, splendid American woman." Clarence Cannon begged the House not to make relief a political football to be kicked about by Congress. As for the investigation of the WPA, the Committee had had but one purpose—to "pin the Bolshevist idea on the Roosevelt administration." According to the Missouri Democrat, an effort to show that the WPA contained subversive elements had run through the hearings like a "scarlet thread." But, as Cannon himself

[101] *Ibid.*, pp. 7,231-7,232.   [102] *Ibid.*, pp. 7,233-7,236.

noted, politicking was inevitable in a preelection year; and in the minds of certain politicians the Federal Theatre had become hopelessly intertwined with that "scarlet thread." Hence it was criticized with a bitterness that surprised even veteran congressmen. In a speech praising the small project in his state, Maine Republican James Oliver remarked on this bitterness and expressed his regret at the "apparent overwhelming opinion of the majority of the House for discontinuance" of the Federal Theatre. Oliver had judged the temper of his fellow representatives correctly. It was not until the following day, however, that the struggle over the Federal Theatre reached its climax in what the *Chicago Daily Tribune* called "one of the most dramatic sessions of more than a decade."[103]

Perspiring from the 96° heat and humidity that forced thousands of sweltering, sleepless Washingtonians out to the grassy cool of Hains Point,[104] Vito Marcantonio reopened debate on June 16 by reading aloud telegrams from drama critics, refuting Woodrum's earlier charges. That "every theatrical critic of note had disapproved of the Project's productions," and that the Federal Theatre had "never produced any productions of distinction with the exception of *Swing Mikado*," simply was not true, said critics from the *New York Times, Forum, The New Yorker, The Nation,* the *New York World Telegram, The Catholic World,* the *New York Daily News, Life* and *Vogue*. Brooklyn Democrat Emmanuel Celler followed with an extensive account of the Project's activities, and finally, New Jersey's Mary Norton rose to offer an amendment reinstating the Theatre. Facing a hostile Congress of which she had been a Democratic member since 1924, the plump, grandmotherly chairman of the House Labor Committee began:

> Mr. Chairman, I do not believe that anything anyone can say tonight is going to change the temper of this House, but I

[103] *Ibid.,* pp. 7,237, 7,261-7,263, 7,265; "Parade of the Left," *Time,* XXXIII (February 20, 1939), 10; *Chicago Daily Tribune,* June 17, 1939, p. 1.
[104] The *Washington Post,* June 17, 1939, p. 1.

beg of you, before proceeding with this bill, stop and consider just what you are doing to 9,000 men and women on this Project.

Point by point Mrs. Norton answered charges against the Theatre, explaining why it deserved to be continued; time after time, her explanations were met with guffaws.[105]

The temper of the House was indeed unmistakable, but the Woodrum forces were taking no chances. For those few who might have been swayed by Project defenders, Everett Dirksen had a ready reply. An avowed critic of the administration, at least for the past year, the young Illinois Republican proceeded to run down a list of play titles remarking in deep, honeyed tones:

A New Kind of Love. I wonder what that can be. It smacks of the Soviets. . . . Then the State Department might well take notice of this—A Boudoir Diplomat. . . . If you want this kind of salacious tripe, very well vote for it, but if anybody has an interest in the real cultural values you will not find it in this kind of junk and I suggest we leave the bill as it is and vote down the amendment of the gentleman of New Jersey.[106]

It was a speech "rarely equalled for bias and ignorance," according to the Catholic periodical, The Commonweal; but the

[105] Cong. Rec., pp. 7,290-7,294, 7,370-7,373; The New York Times, June 17, 1939, p. 12; Chicago Daily Tribune, June 17, 1939, p. 1.

[106] "Dirksen, Everett McKinley," Current Biography, ed. Maxine Block (1941), p. 288. On February 16, 1938, Dirksen announced that he took "rather fine pride" in having voted for WPA, the Social Security Act, AAA, and "a great many other measures that were proposed by the President in the hope of lifting this country from the slough of depression to the high road of prosperity." One year later he switched sides, claiming that the American people were being duped into dictatorship under such New Deal measures as the AAA and NRA, and remained a critic of the Roosevelt administration throughout 1939. See Ben H. Bagdikean, "The Oil Can is Mightier than the Sword," the New York Times Magazine (March 14, 1965), p. 31. For Dirksen's speech, see Cong. Rec., pp. 7,372-7,373.

House applauded lustily.[107] When Massachusetts' Joseph Casey tried to counter Dirksen's attack with quotes from various drama critics, Woodrum moved to limit debate on the amendment to five minutes.[108] William Sirovich, a New York Democrat, former playwright, and advocate of a Department of Science, Literature and Art, began a final plea. But the hour was late; the audience, impatient and unruly; the chairman's gavel, an inadequate check on hoots, catcalls, and boos. In a futile attempt to make himself heard above shouts of "vote," Sirovich's plea for justice to nine thousand theatre workers fell on deaf ears.[109] While Hallie Flanagan and her Washington staff watched from the gallery, the House voted 192 to 56 against the Norton amendment.[110] Then at 1:01 A.M., after the longest session of the year, hoarse, hot, exhausted representatives voted 373 to 21 to accept the Appropriation Committee's relief bill.[111] "An act of defiance toward the White House . . . ," an acknowledgment of the "mounting protest of the general public against high relief costs and relief abuses," said observers.[112] Whatever the interpretation, the Federal Theatre had been doomed by the House.

The Senate alone remained. If the Upper Chamber could be won over, the Project might still have a chance; and Hallie Flanagan aimed to see that it did. With Arts Projects directors, she scrutinized Senate lists for the names of every possible sympathizer. With Howard Miller and her small Washington staff, she went over stacks of records culling material for news releases, reports to WPA officials, information for friendly congressmen as well as for "anyone [else] needing factual ammuni-

[107] See editorial comments in "Farewell to 9,000," *The Commonweal*, xxx (June 30, 1939), 247.

[108] *Cong. Rec.*, p. 7,373.

[109] *Ibid.*, pp. 7,373-7,374; The *Washington Post*, June 17, 1939, p. 1; The *New York Times*, June 17, 1939, p. 1.

[110] Flanagan, *Arena*, p. 355; The *New York Times*, June 17, 1939, p. 1.

[111] The *Washington Post*, June 17, 1939, p. 1; The *New York Times*, June 17, 1939, p. 1.

[112] "Roosevelt's War on Hatch Bill Draws up Battle Lines for 1940," *Newsweek*, xiii (June 26, 1939), 13.

tion." While secretaries feverishly stuffed envelopes with reprints, reviews, and reports, she conferred with Federal Theatre directors, union leaders, Broadway actors, and Hollywood stars.[113] The struggle to save the Federal Theatre had begun.

From Philadelphia, where Yasha Frank had gone to "pass along the word," the Children's Theatre director wrote that the mood of Project employees was "grim and resolute."[114] Detroit reported that Federal Theatre workers had appealed for support from local citizen's groups, the Mayor, the City Council, the Superintendent of Schools, principals and drama teachers, churchmen, Eastern Star leaders, Rotary and Kiwanis Club presidents, stagehand and musicians locals.[115] In New York, Project employees stationed themselves in the Times Square area where, carefully explaining that they were acting on their own time, they solicited signatures to petitions for the Federal Theatre's continuance.[116] Rallying to the cause, the Federation of Arts Unions promised to carry the fight to the Senate and thence to the home state of Everett Dirksen.[117] Organized labor quickly pledged its support; Broadway and Hollywood scarcely had to be asked. Telegrams urging presidential action poured into the White House from Eddie Cantor and from dozens of his fellow entertainers.[118] Helen Hayes, Lee Shubert, Burgess Meredith,

[113] Flanagan to Hester Sondergaard, June 28, 1939; Flanagan to Regional and State Directors, June 28, 1939, RG 69, GSS-211.2.

[114] Frank to Flanagan, June 14, 1939, Flanagan Papers.

[115] Verner Haldene to Howard Miller, June 22, 1929, Flanagan Papers.

[116] The *New York Times*, June 17, 1939, p. 12. For earlier efforts on the Federal Theatre's behalf, see the *New York Times*, June 4, 1939, p. 30; June 7, 1939, p. 4; June 10, 1939, p. 16.

[117] *Ibid.*, June 17, 1939, p. 12; "Federation of Arts Unions Fight for WPA," *Equity*, XXIV (June 1939), 17.

[118] The *New York Times*, June 17, 1939, p. 12; "Roll of Honor," *TAC Magazine*, I (July-August 1939), 8. *TAC* was a publication of the Theatre Arts Committee founded in May 1938. The magazine along with Cabaret TAC were organs of expression for members of the performing arts dedicated to the fight against Fascism at home and abroad. Under the Committee's auspices many of the theatre's best-known representatives lobbied long and hard on behalf of the Federal Theatre throughout June 1939. Previous efforts included a special supplement on the Project in

282

Richard Rodgers, George Abbott, Moss Hart, Clifford Odets, and Harold Clurman were but a few of those petitioning Congressman Cannon to read their endorsement of the Federal Theatre on the floor of the House.[119] From the columns of the *New York Times*, actors, playwrights, and producers issued a joint appeal to the theatre-going public ending with the plea: "If the theatre has ever brought you happiness and joy, join with us in this action; write or wire your Senator NOW demanding the continuation of the Federal Theatre and other Arts Projects."[120] From the west coast, where screen actors, directors, and writers had gathered in a mass rally, telegrams flowed into the capital with signatures running into the thousands.[121] Colonel Harrington issued a statement from Washington in which he reported that the Federal Theatre had given employment to an average of nine thousand people a year since its inception in 1935; that over two thousand five hundred actors, directors, playwrights, and designers had been returned to the commercial theatre; and that, of the ninety-four productions on Broadway during the current season, eighty-eight employed one or more former Federal Theatre workers.[122]

Speedily and inexorably, pressure was mounting. Two days after the House had voted to abolish the Federal Theatre, the press reported that there were "indications" that the administration might try to get the ban against the Theatre "eased" in the Senate along with certain other of the House restrictions.[123]

The report was correct. On June 20, Senator Claude Pepper, an ardent New Dealer and advocate of a Federal Bureau of Fine Arts, began ushering before the Senate Appropriations Commit-

---

TAC Magazine's February issue. See, "The Issue of the Federal Theatre," *TAC Magazine*, I (February 1939), 3; Marc Connelly, "Save America's Theatre," p. 5; "Photographic History," pp. 6-11.

[119] *Ibid.*

[120] The *New York Times*, June 20, 1939, p. 25.

[121] "Roll of Honor," *TAC Magazine*, I (July-August 1939), 8.

[122] The *New York Times*, June 18, 1939, Sec. 1, p. 2.

[123] *Ibid.*, p. 1.

tee a group of well-known stage people. All of those accompanying the Florida Democrat were "theatrical headliners," but Tallulah Bankhead as "the Federal Theatre's Joan of Arc" stole the show.[124] Arriving with both "Daddy," William B. Bankhead, Speaker of the House and a Federal Theatre supporter, and "Uncle John" who was less favorably disposed, the actress set out to convert the Alabama senator with pleas and kisses while flashbulbs popped madly. When, despite her entreaties, "Uncle John" persisted in his refusal to do anything for unemployed actors since those "city fellers in Congress never vote to do anything for the farmers,"[125] his glamorous niece turned to the Committee itself. Her rich, throaty voice almost breaking with emotion, she begged them not to deprive Federal Theatre employees of the chance to "hold up their heads with dignity and self-respect" due every American. Less dramatically but no less sincerely, Blanche Yurka seconded Miss Bankhead's plea. "I do not think anybody questions that the Federal Theatre needs improvement," the actress declared. "But after all, you do not chloroform a child who happened to have the measles. You help that child, you try to build up his strength."[126]

From the antechamber where she had been waiting, Hallie Flanagan was called in to testify. Point by point, she tried to answer charges made during the House Appropriation Committee's investigation. In order to show that the Project did not compete with the commercial theatre, she told of efforts to

[124] The designation is Herman Shumlin's. Interview with Herman Shumlin, November 9, 1961. For further description of the event, see the *New York Times*, June 21, 1939, pp. 1, 24; *New York Herald Tribune*, June 21, 1939, p. 1; "Three Bankheads," *Newsweek*, XIV (July 3, 1939), 13.

[125] Quoted in the *New York Times*, June 21, 1939, p. 1. Senator Bankhead was subsequently reported to have changed his mind and agreed to support the Project. *Ibid.*, June 27, 1939, p. 7.

[126] Hearings Before the Senate Committee on Appropriations on H. J. Res. 326, *Work Relief and Public Works Appropriation Act of 1939*, 76th Cong., 1st Sess. (1939), pp. 49-55 (Senate Hearings on H. J. Res. 326, *Work Relief Act of 1939*).

bring together relief actors and the many Americans unable to afford theatrical entertainment. When, after an introduction from the Federal Theatre, these people eventually went to see commercial productions, the entire theatrical profession would be stimulated. As for the Project's being overstaffed with persons not on relief, Mrs. Flanagan pointed out that 95 per cent of those connected with the Federal Theatre came from relief rolls. While admitting that overhead costs were higher on a professional project than on any other form of work relief, she reminded senators that nine out of every ten dollars appropriated was used for wages, and that admissions were paying an increasing proportion of costs each year. The real value of the Federal Theatre, she insisted, could not be measured in dollars and cents. Yes, rehearsal time for *Sing For Your Supper* had been too long, but the play, which centered around a character called Uncle Sam, had had to be recast almost entirely after cuts. Moreover, in the past months eight Uncle Sams had been returned to private industry and four scripts had been bought by commercial producers so that part of the time the Project lacked both play and actors.[127]

Herman Shumlin of the League of New York Theatres and Frank Gillmore of Actors' Equity testified that the Federal Theatre was not competing with commercial production—the more plays on Broadway, the better the season for everyone, they declared. James F. Brennan explained what the Project had meant to stagehands. A social worker, Sarah Sussman, spoke of the immeasurable good done by performances in hospitals, insane asylums, orphanages, and crippled children's clinics. And Colonel Harrington, trim and tight-lipped, reiterated the Project's accomplishments and explained its apparent shortcomings, until asked by a politely patient Committee to draw up an amendment which would permit the Theatre Project to continue in areas where local sponsors would pay all non-labor costs. Since few communities would have either the funds or the inclination

[127] *Ibid.*, pp. 56-70.

to provide the necessary subsidy, it was a recommendation of limited value—but it was a beginning.[128]

In the meantime, theatre supporters under the auspices of the leftist Theatre Arts Committee (TAC) were publicizing their cause with all the drama and devices at their disposal.[129] In Hollywood, the Motion Picture Guilds arranged for two coast-to-coast radio programs on behalf of the Federal Theatre with star-filled casts that included Claudette Colbert, Melvyn Douglas, Ralph Bellamy, Joan Blondell, Henry Fonda, James Cagney, Dick Powell, Patricia Morrison, and Al Jolson.[130] On the other side of the continent, the Federation of Arts Union sponsored a broadcast from New York, sent lobbyists to Capitol Hill, and held mass rallies in Lee Shubert's Majestic Theatre.[131] Telegrams poured into Washington from the League of New York Theatres, the American Federation of Radio Artists, Bishop Francis J. McConnell of the Methodist Episcopal Church, Dr. Samuel Trexler, president of the United Lutheran Synod of New York, Edna Ferber, and Orson Welles.[132] Eleanor Roosevelt used her column to lobby for the Federal Theatre, as did at least eight other columnists including Walter Winchell.[133] In the press and over the radio, the tough-talking commentator reminded the nation that Federal Theatre productions were "important events in the history of the American theatre, and therefore in the history of the American people." "You cannot budget the value of art," proclaimed Winchell. "Shakespeare lives in the hearts of

[128] *Ibid.*, pp. 72-77, 94-96ff.

[129] As a reflection of their efforts see *TAC Magazine*, I (July-August 1939), 2; "Restore America's Theatre," p. 3; Bob Coyne "TAC Around Town," p. 28; "Roll of Honor," pp. 8, 33.

[130] *Ibid.*, p. 8. For a transcript of the broadcast, see "Take it Away, Hollywood," pp. 9-11ff.

[131] *Ibid.*, p. 8; The *New York Times*, June 23, 1939, p. 22.

[132] *Ibid.*; The *New York Times*, June 22, 1939, p. 18; June 23, 1939, p. 3.

[133] *Ibid.*, pp. 8, 33; "Relief: Theatre Lobby," *Time*, XXIV (July 3, 1939), 9.

all men, but who can remember the name of Shakespeare's bookkeeper?"[134]

Variety, insisting that the "WPA'ers" had never furnished Broadway showmen with "any actual competition," rallied to the cause in a further expression of the solidarity and intimacy characteristic of this mercurial and contentious industry that was also an art. Further support came from Tyrone Power who flew from Hollywood to Washington to speak on behalf of the Motion Picture Guild; Raymond Massey who offered to debate Representative Woodrum; and Orson Welles who succeeded in registering his protests in a radio debate with Senators Capper, Schwellenbach, and Keller.[135]

By the end of a week, the list of actors, producers, directors, and critics volunteering their services had run into the hundreds; telephone calls from TAC headquarters had reached the three thousand mark; and the list of signatures on petitions to Congress had climbed to nearly a hundred thousand. From her own understaffed office, which resembled "the city desk of a newspaper fifteen minutes before press time," Hallie Flanagan wrote: "We know now that we have a better than fighting chance in the Senate and a fairly good chance in the House."[136] About the Senate, she was right.

On the afternoon of June 26, the Subcommittee on Appropriations reported to the Committee a much amended version of the House Relief Bill in which the Theatre, like the other Arts Projects, was to be continued if local sponsorship were forthcoming. Two days later debate began on an amendment submitted by Senators Wagner, Downey, and Pepper calling for no more than 1 per cent of the entire relief appropriation to be set aside for the Arts Projects, all of which would be financed exclusively by the WPA.[137] This amendment, the Federal The-

---

[134] Quoted in Senate Hearings on H. J. Res. 326, *Work Relief Act of 1939*, p. 53.

[135] *Variety*, June 28, 1939, p. 49; the *Washington Post*, June 26, 1939, Sec. 2, p. 1; "Roll of Honor," *TAC*, I (July-August 1939), 8, 33.

[136] Flanagan to Hester Sondergaard, June 28, 1939, RG 69, GSS-211.2.

[137] The amendment was sponsored by Robert Wagner (Democrat, New

atre's best hope for survival, was a modest and reasonable request. The attack which it precipitated was neither. In a speech reminiscent of his days as patent medicine salesman and sideshow barker, Robert R. Reynolds of North Carolina reminded his fellow senators that the Federal Theatre was being used by "clever communists" to destroy American institutions. Although the project in his own state was, of course, "meritorious," he hastened to assure his listeners that such was not the case with projects elsewhere. On the contrary, the Theatre Project was controlled by Communists who used plays as vehicles for "spreading the doctrine of communism at the expense of the American taxpayer." That fact alone, he insisted, should compel the Senate "to condemn the . . . project to the ash can of oblivion."[138] Hopelessly uninformed and irresponsible, Reynolds' red-baiting remarks were thoroughly consistent with his self-appointed role as defender of Americanism. They did not go unanswered.[139]

"What we have to fear in America is fear itself," declared short, stocky Pat McCarran quoting the President and looking straight at Reynolds—fear produced by those who are "forever and always . . . using the bugbear of communism to scare someone in order that they themselves might rise up and thus be held up as the champions against the so-called dangers of communism."[140] Armed with information furnished by Federal Theatre officials, the Project's champions rallied to its defense. If the

---

York), Sheridan Downey (Democrat, California), and Claude Pepper (Democrat, Florida). *Cong. Rec.*, p. 8,084.

[138] *Ibid.*; for Reynolds' earlier attack see pp. 3,956-3,957. Information on Reynolds can be found in the following: "Feather in a Hat," *Time*, XXXIII (February 13, 1939), 16; "The Vindicators," *Newsweek*, XIII (May 1, 1939), 16; Robert McCormick, "Buncombe Bob," *Colliers*, CI (May 21, 1938), 36; "Reynolds, Robert Rice," *Current Biography* (1940), pp. 680-682; *Asheville Citizen-Times*, November 23, 1958, Sec. D, p. 1; Reynolds' newspaper, *American Vindicator*, April 1939.

[139] Reynolds' attack was also sufficient cause to bring the cloture rule into effect. *New York Herald Tribune*, June 29, 1939, p. 1.

[140] *Cong. Rec.*, pp. 8,034-8,035; the *Washington Post*, June 28, 1939, p. 1. McCarran was a Democrat from Nevada.

Project were eliminated entirely, seven thousand men and women on relief would lose their jobs, Claude Pepper declared. Such deprivation was totally unnecessary, for the bill already included a loyalty oath which would suffice to reduce the alleged Communist threat.[141] James Mead of New York doubted if such a threat existed at all. Presenting a complete breakdown of the various unions represented on the New York Project, this one-time Progressive and staunch Roosevelt supporter explained that with the majority of employees belonging to old, established theatrical unions, the number of Workers' Alliance members who were Communists was, at most, negligible. The long list of Project sponsors, continued the senator, should be sufficient refutation of Communist domination.[142] James J. Davis agreed—with some qualifications. Although the Pennsylvania Republican had been thoroughly convinced in 1936 that "those who were of the extreme radical type" controlled the New York Project, he now insisted that with the new loyalty oath, Congress was "on the eve of saving these theatrical projects from the extremists." "Let us clean house," he begged, but "let us not throw these men of the stage out on the street."[143]

Such words coming from a man who had denounced the Federal Theatre on the floor of the Senate three years before was too much for Reynolds. Rising to his feet, this super-patriot from the North Carolina mountains began quoting the more incriminating portions of testimony given before the Dies and Woodrum Committees, dwelling at great length on the testimony of a witness who claimed that a supervisor belonging to the Workers' Alliance had urged her to date a Negro. The attack reached new heights—or, more accurately, new depths—with a description of the Project's "unsavory collection of communistic, un-American doctrines, its assortment of insidious and vicious ideologies," its "putrid plays . . . spewed from the gutters of

141 *Ibid.*, pp. 8,085-8,086.
142 *Ibid.*, p. 8,086. Mead had previously taken Reynolds to task for his earlier (April 7th) attack. See p. 3,959.
143 *Ibid.*, p. 8,088.

the Kremlin" and advertised on marquees which were, of course, "red." Not only was the Federal Theatre pro-Communist, the senator asserted, but it was also unprofitable. Box-office receipts amounted to "virtually nothing" and "approximately 99.99 per cent of this expenditure was dead loss." Admitting that there was "no lady in America of higher character than Mrs. Flanagan," he declared that what the Project needed was "someone with old-fashioned, common horse sense rather than some college professor."[144]

One after another the Federal Theatre's supporters rose to reply, when finally Senator Henry F. Ashurst, an Arizona Democrat and chairman of Judiciary Committee, took the floor. He urged his fellow legislators not to go on record as censors of art. "The stage is art. Art is truth," declared the Rangeland Scholar, "and in the final sum of worldly things only art endures; the sculptures outlast the dynasty, the colors outlast Da Vinci, 'the coin outlasts Tiberius.' "[145]

On that note of oratorical eloquence the Senate settled down to a discussion of whether 1 per cent of the appropriation should go to the Arts Projects or only three-fourths of 1 per cent. They decided on the smaller amount. Senator Wagner made a final appeal for the Federal Theatre; a voice vote was taken; and the amendment passed. After a thirteen-hour session, during which many of the House's more drastic changes were nullified, a group of tired senators unenthusiastically voted 54 to 9 in favor of the Relief Bill.[146] They turned homeward from Capitol Hill only a few hours before papers hit the newsstands with word of Hitler's plan for the "peaceful" return of Danzig to the Reich. With Austria and Czechoslovakia already in German hands and Poland about to go down, war clouds were fast gathering. In the urgency of another world war, relief would be unnecessary and reform slowed down. But for Federal Theatre supporters it was a time for celebration.

[144] *Ibid.*, pp. 8,088-8,096.   [145] *Ibid.*, pp. 8,095-8,096.

[146] *Ibid.*, pp. 8,089, 8,099-8,101; The *New York Times*, June 29, 1939, p. 1.

Although they had won the battle, victory proved as elusive as ever. The bill, which provided all Arts Projects with roughly one-third of the funds they had received the previous year, was immediately referred to a conference committee. House conferees had already made it known that they would not "budge" on four items, one of which was the Federal Theatre. Should they prove adamant, there was little reason to think that, with the present fiscal year ending at midnight on the following day, a Senate Committee would jeopardize the jobs of two and one-half million WPA employees to save those of nearly eight thousand Theatre workers.[147]

In Washington, speculation as to the verdict ended by noon the following day. The report submitted to the House read:

> The conference agreement restores the provision of the House bill, with modifications in the case of the theatre project under which none of the funds made available by the joint resolution shall be available after June 30, 1939, for the operation of any theatre project. Exceptions are made, however, in the case of employees who may be carried on the payrolls during the months of July in administrative or supervisory capacity and for certified relief workers who may be paid up to October 1, 1939.[148]

Obviously there had been a compromise of sorts: Senate conferees had consented to the abolition of the Theatre Project after Woodrum had agreed to the payment of three months' salary to all relief workers.[149]

[147] The *New York Times*, June 30, 1939, p. 1; the *Washington Post*, June 30, 1939, p. 1.

[148] Conference Report Submitted in the House (H. Report 1005), *Appropriation for Relief, Work Relief, and for Loans and Grants for Public Works Projects, Fiscal Year 1940* in *Miscellaneous House Reports*, 76th Cong., 1st Sess. (1939), p. 18.

[149] Woodrum had helped the compromise along by showing Senate conferees what he had learned about the Arts Projects in the course of his investigation of the WPA. Material he produced included a book from the Art Project "consisting of two views of fifty or more models in the nude" and copies of plays produced by the Federal Theatre allegedly

A few hours later, the victorious Woodrum presented the bill to the House as it was reported by conference. Of the Federal Theatre, he remarked that while many of the projects, particularly those in smaller communities, had done splendid work in performances before schools, colleges, and CCC camps, the Project was not to continue. Unreasonable costs, the "ridiculous" length of time spent in rehearsals, and the "amateurishness" of the people involved in many of the larger projects made them "indefensible," to say nothing of subversive. Representatives Celler, Sirovich, and Marcantonio of New York objected in vain. Refusing to yield, Woodrum ended debate with the remark: "I want the Federal Government to get out of the theatre business, but I am willing to help actors and actresses who can't support themselves."[150] The House responded with a tremendous ovation and proceeded to other matters. After less than an hour's debate, during which any attempt to defend the WPA met with cries of derision, a "shouting, cheering majority" passed the bill by a vote of 321 to 23 and Woodrum was promptly showered with congratulations from fellow representatives. In a "raucous" fourteen-hour session the House then went on to take another slap at the administration, by passing a Neutrality bill with an arms embargo strongly opposed by the President.[151]

With only a few hours left before the work relief agency was doomed to expire, the Senate debated the bill. The Federal Theatre might have gone unmentioned had it not been for a lanky, young senator from West Virginia whose tender age and jaundiced attacks on the WPA—forty-seven speeches in eight days— had earned him the title of "Baby Terror" in 1936. In the course of his latest tirade, Rush Holt pulled out Mrs. Flanagan's old articles and plays which had been rehashed in the Dies Com-

---

showing that the Project had been used to disseminate Communist propaganda. See the *New York Times*, June 30, 1939, p. 1.

[150] *Cong. Rec.*, p. 8,456.

[151] The *New York Times*, July 1, 1939, p. 1; "Roosevelt's War on the Hatch Bill Draws up Battle Lines for 1940," *Newsweek*, XIII (June 26, 1939), 13-14.

mittee, along with that much discussed phrase from *Shifting Scenes*, "the strange and glorious drama that is Russia," all but calling the Federal Theatre Director a paid agent of the Kremlin. As examples of the "red" propaganda she had authorized, the West Virginia Democrat repeated the old stock company titles which his colleagues in the House had found so "salacious," unwittingly refurbishing the list with such classics as Sheridan's *School for Scandal* and Molière's *School for Wives*. The harangue went unanswered.[152]

Finally, at 7:30 P.M. thirty-three senators unanimously passed the Relief Bill in the exact form in which it had been reported by conference the night before. Then they proceeded to "talk to death" a bill to extend the President's monetary powers. At 10:00 P.M. the bill went to the White House complete with provisions for dropping all workers of eighteen months or more, requiring a loyalty oath of all those hired for relief work, preventing politics in relief, earmarking appropriations, limiting administrative expenses, abolishing the Theatre, and making all other Arts Projects dependent upon the financial support of local sponsors.[153] In a rather caustic statement, the President pointed out that he "obviously" could not withhold his signature and thereby stop the entire system of work relief. Singling out four provisions for comment, Roosevelt called the abolition of the Theatre, "legislation against a specific class" and "discrimination of the worst kind."[154] But he had to yield. A "fundamental victory for the House conservatives," said the *Washington Post*; a "NEW DEAL REBUKE," read the headlines of the *Chicago*

[152] *Cong. Rec.*, pp. 8,392 *passim* 8,402. Holt's attitude toward the WPA is amply documented in "Fraud v. Fraud," *Time*, XXVII (March 23, 1936), 21; "WPA: 'Baby Terror' Airs West Virginia Laundry in the Senate," *Newsweek*, VII (March 7, 1936), 14-15; Raymond Clapper, "Politics in the WPA," *Review of Reviews*, XCIII (April 1936), 35-36.

[153] The *New York Times*, July 1, 1939, p. 1; the *Washington Post*, July 1, 1939, p. 1; the *Evening Bulletin* (Philadelphia), July 1, 1939, p. 1.

[154] "Presidential Statement in Signing Work Relief Bill, Pointing Out Hardships Imposed Therein, June 30, 1939," *The Public Papers and Addresses of Franklin D. Roosevelt*, comp. Samuel I. Rosenman (New York: Macmillan, 1941), VIII: *War and Neutrality* (1939), pp. 376-377.

Daily Tribune; "manhandling of the WPA . . . an act of defiance toward the White House . . . ," declared *Newsweek*.[155]

With news of the bill came orders for an immediate shutdown of all activities in Federal Theatres across the country. From Washington headquarters, where files had been discontinued and remodeling begun in a most unbureaucratic haste, Hallie Flanagan—gallant even in defeat—sent out hurried instructions to state and regional directors:

> We are at this moment telephoning all of you exactly what to do in the matter of personnel and equipment. Call on the loyalty, strength, high imagination and courage which is yours and that of your workers—*do not give up*. We feel that it is a triumph to get our security people carried for three months. During that time they will want to . . . leave a fine record and a magnificently orderly project. I would like every record in order, every costume pressed, every person proving his high efficiency.
>
> You know better than I can tell you how I feel about you and your project.[156]

Thousands of jobless and indignant theatre workers were in no mood to acquiesce quietly. At the Adelphi Theatre on West

[155] The *Washington Post*, July 1, 1939, p. 1; *Chicago Daily Tribune*, July 1, 1939, p. 3. During this one weekend of June 30, Congress had stripped Roosevelt, at least temporarily, of his control over the nation's currency; upset his hope of obtaining a Neutrality Act without the old mandatory arms embargo; forced him to sign a Tax Bill, which did not include the increase for which he asked, a Farm Bill appropriating $350,000 more than he had requested, and, of course, the Relief Bill. See "Rebellious Congress Stymies Pet Plans of the President," *Newsweek*, XIV (July 10, 1939), 11.

[156] Flanagan to Regional and State Directors, June 30, 1939, RG 69, GSS-211.2. Needless to say, Mrs. Flanagan followed her own instructions. She wrote to each union leader personally thanking him for his cooperation. Aided by her small staff, she worked with Federal Theatre personnel to repair and conserve equipment in each state and to put records in order. Memorandum, Flanagan to F. C. Harrington, Florence Kerr and Lawrence Morris, July 29, 1939, RG 69, GSS-211.29, Miscellaneous Correspondence.

Fifty-Fourth Street, where the notorious *Sing For Your Supper* was making its last stand, Federal Theatre workers chose the moment after the hit song, "Papa's Got a Job," to make their announcement. "Papa" had been hoisted high in the air by neighbors celebrating his having finally found work on the WPA, when suddenly the action stopped. The producer stepped out to the footlights and announced: "Yes, 'Papa' had a job—but they're taking it away from him at 12 o'clock tonight!" Then at the conclusion of the performance, the audience joined the cast in singing "Auld Lang Syne." At the Maxine Elliot, where *Life and Death of an American* was playing before an almost full house, the director announced to a sober audience that the Federal Theatre was no more. Its members, like the hero of the play, had only wanted "the right to live as decent human beings." And at the Ritz Theatre on West Forty-Eighth Street, where *Pinocchio* was to be given for the last time, Yasha Frank announced to an overflowing audience that the Federal Theatre had been abolished. The play went on, but the puppet, Pinocchio, instead of becoming a living boy as on former nights, died—symbolizing the fate of the Federal Theatre—while the cast chanted: "So let the bells proclaim our grief/ That his small life was all too brief." In full view of the audience, stagehands knocked down the sets and actors intoned: "Thus passed Pinocchio. Born December 23, 1938,[157] died June 30, 1939. Killed by Act of Congress." Then actors and crew walked out of the theatre carrying placards with such slogans as "WANTED—REPRESENTATIVE CLIFTON A. WOODRUM FOR THE MURDER OF PINOCCHIO." At Duffy Square the "funeral march" halted, the demonstrators sang the national anthem and walked sadly away into the night.[158]

[157] December 23, 1938, was the opening date of the play.
[158] The *New York Times*, July 1, 1939, p. 2; the *Washington Post*, July 2, 1939, p. 1; the *Evening Bulletin* (Philadelphia), July 1, 1939, p. 2.

CHAPTER SEVEN

Art, Relief, and Politics: Conflicting Forces Examined

THE brief story of the Federal Theatre was as dramatic as any play it staged. It would never have opened but for the economic crisis which thrust into power men who believed that the federal government had a responsibility to provide for its citizens. These men—the President and his Relief Administrator— knew that theatrical people as well as construction workers had lives and talents worth preserving; and they were determined to give the American people the benefit of that talent in a "free, adult, uncensored theatre." The realization of this ambitious ideal was begun under the direction of a Vassar professor and others like her who saw in the administration's proposal an opportunity to create a decentralized American theatre relevant to the lives of a new and receptive audience beyond the narrow confines of Broadway—an institution capable of continuing as an integral part of a particular community long after the need for relief had passed. Pressed by the plight of the unemployed, thoughtful men and women of the theatre had embodied these beliefs and hopes in a plan, translated that plan into bureaucratic forms, and found directors to run a federal relief venture as a theatre. When hosts of destitute players descended upon the old four-story building in New York that had once housed the Bank of the United States, or queued up before Project headquarters in Cincinnati, Providence, Tampa, or San Francisco, paper plans had become reality.

But between plan and reality were unplanned differences. Instead of strategically placed regional centers with a surrounding network of community theatres, huge metropolitan projects grew up, dwarfing smaller units scattered about the South and Midwest. Directors, eager to experiment outside the commercial

296

confines of Broadway, had to work within the administrative confines of Washington. Bureaucratic demands were not merely trying, they were also stifling: for example, regulations prevented the New York Project from sending some of its five thousand members to needy troupes in other states. There were other non-artistic problems too: theatrical unions, vacillating between fear of competition and contempt for another "free show thing," cooperated hesitantly at best; WPA officials, pressed to get the new work program under way, never seemed to understand fully the difference between a theatre project and a road-building project. Nevertheless, out of resultant arrangements, hastily contrived compromises, and ingenious adaptations came productions—sometimes tritely done commercial standbys, often ambitious new American plays, and always the uniquely appropriate Living Newspapers.

Only months removed from relief rolls, 12,500 federal showmen were presenting plays in six different languages to a weekly audience of 350,000 spread over nearly thirty states by the summer of 1936. Three years later, 2,660 Federal Theatre graduates had returned to private industry—some to Hollywood or Broadway, some to community theatres, others to radio, and still others, the recipients of fellowships, to theatrical research. The nearly eight thousand who remained played before a wide and disparate audience from the gaudy lights of Gotham across Illinois farmland and into the hills of Georgia and Maine. They taught hospitalized children how to manipulate marionettes with their paralyzed hands, and they captured the imagination and gratitude of people like the old Florida woman who shyly explained to a visiting troupe: "We're afraid to interrupt living actors [with applause]. It don't seem polite."[1]

An elderly woman who had never seen living actors, a little girl struggling to manipulate dolls on wires, a sunburned con-

---

[1] Flanagan to Alva Adams, June 21, 1939, RG 69, FTP Records, NOGSF; Senate Hearings on H. J. Res. 326, *Work Relief Act of 1939*, pp. 56-58, 64; Flanagan, *Arena*, pp. 102, 240.

struction worker at the Birmingham première of *It Can't Happen Here*—these were the people for whom this People's Theatre was intended. In the four brief years of its existence, they went thirty million strong to a theatre as varied in style, content, and quality as democracy itself. Most of these play-goers liked what they saw; and they expressed their approval in crudely printed notes from reform schools, succinctly worded petitions from faculty members at Harvard University, and mounting totals at Federal Theatre box offices.[2]

But for those on the stage as well as for those in the audience, the value of the Federal Theatre was not to be measured in monetary terms alone. To the young and gifted, the Project offered a chance to develop talents when not to do so meant stagnation for the individual and cultural loss to society. To the many more who were older and technologically displaced, it provided temporary security and frequently a chance to put old skills to new use. For the Negro artist, it meant all these things and more.[3] Even the best-known had found acting a hazardous profession long before the depression. Audiences were poor and theatres never able to support the most talented group for more than a short time. But with the advent of the Federal Theatre came money for fresh designs and productions, time for rehearsals, sufficient casts, and above all, the professional opportunities heretofore lacking. Harlem's LaFayette Theatre, long the home of Negro players, producers, and composers, flourished anew. And from Los Angeles, Chicago, San Francisco, Seattle, Hartford, Philadelphia, Newark, Boston, Raleigh, and

[2] During June and July 1939, letters, telegrams, and resolutions supporting the Federal Theatre flowed in by the hundreds; from the hospitals, settlement houses, homes for the aged, destitute, and orphaned; from veterans organizations, universities (MIT, Reed, Holyoke, Boston, Oregon, et cetera), religious, civic, and labor organizations; and from prominent individuals. See Memorandum, Robert Schnitzer to Flanagan, July 29, 1939, RG 69, FTP Records, NOGSF.

[3] For a discussion of the Project's contribution to the Negro actor, see Edith J. R. Isaacs, "The Negro in the American Theatre: A Record of Achievement," *Theatre Arts Monthly*, XXVI (July 1942), 460-473.

Birmingham came productions that were often lively and sometimes hugely successful. Moreover, with each success came a
growing and often enduring consciousness of what the Negro
artist could achieve if but given a chance.[4] In short, Harlem's
Perry Watkins no less than New York's Howard Bay discovered what financial security, time, and a chance to work
could mean to the young designer.[5] At a time when the Negro
was not always guaranteed equal access to the benefits of other
New Deal agencies, the record of the Federal Theatre was
particularly impressive.[6]

Yet despite all its accomplishments, this WPA Theatre Project
was consigned to the "ashcan of oblivion"—to use Senator
Reynolds' picturesque terminology. The question, of course, is
why? Ostensibly the answer lay in the refusal of Congress to
appropriate money for an ill-run, inefficient, and presumably un-
American institution. Subversive tendencies, unreasonable costs,
excessive length of rehearsals, amateurish actors, and "trashy"
productions were the specific charges made by House Appropriations Committee spokesman, Clifton A. Woodrum.[7] That Woodrum also considered the Project competitive with private enterprise is a matter of record.[8] These considerations, given the
predisposition of certain members and the nature of the testimony heard, were undoubtedly influential in the Committee's
decision to ban the theatre. About the objective validity of
these allegations, however, there is much less certainty.

[4] Interview with Venzuella Jones, November 17, 1961.

[5] Watkins went on to design *Mamba's Daughters* for Guthrie Mc-
Clintic; Bay, *The Little Foxes* starring Tallulah Bankhead. Bay was also
awarded a Guggenheim Fellowship on the basis of work done on the
Theatre Project as was Living Newspaper writer, Arthur Arent.

[6] See, for example, John A. Salmond, "The Civilian Conservation
Corps and the Negro," *The Journal of American History*, LII (June
1965), 75-88; Allen Francis Kifer, "The Negro Under the New Deal,
1933-1941" (unpublished Ph.D. dissertation, University of Wisconsin,
1961).

[7] *Cong. Rec.*, 76th Cong., 1st Sess. (1939), pp. 7,166, 8,456.

[8] House Hearings on H. J. Res. 209 and 246, *Additional Relief Appropriations, 1939*, p. 151.

To state, as did Woodrum, that the Federal Theatre had produced nothing of merit save *Swing Mikado*, and to suggest that such was the verdict of "every theatrical critic of any note" is to indulge in a patent disregard for plain and simple facts.[9] The virtually unqualified praise bestowed on *Murder in the Cathedral, Dr. Faustus, One-Third of a Nation, Prologue to Glory, Pinocchio*, Harlem's *Macbeth* and *Androcles and the Lion* is a matter of record. *It Can't Happen Here, Big Blow, Haiti, Follow the Parade, Run, Little Chillun*, and *On the Rocks* were but a few in a long list of shows which pleased playgoers and critics alike. This could not be said of every Federal Theatre production. In New York and elsewhere there were undistinguished plays unimaginatively produced. Such productions were perhaps most numerous where talent and technical facilities were in short supply and directors clung timidly to standard stock or revivals. But even on smaller projects, choice of plays had improved with the establishment of the Play Policy Board; production standards, with a session at the Federal Summer Theatre in Poughkeepsie and loans from the National Service Bureau. By late 1938, more and more projects were beginning to see the fruits of Hallie Flanagan's insistence on experimentation and retraining. Further proof of progress came only six months before the Project ended with a letter from a self-confessed old-fashioned stock company director who proudly wrote that he was now ready to try "something with new techniques and community interest"—perhaps a San Francisco version of *One-Third of a Nation*.[10]

If such requests were a tribute to Hallie Flanagan's faith in the capacity of Federal Theatre workers to grow, the Project's overall production record was an even more emphatic testimony to her determination to shun what Woodrum called "small trashy kind of stuff."[11] During the early months of the Project,

[9] *Cong. Rec.*, p. 7,166.
[10] Charles King to Flanagan, December 28, 1938, RG 69, FTP Records, NOGSF.
[11] *Cong. Rec.*, p. 7,166.

when outside supervision had been minimal, old stock company standbys had been the understandable choice of directors and casts entrenched in old habits and methods. But even in these early months, when play choices were least commendable, the Federal Theatre never produced all of the titles cited by its congressional critics.[12] And by 1937, Shaw and O'Neill cycles had long since replaced *Up in Mabel's Room* or *Aaron Slick from Punkin Creek*. Indeed, of the 830 major titles produced by the Federal Theatre, a sizable portion consisted of classical drama, children's plays, dance dramas, religious plays, Living Newspapers, puppet shows, foreign-language plays, and historical pageants; a far smaller portion, of musicals and revues.[13] What the feather-bedecked Mikado and his sarong-clad ladies from Chicago contributed to the educational and cultural life of the nation is perhaps debatable; that 326,000 people found them rollicking entertainment is not. It is ironical indeed that those plays designed to contribute most directly to the nation's education were the highly controversial Living Newspapers. Always propaganda and often art, they have remained in the judgment of some critics perhaps the Federal Theatre's most significant contribution to dramatic form.[14] However inappropriate choice and treatment of subjects may have been from a political standpoint, the Living Newspapers were most certainly not the kind of plays of which Woodrum complained; "small trashy kind of stuff" seldom creates the kind of antagonists inspired by the theatrically brilliant *One-Third of a Nation*.

[12] Flanagan to Paul Green, July 13, 1939; Flanagan to Burns Mantle, August 15, 1939, Flanagan Papers.

[13] For a complete breakdown of Federal Theatre productions see *Arena*, pp. 377-434. An alphabetical listing of plays presented through March 15, 1939 is contained in House Hearings on H. J. Res. 209 and 246, *Additional Relief Appropriations*, 1939, pp. 128-137.

[14] Allan Lewis, *American Plays and Playwrights of the Contemporary Theatre* (New York: Crown Publishers Inc., 1965), p. 103; John Gassner maintains in an essay on modern American drama that the Federal Theatre through its Living Newspapers "gave rise to the one original form of drama developed in the United States." See Gassner, *Treasury of the Theatre*, pp. 780-781.

301

Caliber of acting, like quality of productions, varied; but "amateurish" is hardly a suitable adjective when applied indiscriminately to the efforts of these federal players. Undeniably, perhaps unavoidably, the Federal Theatre had more than its share of unqualified personnel during the initial months of the Project. Elmer Rice, hard pressed to get people on the payroll and confident that the incompetent and inexperienced could be easily removed, virtually opened the New York Project to anyone enterprising enough to come up with the necessary paper qualifications. In California, actors from the Pasadena Playhouse found admittance to the Los Angeles Project under Playhouse director Gilmor Brown far too easily to suit the west coast branch of Equity. In some small centers throughout the South and Midwest, directors were sometimes forced to supplement a company with non-professional actors or have no unit at all. By the summer of 1936, however, the process of weeding out had begun; smaller units were shut down entirely and qualified actors transferred to other units.

With each successive reduction in WPA rolls, actors of dubious qualifications and ability were dismissed wholesale. Given the tenacity with which a militant and highly organized minority fought for their jobs, some few worthless individuals undoubtedly managed to remain on the Project. Certain Equity officials were convinced that such was the case when, despite the number of experienced professionals eligible for employment, Federal Theatre officials persisted in retaining a small, talented group of youngsters on the grounds that they were indispensable for a balanced company.[15] On the whole, however, union officials had little cause for complaint. Of all Federal Theatre employees, 95 per cent were from relief rolls. Of these, 80 per cent belonged to accredited theatrical unions despite the fact that the Project required a variety of non-theatrical personnel for

[15] Typical of those in Equity holding this view is Maida Reade, then a member of the Council. Interview November 15, 1961.

302

clerical and other jobs.[16] Thus it would seem that those seeking an explanation for inferior performances might better cite the need for retraining thousands of middle-aged performers rather than the amateurism of these unemployed veterans of show business.

Still more basic, of course, was the fundamental incompatibility of relief and theatre. Whatever their age and experience, actors on the New York Project were subjected to lengthy rehearsal periods that distressed Federal Theatre officials and congressional critics alike. But what the latter failed to appreciate was that the many restrictions imposed by both government and unions made theatrically sensible work schedules almost impossible. Unable to pay more than its monthly wage of $91.10, the Project had sought to meet union demands for prevailing wage rates by adjusting the hours of employment. Since prevailing wages also varied with locality, stagehands wound up working 68 hours in New York, 80 in Chicago.[17] Whatever the locality, the different schedules of each group had to be meshed so as to fit into the time allotted for rehearsal and play production. Mindful of these difficulties, Chicago unions were at first inclined to let employees work overtime in the interests of production. But even this boon was forfeited when it became apparent that under the government's complicated timekeeping rules, a stagehand responsible for working only 76 hours might put in as many as 120 hours and still be docked one-half hour if he were five minutes late at a scheduled time.[18]

The results, naturally enough, were scrupulously punched time clocks, chaotic working conditions, and prolonged rehearsals, particularly in New York where *Sing For Your Supper*, further delayed by cuts and replacements, dragged on for the

[16] Senate Hearings on H. J. Res. 326, *Work Relief Act of 1939*, pp. 57, 59.

[17] Kondolf to Miller, June 9, 1937, RG 69, GSS-211.2; The *New York Times*, May 28, 1939, Sec. 10, p. 1.

[18] Kondolf to Miller, June 9, 1937, RG 69, GSS-211.2. For a discussion of this problem and its consequences, see Atkinson, "FDR'S WPA FTP," the *New York Times*, May 28, 1939, Sec. 10, p. 1.

interminable period of eighteen months. What the scandalized Woodrum failed to point out to his fellow representatives was the fact that the much damned *Sing* was an exception. According to the Committee's own investigators, the average length of rehearsals for the Los Angeles Project was less than six weeks; in Chicago, about two months.[19] Strictly speaking, the length of rehearsal time would have been of little import had the Committee chosen to regard the Theatre Project as purely a relief venture providing sustenance for indigent theatrical people. Actors, musicians, stagehands, box-office and wardrobe attendants received their $23.00 weekly regardless of whether the play was in rehearsal or production.[20] But then rehearsals, unlike productions, brought in no admission receipts.

Obviously, this whole question of excessive costs and poor administration is exceedingly difficult to unravel. As a work project, the Federal Theatre was undeniably more expensive than direct relief; as a professional project, it was also more expensive than other work programs. For example, the wpa paid $1,250 to support a Federal Theatre employee for an entire year; $732 to support a construction worker—a further supplement was paid to the latter by the local sponsoring agency. Admitting this, Hallie Flanagan could counter with a few statistics of her own. Throughout its four-year history, the Project had employed an average of ten thousand workers yearly, each of whom supported an average of four dependents at a total cost of $46 million— approximately the cost in 1939 of a single battleship. Broken down on a yearly basis, this figure amounted to an annual cost of roughly $10 million, 90 per cent of which went for wages. To be sure, the Federal Theatre, as a federally sponsored project, received no sponsor's contributions, but it had taken in admissions amounting to $3 million when finally permitted to do so by the Treasury Department. In addition, during the first four

[19] [E. W. Ericson], untitled report on the Federal Theatre in Chicago, April 30, 1938; F. H. Smith to Edward Taylor and Cedric F. Johnson, June 1, 1939, regarding the California Project; RG 233, HAC, WPA.

[20] This is an approximate sum.

months of 1939, 10 per cent of all Project expenditures, a sum equal to all non-labor costs, had been covered by box-office receipts. In other words, those productions charging admissions —roughly one-third of all Federal Theatre shows—were taking in enough money to pay the cost of theatre rentals, costumes, lights, advertising, stage construction, and other operational costs.[21]

If such arguments seemingly failed to answer the Committee's charges, the explanation may lie not in financial statistics but in the fundamental dichotomy between relief and theatre. As a relief project, the Federal Theatre was expected to relieve distress and prevent suffering by providing employment—not go "touring over the country from place to place, charging admissions at cut rates in open competition with the theatrical industry."[22] As a theatre, it was expected to run financially successful units drawing admissions from full houses, apparently without benefit of theatre parties. And as a tax-supported institution, it was expected to expand theatrical services beyond large metropolitan centers to towns and cities throughout the nation. Financially contradictory, such expectations could hardly have been satisfied by the most tightly run enterprise—and that the Federal Theatre was not.

A hastily created relief project, it suffered from contradictions inherent in its origins. Precisely because the WPA was a relief program, Hopkins had encouraged his staff to get people on the payroll as quickly as possible; administrative refinements could come later. Refinements did come on the Federal Theatre, as on other projects, when efficiency-conscious directors began tightening operations, exchanging equipment, and weeding out the incompetent. But the time Hopkins had counted on simply did not exist in sufficient measure. The administrative streamlining

[21] Senate Hearings on H. J. Res. 326, *Work Relief Act of 1939*, pp. 57 *passim* 66.

[22] House Hearings on H. J. Res. 209 and 246, *Additional Relief Appropriation, 1939*, p. 151. See pp. 143 *passim* 161 for assumptions voiced by various members of the House Appropriations Committee.

305

of any new institution is not accomplished quickly, no matter how secure its future. An emergency program of uncertain duration, the WPA—and the Federal Theatre—had no future. Even those administrators convinced of what a work program could accomplish on a short term basis found it difficult to plan ahead intelligently. Those less imaginative and dedicated simply did not try.[23] For those whose first concern was theatre, additional bureaucratic controls, created in the interest of efficiency and economy, all too often seemed additional obstacles to production. Thus, as an emergency relief project and as an artistic enterprise which traditionally defied tidy organization charts, the Federal Theatre was hardly a model of administrative efficiency. Despite numerous reorganizations, the huge, unwieldy New York Project never lost the air of controlled hysteria which permeated every facet of its operations. Administrative jealousies between New York officials and representatives from the National Service Bureau often went unchecked. The resulting scandal was not the high cost of equipment stacked in theatrical warehouses, but the fact that so little of that equipment left the five boroughs.

Even if the Project had been guilty of inefficiency and extravagance, Congress chose a strange way to economize. Had the Wagner amendment passed, the appropriation for the entire Arts Project would have amounted to only three-fourths of 1 per cent of the entire WPA appropriation for fiscal 1940. Although the amendment ultimately failed, the sum which was to have been divided among the Arts Projects—approximately $11 million—was never deducted from WPA funds.[24] What Congress did accomplish for the American taxpayer was to leave idle nearly eight thousand theatrical workers and a plant spread over twenty states which included nearly $1 million worth of physical equipment.

The fact is that the Federal Theatre was not abolished for

[23] Florence Kerr, tape recording, November 6, 1963, Archives of American Art.
[24] Flanagan, *Arena*, p. 334.

306

purely financial reasons; nor were its merits and demerits objectively assayed by a majority of the House Appropriations Committee. That so summary an investigation of so complicated an organization yielded imprecise, incomplete, and frequently incorrect findings is hardly surprising. There is little reason, however, to suppose that accurate findings would have resulted in an impartial evaluation or a different verdict. Stripped of pious rationalization about economy and efficiency, the ban on the Federal Theatre was primarily a political reaction; and politically, the Federal Theatre was vulnerable.

Created at the high tide of New Deal reformism, the Federal Theatre enjoyed not only the virtues but also the faults and fortunes of the Presidential program of which it was a part. Idealistic, imaginative, and highly experimental, it bore the stamp of that dedicated group of public servants whose belief in human possibility had energized Washington since the "renaissance spring" of 1933. Above all, it aspired—boldly, creatively, and perhaps unrealistically—to be more than a relief measure. It aspired also to reform. A temporary agency designed to give work to indigent theatrical people, it was somehow to become a permanent institution—a true People's Theatre shaping the social and cultural pattern of the nation. But the overwhelmingly Democratic Congress which turned over to the President $4 billion for relief in 1935 gave him no mandate for a national theatre. Some congressmen and many Americans opposed the very idea of federal support for the arts; others opposed the whole concept of work relief; and still others were indifferent to both. Handicapped by the speed and circumstances of its birth, surrounded by controversy, the Federal Theatre could do little to convert these potential antagonists in the first two years of its existence. In the last two, the task was no easier.

Enthusiasm for the New Deal began to wane in 1937. Middle-class citizens, distressed by the recession of 1938, alarmed by the growing power of labor, and irritated by relief burdens, dealt Roosevelt a heavy blow in the November elections of 1938. Congress, torn by the Supreme Court fight and antagonized by

307

the purge, shared in the nation's discontent. By 1939 a newly invigorated and highly aggressive coalition of conservatives sniped away at the President's program forcing the administration on the defensive. As a New Deal measure, a relief project, and an artistic venture, the thrice-damned Federal Theatre provided an easy target for the administration's opponents, economy advocates, relief revisionists, and super-patriots. By the time the House committees had completed their much publicized investigations, no amount of lobbying on the part of Project supporters could change the verdict.

Those who finally voted to accept the Appropriation Committee's ban obviously did so for various reasons. Conservatives, unable to accept the extent and nature of government involvement in virtually every aspect of social and economic life, unquestionably regarded curtailment of the Arts Projects as a desirable act of retrenchment. For economy-conscious congressmen, frustrated in most efforts to cut expenditures in a preelection year, the ban was an expression of intent, a step in the right direction. As opponents of work relief, especially on the federal level, their vote against the Federal Theatre was consistent if not inevitable. To others who believed that the Arts Projects' sole function was a purely humanitarian one, continued support of a Theatre Project with a reformist rationale and aspirations of permanence was understandably distasteful. Mindful of public weariness with relief and influenced by charges of wastefulness and radicalism, they acquiesced in the Committee's decision with an easy conscience. As North Carolina's Senator Josiah W. Bailey declared: "The object of the WPA is to relieve distress and prevent suffering by providing work. The purpose is not the culture of the population."[25] The heated and hostile atmosphere of the House debate would suggest, however, that passion rather than principle was the dominant factor in that body's decision. For many during that raucous, rancorous session, the ban on the Theatre, like the embargo in the Neutral-

[25] Josiah Bailey to Gerald W. Johnson, July 6, 1939, Josiah Bailey Papers, Duke University.

ity Act and provisions in the Tax and Farm Bills, provided another opportunity to take a slap at the administration. For many more, it was an unthinking act made in the assurance that art did not count for much and that, in any case, their own constituents would be little affected. "Culture," spat one congressman in response to Wagner's plea for the Arts Projects. "What the Hell—Let 'em have a pick and shovel."[26]

This was not the response of an inconsequential minority. Roosevelt himself acknowledged the prevalence of widespread congressional anti-intellectualism in a letter written to Nelson Rockefeller more than a week before the Relief Bill was reported to the House. Full of praise for the "amazingly constructive" accomplishments wrought by these federally supported artists throughout the nation, the President pointed out that it was "extremely difficult" for the average senator or representative to realize the importance of continuing the Projects in some form. "I suppose these elected Legislators are representing the view of their constituents, for the simple reason that the average voter does not yet appreciate the need of encouraging art, music, and literature." "Unfortunately," he continued, "there are too many people who think that this type of white collar worker ought to be put to work digging ditches like everybody else. . . . We need all the help we can get to educate the Congress."[27]

In a last-minute educational effort, theatrical supporters had done their best, but to no avail. Given the dimensions of their task, the remarkable thing is not that the Theatre was abolished, but that the other Arts Projects, however much curtailed, managed to survive. The Federal Theatre, after all, had no monopoly on unfavorable publicity. During the 1937 cuts in New York City, musicians, writers, and artists protested, picketed, sat-down, fasted, and even imprisoned a WPA official until the harassed administrator agreed to intercede on their behalf—all with a militant abandon that made them front-page news for

[26] The *Washington Post*, June 21, 1939, p. 2.
[27] F.D.R. to Nelson Rockefeller, June 6, 1939, Roosevelt MSS, Nelson A. Rockefeller File.

nearly a week.[28] And from the Dies Committee, the Writers' Project had received its full share of publicity, as witnesses declared that the Communist Party had 40 per cent of those employed on the New York Project in its clutches.[29] When some of these same witnesses were paraded before the House Appropriations Committee in a repeat performance, stories of Communist machinations once again became headline news. Whatever the effect of this publicity, there is little reason to believe that it was outweighed by a greater congressional appreciation for the contributions of the other arts. A good many legislators may indeed have recognized the worth of the much commended state guidebook series. But few opponents of the theatre were likely to have recognized the importance of a federally subsidized Writers Project for the young and promising John Cheever, Ralph Ellison, and Richard Wright; still fewer the value of an Art Project for Jackson Pollock, Willem de Kooning, Philip Guston, Jack Levine, and Ivan Albright.[30]

In short, the Federal Theatre was vulnerable not because congressmen believed Beethoven superior to Shakespeare, but because this unfortunate Project was surrounded by too much controversy and supported by too few constituents. A far larger enterprise than the other Arts Projects, the Federal Theatre attracted greater publicity in part because of its size, but primarily because it was theatre. A pro-labor bias in the account of labor disputes in the *New Jersey Guide* was simply less dramatic, less far reaching in its impact than the huge masks depicting the Supreme Court Justices in *Triple-A Plowed Under*, or excerpts from the *Congressional Record* read against a grimly realistic cross section of a New York tenement. By the same token,

[28] The *New York Times*, June 22-27, 1937.

[29] *House Un-American Activities Committee Hearings*, II, 981-1,026; The *New York Times*, September 16, p. 1.

[30] When the Art Project closed, most paintings were allocated to various tax-supported institutions. Apparently because of the lack of time available for allocation, some canvases remained on hand, and were stored by the Procurement Division which subsequently sold them for the price of the canvas. An Ivan Albright was reportedly bought in Chicago for approximately $4.00.

310

Henry Alsberg could edit or rewrite an offending passage in a guidebook before publication, and at Hallie Flanagan's insistence, Federal Theatre directors could make comparable revisions in a script, but in the actual performance, the inflection of an actor's voice and subtle nuances of manner often conveyed the original bias. Thus, unwittingly and perhaps uncaringly, the New York City Project early acquired for itself—and for the rest of the Federal Theatre—a reputation for radicalism which a renewed emphasis on historical pageants, classical drama, and children's plays could never fully erase.

Magnified by congressional investigations, this radical image undoubtedly contributed to the Project's demise. But the worst indiscretions of New York leftists and the best efforts of Washington's super-patriots would have been of less consequence had the Federal Theatre had strong and articulate grass roots support. Unfortunately it did not. Restricted initially to those areas where twenty-five qualified professionals could be formed into a local company, forced subsequently to disband these small and often artistically inferior units, handicapped in its efforts at geographical expansion, the Federal Theatre remained a highly centralized institution. As such it could count on the active support of congressmen from New York, California, Illinois, and a few other states which local projects had served loyally and well. But the backing of 56 out of 192 members of the House was simply not enough. The more geographically dispersed Writers' Project, on the other hand, could present every congressman in Washington with a guidebook to his particular state.

The contrast offered by the Art Project was even more striking. During the fall of 1935, an Art Project representative, Thomas Parker, had traveled throughout the artistically barren South exploring possibilities for WPA projects. Undeterred by the sparsity of good painters, Parker had formed advisory committees of artistically knowledgeable citizens in major towns and cities and, with the wholehearted backing of the particularly local group, set up his one, two, or three qualified artists as di-

rectors of Community Art Centers.[31] The local headquarters
for lectures, art classes, ceramic workshops, local shows, and
traveling exhibitions, these Community Art Centers spread from
the South into the North, Midwest, and Far West, sometimes
forming the basis for permanent gallery-museums.[32] By 1939
four hundred and twenty-five Art Project workers staffed eighty-
three Community Art Centers in twenty-one states. Their activities, along with those of mural painters and Project workers
preparing the Index of American Design, so expanded services
that the Project's director, Holger Cahill, could boast of operations in forty-one states and the District of Columbia.[33] The
impact of these figures on congressional thinking cannot be
measured; but neither should one ignore the fact that Woodrum's
theatrically unproductive Virginia had its Community Art Centers and guidebook. Whatever the relative merits of these considerations, the outcome was the same: the Federal Theatre
had been abolished; the other Arts Projects allowed to continue
under local sponsorship.

For Hallie Flanagan it was a bitter defeat. Having nourished
the Project from a paper plan to a professionally respectable
production unit, she realized how far from perfect it was. But
she also knew that Congress had treated the Federal Theatre
as a political issue rather than a cultural or human one. The
WPA, she thought, was also culpable. Fearful for the future of
the relief organization, officials had consented to the ban on
the Theatre Project when the House Appropriations Committee
promised to eliminate certain administrative restrictions favored
by Congress and soft-pedal discussion of such matters as the
high non-relief cost of the North Beach Airport or the WPA
building at the World's Fair. Suspecting, too, that the attacks
of certain Southerners might have been prompted by resent-

[31] Thomas Parker, tape recording, October 14, 1963, Archives of
American Art.
[32] Holger Cahill, Report on Progress of Federal Art Project, February 16, 1936; "The WPA Art Program—A Summary," October 1,
1940, Mildred Baker Papers, Archives of American Art.
[33] Ibid.

ment at the equality of opportunity enjoyed by Negro players, she was convinced that the Federal Theatre was abolished primarily because of the "vicious report of a biased committee and the mass action of a great many other people in Congress . . . taken in by false fears [of communism]." Had congressmen known they were getting a "prejudiced and distorted" report, had they only realized that this much damned Project was not a "red menace" but "the beginning of an American Theatre," Hallie Flanagan was confident the outcome would have been different.[34]

It was a naïve hope, and one particularly characteristic of her. Out of an enforced union of art and government, this indomitable woman had labored at great personal cost to bring forth an American Theatre relevant enough to the lives of its audience and regional enough in its local roots to insure institutional permanence. Shaped more by the circumstances of relief than the concept of regionalism, the theatre that emerged was heavily centralized—a condition for which Hallie Flanagan could hardly be blamed. Relevant if not widespread, the Project's largest unit soon acquired a reputation for radicalism that dismayed WPA officials and delighted professional red-baiters. For this, Hallie Flanagan as chief architest and administrator was in part responsible. Dedicated to the idea of an involved, socially committed theatre, she failed, as do many idealists, to appreciate the political and administrative context within which such a theatre would have to be created. Artist and liberal as well as administrator and bureaucrat, she invariably placed theatrical daring above administrative safety, neglecting, as in the case of *Injunction Granted*, to clamp down on talented and politically irresponsible subordinates until convinced that her confidence had been misplaced and the Project's reputation impaired. Had she been aware in the early years that "false fears" of communism would contribute to the Federal Theatre's undoing, she might have acted sooner and with a firmer hand. She might

[34] Flanagan, *Arena*, pp. 335, 353; Flanagan, "Congress Takes the Stage," the *New York Times*, August 20, 1939, Sec. 9, p. 1.

even have appreciated the predicament of WPA officials responsible for defending this controversial venture to unsympathetic congressmen. But there is little reason to suppose that she could have changed either her goal or her assumptions about the proper role of theatre in society.

A dynamic leader and a woman of incredible will, she brought to the Project and drew from it the vitality, creativity, and sheer enjoyment that made this imperfect, highly conspicuous institution what it was. Without Hallie Flanagan, the Federal Theatre would have been a constituentless and, in all probability, a controversial relief project still subject to the political vicissitudes of the New Deal. Less successful as a theatre, it might have been more successful as relief, managing, as did the other Arts Projects, to continue into the war years. But Hallie Flanagan would never have been content to "play it safe." Because of her, this depression-born venture achieved a power, originality, popular appeal, and capacity for service that made it an incomplete but unmistakable reflection of the kind of theatre initially envisioned. Without her and those on the Project like her, the tragedy of its demise would not have been so great because the goals envisioned, and in some measure attained, would not have been so ambitious.[35]

[35] For Hallie Flanagan the tragedy was compounded by personal loss. Eight months later, Philip H. Davis died of a heart attack. Completely devoted to her husband, she had endured separation and the severe physical and emotional burdens associated with her job as Federal Theatre Director only because of his unfailing support and encouragement. Left with Davis' three young children, she went to Smith College in 1941 as dean and professor of drama. Four years later she was stricken with Parkinson's Disease.

Bibliography of Works Cited

1. Manuscripts

Josiah M. Bailey Papers, Duke University.

Mildred Baker Papers, Archives of American Art, Detroit Institute of Art.

Federal Theatre Project Records, National Archives. Catalogued as Record Group No. 69: Records of the Work Projects Administration, Records of the Federal Theatre Project.

Hallie Flanagan. Personal Papers, Poughkeepsie, New York. Now located in New York Public Library Theatre Collection at Lincoln Center for the Performing Arts. (The Flanagan Papers are, at present, in the process of being catalogued; some are already accessible to the public.)

House Appropriations Committee Records, National Archives. catalogued as Record Group 233: Records of the House of Representatives.

Elmer Rice. Personal Papers, Stamford, Connecticut.

Franklin D. Roosevelt Manuscripts, Franklin D. Roosevelt Library, Hyde Park, New York.

Aubrey Williams Papers, Franklin D. Roosevelt Library, Hyde Park, New York.

Works Progress Administration Records, National Archives. Catalogued as Record Group No. 69: Records of the Work Projects Administration.

2. Government Documents

Congressional Intelligence. *1939 Factual History of the Federal Government*, 76th Cong., 1st Sess., 1939.

Congressional Record. Vol. 75 (72nd Cong., 1st Sess.), Vol. 80 (74th Cong., 2nd Sess.), Vol. 84 (76th Cong., 1st Sess.), 1932, 1936, 1939.

U. S. House of Representatives, Committee on Patents. *Department of Science, Art, and Literature*. Hearings on H. J. Res. 29, 75th Cong., 3rd Sess., 1938.

————. *Conference Report, Appropriation for Relief, Work Relief, and for Loans and Grants for Public Work Projects, Fiscal Year 1940.* Report No. 1005 in *Miscellaneous House Reports*, 76th Cong., 1st Sess., 1939.

————. Special Committee on Un-American Activities. *Investigation of Un-American Propaganda Activities in the United States.* Hearings on H. Res. 282. Vols. 1, 4, 75th Cong., 3rd Sess., 1938.

————. Special Committee on Un-American Activities. *Report of the Special Committee on Un-American Activities—Pursuant to H. Res. 282*, 75th Cong., 4th Sess., 1939.

————. Sub-Committee of the Committee on Appropriations. *Further Additional Appropriations for Work Relief and Relief, Fiscal Year 1939.* Hearings on H. J. Res. 209 and 246, 76th Cong., 1st Sess., 1939.

————. Sub-Committee of the Committee on Appropriations. *Investigation and Study of the Works Progress Administration.* Hearings on H. Res. 130, Pt. 1, 76th Cong., 1st Sess., 1939-40.

————. Sub-Committee of the Committee on Appropriations. *Work Relief and Relief for Fiscal Year 1940.* Hearings on H. J. Res. 326, 76th Cong., 1st Sess., 1939.

————. Sub-Committee of the Committee on Appropriations in Charge of Deficiency Appropriations. *First Deficiency Appropriation Bill of 1936.* Hearings on Pt. 2, Emergency Relief, 74th Cong., 1st Sess., 1936.

U. S. Senate. Committee on Appropriations. *Supplemental Appropriations: Relief and Work Relief, Fiscal Year 1938.* Hearings on H. J. Res. 596, 75th Cong., 3rd Sess., 1938.

————. Committee to Investigate Unemployment and Relief. *Department of Public Works, . . .* Hearings on S. 1265, 76th Cong., 1st Sess., 1939.

————. Committee on Appropriations. *Work Relief and Public Works Appropriation Act of 1939.* Hearings on H. J. Res. 326, 76th Cong., 1st Sess., 1939.

316

3. Newspapers

American Vindicator. April 1939.
Asheville Citizen-Times. November 1958.
Brooklyn Eagle. 1938-1939.
Chicago Daily News. 1937.
Chicago Daily Tribune. 1936, 1938-1939.
Daily Worker. 1936-1939.
Evening Bulletin (Philadelphia). June-July 1939.
New York American. 1936.
New York Daily Mirror. 1936-1939.
New York Daily News. 1936-1939.
New York Evening Journal. 1935-1936.
New York Herald Tribune. 1935-1939.
New York Journal and American. 1936-1939.
New York Post. 1936-1939.
New York Sun. 1936-1939.
New York Times. 1931, 1934-1939, 1950, 1964.
New York World Telegram. 1936-1939.
St. Louis Post-Dispatch. August 1938.
Variety. 1935-1939.
Wall Street Journal. January 1939.

4. Periodicals

"The American Theatre in Social and Educational Life: A Survey of its Needs and Opportunities," *Theatre Arts Monthly*, XVII (March 1933), 235-242.

Ames, Richard Sheridan. "Uncle Sam's Success Story," *Robert Wagner's Script*, XX (October 22, 1938), 6-7.

Anderson, Paul Y. "Behind the Dies Intrigue," *The Nation*, CXLVII (November 12, 1938), 499-500.

———. "Fascism Hits Washington," *The Nation*, CXLVII (August 27, 1939), 198-199.

———. "Investigate Mr. Dies!," *The Nation*, CXLVII (November 5, 1938), 471-472.

"Authorized Spokesman," *Equity*, XXIII (October 1938), 15.

Bagdikean, Ben H. "The Oil Can is Mightier than the Sword,"

the *New York Times Magazine* (March 14, 1965), pp. 30-31ff.

Baker, George Pierce. "The 47 Workshop," *The Century Magazine*, CI (February 1921), 417-425.

Bellamy, Francis R. "The Theatre," *Outlook and Independent*, CLI (January 23, 1929), 140.

Benchley, Robert. "No Fights This Time," *The New Yorker*, XIII (January 29, 1938), 23.

Bodeen, Dewitt. "New York Stage: *Life and Death of an American*," *Robert Wagner's Script*, XXI (June 10, 1939), 27.

Brandt, Raymond P. "The Dies Committee: An Appraisal," *The Atlantic Monthly*, CLXV (February 1940), 232-237.

Britt, S. Henderson and Seldon C. Menefee, "Did the Publicity of the Dies Committee in 1938 Influence Public Opinion?," *The Public Opinion Quarterly*, III (July 1939), 449-457.

Brown, Heywood. "Uriah Comes to Judgment: Dies Committee," *The New Republic*, XCVI (September 7, 1938), 129-130.

Brown, John Mason. "The Four Georges: G[eorge] P[ierce] Baker at Work," *Theatre Arts Monthly*, XVII (July 1933), 537-557.

"Budget: The President and the Republicans Preach Thrift to Embarrassed Democratic Spenders," *Newsweek*, IX (May 1, 1937), 7-8.

Burr, Eugene. "From Out Front," *The Billboard*, XLVIII (May 2, 1936), 18.

Can You Hear Their Voices?, *Theatre Guild Magazine*, VIII (July 1931), 24-25.

Clapper, Raymond. "Politics in the WPA," *Review of Reviews*, XCIII (April 1936), 35-36ff.

Clark, Barret H. "Broadway Brightens Up a Bit," *The Drama Magazine*, XIX (March 1929), 170-171.

"The Colleges Protest," *Theatre Arts Monthly*, XV (July 1931), 535-536.

"The Congress," *Time*, XXIV (November 19, 1934), 12.

"Congress Applies the Brakes to the New Deal," *The Congressional Digest*, XVIII (March 1939), 65-67.

"Congress Leans Toward the 1940 Campaign," *The Congressional Digest*, XVIII (January 1939), 1-3.

"Congress Moves to Control Relief," *The Congressional Digest*, XVIII (February 1939), 35-36.

Connelly, Marc. "Save America's Theatre," *TAC Magazine*, I (February 1939), 5.

Cooke, Alistair. "A National Theatre on Trial," *Fortnightly* (December 1936), 726-731.

Coyne, Bob. "TAC Around Town," *TAC Magazine*, I (July-August 1939), 28.

de Rohan, Pierre. Untitled editorial, *Federal Theatre*, I, No. 2 (December 1935), n.p.

————. Untitled editorial, *Federal Theatre*, I, No. 3 (January or February 1936), n.p.

"The Dies Committee Mess," *The New Republic*, XCVI (August 31, 1938), 90.

"Dirksen, Everett McKinley," *Current Biography: Who's News and Why*. Ed. Maxine Block. New York: The H. H. Wilson, Co., 1941.

"The Elmer Rices Buy a Theatre for *Judgement Day*," *Newsweek*, IV (August 11, 1934), 20.

"Equity Faces Long, Hard Fight Over WPA," *Equity*, XXIV (February 1939), 3.

"Equity Fight WPA Cuts," *Equity*, XXIV (January 1939), 5-6.

"Equity's Twenty-Sixth Annual Meeting," *Equity*, XXIV (June 1939), 5.

"Farewell to 9,000," *The Commonweal*, XXX (June 30, 1939), 247.

"Feather in a Hat," *Time*, XXXIII (February 13, 1939), 16.

"Federal Project and The Devil Receive Their Due," *Newsweek*, IX (January 23, 1937), 30-31.

"Federal Pulmotor for Arts," *The Literary Digest*, CXX (October 12, 1935), 24.

"The Federal Theatre Makes an Exciting Play of the Housing Problem," *Life*, IV (February 14, 1938), 24.

"Federation of Arts Unions Fight for WPA," *Equity*, XXIV (June 1939), 17.

Ferguson, Otis. "You've Got to Have a Place to Live," *The New Republic*, LXXXXIV (February 16, 1938), 46.

Fiske, Harrison Grey. "The Federal Theatre Doom-Boggle," *The Saturday Evening Post*, CCIX (August 1, 1936), 23ff.

Flanagan, Hallie. "Blood and Oil," *Theatre Guild Magazine*, VIII (December 1930), 27-29.

———. "The Dragon's Teeth," *Theatre Guild Magazine*, VIII (February 1931), 24-27.

———. "Experiment at Vassar," *Theatre Arts Monthly*, XII (January 1928), 70-71.

———. "Federal Theatre Project," *Theatre Arts Monthly*, XIX (November 1935), 865-868.

———. "Federal Theatre: Tomorrow," *Federal Theatre*, II, No. 1 (1936), 5-6ff.

———. "The People's Theatre Grows Stronger," *Federal Theatre*, I, No. 6 (May 1936), 5-6.

———. "A Report of the First Six Months," *Federal Theatre*, I, No. 4 (March 1936), 5-16.

———. "Theatre and Geography," *American Magazine of Art*, XXXX (August 1938), 464-468.

———. "A Theatre for the People," *American Magazine of Art*, XXIX (August 1936), 494-503.

———. "A Theatre is Born," *Theatre Arts Monthly*, XV (November 1931), 908-915.

———. "The Tractor Invades the Theatre," *Theatre Guild Magazine*, VIII (December 1930), 36-38.

"The Fortune Survey: XIX," *Fortune*, XIX (March 1939), 66-69ff.

"Fraud v. Fraud," *Time*, XXVI (March 23, 1936), 21.

Garrett, Garet. "Federal Theatre for the Masses," *The Saturday Evening Post*, CCVII (June 20, 1936), 8-9ff.

Gellhorn, Martha. "Federal Theatre," *Spectator* (London), CLVII (July 10, 1936), 51-52.

Gilder, Rosamond. "The Federal Theatre," *Theatre Arts Monthly*, XX (June 1936), 430-438.

⸻. "Who's Who in the Tributary Theatre," *Theatre Arts Monthly*, XXVI (July 1942), 460-464ff.

Heiberg-Jurgensen, Kai. "Drama in Extension," *The Carolina Play-Book*, Memorial Issue (June-December 1944), 54-62.

Hunter, John O. "Marc Blitzstein's *The Cradle Will Rock* as a Document of America, 1937," *American Quarterly*, XVIII (Summer 1966), 227-233.

Isaacs, Edith J. R. "Come of Age!," *Theatre Arts Monthly*, XVIII (July 1934), 478-488.

⸻. "*Dr. Faustus*—Broadway in Review," *Theatre Arts Monthly*, XXI (March 1937), 184-185.

⸻. "Portrait of a Theatre: America—1935," *Theatre Arts Monthly*, XVII (January 1933), 32-42.

⸻. "The Negro in the American Theatre: A Record of Achievement," *Theatre Arts Monthly*, XXVI (July 1942), 460-473.

⸻. "Who Killed Cock Robin?—Broadway in Review," *Theatre Arts Monthly*, XXII (March 1938), 173-174.

"The Issue of Federal Theatre," *TAC Magazine*, I (February 1939), 3.

"Its Most Useful Citizen," *Little Theatre Monthly*, II (April 1926), 64.

Koch, Frederick H. "Drama in the South," *The Carolina Play-Book*, Memorial Issue (June-December 1944), 7-19.

⸻. "Making a Regional Drama," *Bulletin of the American Library Association*, XXVI (August 1932), 466-473.

⸻. "Toward a New Folk Theatre." Reprinted from the *Quarterly Journal of the North Dakota University* (1930).

Kolodin, Irving. "Footlights, Federal Style," *Harper's Magazine*, CLXXIII (November 1936), 621-631.

Krutch, Joseph Wood. "Elmer Rice and the Critics," *The Nation*, CXXXIX (November 21, 1934), 580.

———. "The 'Living Newspaper,'" *The Nation*, CLXVI (January 29, 1938), 137-138.

———. "The Prosecution Rests," *The Nation*, CXXXVI (February 8, 1933), 158-160.

———. "The Swing Mikado," *The Nation*, CXLVIII (March 18, 1939), 329.

Lavery, Emmet. "Communism and the Federal Theatre," *The Commonweal*, XXXVII (October 7, 1938), 610-612.

Lindley, Earnest K. "The New Congress," *Current History*, XLIX (February 1939), 15-17.

Littell, Robert. "Brighter Lights: Broadway in Review," *Theatre Arts Monthly*, XIII (March 1929), 164-176.

Lorentz, John. "Arts Unions Offer Sincere Thanks," *Equity*, XXIV (May 1939), 4.

McCarty, Barclay. "Three Designs for Living: Broadway in Review," *Theatre Arts Monthly*, XII (April 1933), 257-264.

McCormick, Robert. "Buncombe Bob," *Colliers*, CI (May 21, 1938), 36-38.

McLaws, Lafayette. "A Master of Playwrights," *The North American Review*, CC (September 1914), 459-467.

"Milestones," *Time*, LVI (October 16, 1950), 93.

"Mr. Rice Resigns," *The Nation*, CXLII (February 12, 1936), 174.

"More Dollars for Dies," *Colliers*, CIII (January 14, 1939), 50.

Moses, Montrose J. "Native Drama," *The Carolina Play-Book*, XVI (March-June 1943), 64.

Mullen, John. "A Worker Looks at Broadway," *New Theatre*, III (May 1936), 25-27.

"The National Theatre Approaches Reality," *The Literary Digest*, CXIX (June 22, 1935), 23.

"Newspaper into Theatre," *The Nation*, CXXXXIV (March 6, 1937), 256.

"A New University Theatre," *Theatre Arts Monthly*, XVIII (September 1934), 702-703.

"Notice to H. Huffman & Co. 'Keep Out!,'" *Equity*, XXII (December 1937), 12.

"Once Upon a Time," *The Saturday Evening Post*, CCIX (June 26, 1937), 22.

. . . *One-Third of a Nation*, *Time*, XXXI (January 31, 1938), 40.

"Parade of the Left," *Time*, XXXIII (February 20, 1939), 10-11.

"Photographic History [of the Federal Theatre]," *TAC Magazine*, I (February 1939), 6-11.

"*Power* is WPA Ownership Propaganda," *Life*, II (March 22, 1937), 22-23.

"The Presidency," *Time*, XXIV (November 19, 1934), 11.

"Project to Continue on National Basis," *Equity*, XXI (May 1936), 8.

"Rebellious Congress Stymies Pet Plans of the President," *Newsweek*, XIV (July 10, 1939), 11.

"Relief: For 1940," *Time*, XXXIII (June 26, 1939), 19-20.

"Relief: Theatre Lobby," *Time*, XXIV (July 3, 1939), 8-9.

"Restore America's Theatre," *TAC Magazine*, I (July-August 1939), 3.

Rice, Elmer. "Theatre Alliance: A Cooperative Repertory Theatre Project," *Theatre Arts Monthly*, XIX (June 1935), 427-433.

―――. "Towards an Adult Theatre," *The Drama Magazine*, XXI (February 1931), 5, 18.

"Roll of Honor," *TAC Magazine*, I (July-August 1939), 8, 33.

"Roosevelt's War on Hatch Bill Draws up Battle Lines for 1940," *Newsweek*, XIII (June 26, 1939), 13.

Salmond, John A. "The Civilian Conservation Corps and the Negro," *The Journal of American History*, XLI (June 1965), 75-88.

Seldon, Samuel. "Frederick Henry Koch: The Man and His Work," *The Carolina Play-Book*, Memorial Issue (June-December 1944), 1-5.

"The Sheppard Committee Reports on Use of WPA Funds in Politics," *The Congressional Digest*, XVIII (February 1939), 40.

"Should Existing Methods of Administering Relief Funds be Changed: The Gallup Poll," *The Congressional Digest*, XVIII (February 1939), 52.

"Should Existing Methods of Administering Relief Be Changed: the *Washington Post*," *The Congressional Digest*, XVIII (February 1939), 53.

Skinner, Richard D. "The Play: *Judgment Day*," *The Commonweal*, X (September 28, 1934), 509.

————. "The Play: *We, the People*," *The Commonweal*, XVII (February 8, 1933), 411.

"Smart Uncle Sam," *The Literary Digest*, CXXI (May 9, 1936), 25.

Smith, Boyd. "The University Theatre as it was Built Stone upon Stone," *Theatre Arts Monthly*, XVII (July 1933), 521-536.

Smith, Paul Gerard. "Backstage of the Federal Theatre," *Robert Wagner's Script*, XXI (May 6, 1939), 16-17.

"Spirit of New York Workers Praised by National Director," *Federal Theatre*, I, No. 1 (November 25, 1935), 1-3.

"Still a Mess," *The New Republic*, XCVI (September 28, 1938), 198.

"Taxes and Neutrality," *The Congressional Digest*, XVIII (April 1939), 97-100.

"The Theatre," *New Masses*, XX (August 4, 1936), 29.

"Theatre Arts Bookshelf: *Can You Hear Their Voices?*," *Theatre Arts Monthly*, XV (November 1931), 952.

"This is No Time for a Cut on the Project," *Equity*, XXIII (December 1938), 3.

"Three Bankheads," *Newsweek*, XIV (July 3, 1939), 13.

TRB, "Demagoguery on the Chesapeake," *The New Republic*, XCVI (August 31, 1938), 102.

"The Tributary Theatre . . . ," *Theatre Arts Monthly*, XVII (July 1933), 566-578.

"Two 'Baker Maps', " *Theatre Arts Monthly*, XVII (July 1933), 552-553.

"Two Playwrights with a Difference," *The Literary Digest*, CXV (February 11, 1933), 15-16.

"Unemployed Arts," *Fortune*, XV (May 1937), 108-117ff.

Vernon, Granville. "*Injunction Granted*: Latest Edition of the Living Newspaper is Out and Out Propaganda of the Left," *The Commonweal*, XXIV (August 21, 1936), 407.

———. "The Theatre: *One-Third of a Nation*," *The Commonweal*, XXVII (February 4, 1938), 414.

"The Vindicators," *Newsweek*, XIII (May 1, 1939), 15-16.

W[agner], R[obert]. "*Two-A-Day* Twice," *Robert Wagner's Script*, XX (December 1938), 13.

Watson, Morris. "Living Newspaper," *Scholastic*, XXIX (October 31, 1936), 8-9.

Wolfe, Thomas. "The Man Who Lives With His Idea," *The Carolina Play-Book*, Memorial Issue (June-December 1944), 15-22.

"The World and the Theatre: Dedication of G[eorge] P[ierce] Baker]—National Theatre Conference . . . ," *Theatre Arts Monthly*, XVII (July 1933), 483-491.

"The World and the Theatre: Reforming the Theatre," *Theatre Arts Monthly*, XVII (May 1933), 331-333.

"WPA: 'Baby Terror' Airs West Virginia's Laundry in the Senate," *Newsweek*, VII (March 7, 1936), 14-15.

"WPA's New Show . . . *One-Third of a Nation* . . . ," *The Literary Digest*, CXXV (February 12, 1938), 21-22.

Wyatt, Euphemia Van Rensselaer. "The Drama: *One-Third of a Nation*," *The Catholic World*, CXLVI (March 1938), 728-729.

5. Books

Aaron, Daniel. *Writers on the Left*: *Episodes in American Literary Communism*. New York: Harcourt, Brace and World, 1961.

Arent, Arthur and the Living Newspaper Staff. *Injunction*

Granted. New York: Federal Theatre Project Play Bureau, 1936.

Baker, George Pierce. *Dramatic Technique.* New York: Houghton Mifflin, Co., 1919.

Blum, John Morton. *From the Morgenthau Diaries: Years of Crisis, 1928-1938.* Boston: Houghton Mifflin Co., 1959.

Burns, Arthur E. and Edward A. Williams. *Federal Work, Security and Relief Programs.* Washington: U. S. Government Printing Office, 1941.

Carter, Jean and Jess Ogden. *Everyman's Drama: A Study of the Noncommercial Theatre in the United States.* New York: American Association for Adult Education, 1938.

Charles, Searle F. *Minister of Relief: Harry Hopkins and the Depression.* Syracuse, N.Y.: Syracuse University Press, 1963.

Cheney, Sheldon. *The Art Theatre.* New York: Alfred A. Knopf, 1925.

———. *The Theatre.* New York: Longmans, Green and Co., 1930.

Clurman, Harold. *The Fervent Years: the Story of the Group Theatre and the Thirties.* New York: Hill and Wang, 1957.

Derber, Milton and Edwin Young, eds. *Labor and the New Deal.* Madison: University of Wisconsin Press, 1957.

de Rohan, Pierre, ed. *Federal Theatre Plays: Prologue to Glory, One-Third of a Nation, Haiti.* New York: Random House, 1938.

———. ed. *Federal Theatre Plays: Triple-A Plowed Under, Power, Spirochete.* New York: Random House, 1938.

Dies, Martin. *Martin Dies' Story.* New York: Bookmailer, 1963.

Egbert, Donald Drew and Stowe Persons, ed. *Socialism and American Life.* 2 vols. Princeton, N.J.: Princeton University Press, 1952. I.

Farley, James A. *Jim Farley's Story: The Roosevelt Years.* New York: McGraw-Hill, 1948.

Flanagan, Hallie. *Arena.* New York: Duell, Sloan, and Pearce, 1940.

———. *Dynamo.* New York: Duell, Sloan, and Pearce, 1943.

———. *Shifting Scenes of the Modern European Theatre.* New York: Coward McCann, Inc., 1928.

Gard, Robert E. and Gertrude S. Burley. *Community Theatre: Idea and Achievement.* New York: Duell, Sloan, and Pearce, 1959.

Gassner, John, ed. *A Treasury of the Theatre From Henrik Ibsen to Arthur Miller.* New York: Simon and Schuster, 1956.

Gellerman, William. *Martin Dies.* New York: The John Dey Co., 1944.

Gill, Corrington. *Wasted Manpower.* New York: W. W. Norton & Co., 1939.

Green, Harriet L. *Gilmor Brown: Portrait of a Man—and an Idea.* Pasadena, California: Burns Printing Co., 1933.

Himmelstein, Morgan. *Drama Was a Weapon: The Left-Wing Theatre in New York, 1929-1941.* New Brunswick: Rutgers University Press, 1963.

Hopkins, Harry. *Spending to Save.* New York: W. W. Norton & Co., 1936.

Howard, Donald S. *The WPA and Federal Relief Policy.* New York: Russell Sage Foundation, 1943.

Howe, Irving and Lewis Coser. *The American Communist Party: A Critical History.* Boston: Beacon Press, 1957.

Hughes, Glenn. *A History of the American Theatre, 1790-1950.* New York: Samuel French, 1951.

———. *The Story of the Theatre: A Short History of Theatrical Art from Its Beginnings to the Present Day.* New York: Samuel French, 1928.

Ickes, Harold L. *The Secret Diary of Harold L. Ickes.* 3 vols. New York: Simon and Schuster, 1954. II: *The Inside Struggle, 1936-39,* 1954.

Kempton, Murray. *Part of Our Time.* New York: Simon and Schuster, 1955.

Kinne, Wisner Payne. *George Pierce Baker and the American Theatre.* Cambridge: Harvard University Press, 1954.

Koch, Frederick Henry, ed. *Carolina Folk-Plays*. New York: Henry Holt and Co., 1941.

Koestler, Arthur. *Arrow in the Blue: An Autobiography*. London: Collins Press, 1952.

Krutch, Joseph Wood. *The American Drama Since 1918: An Informal History*. New York: George Braziller, Inc., 1957.

Lens, Sidney. *Left, Right and Center: Conflicting Forces in American Labor*. Hinsdale, Ill.: Henry Regnery Co., 1947.

Leuchtenburg, William E. *Franklin D. Roosevelt and the New Deal, 1932-1949*. New York: Harper and Row, 1963.

Lewis, Allan. *American Plays and Playwrights of the Contemporary Theatre*. New York: Crown Publishers, Inc., 1965.

MacCracken, Henry Noble. *The Hickory Limb*. New York: Charles Scribner's Sons, 1950.

MacGowan, Kenneth. *Footlights Across America: Towards a National Theatre*. New York: Harcourt, Brace and Co., 1929.

MacKaye, Percy. *The Playhouse and the Play and Other Addresses Concerning the Theatre and Democracy in America*. New York: The Macmillan Co., 1909.

Mantle, Burns, ed. *The Best Plays of 1932-33 and The Yearbook of Drama in America*. New York: Dodd, Mead and Co., 1933.

————. ed. *The Best Plays of 1933-34 and the Yearbook of Drama in America*. New York: Dodd, Mead and Co., 1934.

Markov, P. A. *The Soviet Theatre*. London: Victor Gallancz Ltd., 1934.

Merton, Robert K. *Social Theory and Social Structure*. Glencoe, Ill.: The Free Press, 1949.

Ogden, August Raymond. *The Dies Committee: A Study of the Special House Committee for the Investigation of Un-American Activities, 1938-1944*. Washington: The Catholic University of America Press, 1945.

Overmyer, Grace. *Government and the Arts*. New York: W. W. Norton & Co., 1939.

The Public Papers and Addresses of Franklin D. Roosevelt. Comp. Samuel I. Rosenman. 13 vols. New York: Macmillan,

1938-1950. IV: *The Court Disapproves* (1935); VI: *The Constitution Prevails* (1937); VII: *The Continuing Struggle for Liberalism* (1938); VIII: *War—And Neutrality* (1939).

Rabkin, Gerald. *Drama and Commitment: Politics in the American Theatre of the Thirties.* Bloomington, Ind.: Indiana University Press, 1964.

Rice, Elmer. *The Adding Machine: A Play in Seven Scenes.* Garden City, N.Y.: Doubleday, Page and Co., 1923.

———. *Judgement Day.* New York: Coward McCann, Inc., 1934.

———. *The Living Theatre.* New York: Harper and Bros., 1959.

———. *Street Scene.* New York: Samuel French Ltd., 1929.

———. *Two Plays: Not for Children and Between Two Worlds.* New York: Coward McCann, Inc., 1935.

———. *We, The People.* New York: Coward McCann, Inc., 1933.

Rosenman, Samuel I. *Working With Roosevelt.* New York: Harper and Bros., 1952.

Schlesinger, Arthur M., Jr. *The Coming of the New Deal.* Boston: Houghton Mifflin Co., 1959.

———. *The Politics of Upheaval.* Boston: Houghton Mifflin Co., 1960.

Seldon, Samuel and Mary Tom Sphangos. *Frederick Henry Koch: Pioneer Playmaker—A Brief Biography.* Chapel Hill, N.C.: University of North Carolina Library, 1954.

Sherwood, Robert E. *Roosevelt and Hopkins.* New York: Harper and Bros., 1950.

Slonim, Marc. *Russian Theatre From the Empire to the Soviets.* New York: The World Publishing Co., 1961.

Timmons, Bascom N. *Garner of Texas: A Personal History.* New York: Harper and Bros., 1948.

Wechsler, James. *The Age of Suspicion.* New York: Random House, 1953.

Whitman, Willson. *Bread and Circuses.* New York: Oxford University Press, 1937.

Wittler, Clarence J. *Some Social Trends in WPA Drama*. Washington: The Catholic University of America Press, 1939.

6. Interviews and Tape Recordings

Arent, Arthur. Interview, November 11, 1961.
Barber, Philip. Interview, November 14, 1961.
Bay, Howard. Interview, November 16, 1961.
Brown, John Mason. Interview, November 10, 1961.
Cahill, Holger. Tape Recording, April 15, 1960. Archives of American Art, Detroit Institute of Art.
Connelly, Marc. Interview, November 10, 1961.
da Silva, Howard. Interview, November 14, 1961.
Flanagan, Hallie. Interview, November 13, 1961.
Freedley, George. Interview, December 29, 1960.
Handlesman, Sam. Interview, November 16, 1961.
Jones, Venzuella. Interview, November 17, 1961.
Kerr, Florence. Interview, February 2, 1962.
Kerr, Florence. Tape Recordings, October 16, 18; November 6, 1963. Archives of American Art, Detroit Institute of Art.
Parker, Thomas. Tape Recording, October 14, 1963. Archives of American Art. Detroit Institute of Art.
Reade, Maida. Interview, November 15, 1961.
Rice, Elmer. Interview, November 15, 1961.
Roosevelt, Eleanor. Interview, November 8, 1961.
Sherman, Hiram. Interview, November 15, 1961.
Shumlin, Herman. Interview, November 9, 1961.
Ullman, James R. Interview, November 17, 1961.

7. Miscellaneous Materials

Copeland, Aaron, et al. "Marc Blitzstein Remembered," *Program for the Marc Blitzstein Memorial Concert, Philharmonic Hall, Lincoln Center for the Performing Arts*. New York: Saturday Review, Inc., 1964.
de Rohan, Pierre. *First Federal Summer Theatre . . . A Report*. New York: Federal Theatre National Publications, [1937].
Dycke, Marjorie Louise Platt. "The Living Newspaper: A Study

of the Nature of the Form and its Place in Modern Social Drama." Unpublished Ph.D. dissertation, New York University, 1947.

Federal Theatre Project. *Highlights of the First Production Conference of the New York City Unit of the Federal Theatre Called by Hallie Flanagan, National Director and Philip W. Barber, New York Director.* New York: Play Bureau of the Federal Theatre Project, [1936].

Flanagan, Hallie. Autobiographical Notes for Jane Mathews. Winter, 1962.

Kerr, Florence. Letter to Jane Mathews, April 10, 1962.

Kifer, Allen Francis. "The Negro Under the New Deal, 1933-1941." Unpublished Ph.D. dissertation, University of Wisconsin, 1961.

"Marc Blitzstein Discusses His Theater Compositions." Spoken Arts, Recording No. 717.

Saul, Oscar and Lou Lantz. *The Revolt of the Beavers.* New York Public Library Theatre Collection at Lincoln Center, typewritten, 1936.

INDEX

Abbey Theatre, influence on American theatre, 16, 24, 25

Abbott, George, supports Federal Theatre Project, 283

Actors' Equity Association, 203-04, 207, 302; relations with Federal Theatre Project, 38; members charge Communist influence in Federal Theatre, 78; president repudiates charges of Communist influence in Federal Theatre, 79; prevents members from demonstrating against cuts, 103, 120; fights for preservation of Federal Arts Project, 269; *see also* Gillmore, Frank; Meredith, Burgess; unions

Alsberg, Henry, directs Federal Writers' Project, 28; testimony before Dies Committee, 223, 226, 232

American Federation of Musicians, supports Federal Theatre, 80; *see also* unions

American Federation of Radio Artists, supports Federal Theatre, 286

Andrews, Charles O., objects to portrayal in *One-Third of a Nation*, 172-74

Androcles and the Lion, 240, 300; Seattle production, 153-54

Arent, Arthur, 109, 114, 170, 299*n*

Ashton, Herbert, 151, 184

Ashurst, Henry F., defends Federal Theatre, 290

Atkinson, Brooks, 38, 128; criticizes closing of *Ethiopia*, 69; on inactivity of New York Project, 169; defends Federal Theatre, 269-70

Audience Research Department, 101

Awake and Sing, 240

Bacon, Robert L., attacks *Triple-A Plowed Under*, 72, 77

Bailey, Josiah, 308; burlesques *One-Third of a Nation*, 174-75

Baker, George Pierce, invites Hallie Flanagan to Harvard, 15; 47 Workshop, 16, 24; wants a national theatre, 26

Baker, Jacob, 12, 17, 30, 40-41, 46, 48, 49; discourages production of *Ethiopia*, 63-66; dismissal, 87, 93

Bankhead, John, 284

Bankhead, Tallulah, defends Federal Theatre, 284

Bankhead, William B., 284

Barber, Philip, 39, 70, 105, 110, 112, 140; backs *Triple-A Plowed Under*, 70-71

Bassa Moona, 108

Battle Hymn, 81, 106

Bay, Howard, 170, 299, 299*n*

Big Blow, 239, 262, 300

Blankfort, Michael, 81

Blitzstein, Marc, 123*n*, 165; *see also Cradle will Rock*

Brennan, James J., 285

Broun, Heywood, 16

Brown, Gilmor, 26, 30, 37, 40, 84, 87, 128, 164

Brown, John Mason, 16, 38, 271

Burton, Ralph, investigates for Woodrum Committee, 265-66, 270-71

Byrd, Harry F., objects to portrayal in *One-Third of a Nation*, 172ff

Byrnes, James F., 177, 196, 252; opposes Federal Arts Projects, 258-59

Cahill, Holger, 28, 312; *see also* Federal Art Project

Can You Hear their Voices?, Vassar production, 20-22; in-

333

abolition of Federal Theatre, 281ff, 294-95, 312-13
Flax, 144, 154
Fletcher, Lois, 91-92
47 Workshop, 15ff, 24
Francis, Arlene, 108
Frank, Yasha, 154, 240, 243, 282, 295

Garner, John Nance, 127, 258
Geddes, Virgil, 105ff
Geer, Will, 124
Gerwing, George, evaluates Los Angeles project, 83; acting regional director in the East, 149-50, 154, 164, 168; resigns, 245*n*
Gifford, Charles L., 278
Gilder, Rosamund, 37, 40, 87
Gill, Corrington, 93, 183, 190
Gillmore, Frank, 12, 38, 51-52, 79-80, 285
Gold, Michael, 81
Goodman, Edward, 105-06
Green, Paul, 25, 34, 115
Grinnell College, 13ff, 17

Haiti, 199, 238, 308
Hammond, Percy, 38
Harrington, F. C., 250, 250*n*, 259, 274, 283, 285
Hart, Moss, 283
Hart, Walter, 106, 129-30, 139-40
Hayes, Helen, 282-83
Healey, Arthur D., 226
Holt, Rush, 292-93
Hopkins, Harry L., background and concern for unemployed artists, 3-4; proposes work program, 8-9; discussed subsidized theatre, 12; wants Hallie Flanagan to direct Federal Theatre Project, 27; discusses role of Federal Theatre, 32; addresses Iowa Theatre conference, 32-33; urges WPA cooperation with Arts Projects, 57-58; urges decentralization of Federal Theatre

Project, 60, 179, 243; decides against producing *Ethiopia*, 67-68; before House Appropriations Sub-Committee, 77-78; pleased with Federal Theatre, 86-87; promises better support of Federal Theatre, 87, 93; orders personnel cuts, 102-03; transfers administration of New York Project to Hallie Flanagan, 104; political ambition, 134-36, 187; attends Federal Theatre productions, 109, 114-15; relations with Congress, 119, 160; supports Vassar workshop, 125-26; encourages Living Newspaper on housing, 115, 169; illness, 134, 162-63; concerned with radical reputation of New York Project, 131*n*, 133, 136-37
Horse Eats Hat, 108
House Appropriations Subcommittee Investigating the WPA (Woodrum Committee), 263, 264-68, 270-72
House Committee on Un-American Activities (Dies Committee), 198-235; hearings on Federal Theatre, 200-05, 214-23; criticism of hearings, 212, 233; report on Federal Theatre, 225-26; reaction to hearings, 225; effect of hearings on Federal Theatre, 232-35; investigations, 250, 251
Houseman, John, 75, 105-06, 108, 109, 123, 124, 133, 158, 165, 165*n*
How Long, Brethren?, 115, 120
Howard, Sidney, 16, 37, 131
Huffman, Hazel, testimony of, 200-03, 225; mentioned, 206, 215, 219
Hughes, Glenn, 25, 33
Humphrey, William Harrison, 203
Hunter, Howard, 132, 189, 190
Hymn to the Rising Sun, 115

337

338

106, 118, 300; New York production acclaimed, 74-75

National Service Bureau, 254, 300, 306; functions of, 148-49, 149*n*
national theatre, lack of, vii, viii; hopes for, 12, 26, 29; emphasis on regional organization, 30
National Theatre Conference, 26
National Youth Administration, 36, 56
Negroes, and Federal Theatre, 38, 150, 153-54, 156, 265, 268, 298-99
Ness, Ole, 154, 155, 164, 269
New York City Project of the Federal Theatre, delays in establishing, 47-54, 57; union difficulties, 50-53; criticism of, 53-54, 109, 112, 131*n*; and *Ethiopia*, 62-68; disturbed by demonstrations, 65, 102, 103, 120-21, 246-47; and *Triple-A Plowed Under*, 70-73; praised for *Chalk Dust* and *Murder in the Cathedral*, 74-75; troubled by malcontents, 74; rightist activities in, 74; acclaimed for *Macbeth*, 76; morale boosted by success, 81; public enthusiastic over, 86; and *It Can't Happen Here*, 97-99; disrupted by reorganization of, 102-07, 120-21, 129, 130, 139; praised for *Horse Eats Hat*, *Faustus*, *Power*, and others, 107-09, 113-15; problems with *Injunction Granted*, 109-13; criticized for *Revolt of the Beavers*, 116-17; praised in *Fortune*, 118-19; unable to open *Cradle Will Rock*, 122-25; appointment of George Kondolph as director, 131-34, 137; curtailment of program because of reorganization, 141-42; retrenchment of, 162; inactivity of, 167ff; *One-Third*

of a Nation acclaimed, 169-71; efforts to broaden support, 187-88; productions of, 237-41; cuts of personnel in, 102ff, 120ff, 246ff, 275; *Big Blow, Androcles and the Lion, Pinocchio*, and others well received, 238-42, 262; attitude toward those outside New York, 253-54; alleged communist influence in, 200-05, 227-32, 265-66, 271-72; struggle for continuation of, 282; reaction to ending of, 294-95; length of rehearsals, 269-70, 285, 303-04; effectiveness of opposition, 306; *see also* Federal Theatre Project
Niles, David, 124, 136-37, 158ff, 166ff, 183, 190, 199, 209, 223
Norton, Mary, 279-80
Norvelle, Lee, 84

On the Rocks, 300
One-Third of a Nation, 144, 169-71, 171-77, 199, 220, 237-39, 300, 301
O'Neill, Eugene, 16, 143-45, 151, 156, 301
O'Shea, Madalyn, 106

Patents Committee Hearings, 166-68
Pepper, Claude, 232, 283-84, 289
Pinocchio, 154, 156, 240-41, 262, 295, 300
Play Policy Board, 96, 96*n*, 182-83, 190, 243, 300
Post, Langdon, 115, 170
Power, 109, 113-15, 138, 153
Processional, 226, 227
Professor Mamlock, 115
Prologue to Glory, 144, 199, 211, 238-39, 241

Ready! Aim! Fire!, 156
relief, public reaction to, 252; con-

Taylor, Edward, 261

Theatre Arts Committee, lobbies for reinstatement of the Federal Theatre, 286-87

Theatrical research program, 38

Thomas, J. Parnell, 196, 199, 200, 202, 207, 209, 210, 221

Thompson, Virgil, 123

Todd, Michael, 242, 242n

Townsend, John G., 177, 177n

The Tragical History of Dr. Faustus, 108-09, 118, 138, 300

tributary theatre, 26; *see also* community theatre, university theatres

Triple-A Plowed Under, 70-73, 77, 81, 106, 310

Trojan Women, 95

Tydings, Millard, 172-73

Ullman, James, 245n, 247, 255, 257-58

unions (theatrical), concerned with wages and hours, 8, 36, 51-52, 303; Dramatist Guild, 38; Chorus Equity, 38; fear competition from Federal Theatre, 50-51; object to amateurs on Project, 56; exert pressure to continue national project, 80; demand professional experience be taken into consideration on cuts, 121; protest cuts, 246; try to get Federal Theatre reinstated, 282ff, 286

university theatres, 37; growth of, 24, 25

Unto Such Glory, 115

Vassar College Experimental Theatre, 13, 17, 20ff

Verdi, Francis M., 203-04, 206-07

Voorhis, Jerry, 278

Wagner, Robert, 79, 290

Walk Together Children, 75

Walton, Charles, 204, 271-72

Ward, Lem, 171, 240

Watkins, Perry, 299, 299n

Watson, Morris, 62, 63, 105-06, 110-13, 110n, 111n, 167

Welles, Orson, 75, 108, 109, 123, 124, 158, 165, 165n, 286ff

Whitcomb, Bess, 154

Williams, Aubrey, 40, 48, 67-68, 132-33, 136, 159, 168, 176-77, 183, 192

Winchell, Walter, 231, 286-87

Woodrum, Clifton, 77, 250, 251, 260-61, 274, 277, 292, 295, 299, 300

Woodward, Ellen, 93, 114, 123, 128, 131ff, 136-37, 164ff, 181, 183, 185n, 186, 191, 192, 210, 212, 214-17

Workers' Alliance, recruits project personnel, 52-53; demonstrates against cuts, 120; influences New York Project, 199, 201-05, 207, 225, 228ff, 232, 265-66, 271; influence on Federal Theatre Project, 289

Works Progress Administration (WPA), origins of work relief program, 5, 8, 9; establishment, 9ff; and unemployed artists, 9, 10; reaction to relief bill, 39-40, 276; and administration of the Federal Theatre, 40-41; state officials and Federal Theatre, 44-45, 47, 87, 142n, 151, 152, 152n, 153-54, 163ff, 185-86, 185n, 257-58, 262; congressional criticism of, 77, 80, 119, 249-53, 275; tightens control over Federal Theatre, 131-33, 136-37; uncertain future of, 159, 161, 196; policy concerning nationwide touring program, 181, 183, 190-91, 196-97; on regional tours, 191-93, 197; relations between local administrators and Federal Theatre, 183, 184-85, 188-89, 190; response to Dies